Take a Look at Me Now

Anita Notaro

TRANSWORLD IRELAND

TRANSWORLD PUBLISHERS
61–63 Uxbridge Road, London W5 5SA
A Random House Group Company
www.rbooks.co.uk

TAKE A LOOK AT ME NOW
A TRANSWORLD IRELAND BOOK: 9781848270114

First published in Great Britain
in 2007 by Bantam Press
a division of Transworld Publishers
Transworld Ireland edition published 2008

Copyright © Anita Notaro 2007

Anita Notaro has asserted her right under the Copyright, Designs and Patents Act 1988 to be identified as the author of this work.

Addresses for Random House Group Ltd companies outside the UK
can be found at: www.randomhouse.co.uk
The Random House Group Ltd Reg. No. 954009

The Random House Group Limited supports The Forest Stewardship
Council (FSC), the leading international forest certification organisation.
All our titles that are printed on Greenpeace approved FSC certified paper
carry the FSC logo.
Our paper procurement policy can be found at
www.rbooks.co.uk/environment

Typeset in 12/15pt Ehrhardt by
Falcon Oast Graphic Art Ltd.

Printed in the UK by CPI Cox & Wyman, Reading, RG1 8EX.

2 4 6 8 10 9 7 5 3 1

Anita Notaro always knew she wanted to write, but only began to take it seriously when she became a journalist and television producer with RTE, Ireland's national broadcaster. During her time there she directed most of the major entertainment and current affairs programmes, including the Eurovision Song Contest and the 1997 General Election.

She left in 2002 to become a writer and her first three novels, *Back after the Break*, *Behind the Scenes* and *The WWW Club*, have all been published by Bantam Books. She has also written several stories for children for DEN TV, and when she can't stand the isolation she hangs around with the cast and crew of *Fair City* – Ireland's No. 1 TV soap – where they take pity on her and let her direct a few episodes.

www.transworldireland.ie

Also by Anita Notaro

Back after the Break
Behind the Scenes
The WWW Club

and published by Bantam Books

This book is about the unbreakable bond between sisters
and I'm lucky enough to have that three times over so,
Jean, Lorraine and Madeleine,
this is for you with love and thanks

1

ALISON

ALISON WAS HAPPY. REALLY HAPPY, IN A LAUGH–OUT–LOUD kind of way. Not just pretend happy – like when she was a child and lived in a make-believe world. Or peer-pressure happy – when in her teenage years acceptance was everything. She felt like a snake shedding its skin as she wriggled her toes in the gritty sand on a deserted south Dublin beach. Years of worry finally seemed to evaporate and the needle-sharp air whipped away the last of her anxiety.

Today was all about new beginnings. She smiled, just for the sake of it. It felt unfamiliar. Ali had got used to smiling on demand. Sometimes that expression meant reassurance for Lily, her twin sister, who relied on her totally. Other times it was all about comfort and protection for her darling child. And in the last few years, she'd become an expert at the seductive smiles she used often on the men in her life. But not any more: from now on there was no need.

'Mummy, look, I fly.' Her three-year-old son stretched out his arms and glided towards her, dipping from side to side. No smile of approval needed there today, Ali noticed. She watched as he fluttered past, utterly content in his own little world. All the kisses and smiles and love and security she'd given freely since the day he was born meant he was turning into the most confident, gorgeous little man.

'Come on.' Alison jumped up. 'Let's fly out to sea together.' She quickly tidied up their belongings, tucked an almost empty purse into her pocket and ran out ahead of Charlie, still hardly able to believe their luck had changed so hugely.

'Come on, you can do it,' she shouted encouragingly and bobbed about like a kite in a gale-force wind. Charlie ran towards her and she held out her arms for him. Cackling, he tried to dodge past and Alison picked him up and swung him round in circles until they were both out of breath.

'Drunk,' he announced, copping on quickly to their favourite game.

'No, you're not!' She tickled her bright-eyed boy. 'You're just dizzy.'

'Drunk,' he squealed again, trying in vain to stay upright.

Alison grabbed him before he hit the sand and threw him in the air. 'I love you, Charlie.'

'Love you lots . . . like jelly tots . . .' He wrapped his fat little arms round her neck and she smelt him, the way she always did, just behind his left ear.

'. . . but not as much as vodka shots.' Alison smiled and finished the rhyme for him. Her sister Lily had taught him that one and he repeated it a zillion times, although Alison had no idea what the teachers in playschool made of it. Still, it was typical of Lily's zaniness and Alison loved it that the two most important people in her life shared the same sense of fun. She could still hear her sister's throaty laugh from when Charlie had demanded 'wodka shots' in a sweet shop one day.

Now he wriggled to get down. 'Come on.' She looked around and checked their belongings again. The beach at Sandymount Strand was strangely silent, except for a lone dog walker, hands in pockets, way down towards the towers. 'Let's go catch the waves.'

'Bucket, want my bucket.'

Alison ran back and picked up the little yellow fireman's hat that they'd found earlier.

'Here's your bucket.' He was happy.

They headed across the cool, golden carpet. Alison loved it here when the tide was out. You could nearly walk to Holyhead, in Wales – at least that was what her mother used to tell her.

Charlie toddled along beside her. Progress was slow but steady, halted every minute or so by things she'd never have noticed.

'Hell.'

'Yep, that's a shell. Put it to your ear and see if you can hear the sea.'

'Sea.' He pointed.

'The sea is far away.' She ruffled his hair. 'Some day I'm going to take you on a big boat across the ocean.'

'Boat.'

'Or maybe an aeroplane. Would you like that?'

'Whoosh.' He was gliding again.

'You know something, darling, it's all going to be OK.'

'OK.'

'More than OK. Perfect.' She wondered what Lily would say when she told her that all their worries were over. Alison was almost more excited for her twin. Lily had so many dreams.

She held Charlie's hand but it wasn't long before he wanted to be free.

'Charlie, we're going to be fine. Mammy's going to look after us all.' She picked him up and cuddled him tight.

'Ow, put me down.' Charlie squirmed and was off exploring again in seconds.

Alison showed him a jellyfish and he ran away screaming, and then almost toppled over as he looked back through slatted fingers once he was holding her hand for safety.

'Today it all finally worked out for us, Charlie.' Her shoulders sagged and her neck felt looser. She couldn't wait to see her sister's face and she hugged her secret to herself with childlike glee.

'Ice cream?' the child asked hopefully.

'Yes, we'll go home on the Dart and then stop at Mrs O'Neill's shop and get wafers, how's that? And later on we'll have tea. What would you like?'

'Chips.' He was being economical with words these days.

'OK, chips it is, but from next week on we're going to be healthy. I'm going to feed you vegetables and lots of lovely meat and fish and—'

'I want chocolate buttons.'

'Well, only if you're a very good boy for your mammy.'

He nodded much more solemnly than he should have had to. 'Charlie very good.'

'Yes, you are, you're the best boy.' Alison picked him up and hugged him. She felt vaguely uneasy that she didn't have anything to worry about. No more saying no to him all the time and no more trying to curb her sister's enthusiasm either.

'Down.'

She did as ordered, settling for a feel of his baby curls as they strolled along.

'Sea.' It was his word of the day.

'Yep.'

'Splash.'

'I think it's too far away to splash, love.' She chased him further out, their arms and legs a jumble as she pretended to be an octopus, just like in his current favourite movie. The evening sun warmed their backs and the soft breeze made Charlie's curls tickle his neck. Alison giggled with him as he pushed his hair away and tried to dodge her embrace.

She ran it all through in her head again. Today had been a good one – scratch that, today had been the best in years.

She made mad plans as they meandered along, Charlie in his magical little world and Alison in hers. She'd come for a walk here to sort it all out in her head before she told her sister. Lily would be very emotional, Alison knew, so she needed to be careful.

'Wa-ter.' Her baby focused her mind again and the daydream and all her plans for a storybook ending for the three of them disappeared for the moment.

'Yes, the tide's coming in, we'd better get back or we'll get wet.' Alison laughed and looked around, surprised to find that they were on their own little desert island. Even the sun had abandoned them.

'Come on, love.' She took his hand. 'Mammy was dreaming. There's a big patch of sand over there.' She started to walk and quickly realized that the level they were on was higher than anything else around them.

'Come on, Charlie, Mammy'll carry you. We need to get back to the beach.' He felt cooler as she picked him up and held him close. He dropped his yellow toy and screamed.

'Bucket!'

'It's OK, I've got it.' She reached down but the yellow hat was being carried in by the tide.

'Gone,' Charlie said, as if he'd lost a fortune.

'It's OK, it'll be waiting for us on the beach, I promise.' She held him tight and cursed her stupidity. It seemed like they were miles out. She started to wade into the water. It was only just past her ankles but the stretches of sand were fewer now. She moved as quickly as she could with a three-year-old and a gypsy skirt hindering her progress.

'Charlie, love, I'm just going to put you down for a moment, while I tuck in my—'

'Nooo!' He wasn't budging. She hitched up as much fabric as she could and kept moving. They seemed to be getting nowhere. Her eyes scanned the horizon for back-up, just in case, but she couldn't see anyone. What a silly thing to do, she thought again, so unlike her normally sensible-to-the-point-of-driving-you-mad approach to life. She searched in vain for their pile of clothes to use as a landmark, but a faint mist now blurred the horizon and even the hum of commuter traffic on the nearby Strand Road sounded miles away.

Panic set in quite quickly then. It seemed as if she was pushing against the water and it was slowing them down. Her skirt felt like lead and she cursed silently once more, trying to remain calm. 'It's OK, darling,' she kept repeating. 'Just hold on tight to Mammy.'

'Cold.'

'I know, love, but we'll be on the beach soon and your jumper is there.' She kissed his head absentmindedly and tried to increase her pace. 'Silly Mammy.' She smiled at him encouragingly. 'We walked too far but don't worry, we're nearly there.' The next step saw them both almost topple over. The levels had changed again. It was deeper here. They seemed to be making no real progress. She closed her eyes and tried to think logically. For once, nothing came.

The wind increased and her colourful skirt rubbed

against her, hurting her legs. She felt her mobile phone through the thin cotton and grabbed it, staring at the face for a second. It seemed ridiculous to call for help but Alison realized she was frightened. It was darker now, or at least the pewter sky made it seem so. She dialled the emergency services, feeling a complete fool.

The calm, motherly woman tried to keep her talking, but Alison's breathing was heavy with fear and exertion and speaking was suddenly an effort.

'Stay on the line, that's a good girl. I'm just going to radio for help. I can still hear you, don't worry.' She was back to Alison in a second.

'What's your little boy's name, Alison?'

'Charlie.'

'And how old is he?'

'Three, but he's small and I'm scared and—'

'Just try and stay where you are. Are you wearing anything brightly coloured, by any chance?'

'Yes, a yellow T-shirt.'

'Good, that's good. Don't worry, Alison, help is on the way.'

She kept her voice even and used Alison's name all the time, asking questions to distract her, like what her home telephone number was and who would be there.

Alison gave it automatically, then panicked. 'My sister, Lily, but please don't ring her, she'll be frightened and I don't want to—'

'It's OK, don't worry, I won't call anyone. I just—'

'I'm trying to walk fast, honestly I am, and I'm so sorry to be troubling you like this. It's just that I don't seem to be getting anywhere and Charlie's heavy and—' She was out of breath now.

'It's no trouble, don't worry. Can you put him up on your shoulders? That might make it easier.'

'I'll try, but I'll have to— Wait . . . Hold on a minute.' Alison clutched the phone and hoisted the baby up. 'Just hang on to Mammy, love, that's a good boy.' Charlie screamed and kicked her in the face and grabbed her hair. The phone fell out of her hand and disappeared beneath the froth.

'Help!' Alison screamed after it, hoping the woman could still hear.

The water was rising, but at least with the baby on her shoulders Alison could wade a bit faster. Big boulders of cloud turned day to night, a late summer evening into a December dusk.

She was moving forward, or at least she thought she was, but it seemed to be in slow motion and the landscape was becoming more blurred. Her shoulders ached from the weight. After what seemed like ages, she heard a noise. It sounded like a boat. Alison was frantic by this stage.

'Over here,' she waved and thrashed about, unsure where the sound was coming from. Charlie was almost hysterical. The water was now above her waist, and even standing firm was getting more difficult.

'It's OK, love . . . Charlie, look, darling, here's the big ship and it's going to take us home.' As she spoke Alison realized the noise was coming from above. It had started to rain, but her eyes were wet anyway, even before she looked up.

'Help' seemed to be the only word she knew, and she was hoarse from shouting it. The noise was deafening now and Charlie was very frightened. Alison saw an action-man figure on a rope, dangling dangerously over her head. She felt weak with relief. Charlie was going to be safe and dry and Lily wouldn't have to worry. Alison would take care of them both, just as she always had.

'Thank God,' she screamed. 'Take him first, please take him first!'

She tried to hold up her precious bundle. The man was nearly on top of them. Alison couldn't hold on, her arms were almost out of their sockets. The water was cold on her breasts. Charlie kicked and screamed and she swallowed a mouthful of dirty water.

'Hold the baby in your arms and I'll take you both,' was what she thought he said, but now Alison was the hysterical child.

'Nooooo!' She forced her arms up once more, holding Charlie up to him in a vice-like grip. Her hands were numb and she couldn't feel her fingers. 'Please, take him first, please, I can't hold him for much longer.' She thrust her baby towards him, begging him with her eyes. 'Please, I'm OK, just don't let anything happen to my baby.'

'Hold on, I'll be back for you in a jif.' The wind carried

his words away. He was saying something else and Alison was trying to lip-read through her tears and the noise and the stinging rain. He swooped on them and had Charlie in an armlock an instant later. She watched as he fastened her precious child to his waist.

'Don't panic, Alison, I've got him. Are you OK? Can you stay standing?'

'I think so. My skirt is . . .' She swayed, feeling faint from the effort and weak with relief that her little boy was safe at last.

'Take it off,' he yelled and she tried to kick her legs free.

'Be careful with him, please,' she begged again. 'My sister will be . . .' She couldn't speak.

'You're both safe, just stay calm and don't worry. I'll be back before you know it.' His smile was reassuring but seemed to come from far away and Alison watched her baby get smaller and smaller, saw his arms and legs flail like a battery-operated plastic doll. Her own arms didn't seem to want to go back into their normal position, as if they'd been wrenched too far from their sockets. The current was stronger now.

Please God, don't let my baby die, and let my sister know I love her, Alison prayed out loud in a strangled voice as she willed her only child up to safety and the icy water pulled her down.

2

WILLIAM AND BETH

A PUPPY BARKING GOT THE DAY OFF TO AN EARLY START for William Hammond. It took a few seconds before he realized it was the alarm on his phone. He jumped up, feeling the tension before he was fully awake. Yawning, he flicked open the phone to kill the yelp. A photo of two adorable Jack Russell puppies complete with cowboy neckerchiefs greeted him. He half smiled, half grimaced as he thought about hitting the snooze button, wishing that such a simple luxury was his this morning.

'Cup of tea.'

It wasn't a question. Beth, his wife, always had to work at being cheerful in the mornings, so she usually glided in, humming a tune, trying to pretend she was fully awake. Her dark hair was piled on top of her head in a knot and she was wearing pink fluffy pyjamas and a ridiculous pair of slippers with smiley faces – a Christmas present from the kids.

'Very fetching hairstyle.' He stretched out his arms.

'Isn't it?' She winked. 'Shame you're rushing away.'

Tea by the bed for him was part of the routine. William was in theatre today and as usual Beth had set her alarm to go off fifteen minutes earlier than his. Even though his work had been part of their lives from the start, William liked it that she still fussed over him. It meant she appreciated the weight he carried around with him on days when it really was a matter of life or death.

He took the china mug without a word, handing Beth his phone in return. 'Have a look at the latest offering from those conniving characters we call our children.'

'What is it this time?'

'More puppies. They never give up.'

'Well, maybe we should—' She stopped even before she saw the look on his face. 'OK, OK, another time, don't get stressed.' She kissed him on the head. 'I'll just get breakfast organized.'

'Thanks.' He sipped the hot liquid then glanced at the time again. 'Actually, I'd better jump in the shower or I'll be running behind before I even start.' He was out the door ahead of her, cup in hand. Without stopping in case she was tempted to climb back into bed, Beth pulled open the heavy curtains and yanked at the blind. It was almost morning. Quickly, she plumped the pillows and folded back the duvet, then opened the top of the big bay window to air the room. There was already another one open on Will's side. He liked fresh air and she didn't care, although sometimes, especially in winter, she longed for that peculiar warm human smell that had always been part of her room as a little girl.

19

In the kitchen, porridge glugged away on the stove. Beth loved everything about this room – the warmth, the clutter and the feeling of freshly baked bread she always thought you got just from looking at an Aga. Come to think of it, she hadn't baked in ages. She resolved to have a major baking day later in the week – breads with olive oil and rosemary; Madeira cake with coconut icing, the one that Harry loved. Oh, and she'd get in the mood by doing a big steak and kidney pie for William tonight, even though he was always watching his weight. She'd lie and tell him it was low-fat pastry. Looking around, Beth flicked an imaginary speck of dust and smiled to herself. She felt safe here.

'Hi, Mum,' a sleepy voice interrupted the early morning reverie.

'Hi, love, what are you doing up? It's still the middle of the night.'

'Then why are you up?' Harry Hammond dug his knuckle into his eye in an effort to wipe the sleep away.

'Daddy's in theatre today. You know I always make him breakfast before he operates.' Beth crouched down to inspect her son. 'Why don't you go back to bed? You've another two hours, at least.'

'I'm not tired any more.'

'Well then, have a glass of juice,' she handed him the one she'd just finished squeezing for Will, 'and go inside to the playroom and watch some TV until Daddy's had a chance to relax. Isn't that programme on early in the morning – the one with the warriors?'

'Dunno.' He shrugged. 'I'm hungry.'

'Well, go check and I'll bring you in pancakes and hot chocolate as a special treat as soon as Daddy's gone.' William didn't approve of her constant spoiling of the kids. 'How's that, will your hunger wait for five minutes?' she teased.

'Thanks, Mum.' He was an easy child. Early morning TV was a treat, and without his big sister Winnie owning the remote it was heaven.

'Morning, Harry, what has you up?' William appeared, fixing his tie and draping the jacket of his dark grey suit over a chair. He looked handsome and alive and definitely someone you'd notice.

'Nothing,' the little boy mumbled and wandered off, already in his own early morning, action-man world.

Beth placed a fresh glass of juice in front of her husband and brought the teapot over to the table.

'Actually I think I'll switch to coffee, if there's any going.'

'Yep.' His wife handed over the cafetière she'd just filled for herself. 'What's this about? You never drink coffee in the morning.'

'I know. But I'm tired today. Don't have the energy, for some reason.'

'Well, you look rested and ready to take on the world.' She always envied him his get-up-and-go attitude. She'd struggled with mornings all her life and Harry was the same, much to William's irritation. 'Did you sleep?' she asked her husband.

'Yes, I did actually. Soon as my head hit the pillow. But you know how it is. I never really relax the night before a big one.'

'Will it be a long day?' Beth set the porridge down beside him and checked again that he had everything he needed. She moved the milk jug and honey closer to his hand.

'Shouldn't be too bad. If there are no complications I'll be home for dinner.'

Beth knew he probably wouldn't be. Her husband was the most committed surgeon she'd ever met, and she had got to know quite a few over the years. He wouldn't leave tonight till he was 100 per cent happy with everything and everybody. She knew that the operation was the removal of a tumour from a thirty-two-year-old man who had been diagnosed with cancer despite being super healthy and very fit. It was the position of the tumour, close to a major artery, that was the main concern. William told her all about his patients. They were his other family and she took an interest in their lives too. Matt Jennings was an engineer, she knew. Very successful, according to William. His wife was expecting their second child. Beth always said a prayer for the family on the day of an operation. It was very hard on them as well.

'Where's Harry gone? Back to bed?'

'No, he couldn't sleep. He's watching TV.' She put the wholewheat toast down and picked up William's porridge bowl. As before, she moved the necessary accompaniments closer and took the milk and honey to her side of the table.

'He watches too much TV.'

'He'll be fine,' Beth soothed. 'He's like me. Needs to come round slowly.'

'I can't understand that. I think he's not getting enough rest, he plays those computer games all evening.'

'He doesn't. I monitor him carefully, you know that. Anyway, he has rugby after school. No shortage of fresh air today.'

'How's he doing at it?'

'Fine. The coach says he's keen.' She realized William hadn't seen him play in ages. 'You should try and get to his match on Saturday. He'd love it.'

'Well, I'll see what I can do, but last time I saw him play soccer he spent most of the match shouting at his mates on the sidelines. If I'd been the referee I'd have sent him off.'

'He was probably bored,' Beth said, laughing. That was Harry, always teasing someone, always up for a laugh. She heard the newspaper arrive and went to fetch it to distract her husband from the 'when I was a child' lecture.

'Stop worrying.' She kissed his head and handed him the paper. 'Harry is a well-adjusted little boy. Just like you were,' she teased.

He grinned at her and said nothing. Beth knew him so well. He liked that.

'More coffee?'

'Eh, no, thanks. Can't afford to be jittery.'

She poured herself a first cup and came to stand beside him to check what had made the front page today. Nothing major, she suspected, having heard the early morning radio bulletin while her husband showered.

It was all about the Middle East and the war on terror. Definitely nothing new there. She sat down again and munched on her wholegrain toast, spooning honey on after one bite in an effort to liven it up.

BOY RESCUED FROM SEA BUT WOMAN DROWNS. William glanced at the small insert in the bottom right-hand corner of the front page.

'Anything interesting?' Beth asked.

'No. Some woman drowned on Sandymount Strand last evening. A child was rescued, seemingly.'

'That's awful. Who was she?'

'No name given. Details are sketchy. An air-sea rescue unit tried to save her.' William sipped his coffee. 'Oh and house prices rose again last month.' He was reading the index.

'What's new? We're so lucky, you know.'

'What, the house?' He glanced around.

'The house, our holiday home. Two healthy kids, no money worries, everything.' Beth sighed. 'Some poor family without a mother or daughter this morning.' She shook her head to rid herself of morbid thoughts and stood up just as her husband did.

'I know we're lucky.' He kissed her cheek. 'And you keep us all on the straight and narrow.' It was true. Beth was a wonderful wife and mother. He patted her backside. 'See you later. And don't go out with that hairstyle. You'll frighten the birds.'

'Very funny.' She walked him to the door. 'Mind your-self driving home tonight. You'll be tired.'

'I'll call you before I leave.'

'Hope it all goes well.' She never quite knew what to say when he would be working to save someone's life.

'Yeah,' he sighed. 'Me too.'

He did look tired, she noticed, which wasn't like him at all. That was her territory. Normally he was a powerball of energy.

Beth closed the door and went to switch on the TV in the kitchen while she made hot chocolate and pancakes for herself and Harry. She wanted to hear if there was any more news on that poor woman who'd drowned.

3

RICHARD AND DAISY

RICHARD KEARNEY WAS ALLERGIC TO EARLY MORNINGS, which was unfortunate because his livelihood depended on them just now. He didn't have to face one today, however, because it had long since disappeared. Opening his eyes gingerly, he glanced at the clock, then blinked, because he knew he was reading it upside down or something. Also, the face looked funny, sort of wavy. Before he could work it out his phone rang. By the time he realized it was ringing it wasn't.

'OK, concentrate,' he mumbled, trying to work out what day it was and where he was supposed to be. He had a dull but definite ache at the back of his head and someone had packed his mouth with cotton wool like they did at the dentist. Yawning, he shook his head, trying to clear the debris. His tongue felt like a rice cake. He got out of bed slowly and glanced at the clock again. Now that he was upright he realized why it looked odd. It was immersed in a pint glass of water. He was sure that had been hilarious at three o'clock this morning.

'Hi, babe.' He wasn't surprised to hear the strange female voice mutter from under the duvet, because he definitely remembered the great shag he'd been having just before he realized he couldn't perform, and passed out.

'What day is it?'

'What?'

'Today, what day is it?' He was already looking for his clothes.

'Thursday, why?'

'Fuck, are you sure?'

'Sure I'm sure, and do you know why?' A tousled blonde head peeked out at him.

'No idea.' He grabbed his boxers.

''Cause yesterday was Wednesday.' The pretty blonde girl giggled. 'Come back to bed, pleeeeease?'

'Can't, Viv, sorry. I'm already in big trouble.' He was out the door and halfway to the shower before she could work out her next move, which was normally to pull back the duvet and show her man exactly what sort of incentive she was offering.

Richard hit number three on his speed dial with his face screwed up, as if in real pain. 'Hello, Maggie?' he said tentatively, taking it as a good sign that she'd actually answered when she'd seen his name come up on her mobile. 'Look, don't ball me out, I swear I'm on the way,' he told his manageress, the only woman in the world he was afraid of, even though he was the boss. Maggie ran the café with a rod of iron and he'd never admit it but it was exactly what he needed. He was turning on the shower, grabbing towels and trying to clean his teeth while making the call.

'Hello, Mags.' He glanced at the screen, cursed and dialled again.

'Maggie, look, just hear me out . . . Hello, hello? Fuck!' he roared and flung the phone down. Luckily the rug broke its fall. In the shower he tried to think logically. He was supposed to open up this morning. God, she was going to kill him. There wasn't an excuse on the planet that would win her round today.

Ten minutes later he'd sort of dried himself and dressed in the only clean shirt he could find.

'Viv, honey, I'm sorry but I've got to go.' She was fast asleep. He didn't have time for this shite, so he shook her awake.

'What time is it? Richard, stop, you're hurting me.' She sat up quickly.

'Listen, gotta go. Here's some money for a taxi. Take your time, have coffee, whatever. I'll ring you.' He thought about kissing her but realized he couldn't be bothered. 'Pull the door after you,' he shouted as he picked up his keys and wallet and checked he had his phone.

On the way in he thought about the night before. It had been fun. His best mate, Tom Dalton, was the latest big thing on radio and got invited to everything, and invariably Richard tagged along.

'Hey, bud, what time is it?' his mate greeted him. He'd

dialled the number at the first red light he'd encountered, and hoped there were no cops lurking because his hands-free kit was busted.

'It's half nine and you, ye bollocks, don't have to be anywhere till tonight, I'd say.' Richard laughed and his tension eased as the slagging started. He enjoyed it and could give as good as he got any day.

'Yeah, I just left her, actually,' he admitted in response to a question about Viv and what they'd been up to. 'How about you?'

Tom had been just as successful, it transpired, and they complimented each other on their pulling power – as you do – although Richard didn't mention his inability to do anything about it once he'd gotten Viv into the sack.

'Gotta go, I'm there and I'm in for a shitload of grovelling,' he sighed.

'Maggie?' Tom laughed.

'Don't mention the war. She'll bleedin' lynch me.'

'You're the boss, remember?' They all knew Maggie. Tom was terrified of her too. 'Why do you keep her?' he asked Richard. 'She'd do your head in.' It wasn't the first time they'd had this conversation.

'I need her. She saves me a fortune and besides, she's the most efficient woman I've ever met in my life.' Richard's head was throbbing again. 'Anyway, talk to you later.' He parked on a double yellow and tried to stroll nonchalantly towards the coffee shop. He pushed against the door but it wasn't going anywhere. It was only then that he noticed there were no lights on.

'Richard, over here.' He looked across the green and saw Hazel, his chef, and Lucy, his zany waitress, smoking and drinking coffee without a care in the world. Tommo, their kitchen porter – dogsbody really – sat on a bench nearby, texting. His girlfriend, Richard suspected. It was what he did most of the time at work anyway. Richard ran over to them, without stopping to admire the pretty enclosed park that they were lucky enough to have opposite the café. In summer, this hidden gem made Ringsend a haven for students, local office workers and hassled mothers trying to keep kids busy. Its proximity to the sea added an extra air of languidness, Richard always thought, and meant they did a great business in takeaways – an unexpected bonus that he'd fully exploited, laying on a 'picnic in the park' menu whenever the sun appeared.

'What's going on, where's Maggie? What are you doing sitting here, handing business to that dump across the road?'

Richard kicked at the empty cup Hazel had just set down in order to answer her mobile. He needed a caffeine hit badly himself at this stage. That and a Solpadeine sandwich – definitely not recommended by the manufacturers though.

'Maggie couldn't come in,' Lucy said nonchalantly.

'What?' He heard but didn't understand.

'We rang her, but she said she was busy.'

'So who opened up?'

'No one.' Tommo had stopped texting long enough to stretch out and enjoy the still-warm autumn sun.

Richard was getting angry now. Leaning in closer, he asked in a quiet voice, 'So why the hell didn't someone ring me?'

'We did, loads of times.' Hazel gave him a reproachful look.

'No answer.' Lucy shrugged and blew a dirty grey bubble in his direction. He wanted to burst it straight into her smug mug.

'You mean the fucking place has been closed all morning?' he asked incredulously, knowing there was no point getting annoyed. It rolled off them anyway.

'It's not even ten o'clock.' Tommo had on his usual dazed and confused look.

'Right.' Richard changed tack. 'I'm here now, so inside and get cracking.' He lunged towards the door and practically flung them in ahead of him once he'd opened up. 'Hazel, get the ovens on. Lucy, lights and music. Tommo, put that fucking phone away and clean up those tables. You're supposed to do them before you go home in the evening anyway. How many times do I have to fucking tell you?'

'I was late last night and Maggie told me to leave them.' The young man had a sullen look on his face and Richard wanted to chuck him out there and then, but Maggie would skin him alive. She really liked the little wanker.

'Well, I make the rules around here and no one goes home until the tables are cleared and the floor is washed, OK?'

31

'Yes, boss. I'll help.' Lucy smiled, the peacemaker as usual.

'And here, Tommo, move my car and be quick about it.' Richard threw the keys in his general direction and prepared to do battle with what was left of the day.

It was three o'clock before he got anything more than a glass of OJ and by that time his head was hanging off. Several of the regulars wanted to know why they hadn't been open early as usual and Dolores, the snooty HR manager from the big software company next door, moaned that she'd had to take clients elsewhere for breakfast.

'Not good enough, Richard.' She flicked back her blonde hair and wagged her finger at him. 'We're your loyal customers, don't forget that. You need us.'

I need you like a dose of the clap, Richard thought. She'd never forgiven him since he'd rejected her advances in the pub one night last Christmas. Hell, he'd left the place without finishing his pint, and that said it all. She was a bow-wow.

'Sorry, Dolores, won't happen again.' He forced a smile. 'Have a Danish on me, why don't you?' Fat cow, he thought as he handed her the pastry.

He had to prise the coffee cup out of the hand of a pensioner at ten past five, because he couldn't cope for a second longer. His eyes were stinging and even hangover food – along with a sachet of Get Up And GO, courtesy of Lucy – hadn't helped him move one bit faster.

He put down the roof of his Audi on the way home in an effort to blow away the fuzz. It took him ten minutes before his shoulders relaxed.

He rang another of his mates. 'Hey, Jim, fancy a quick pint?'

'Yeah, suits me. I've had one helluva day.'

Richard laughed. Jim was wrecked too, it seemed. 'See you in ten. What? No, I'm on the way. I'll get them in.' He hung up and sighed. Christ, what a day. And he had Maggie to face in the morning. Richard rubbed his forehead. Still, a pint would help ease the pain.

His phone rang.

'Hi, Daisy, what's up?' he asked gingerly, knowing he'd have to be careful. His fiancée was razor sharp when it came to his gallivanting, as she called it. She grilled him about the night before.

'No, nothing . . . We went to a couple of gigs, that's all . . . No, I was home early enough. What did you do? How's your mother? No, babe, I couldn't face it. You go . . . No, I haven't forgotten the weekend. It's all organized . . . OK, hon . . . Yeah, I'm gonna hit the sack . . . OK, talk to you then . . . You too, babe.' He flicked the phone shut.

Christ, he'd have to watch himself. Daisy was getting suspicious. It was too much to think about just now. He turned on the radio for some light relief.

'The young woman who drowned last night in Dublin has still not . . .' the newsreader droned.

'No, thank you.' Richard twiddled the dial until he found some mind-numbing sounds.

4

JAMES AND TAMSIN

AS SOON AS HE OPENED THE FRONT DOOR JAMES KNEW something was wrong. It was too quiet. Even in their childless, coffee and cream home there were normally dogs on the rampage and a TV or radio droning. At the very least there would be music. Tamsin adored music. He knew immediately that this silence could mean only one thing.

'Anyone home?' His voice sounded falsely bright. 'Tamsin, darling, where are you?' She came to greet him most evenings, was usually smiling no matter what the day had brought and almost always flanked by an animal or two.

'I'm in here.' The childlike voice was barely audible. His heart started thumping and he dropped his briefcase and threw his jacket off as he moved quickly towards the bedroom.

She was curled up like the child she craved. Her copper hair was matted and her greeny-grey eyes were puffy. He gathered her to him and held her. They stayed that way for several minutes. Neither spoke. There was no need. Her sobs told him what he'd dreaded hearing. He rocked her gently and rubbed her back. 'Shhh, it's OK, baby. It's OK.'

'I just jjjjumped into the shower and I was washing myself and there was . . . blood.' Her sobs were stronger and they jolted him too.

'Did you ring the doctor?'

'No, there's no point, he can't help, he's done all he can.' She looked up at him as if he could solve it somehow. 'Oh James, what are we going to do?'

'I don't know yet, love, but it'll be OK, I promise.' He kissed her head and held her as tight as he could, wishing he could change it for her. For them both.

After a few more minutes he lifted her face to his and kissed her wet eyes. His own were damp.

'Will I make us a cup of tea?'

'Nnnnno. I don't want you to leave me.'

'Fine. Why don't you come into the kitchen with me and I'll bring the duvet and you can curl up on the sofa while I make you some herbal tea?'

She blew her nose and he stood her up gently and fastened the big white robe tightly around her, even though the underfloor heating ensured the house was always toasty. He half carried her towards the big squashy sofa, with the dogs and the duvet trailing behind.

Levi and Wrangler, their two westies, fussed about her and even Pepe, their rescued greyhound, who was usually content to observe the family antics from the comfort of his spongy basket, padded over to be closer to her, as if he could sense her pain.

James barely had time to tuck her in before the smaller dogs claimed their corner of her lap. Pepe sat at her feet and James looked away when he saw them, in case his grief upset her.

He made cranberry and raspberry tea and handed it to her.

They sat for a short while, each lost in their own thoughts, but with them that never lasted long. They shared everything.

'I feel so empty.' Her eyes were the saddest he'd ever seen them. 'As well as that, I feel . . .' She bit her lip. 'I feel such a failure.' She was crying again.

'Darling, you're not a failure.' He had tears in his eyes too. 'You're the best in the world and I love you more than anything and you mustn't torment yourself over this.'

'I know what this means to you, too.' She reached up to wipe his eyes with her hands and then pulled him to her. 'I just feel . . . so awful. It hurts, James. It really hurts.'

'I know, love, I know.'

'What are we going to do now?'

'I don't know. That's for tomorrow.'

'I felt so good this time. I was sure I was . . . pregnant. I dunno, it just felt different.'

'I know, you kept saying that. And I felt good too.' He hadn't told her just how much he was banking on it working this time. In his head he'd made all the plans for their happy-ever-after life.

'I'm so sorry I don't seem to be able to give you the baby you want so much.'

'It's not your fault.' He held her face in his hands. 'It just wasn't meant to be this time, that's all.'

'But it's the end, we both agreed that this was our last attempt.'

He shushed her with his finger on her lips. 'Don't torment yourself about it tonight, there's a good girl.'

'You know what they said.' She was crying again. 'They told us that this was it, really . . .'

'I know, I know,' but he wasn't ready to go there just yet.

'Will we ever survive this?'

'Yes, we will. We have each other and we've got through things before.'

'Not like this, though.' She pressed herself to him. 'I love you, James. I don't know what I'd do without you.'

'I love you too.'

They sat and talked some more and he brought her some soup, which she barely touched.

'Will I make more tea?'

She shook her head. He poured himself a glass of wine and sat down beside her. She said nothing but James knew she didn't really approve.

Tamsin only ever had a drink on special occasions and it was one of the very few things on which they didn't always see eye to eye. James liked an odd glass of wine, especially after a hard day, and he hated having to justify it to her. They argued about it sometimes, particularly if he stopped off with the guys for one after work, which happened only rarely. James knew it would be easier if he didn't drink at all, but he did it anyway and that surprised him. Tamsin's father had been a heavy drinker and he knew that was part of it, but at times she could be bloody unreasonable and occasionally it irked him.

He drained the glass and would have liked another. It had been a bitch of a day, even before all this. But instead he helped her back to bed and kissed her red eyes and washed her face with a warm flannel.

'I haven't cleaned my teeth.'

'Let me see.' He was teasing her. 'I think they'll survive till the morning. Unless you've been eating toffees?'

She shook her head.

'OK, snuggle in there.' He fixed her pillows. 'Will I make you some cocoa?'

'Yes, please.'

'Coming up. Want a chocolate biscuit to go with it?' He tried to encourage her to eat but she shook her head.

By the time he came back she was fast asleep. He took a mouthful of the stuff and grimaced, then decided to leave it beside her for the moment. He ran his hand gently across her face and smoothed her hair. Even in rest she looked troubled and he kissed her hair and wished again that he could take away her pain.

After cleaning his own teeth and splashing his face he wandered round the place for a bit. He really wanted to channel-hop mindlessly for an hour or two until he found one of those reality TV shows, but he knew Tamsin would reach for him, even in her sleep, and be disturbed if he wasn't there. Yawning, he climbed into bed beside her, having locked up and made sure the monsters had peed.

He turned on the TV, keeping the sound low. Even though he was exhausted James knew he wouldn't sleep at this time of night. Too much pent-up energy and emotion. The nine o'clock news was just starting and he caught the tail end of a report on a drowning tragedy. A picture flashed on the screen and he wasn't sure he'd seen it right. His heart started thumping as he waited for more information but the newsreader had moved on to a report about Iraq, so James quickly flicked to the other Irish channels to see if there was news on any of them. RTE 2 was showing sport and TV3 another of those American sitcoms. He flicked back and waited for the headlines at the end of the bulletin but there was no mention of the story again.

Eventually he turned off the TV along with his bedside lamp and lay there in the darkness, wide awake. James knew he wouldn't sleep until he found out for sure. He could still clearly see the picture that had been on screen a few minutes earlier. It looked awfully like Alison. Throwing back the duvet, he padded downstairs again and waited impatiently for some late news headlines. He kept telling himself he was being ridiculous.

5
DAVE AND MARIE

THE PUB WAS HEAVING. IT WAS LIKE THIS EVERY THURSDAY and Dave Madden loved it. So did Marie, his wife. The only thing that annoyed him was the bloody smoking ban. Every time he thought about that feckin' former Minister for Health Micheál Martin he fumed. And very little annoyed Dave. 'Chill out, love,' he was always telling the missus, who took everything in life personally and was constantly letting things get to her.

'Just goin' outside for a smoke. Want another drink?' he asked her now.

'No, thanks. What's up with you? You've a face like a bag of hammers.'

'I'd just rather be havin' my pint inside. With you, my love,' he added for good measure, giving her a kiss. 'Lookin' good tonight, babe.' Dave always said the right thing. His wife was very sensitive about her appearance and especially about her weight, since she'd hit the change a few months ago. Years of putting his foot in it – mostly in jest, mind you – meant he now had the patter off by heart, even if he didn't really think she was hot totty any more.

Marie Madden smiled at her husband. He was the looker and they both knew it. Even after all this time she still liked being seen in public with him. At forty-eight he still had a lot of hair – his own – and soccer coaching, cycling and the local golf club meant he had the body of a thirty-year-old. He was one of the most popular guys in the area, and she was glad she'd caught him young. Dave had turned heads ever since they'd started dating as kids and that hadn't diminished one bit as he got older. In fact, Marie thought he got better-looking as he aged. If only she could say the same about herself. She sighed, hating the fact that she was pushing fifty. Today she felt about seventy. Her joints ached and when she'd looked in the mirror earlier she saw that her jowls were getting more droopy by the day and the lines around her eyes made her seem permanently tired, whereas her husband was fresh-faced and full of energy.

'Joan?' Dave finished his chat with a fellow golfer and turned his attention to Marie's sister, who was on the Bacardi Breezers.

'No, Dave, you're grand.'

'Another diet?' It was the only time she ever refused a drink.

'Sort of, I'm trying to look my best. Actually,' she leaned towards him, 'I've met a fella and he's here so I don't want to get langers.'

'Who is he? Do I know him?' Dave looked around the velour-infested lounge.

41

'No, but I'll introduce you later, maybe.' Joan was playing it cool. She was a glamorous blonde in her mid-forties, divorced with a teenage son who was a handful, and she was worried about scaring yet another guy off by appearing too eager.

'Can't wait. You seem to be playin' a blinder.' He winked at her and squeezed her shoulder. 'Let me know if you want me to make him jealous,' he teased, having heard the girls talking about the subject more than once over a few bottles of wine and a Chinese takeaway in his kitchen. 'OK then, off to freeze me balls off.' He picked up his glass and took a gulp before heading outside.

Normally he knew everyone here and there was no shortage of conversation, but tonight a visiting football team was up from Tipperary or somewhere and after a few nods and a 'How's she cuttin', Dave?' – a culchie greeting that he despised – he found himself without a mate.

He lit a fag and inhaled deeply. Dave had been smoking since he was fourteen and even now, all these years later, he still got as much pleasure out of every drag.

There was nothing to match the first fag of the day; that was the one he enjoyed most. Recently Marie had been complaining about the smell of smoke and talking about getting a patio done outside, so he supposed it was only a matter of time before he was having that one outdoors too. The bloody country had gone mad, what with all the recycling and taxes on plastic bags and everything. Stop moaning, he chided himself. You sound like an oulfella.

Dave wished there was a seat so he could sit and relax. But since the fancy awnings had gone up and the patio heaters had been installed there wasn't a hope. Too many yuppies out here most nights now. And Thursday was practically the start of the weekend, with all the money in Ireland these last few years. He listened to a gang of guys in suits discussing the price of houses and how a three-bedroomed semi in Drumcondra had recently sold for a million and his spirits soared. It had been great being in the building trade these last few years and business was showing no signs of slowing down, no matter what the experts were saying.

He leaned against the wall, trying to ease the strain on his back. Like his wife, Dave wasn't a fan of getting older but unlike Marie he worked hard at looking after himself. Marie sat around and talked about getting fit, mostly while eating a packet of chocolate chip cookies and on the phone to Joan, whereas Dave got up off his arse and did something about it. A lot of money went on clothes, too, and he used products on his face, unlike most of his mates. He liked it that women still looked at him when he walked into a room. A well-cut jacket and decent shirt worked wonders, he'd long since decided.

'How's it going?' his old pal John Brophy greeted him. 'Are you golfing at the weekend?'

'No plans. You?'

'Might play a round on Sunday morning if you're interested?'

'Ah, I think I'll pass.'

'Still not feeling great?'

'No, and don't say anything to the wife. You know what women are like.'

'I do, yeah.' His pal indicated the almost empty glass. 'Another one?'

'No, thanks.' Dave grinned. 'I'm tryin' to cut down.' He patted his stomach.

'And I'm Muhammad Ali.' John put up his fists and did a little dance.

'You're pathetic,' Dave told his pal, but it wasn't meant.

'We can't all be Brad bleedin' Pitt.' John gave his mate a few playful slaps on the face. 'Smooth as a baby's bum. All those face scrubs must be worth it, eh?' John loved to tease Dave about not looking his age. 'Anyway, I'll see you inside. The missus'll be looking for me.'

'Take it handy.' Dave laughed. He spotted an empty table and sat down to enjoy another fag and finish his pint in peace. He watched the group of suits again. Marks and Sparks, he reckoned, noticing the way most of the jackets were cut and the trousers hung. Good basic work gear but not for him. He only wore Boss or Armani. Not that he wore suits to work, except when he had meetings. Marie always teased him that he was the only man she knew who ever noticed what other men wore, but he'd always been that way, even when he didn't have a bean.

A copy of the *Evening Herald* had been left behind. He lit another cigarette and glanced at the front page.

WOMAN DROWNS TRYING TO SAVE CHILD, he read, and glanced at the picture. She looked young. It was only when he read the caption that it hit him. *Alison Ormond – accident or suicide?* Typical bleedin' tabloid sensationalism was his first reaction. Then he looked again.

Jesus Christ, he thought. He jumped up, stamped out the cigarette and moved into the light to read it properly. It must be another Alison, with the same name, he decided, because the picture looked nothing like her. But as he scrutinized it he realized it was definitely her. The eyes gave her away.

He scanned the article, then turned to page two as instructed. The details were sketchy. A woman had phoned the rescue services after she was stranded out at sea when the tide came in on Sandymount Strand yesterday evening. Her young son was with her. Alison didn't have any children, so he was hopeful again. It must be a mistake, he decided, still staring at the black and white photo. Her hair was different, she looked younger – but it was Alison all right, he'd bet his life on it. Dave was gutted. Alison Ormond had been his friend, his confidante, his lover. It didn't bear thinking about that she was dead.

6

LILY

I WAS THE ZANY ONE IN OUR SMALL FAMILY UNIT, OR SO MY sister said. I preferred easy-going. Alison worried enough for both of us, and anyway she was such a doer that there were very few decisions left over for me to make, so it was easy to be a bit of a slouch. My twin had very definite views on life and she was extremely hard to say no to, so most of the time I simply went along with things. It suited me, I suppose. Certainly it made my life easier, although occasionally I wanted to shout, 'No, that's not what I want.' But I never did. On the plus side my sister was the kindest, most generous person in the world and would do anything – literally – to help the few people she really loved, namely me and Charlie, her son.

Alison and Charlie and I were good together. Since he'd come along, my sister had relaxed a bit. Also she'd had to depend on me a bit more, which was – surprisingly – a nice feeling.

That night, I was indulging in my favourite hobby – fantasizing about what I'd do if I won the lotto – and so I remember the split second life as I knew it changed for ever. The kitchen was full of the smell of rosemary and garlic and good olive oil, as I attempted to perfect a new bread to go with the supper Ali had promised. Really I was just killing time – and cooking was one of the few things that totally absorbed me. I'd watched TV for a while but I couldn't concentrate. Something was going on with Alison and I wanted in on the action.

When I heard a noise I flung open the door – even though my sister was always telling me to look through the peephole first – and reached out to take whatever was thrust at me. Ali always came home with the baby in one arm and a load of shopping in the other and usually relieved herself of whichever was causing her the greatest strain, which most evenings was the bundle that wriggled. She never used her keys when she knew I was there. Once loaded up from the car she just waited until one of our neighbours was coming or going and usually signalled her arrival by kicking the door of the apartment.

'And what time do you—' It took me a moment to realize it wasn't her. At first I looked over their shoulders, expecting to see a shamefaced Ali apologizing for giving me a fright. But the hall was deserted. I think I took a step back then, maybe because I saw something in the blank pages of their faces, although even in my wildest imaginings – and I'd had some – I could never have envisaged the full horror story they'd come to deliver.

'How did you get in?' I decided they couldn't be looking for me because they hadn't rung our buzzer.

'One of your neighbours was going out,' the older, male officer explained quietly.

'We're looking for Lily Ormond.' The voice of the female Garda sounded matter-of-fact, just like I'd heard many times on *The Bill*.

'What's happened?'

'Can we come in?'

I stepped back further. 'Please, tell me, has there been an accident?'

The grey-haired man nodded and introduced them both.

'Where is she? I need to see her . . .' I could feel panic beginning to surface.

'Maybe we could go somewhere for a moment.' The young woman looked too nice and too innocent for what I suspected she was about to say. A car accident had been my first thought. 'You might like to sit down . . .'

'The baby, where's Charlie?' I remember shouting then, unable to believe I'd forgotten him even for a second.

'The baby's fine,' the man said quickly. I knew then that it had to be Ali and I backed away from them, not wanting to hear what they seemed intent on telling me.

They sat me down and explained as gently as they could that my sister – my lifelong friend, my soulmate – was dead.

'No,' I said softly and then the word kept getting louder in my head until I realized I was screaming it at them. All of a sudden the chair seemed to disintegrate underneath me and I felt myself slithering, jelly-like, to the floor.

* * *

They did everything they could, held my hand, made tea, let me cry, while explaining in quiet voices what had happened while I'd been watching *EastEnders* and sucking clove drops. Afterwards, they stayed for ages and tried to persuade me to let them call someone to come and stay with me, but I couldn't think of anyone. Sally, my best friend, was living in Australia and Orla, my old school pal, was working in a hotel in Brighton.

'You must have some family?' they prodded gently. 'Other brothers and sisters . . . an aunt or uncle maybe?'

But I couldn't think of anyone – no one I wanted, that is.

'There was just the two of us . . . and Charlie . . .' My voice trailed off. How could I make them understand that the only one who could have helped tonight was the person they'd just taken away with their calmly delivered missile?

'I have to see the baby, make sure he's all right.' I stood up and felt my head go light. 'Will you take me, please?' I grabbed my handbag and ran a comb through my hair, as if it mattered.

When I saw him he looked frightened, even though the Filipina nurse told me she'd been with him all the time.

'Lily!' He held out his arms and I grabbed him. The tears came then and they all tiptoed out to give me space, although what I needed was the claustrophobia of my sister's arms around me, the way she'd done a million times, like when Mum died, or my father was in one of his moods.

'Mammy Lily.' Charlie kept repeating my name as he cried and clung on for dear life to me. Usually, he wasn't able to tell us apart when he saw Alison and me together and it had become a guessing game that the three of us played all the time. He called Ali Mammy and me Mammy Lily even though sometimes he looked at us both when he shouted one of our names, as if covering all his options. What I saw was that hers were the eyes that lit up like beacons each time she spotted him, and she was the one who looked at him with exquisite tenderness and had pale grey circles because she'd never slept soundly at night since he'd come along. He, however, saw us as identical, as most people did, yet on this truly awful night he knew I wasn't her.

'Mammy gone' was all he said.

'It's OK, Charlie, I'm here.' I held him as close as I could without hurting him. 'Mammy Lily is here.' I rocked him back and forth and tried to stop crying. Eventually, he struggled free.

'Mammy gone sea.' He pointed out the window. I kissed him and mumbled something stupid.

'All gone,' he repeated in that wondrous voice he used when he'd eaten all the crisps in the packet and then couldn't believe it was empty.

'Mammy's in Heaven,' I told him gently but he didn't do religion.

'Mammy's in the water.' He looked bewildered. 'The man in the sky took me away.'

They'd told me about the attempted rescue but my mind was refusing to go there yet. Now I thought about how scared he must have been and how frightened my sister must have felt too. I tried to stop the pictures forming in my head but all I could see was her face in the water. Suddenly it felt like I was drowning and the panic made me throw up with fear and desperation. We both sat there, shivering, until they came back in and took him from me and cleaned both of us up and changed the bed and tried to make me drink hot, strong tea.

It was much later when I realized that without Charlie I might not have been able to cope. Having him gave me a focus on that pitch-black night. They wanted to keep him in for observation and because I wouldn't leave him I ended up crashing out beside him on the too small, rubbery bed. All night I went over and over things in my head. Alison had been so happy when we'd spoken at lunchtime. She'd rung to ask if I'd be at home that evening.

'I'm not babysitting' had been my instant response.

'I'm not asking.' Alison had laughed. 'I just want to talk to you.'

'What about?' I was wary. Talking usually meant she had another plan for us.

'Nothing bad, don't worry.' She'd paused, as if about to say something, then seemed to change her mind. 'I'll tell you all tonight. It's good, you'll be happy.'

'You're looking for something,' I'd said and both of us giggled, knowing it was much more likely to be the other way round. 'Don't tell me,' I'd teased her. 'You want to borrow my petrel-blue mini with the silver buttons?'

'Only if you'll lend me your white spangly top to go with it,' she'd snorted, referring to the first item in my wardrobe she'd take a pair of scissors to, given half a chance.

So I'd relaxed and looked forward to the evening. Alison had said we'd order in Italian – which was why I'd been messing around with some new bread – and had offered to bring home a bottle of wine. Such extravagance was not usual for my sister, except where handbags were concerned. It made this whole thing even harder to comprehend.

The groaning doors and squeaky soles on lino provided me with a lifeline that night, reminding me that normality still existed in a world that had stopped for me. I don't think I could have stayed alone in the flat. As it was I curled up in a corner of the bed with the TV on, and only realized I'd slept when I woke up very early feeling cold and shivery despite the stifling hospital temperature.

A new nurse brought me more strong tea and buttery toast and left me a makeshift toilet bag, which at least allowed me to clean my teeth and comb my hair, although the smell of sick still clung to me. While they did a final check on Charlie, I sat in a faded velour seat by the window and tried to make a mental list of things I needed to do. Even that felt strange. Alison was the list-maker and a million other things besides. She was the organizer, the doer, the charmer, the communicator. Without her I felt ten years old again. I wanted someone to bring me breakfast of a boiled egg and soldiers, or at the very least jolly me along, the way she used to when we were kids and my father was on the warpath.

'Come on, Lily, eat your vegetables, otherwise we'll be in trouble with Dad.'

'Don't want them. I hate broccoli.'

'OK, tell you what, give it over to me.' My sister expertly cleared my plate on to hers. 'Here, you have my chicken, you like chicken.' She had it all sorted in an instant.

'Good girl, eat up and be very quiet. Dad's in a bad mood tonight. And if you're good we could sneak a book up to bed later and read without anyone knowing. How about that?'

It was just one of a thousand times she'd made it all OK for me.

The nice female Garda, Susan Malone, knocked on the door then. The clock on the wall told me it was almost eight a.m. She looked even more fresh-faced, whereas I felt I'd withered overnight.

'Are you still on duty?' I was surprised.

'Nearly finished,' she told me. 'I just wanted to make sure you were all right and take you home, or wherever you need to go.'

'Thank you.' I was amazed by all the kindness. 'Home would be good, I suppose.'

'There'll be phone calls to make, things to organize . . .' She trailed off.

'I guess so,' I agreed, even though action of any kind seemed beyond me right then.

The sister on duty gave me her direct line in case I needed to talk to anyone about Charlie, and then we left to face the most dreaded day of my life so far.

Aunt Milly, that was who I'd call, I decided after letting several cups of tea go cold while I sat with the phone in my hand. It was the easiest, and besides, she just might know what to do or where to start.

When our mother died just before our fifth birthday, it had been Aunt Milly who'd kept us going. She was Mum's younger sister, the one who'd stayed in the family home in Cork and looked after our elderly grandparents. Milly was a giver, everyone said so. 'It's all she knows, poor thing,' Ali had told me a couple of months ago, when we'd been discussing the family. 'She deserves to be looked after herself for a change.'

I hadn't given it much thought at the time.

Now I was nervous about phoning her, because it had been so long since I'd been in touch. What if she wouldn't help me? I dialled while reciting a childhood prayer that Ali and I used to say every night when we needed guidance.

'Aunty Milly, I have some terrible news,' I blurted out as soon as pleasantries were out of the way.

'What's up, child?' The soft, lilting Cork brogue was my undoing.

54

'It's Ali, she . . . she's dead.' I felt my eyes fill up saying it for the first time. I bit hard on my lip.

'Jesus, Mary and Holy St Joseph, what are you saying to me?'

'She drowned . . . last night. She got caught too far out and . . . and they couldn't get to her in time.' I tried to hold it together. 'The baby's OK, though,' I told her quickly.

'She had the baby with her?'

'Yeah . . .' I gulped as I watched him watching me. 'But he's fine, don't worry. He was in hospital, but just for observation. He's here beside me, glued to the cartoons on TV.'

'Oh my poor pet, I can't believe what you're telling me. I was only talking to her last week.'

'Aunt Milly, will you come up?' I wasn't sure I'd ask, but I needed a mother so badly right now.

'Of course, child. I'll come today. Let me get a few things together here and organize one of the neighbours to keep an eye on the dog.'

Horace. That was all I could think of then. Ali hated Aunt Milly's dog, said he made Dennis the Menace's dog Gnasher seem attractive. She always insisted he had the personality of Maggie Thatcher. All the neighbours hoped he'd get lost some day and constantly left her front gate open, Ali claimed.

'Thanks.' I jerked myself back to the present. 'It's just I . . . can't really cope on my own.'

'I'm on the way, don't fret yourself. I'll probably be on the lunchtime train and then I'll get a taxi. Just give me directions again, I know I have the address here some-where.' I could hear her rooting around for a pen and paper. 'Sorry, love, I'm all addled. Here it is. Now, give me your phone number first.'

We chatted for a while longer and I gave her what little information I had and she promised to ring me back as soon as she'd made arrangements.

Next I called our other aunt, my father's only sibling.

'Aunt Rose, it's Lily . . . Lily Ormond,' I felt I should add. We hadn't seen each other in yonks.

When I told her I could tell she was shocked, but she was much more controlled in her emotions. Just like my father, I thought bitterly. Ali said it was all they knew. Apparently their own parents had never been affectionate to either of them. As I answered her questions I gave thanks for my own lovely mother, who'd given us every-thing during those first crucial years before she died.

We spoke for a little while and I promised to ring back later when I knew more. Rose offered to come over but I explained that Aunt Milly was on the way.

'I'll go to mass this morning for the poor unfortunate girl.' It was meant to be compassionate but the way she said it made it sound as though Ali had done something to deserve this. I pictured Rose's thin lips slicked over with too much red Max Factor lipstick, the one I used to coat my dolls with when we were little and she wasn't looking.

'Thanks,' I said now because I couldn't think of any-thing else. 'Say one for me.'

'Of course I will.' She made no mention of Charlie but that didn't surprise me. Rose had never approved.

'And Charlie,' I said tightly.

'Yes.'

Talking to her always unnerved me. Her voice was too like my father's. I could still hear him, even now.

'What did I tell you about making noise after bedtime?'

My father seemed to constantly patrol the house.

'It's only seven thirty. I want to go out and play.'

'You will stay in your room and study and be quiet, otherwise you'll get no supper.'

'Lily, shush. Come here,' Ali called. 'Don't annoy him. Let's play quietly by ourselves.'

Ali always said it was simply that he couldn't cope with twin girls. Control was the only way he knew where youngsters were concerned. But we were good, always quiet, always obedient. I tried to rid myself of the unwanted thoughts and went to check on the baby. Charlie was still engrossed in the cartoons. Ali rarely let him watch that sort of stuff, and it was working to my advantage now. He was enthralled by it, sitting mesmerized on a cushion with his juice, locked into his own uncomplicated little world of cats chasing mice and dinosaurs in skirts.

Next up I phoned my boss. The more I said it out loud, the easier it got to say and the harder it was to believe. Stephen Pritchard was already at work in

57

the big glass building where I was employed as a chef.

'Stephen, we had bad news last night. My sister, Alison, was killed. She drowned. It's been a lot to take in, so I'm afraid I won't be in for a while.'

Everyone I rang had the same reaction. Disbelief. Shock. Sympathy. After several more calls I was exhausted and teary again. I made coffee for a change and tried to think what to do next. Sally would know, but Sydney was so far away. I'd have to tell her but I couldn't face it yet, because I knew she'd be devastated. She had only brothers and looked on Ali as her big sister too. I wished she hadn't gone away. I tried Orla again. She shared a house in Brighton when she wasn't staying over at the hotel where she worked, but there was no reply and her mobile was off so I left a message asking her to call me urgently. I hoped she'd be able to come home.

I'd no idea what to do about Alison's work. I knew so little about it really: another sign of my sister's competency. She juggled her life effortlessly, whereas I just about managed. Eventually I called Violet, the girl who helped out part-time. She burst into tears and I found myself in the role of comforter for a change, which kept me going for another little while. After we'd talked for ages, Violet offered to phone clients of The Haven, the little beauty salon Alison had invested so much in. She also promised to put a notice in the window and we quickly worded it together.

Everyone wanted to know about the funeral and I

hadn't a clue where to start. I'd been worried about that during the night. There wasn't much money in either of our accounts and as far as I knew neither of us had any life assurance. I'd no idea what funerals cost anyway. The only person I could think of to ring was Brian Daly. He'd been our family solicitor for years and Alison had gone to him for advice when she was setting up the business. As far as I could remember they were in regular contact, although I hardly knew him.

He seemed completely thrown by the news. He told me in a low voice that he'd had a long meeting with Alison only yesterday.

'Really? She phoned me at lunchtime.' I started to cry again. 'She was in great form,' I said through my sniffles. I wondered if he knew what was going on, or what it was that Alison had wanted to talk to me about. Brian immediately offered to call round to the flat. I was glad to have someone in authority nearby, even though I felt he might be a bit intimidating. He was quite serious, from what I could remember, but I dismissed my fears. I needed someone like him right now; I was completely out of my depth.

He arrived in less than an hour. I had barely showered and changed when he rang the bell.

He asked me to tell him again what had happened and he pressed me for details I didn't have. When I got upset he seemed quite distressed, as if it were all his fault, and kept telling me not to worry, he could easily find out all he needed to know from the police. When I eventually voiced my concern over the funeral he assured me that there was plenty of money and instructed me to send all the bills directly to him.

'Are you certain?' I was amazed. As far as I knew, we were broke. My job paid well enough but I just seemed to fritter it away and Ali had used every cent she'd saved on the business and that hadn't yet made any profit.

'There's plenty of money to take care of things, Lily. Your father's estate . . .'

'You mean there's actually a bit of his money that he didn't leave to the donkey sanctuary or some other useless charity?' I knew my voice held a not very well-disguised sneer.

'Lily.' He sat down beside me. 'I know this is very hard for you. I can hardly believe it myself.' His eyes were sad. 'She was so young and yesterday when we met she was alive and happy and looking forward to life.' He stopped and closed his eyes for a second. 'She had everything going for her.' He was watching me carefully again.

'No, she hadn't.' I wasn't letting him get away with anything. 'You've no idea how hard it's been for her since the baby came along. All she did was work and worry about Charlie's future and . . .' I stopped, afraid the tears would take over again. My sister had struggled for so long and now, just as things seemed to be picking up, it had all been taken away from her.

'I did know something of her efforts and I know how courageous she was.' He seemed to search for the right words. 'Things were hard, I'm aware of that. I just want you to know that I'm here to help.'

'Hard, how would you know?' I was pissed at him and I'd really no idea why. Maybe it was because he'd been my father's confidant. It never mattered anyhow: the fact was that anyone who mentioned my father's money generally got it on the chin from me. Ali was always telling me to chill in that regard.

'I'm sorry, I guess I'm just all screwed up at the moment,' I told him then. 'I've no idea how I'm going to deal with this. What am I supposed to do with Charlie, for instance? He needs a mother and I need to work. Up to now I've only ever given a dig out in the evenings, when she had to see clients in the salon. Anyway, I've no idea how to look after a baby,' I said petulantly. It wasn't even true, I helped out with Charlie all the time. I just felt overwhelmed by responsibility and I'd no one to turn to.

'And to think I didn't even want kids myself,' I said, more to shock him than anything else. But that bit was at least half true: kids had never really been on my agenda, even though I loved my nephew to bits. I was just afraid that I wouldn't be able to cope, or worse still, would cope the way my father had.

I felt an awful loneliness creep over me then. My twin sister had been the other half of me; having her meant I was never really alone.

'Look.' He moved closer to me. 'We need to sit down and talk about a lot of things just as soon as you feel you're ready. We can arrange a childminder for Charlie, Alison left instruc—'

'I know what Alison wanted, and when she was here I wanted it too. She always made everything sound possible. But what about now, what's going to happen to us now?' I jumped up, all the frustration of the past twelve hours hitting me in one blow. 'I can't go on. You don't understand. Alison was the leader, she did all this – the flat – everything.' I ran out of steam and sat back down. 'I don't even know how much the mortgage was, can you believe that? All I did was contribute a sum each month and she figured out the rest. Stupid, I know, but she liked being in control and I'm just . . . lazy, I guess. I don't even know if we had any insurance.' I lowered my head, hating every moment of this. It felt like I was begging.

'Lily . . .' He tried to take my hand to comfort me, but I pulled away. His dark eyes were kind. 'Lily, money isn't a problem, I promise you. Please understand that. I can let you have an advance, whatever you need.'

'I don't want your charity!' I jumped up. Once again I'd no idea why I was shouting at him; he'd never been anything but nice to me. 'Do you know what I want more than anything else in the world? I want my life back to the way it was this time yesterday.' I swallowed hard. 'I want my sister back,' I whispered, then stumbled from the room because I was afraid that if he tried to comfort me again I'd cry and never stop. When I returned he was sitting on the floor playing with the baby. We both apologized together. It was awkward so I made even more tea and he was very kind and left only after giving me his home as well as his mobile number. He promised to call me later to talk about the funeral, and reiterated that his secretary would take care of all the arrangements: all I had to do was let them know my preferences.

When Aunt Milly arrived it all came gushing out. The warm, roundy woman was the nearest thing to a mammy I'd ever really known. For many years Alison had filled that role, even though she was barely five minutes older. Now, sitting on the floor with Charlie pulled close for warmth, I mourned the mother and twin sister I'd lost way too soon.

7

WILLIAM AND BETH

IT WAS ALMOST NINE WHEN WILLIAM ARRIVED HOME, exhausted. As soon as she heard his car on the gravel Beth ushered the children upstairs, feeling guilty that she hadn't noticed the time. They'd been playing Scrabble, Harry's addiction of the week. Winnie preferred to play her games on the computer, but William didn't approve. Initially she'd joined in rather reluctantly but soon all three were having fun and teasing Harry over his spelling. Now Beth quickly tidied away the game, despite their protests.

'Come on, Harry, don't slouch. It's way past your time anyway.'

'Why do we always have to be in bed when Dad comes home? It's not fair.'

'Because, darling, Daddy's been in theatre all day and he needs peace and quiet now to relax. Anyway, it's a school night, you know the rules.'

'I want to see Daddy,' Winnie whined. 'I'm older, I shouldn't have to go to bed with him.' She elbowed her annoying sibling out of the way.

'You will see Daddy, don't worry.' Beth shooed them both up the stairs. 'I promise he'll come and tuck you in later.' Winnie was resisting and she gently moved her daughter forward with a kiss on the head. 'Off you go, there's a good girl.'

'Don't want to.'

'Please, darling, I need to say hello to Daddy first.' Beth knew they played up when she was on her own. If William said hop they hopped and never argued or pleaded.

'Harry,' she said to the boy, who was hovering now too, waiting to see if his sister got her way, 'get out your story and I'll pick up where we left off last night.'

'OK.' He was satisfied at last.

'Winnie, go, you heard me.' She tried to sound stern but it didn't really work.

'Can I stay up late tomorrow night?' Her daughter was always bargaining.

'Maybe. Now scram!' Beth slapped her daughter's bottom playfully.

She checked her dark, wavy hair in the huge hall mirror and wished she'd remembered to redo her make-up. Being in the kitchen with the Aga on all the time always left her with a shiny face. Too late now, she thought, smiling to herself as she opened the front door and waited for her husband, who was on the phone in his car and still had the engine running.

Beth examined her nails and flicked a spot of dirt off her red and white wrapover dress. The style suited her and her glossy red toenails and high sandals painted a pretty picture overall. She was a good-looking woman, well groomed, with an easy smile and a warmth about her that most people commented on.

As she waited she inhaled the spicy autumn scents of cinnamon and lemon around the door. Beth adored being in the garden; it was her sanctuary sometimes and she loved to potter, even though they had a full-time gardener. William decided when they bought this house that the garden would be too much for her and sometimes she was glad and sometimes sorry; sorry when she missed the first snowdrop, or didn't notice the gorgeous purple peony until it was almost too blowzy. Still, the garden was huge, William had been right. And this way it always looked just so, which appealed to him more than her.

'Hello, darling, how did it go?' She kissed him now and searched his face for wear and tear.

'OK, I think. It was tougher than I thought but he should be all right.'

'How was that poor pregnant wife of his?'

'Teary. I did my best to reassure her.' William stretched his muscles. 'I can't wait to get out of these clothes. Have I time for a shower before dinner?' He always asked and the reply was always 'Of course. Then I'll pour you a drink.'

'What's to eat?'

'Steak and kidney pie, your favourite.' She smiled up at her man.

'Great, you make the best pastry ever.'

'Yes, I do,' she lied. Beth didn't know anyone who made

pastry any more. William liked to boast that he'd never eaten processed food in his life and she wasn't about to disillusion him any day soon. Beth often wondered where he thought she got the time to do all she was supposed to, even with a housekeeper. So she said nothing and was considered a domestic goddess by everyone, especially her husband.

'How was your day?' he asked, already halfway up the stairs.

'Oh fine, the usual. I'm just going to read Harry his story, then maybe you'd pop in to say goodnight on your way downstairs?' She smiled. 'They never want me when you're around.'

'OK, will do.'

Fifteen minutes later she was putting the plates to warm in the oven when he strolled into the kitchen. 'I thought I might get out for a cycle tonight, but now I haven't the energy.'

'You push yourself too hard.' Beth was already pouring him a glass of red wine.

'Well, no chance of it after this, that's for sure.' He held up the glass. 'Cheers.'

She searched for her half-empty one. '*Slainte*.' She loved the old Irish toast to health. 'And well done today.'

'Were you at the gym?'

'Yes, then I undid it all by having a slice of pear and almond tart and two milky coffees with Aileen.' She grinned.

'That's my girl.' William kissed the tip of her nose. 'Never worries about the E numbers.'

'Oh, it was homemade, I checked.'

'Homemade along with four million others the same day, I'd say.'

'It must be great to be so self-righteous.' Beth stuck out her tongue at him as she glanced around for her oven glove. 'Still, I enjoyed every crumb,' she told him and he laughed at her cheeky face. Beth was carefree and easy and she loved to tease him about his stiff upper lip. It was one of the reasons he'd fallen for her in the first place.

'Why don't you catch the headlines while I start mashing the potatoes?' she suggested, knowing he'd need to unwind.

'OK,' he said absently, glancing at the wall clock. 'That's just what I need, actually. Fifteen minutes of peace and quiet.' He moved away. 'I haven't heard any news all day,' he said over his shoulder.

'Nothing much happening, as far as I know.' Beth felt hot and sticky and was dying for a bath. 'I'll call you when it's on the table.'

William left the glass down by his favourite chair in the formal sitting room and turned on RTE 1 television. The news had just started and hurricanes and floods seemed to be occupying most of the world. He added a log to the fire and sat back to enjoy being home. He loved this room, with its boxy leaded windows and high ceiling. Despite its size it felt warm and welcoming. The furniture was a mixture of gorgeous antique pieces he'd picked up over the years and the oversized sofas that his wife insisted on. 'I hate sitting on an antique, I'm always afraid I'll spoil it,' she'd told him when he'd tried to protest that the room wouldn't take anything modern.

Still, they did work, he had to admit, sitting back and sipping his drink. It helped that everything was always just right in here. No kids allowed – his rule, not hers.

The stories were the same ones he'd heard that morning on his way in to work so he flicked around. Nothing much on offer except reality TV shows, so he switched back just in time to hear the end of a report on that drowning tragedy he'd read about earlier.

'The woman has been named locally as Alison Ormond, a twenty-nine-year-old mother of one, who was originally from Sligo but now living in Ranelagh.'

William sat up straight and stared at the picture of Alison. It didn't look like her. It failed to show her vibrancy and she wasn't smiling. He started to think about her, then jerked himself back to the present to listen to what was being said. It was more or less what he'd read in the paper but earlier there'd been no mention of a child. He didn't think Alison had any children, at least she'd never said anything about a child to him. But then he knew very little about her, really.

'Dinner's on the table.'

The sing-song voice irritated him but then he was nervous because suddenly Alison seemed to be right here, in his home. William thought about her a lot in private, especially when he heard a particular song, or smelt a certain fragrance, a sort of lemon and lime fruity scent that she always wore. But Alison had been his secret now for a number of years, the one thing that might upset his perfect world. Not any more, it seemed.

'Give me a second.' He sounded sharper than he should have done. The report had ended and he was left with his thoughts again. It was hard to comprehend, really.

'Are you OK?' Beth came scurrying in. 'It's just that everything's ready and I thought you were—'

'Yes, fine, sorry, I just felt a bit . . .' He shook his head. 'A bit faint, that's all.' The lie came easy.

'Have you eaten today?'

'Not much.'

'That's it then. It's probably the wine on an empty stomach.' His wife slapped his hand. 'I'll report you to a doctor if you're not careful.' It was one of her favourite jokes.

'Sorry, darling.' He put his arm on her back as they moved into the kitchen. 'I know you've gone to a lot of trouble.' He smiled absently at her, suddenly unable to stop thinking about Alison.

They had dinner and he drank more than usual. Beth knew something was bothering him, but she didn't ask. He'd tell her in his own time. He had a lot going on in his work and she knew he worried if he wasn't as on top of things as he should be. Her husband liked to be in control, the best at everything he did. Beth watched him as she chatted away about the kids and school and rugby. She

70

knew it suited him not to be asked too many questions tonight and she was used to it.

Later, after a warm shower she came to bed in a sexy short nightdress that her friend Pam had given her for her birthday. It was all black lace and plunging back and front and it made her feel like a mistress. She slipped into bed and inched closer to her husband, kissing him lightly on his back. They usually made love after theatre. 'All that adrenalin,' he'd told her years ago. 'Can't sleep unless I'm fully relaxed.'

'Darling, would you mind if we didn't?' He moved away from her embrace and turned towards her. 'I'm afraid I've had too much to drink.'

'That's not like you.' She kissed him on the cheek and rolled over on her back. 'No problem, I'm whacked any-way. 'Night, love.'

'Goodnight.'

She was soon breathing evenly but he lay awake for ages, thinking about Alison. They'd had a lot of fun these past few years and he knew he'd miss her spark, her easy banter and the way she made him feel. He always felt completely alive with Alison. He supposed he ought to go to the funeral but decided he couldn't possibly risk it.

8

RICHARD AND DAISY

THE NEXT DAY WAS MUCH BETTER FOR RICHARD AND ONCE he had recovered from a very frosty reception by his manageress he felt in top form. He'd gone to bed early – alone – and had the place opened up and fresh coffee brewing by the time Maggie arrived. Richard knew she'd give him hell for a few days but he was prepared to put up with it because having her in charge meant he could come and go as he liked. Also she ran the place like a military barracks, kept a strict eye on wastage and got the best-quality produce from all their suppliers. Nobody in their right mind would knowingly upset her. She was Hillary Clinton in an apron.

As soon as the lunchtime rush was over, Richard rounded up the day's newspapers. He made himself a coffee and sat in a corner, scanning the headlines. It was the picture that first caught his eye.

'Richard, can I talk to you about tomorrow's menu?' Hazel popped out from the kitchen.

'Later,' he said, without lifting his head.

'That's what you said an hour ago,' the chef muttered, annoyed at his curtness. 'I need to ring the suppliers.'

'For Christ's sake, just do it yourself.' He banged his cup down and glared at Hazel, his mind still on the photograph he'd just seen. 'Am I not entitled to a break the same as the rest of you?' She scurried away and Richard felt guilty. Hazel was the best; he should have held his tongue. Now he'd have Maggie blathering on about upsetting the staff, on top of everything else.

He read the headline again. WOMAN DROWNS TRYING TO SAVE SON. Richard never knew she had a child. A little boy, apparently. Three or thereabouts, none of the papers seemed to agree. He tried to think back to when he'd first met her. It was over four years ago. She'd never said anything to him about being pregnant, although come to think of it she had disappeared for months shortly afterwards and never seemed to want to say much about it. He read all the papers but learned nothing new after the first one.

'OK, mate?' Tom Dalton chucked his keys on the table and grabbed a stool.

'What are you doing here?'

'Just on the way in to studio. What's up?'

The whole thing hit Richard all of a sudden. His shoulders slumped.

'Hey, you OK?'

'Yeah, just read something. You remember Alison – Ali, that girl I used to date?'

'Vaguely, why?'

He shoved the paper in Tom's direction to show him the picture. 'She drowned,' he said, unnecessarily since his mate had clearly seen the headline.

'Fuck, how did it happen?'

Richard filled him in.

'Hey, Luce, any chance of a black coffee?' Tom called as he took off his jacket.

'Coming up.'

'So, what's the story? I mean, you hadn't seen her for years, had you?'

'Sort of.'

'What exactly does that mean? I thought you'd given up everything except the occasional one-night stand once you and Daisy got engaged?'

'I had.'

'So?' Tom took the cup from Lucy, who smiled sweetly at him and gave Richard a dour look.

'We sort of . . . kept in touch.'

'What d'ya mean, you texted her once a week or shagged her occasionally?'

'Both.' Richard glanced around nervously. He needed to tell someone. 'She was a hooker.'

'Would you ever fuck off!'

'I'm serious.' Under other circumstances, it would have been worth it to see the look on Tom's face. 'And do you know something, I was really into her.'

'Hang on, not so fast.' Tom tried to piece it all together. 'So, let me get this straight.' He looked at her picture again. 'You were screwing her?'

'Yup.'

'And *paying* for the privilege?'

Richard nodded.

'I don't believe it. You're having me on.'

'I'm not.'

'But, fuck it, Richard, you don't need to pay for sex. Of all of us, you're the one most likely to have it handed to you on a plate.' Tom scratched his head. 'And you're engaged to a model. What the fuck's going on there?'

'Meet me next door for a pint in an hour.' Richard glanced at his watch. 'This place is doing my head in all of a sudden.'

'I'm on at seven. It'll have to be quick.' Tom wanted to hear more.

'Make it half an hour then.'

'No, gimme an hour like you said. I'll tear into work and get things started.' He checked his phone. 'That way I'll have time for two pints.'

'OK.' Both men got up together. Tom left with a casual 'Stay cool,' and Richard headed for the kitchen to make it up with Hazel. He served a few customers and wished he could get away to clear his head. A couple of regulars remarked to Maggie that the boss wasn't his usual talkative self today and she wondered if it was perhaps time to bury the hatchet.

Richard had the pints in and was reading it all again when Tom arrived back.

'So, tell me.' He swung his leg over a stool.

'Let's grab a table.' Richard nodded towards another guy at the bar. 'Keep it quiet.'

They settled into a corner, as far away as they could get from the pumping disco beat.

'There's not much to tell, really.' Richard took a slug of his pint. 'It started about five years ago when I was with that ad agency – Moffats. I needed someone to take out to meet the directors of a major new account I was on the verge of poaching from Vision International. I'd just dumped Marlene, remember? The clients were a family company and were all taking their wives to this dinner.' He thought about his days in the corporate world without a trace of nostalgia. 'All the girls on the scene at the time were either too thick or too intense. A guy in the office mentioned this girl called Alison. Said she was just what I was looking for but that it'd cost me. Suggested I check her out on this website. I contacted her more out of curiosity than anything else.' He laughed and took another swallow. 'As you say, I didn't need to pay for it.'

'Where did you meet her?'

'In a pub, an hour before meeting the clients,' Richard remembered. 'Don't know what I'd have done if she was dog rough,' he laughed nervously, 'although from what the guy had told me I knew she'd be OK. In fact, she was more than OK.' He took a swig of his pint. 'She was gorgeous. I remember being intrigued by her. She wasn't what you'd expect – hell, sure you met her, you know all this. She was so . . . I dunno, independent, I guess. Aloof, maybe.' Richard could still see her now. 'And she wasn't looking for a "commitment". How sexy is that, eh?'

'The one word in the English language guaranteed to kill an erection in five.' Tom grinned, sidetracked for a minute. He swallowed half his pint. 'Anyway, how could she have been looking for anything except money? She was a bleedin' prostitute.'

'She was an escort, very high-class.' Richard didn't know why he felt the need to defend her.

'So, what happened?' Tom signalled the barman and indicated their glasses.

'She came to the dinner with me. Everyone loved her. She was warm and funny. They all assumed she was my girlfriend.'

'Did you have sex with her?'

'Not that night, no.'

'So you paid for a date and didn't even get your leg over? Not like you at all.' Tom laughed.

'We did have sex, of course we did. But she did get jobs where all the guy wanted was a good-looking broad on his arm. Wealthy businessmen, that sort of thing.'

'That's what she told you.' Tom clearly didn't believe him.

'No, honestly, she didn't need to lie. In fact, that was one of the things I liked so much about the whole thing. There was no pretending, no putting on a show. It was all just . . .' He shrugged. 'Natural, I guess.'

'What's natural about paying for sex?'

'What's unnatural about it? It was honest, we weren't fooling each other. No one got hurt. And I'll tell you something for nothing.' Richard played with his beer mat. 'It was fun, it felt really exciting and it suited me.'

'So how long did this go on for?'

'A couple of months after I met her she went back home. Cork, I think, or Sligo. Can't remember. Her aunt or someone was sick and she had to nurse her. I didn't see her for, I dunno, months. Maybe a year even.' Richard drained his glass and looked around, wanting an immediate replacement.

'It's on the way.' Tom fished in his pocket for money.

'Then she texted me to let me know she was back in town and we sort of picked up where we left off.'

'But at this point you'd met Daisy.'

'Only barely, I think. Sure Daisy and I weren't really an item for months. She was going out with that rugby player – Bob Gleeson or Glennon, remember? Anyway, I'd sort of missed Alison, you know.' Richard shrugged, knowing his mate probably hadn't a clue what he meant, judging by the look on his face.

'How come?' Tom paid for the drinks. He was intrigued. This all sounded way too complicated, even for Richard – the original 'drama queen', as he was christened at college.

'She was different. Didn't take herself seriously. We understood each other.' He shifted in his seat. 'Didn't want a fucking ring after three dates.' He laughed. 'You've been there, don't forget. Remember Brenda, the redhead? You said she stalked you for months. Practically had the ring bought after the first date, you told me.'

'Yeah, well, I'd say she could have bought *herself* a diamond or two.' He indicated the newspaper. 'With all the dosh you paid her.'

'Maybe.' Richard was remembering her face. 'I didn't really care about the money. I liked her, she was fun.'

'And the sex?'

'The sex was mind-blowing.' Richard looked thoughtful, then shrugged his shoulders. 'But I've done mind-blowing. I can't explain it, really. The whole thing was just so . . . so easy. Refreshing.' He grinned. 'Not a word I'd normally use to describe a blow job.'

'So, all this time and you never said anything. How come?'

'Nothing to tell, really.'

'Oh yes there was.' Tom grinned. 'And you always tell me things like that eventually. You can't resist it, mate. You like being one step ahead of the rest of us.'

'I kind of liked keeping it to myself.' He flicked the mat and watched it fall to the floor. 'As I said, it was exciting.'

'But you had Daisy to take to all these functions. You didn't need this Alison.' Tom still didn't fully understand the attraction.

'Sure I'd long since left the corporate shite behind. It's been a while since I had to entertain a client.' Richard stared into his pint. 'I don't know why I kept it going.' He thought for a second. 'She was so different to Daisy.' He grinned at his mate. 'Daisy is high maintenance.'

'Aren't they all?' Tom grinned back.

'I suppose I got hooked.' Richard was gulping his drink. 'Hooked on a hooker. How's that for a pun?'

'So what now? Are you cut up about this?' Tom indicated the pile of newspapers.

'I dunno. It's not as though I thought it was going anywhere or anything like that. I hadn't seen that much of her in the last few months.' He ran his hands through his hair. 'Fucking pressure of work and all that. It's just . . . shock, I guess.'

'Well, listen, bud, I gotta get to work.' Tom checked his phone. 'The producer'll be going ape.'

'Sure. I'll hang on here for a while. Maybe have one for the road.'

'Gimme a shout later if you fancy goin' out, OK?'

'Cheers.' Richard raised his glass as his mate gathered up his bits and gave a backward wave. He was about to order another pint then changed his mind. He was getting maudlin. What the hell, he picked up the papers and headed out the door. He needed to get his head around this whole crazy thing and he wasn't going to do that with ten pints inside him.

9

JAMES AND TAMSIN

THE LAST FEW DAYS HAD BEEN A NIGHTMARE FOR JAMES. His beloved Tamsin had disintegrated in front of his eyes. The psychologist who spent her days sorting out other people's problems couldn't seem to get to grips with her own. Every time James saw her he felt guilty. It was as if hearing about Alison's death had opened up a whole new perspective on the double life he'd been leading. And now that it was over, now that it appeared he'd got away with it, he felt like a total jerk. And for the first time in years, he couldn't discuss it with the one person with whom he shared absolutely everything. It was driving him nuts.

Late one evening, after Tamsin had cried herself to sleep again, he rang her best friend, Maria.

'I don't know what to do. It seems like I can't help her.' He felt like crying himself.

'James, give her time. She's in mourning,' Maria soothed. 'Every time this happens it's like another bereavement, the death of a child she already believed was alive and growing inside her.'

'But we hadn't even had it confirmed that she was pregnant.' He felt he had to argue. Trying to get inside his wife's head these past few days had been doing his own head in.

'James, that's a rational male talking. Believe me, it's different for a woman. In her head she had a child the moment the egg was fertilized.'

'I know, I know.' He rubbed his forehead. 'I'm sorry to dump all this on you, it's just that I feel so bloody useless.'

'James, you are the closest couple I know. Hell, you have the ultimate happy-ever-after lifestyle.' It was said without a trace of sarcasm. 'Sometimes I hate the two of you for being so perfect.'

'Yeah.' It made him feel worse.

'So, talk to her.'

'I am, you know what we're like. Everything gets thrashed out. It's just, I'm not sure what's going on in her head. She's sort of withdrawn from me a bit and I'm finding it hard.'

'Well, stop trying to be strong for her. Just . . . be yourself. Hell, I can't give you any advice, James. You know what to do, what to say. You always have.' She screamed at one of her kids. 'So stop worrying,' she came back to him. 'You'll both get through this, I haven't the slightest doubt about it.'

'Thanks, Maria. I guess I just needed to hear someone say that. You're a pal.'

'I'm meeting her tomorrow. I said I'd call round about lunchtime. She just needs lots of love and support right now. And to talk, and talk, and talk.'

'I know. And as I said, we're doing that.' He was worn out and besides he felt useless tonight. 'You know us, the ultimate self-help couple.' He tried to inject a bit of life into his voice. 'Listen, go off to your gang. I can hear them killing each other. And send my best to Dan. We'll see you for a Chinese real soon, OK?'

'Sure. Call me any time. Ta-ra.'

'Bye. Thanks again.' She was already yelling at her two-year-old son to get his head out of the oven. James smiled and felt slightly better.

Next morning, he woke way before the alarm went off and turned over to reach for his wife. Her side of the bed was empty. It had been the same every morning recently. She almost collapsed with tiredness at night but then couldn't sleep for more than a few hours.

James hadn't the energy to get up to be with her, the way he normally did. Today was Alison's funeral. A bit of him wanted to go, just to pay his respects. But what could he say to her relations? 'Hi, I'm James, I was one of her clients' wouldn't go down well, he suspected. He knew nothing about her family, didn't even know if they knew the truth about her lifestyle.

'Hi, darling, how are you feeling?' he asked Tamsin a little while later.

'Sad. I woke up crying.'

'Come 'ere to me.' He wrapped his arms around her and wished for the millionth time that he could take away her pain.

'Come on,' he urged her gently after a while. 'I want you to sit down and watch some good oul breakfast TV while I make tea and toast.'

'I always feel guilty watching daytime telly. It's addictive.'

'Doctor James's orders.' He led her into the sitting room and propped her up on the squashy couch. 'Now, flick,' he handed her the remote and ruffled her hair.

As he made breakfast he watched her through the inter-connecting doors. She looked so small and vulnerable in her polka-dot fluffy dressing gown and matching pyjamas that he'd bought her in Next. She meant everything in the world to him and he still couldn't understand how he'd cheated on her. Oh, he'd tried to justify it to himself many times. It wasn't a real relationship, he argued in his head. Just sex.

'There you go.' He handed Tamsin a tray with freshly squeezed juice, ginger and lemon tea and brown whole-grain toast. He knew exactly what she liked, down to the organic marmalade he'd spread thinly on the bread, just as she did herself.

'What's on?' He glanced at the TV.

'Cellulite.'

'Essential viewing, I would have thought, even if you don't have a trace of orange peel anywhere on your body.' He smiled and kissed her head. 'Enjoy.'

'Are you OK?' She smiled at him sadly. 'I know it's all been about me in the last few days.' She stroked his arm. 'You look tired. I'm sorry I haven't really been there for you.'

'I'm fine.'

'We need to talk about you, too, you know.'

'Later. Let's just concentrate on getting you right for the moment. That's all that's important to me.'

'I love you, James.' She had tears in her eyes. 'I don't know what I'd do without you.'

'You'll never have to.' He crouched down beside her. 'I love you too, darling. With all my heart. And I'm sorry for . . . everything.'

'Please, don't say that.' She was crying openly now. 'None of this is your fault. You've done everything possible to support me.'

'Shush, we're in this together.' He held her close and stroked her hair and wished he could tell her.

'James, are you worrying about something else?' She pulled away from him as if seeing him properly for the first time in days.

'No.' The lie made him feel even more guilty. They were always completely honest with each other. Trust was a huge part of their relationship and he wasn't sure how much longer he could keep this to himself.

It bothered him all day at work. He was edgy and everyone noticed.

'Fancy a pint on the way home?' Colin Johnson, one of the other architects asked casually around six o'clock.

'Yeah, great.' James immediately wondered if he could confide in him. Colin was a solid father-figure type who had always kept an eye on him, had been his mentor, in fact, since he'd joined the practice. But he knew he couldn't do it to Tamsin. Confiding in someone else would be the ultimate betrayal. 'Actually, no,' he said quickly, not trusting himself. 'I'd better get home.'

'How is Tamsin?'

'Not great.'

'You need to talk about it?'

Why did everyone ask him that?

'To an outsider, I mean?' Colin grinned. 'Yes, I know you discuss everything with your wife. I get enough stick about you being the perfect husband from Anne.' He looked at the younger man's worn-out face. 'But sometimes it's good to chat to someone else.'

'Thanks, Colin. I'll remember that.'

'Someone male, who doesn't feel the need to analyse it to death.'

James smiled. He was tempted.

'Sure you can't manage a quick one?'

'Maybe another night.'

'OK, fine.' He patted James's arm as he passed. 'Mind yourself.'

'I will.'

Later that evening, when Tamsin was in bed and he was sure she was sleeping, James opened the phone book and looked up a number. This is mad, he thought, closing the book. I am not ringing a helpline.

He made himself coffee, all the while berating himself for being so weak. What are you like? Any other man would just get on with it. You're a big girl's blouse, that's what you are. He banged down the spoon and went to sit on the couch. After a few minutes spent staring into space he sighed, looked up the number again and dialled.

'Hello, this is the Samaritans. My name is Rita.'

'Hello, eh sorry, I'm not suicidal or anything.' James felt guilty about wasting their time. 'I just need to talk to someone.'

'That's fine. That's what we're here for. Would you like to tell me your name?' She sensed reluctance and said quickly, 'Just your first name and you don't have to, only if you want.'

'No, it's fine. I'm James.'

'Hi, James. How're you doing?'

'Not very well. I just have to tell someone.' He looked around nervously and took a deep breath. 'I've been having an affair.' Just saying the words felt like a huge relief. It was followed immediately by worry. Now that he'd told somebody Tamsin might find out. Oh God, he thought, what if this person knows me? Or worse, knows Tamsin? He felt sick.

'OK.' Rita waited but nothing came. 'And is that a problem for you?'

'I'm married, that's the problem.' He couldn't stop himself. 'I'm married to the most wonderful woman and I love her dearly and we share everything and it's eating me up inside.' He drew a long breath. 'This is in confidence, isn't it? I mean, what if . . .'

'Completely, James. Anything you say to me will not be

repeated. There are no notes taken, nothing. That's why we don't use second names.'

'Thanks.' He felt slightly better. 'It's just that Tam—my wife and I have been trying for a child for a long time and we haven't managed to conceive. It's put . . .' He struggled to find the right words. 'It's put a lot of pressure on our . . . the sexual side of things.'

'I understand.'

'It's just . . . all been about getting pregnant, you know. No spontaneity, no foreplay. Nothing. It's all become . . . a bit mechanical, I suppose.'

'That must be very hard on you.'

'It's been much harder on . . . her. My wife wants a child desperately.'

'And do you?'

'Yes, I think so. Sometimes I don't know any more.' He let out a deep breath. 'Yes, I do, but I can live without it, at least I think I can. It's not the end of the world for me.' There was a long pause. 'But it is for her.'

'That must be tough,' the counsellor said softly.

'So, a few years ago I . . . sort of got involved with someone . . .'

'This is the affair you mentioned?'

'Yes. Well, it wasn't really an affair. Not in that sense. You see, I have everything I could possibly want within my marriage.'

The woman waited.

'I was . . . lonely, frustrated, whatever. I didn't feel able to put all that on to her, so I . . . took the coward's way out.'

'What makes you think you were a coward?'

'Oh, I was. I'm ashamed of myself, really, not being able to control my . . . urges, I suppose.' Another long pause followed by a sigh. 'Well, eventually I did something about it.'

'You met someone else?'

'Yes. No, not really. I made contact with . . . someone . . . through a website.' James closed his eyes. 'I started seeing a woman.' His voice dropped to a whisper. 'Basically what I'm saying is that I paid for sex.' He couldn't think of anything else to say. 'I'm not sure I can do this,' he said eventually.

'That's OK, James. You don't have to.'

'It's just that I have it all,' he said, as if he hadn't heard her. 'Christ, the whole country thinks I'm the perfect husband. And I love my wife. I'd do anything for her.'

'I'm sure you would.'

'I would, honestly.' It seemed important to say it.

'I believe you, James.'

'It's just that this went on and on and I really tried to tell her that it was getting to me, and for once she didn't hear me. And do you know something, Rita?' It seemed important that this stranger thought well of him. 'We do really listen to one another. We're there for each other, twenty-four/seven. But she became sort of obsessed with the mechanics of sex and I found it harder and harder to . . . get an erection, even. I began to doubt myself. And, eventually, I suppose I just wanted someone who, I dunno, found me sexually attractive.' He laughed at the irony. 'So you'd think I'd have had an affair. But I couldn't. I couldn't do that to her and besides, as I already told you, I had everything I wanted. Except sex. So I got it the only way I could. I paid someone to want me in that way.'

10

DAVE AND MARIE

DAVE WENT TO THE FUNERAL. HE FELT HE OUGHT TO. Alison had been very good to him. He never thought for a moment it was because he was paying her. In Dave's mind, they'd been having a mad, passionate affair, kept secret only because he was married.

That morning he'd arrived on the building site dressed in a dark suit with a white shirt and muted tie.

'Lookin' good, boss,' one of the chippies had shouted.

'How much am I paying you?' he yelled over the noise. 'Whatever it is, it's too much.'

'You must be goin' to see the bank manager dressed like that.' Eugene Moran, his foreman, punched Dave playfully on the arm.

'Lay off, will ye, you're filthy.' He brushed his jacket. 'Actually, I'm going to a funeral if you must know.'

'Oh, sorry about that.' He looked questioningly, waiting to hear.

'Just a girl I . . . used to know. Died suddenly.' Dave was sorry he'd mentioned it.

'Old flame, was she?' George the sparks was nearby. 'Or maybe not so old.' Everyone knew their boss was a ladies' man, particularly fond of younger fillies. 'I seen you in the pub the other night chattin' up that Imelda one.'

'No, she bleedin' wasn't, she was just a friend.' Dave was annoyed. 'Get back to work, for fuck sake. We're already over on this job.' He turned to the foreman. 'I'm on the mobile if you need me, Eugene. I'll be back around lunchtime.'

'Right so,' the foreman said in his thick Cavan accent. 'We'll be here.'

In the church he wasn't sure why he'd come. He'd decided he was going to go up and shake hands with the family – mark of respect and all that. But then he had a good look at the woman who made a speech after Communion and he got a fright. She was the absolute spit of Alison. He immediately felt the same attraction that had completely captivated him when he'd first met Alison. She was like an unplugged version of her sister, alive but without the fizzle – understandable under the circumstances, Dave acknowledged to himself. He listened as Lily spoke quietly about what a good sister Alison had been, how she'd been mother and father to her for many years. There were a few bowed heads when she told how they'd been best friends and shared everything, including a love of handbags. About the time they'd taken Charlie for an impromptu picnic, and Ali had filled her favourite pink handbag with egg and sardine sandwiches and the bag had to be thrown out afterwards because it smelt so bad. Dave watched her try to hold back the tears and couldn't take his eyes off her.

It was only at the end when she walked behind the coffin that he was fully convinced it wasn't Alison. This one had a different stride. Alison always had a swagger, a confidence that this girl didn't possess, or if she did it had deserted her today. She looked lost and Dave immediately felt protective towards her. A middle-aged woman walked beside her, rubbing her back, and a small boy clutched her hand and carried a white rose. He didn't seem too upset, just kept looking at the faces and waving at people he knew. Must be the kid, Dave surmised. He'd read the story several times over in the tabloids.

Outside, Dave stayed well in the background and stared at Alison's sister in daylight. She was thinner, and dressed in black she didn't have the same presence. He tried to pinpoint exactly what it was. Class, he decided, or maybe style. He watched as people came over and hugged her, saw the same elegant gestures that Alison had used. She had style all right, but she lacked punch. Alison had always seemed to grasp at life; this girl looked like she was used to being led. She still didn't cry, he noticed, although she looked very fragile and bit her lower lip a lot. 'In need of a good dinner,' his mother would have said.

The little boy played around and brushed off the hugs and kisses as if they were mosquitoes. Mostly he dodged in and out of the crowd and never noticed the pitying glances thrown his way. A few people gave him money and he showed the coins to everyone so that eventually he had a right stash, and he sat on the step and laid his treasure out in front of him. The older woman who'd been with him earlier quickly gathered them up and the child looked as if he was about to cry but changed his mind once the loot was handed to him. He stuffed the coins in his pocket and left his hand there, shuffling them about and stealing a glance at them every now and then when he thought no one was looking. Dave smiled to himself: Alison's boy had the makings of an entrepreneur, a bit like his mother in that respect.

Eventually, Dave decided he had to see the sister face to face. He waited until most of the crowd had disappeared. She was just about to put her dark glasses back on when he found himself in front of her, without really knowing what to say.

'I, eh, was a . . . eh . . . friend of Alison's' was the best he could think of. He could feel his face going red. Fuck it, he hadn't blushed since he'd been refused a dance at the convent disco thirty-five years ago. The sister stared at him with Alison's eyes, except they weren't smiling at him. 'I, eh, just wanted to say how sorry I was.'

'Thank you very much.' She shook his hand. 'I'm Lily.' She looked amazingly composed. 'I'm sorry I don't know your name, Mr . . .'

'Mad . . . Eh, Dave will do.' He was afraid she might have heard his name but she showed no sign, just nodded. 'Thank you, Dave. I'm meeting a lot of Alison's friends for the first time today.' She brushed her hair away and he could have sworn it was Alison standing in front of him. 'I'm afraid it's all been quite a shock.'

'I'm sure it was.'

'Did you know Alison well?' she asked politely.

Dave hadn't a clue how to answer that one. 'Eh, I did, yeah . . . Well, sort of.'

'Lily, love, I'm so sorry.' A woman with dyed red hair grabbed her in a bear hug and Lily smiled at Dave and thanked him again and he melted away to where he could watch her unseen. She fascinated him in the same way her sister had. That fascination had kept him coming back time and time again to Alison – and not just because of the sex.

Later that evening, on his way back from looking over a job with Eugene, he decided he needed a pint. Normally he didn't drink during the week, except Thursdays when he took Marie out. He'd seen too many men with beer bellies and purple, veined faces over the years.

'Fancy a gargle?' he asked now as they reached their cars.

'Don't mind if I do.'

'Com'on then, it's been a bitch of a day. We deserve it.'

'So, was it the funeral then?' Eugene asked as they settled into the snug in Ryan's pub.

'Yeah, hard that.' Dave put down the pints of Guinness and pulled out a stool. 'She was only a young one.'

'Sad. Family?'

'Sister. The spittin' image of her.' Dave finished half the pint in one go and licked his lips. 'And a boy, too. Only a baby really.'

'Tough.' Eugene sighed but said nothing else.

'Thing is, I was sort of . . . havin' a relationship with her.'

'Right.'

'I'd only seen her last week.'

'What happened?'

'She drowned. You probably read about it in the papers.' Dave fidgeted. He would have loved a fag but couldn't be arsed going to all the trouble.

'Think so, yeah.' It was clear Eugene hadn't seen the story.

'I was sort of seeing her, on and off like, for a few years. Keep that to yourself, though.' Dave took another swallow.

'I don't gossip about my boss.' The older man looked straight at him.

Dave signalled for another round. 'Needless to say the missus knew nothing.'

'Aye.'

'Marie and me, we get on great, like, but you know how it is, over the years things change.'

'They do, I suppose.'

'Thing is . . .' Dave fished for money. 'After the kids were born, Marie sort of . . . lost interest, if you know what I mean.'

'I do.' Eugene tried not to look uncomfortable as he sipped his pint and wished he wasn't having this conversation. Where he came from, a small town in the arsehole of rural Ireland, nobody talked like this. Oh sure, everybody knew exactly what was going on in every house for miles around but nobody ever discussed it openly. Dublin was a queer place, he'd long ago decided.

'Fuck it, man.' Dave banged down his glass. 'I'm a healthy, normal male. And there's no shortage of women where I'm concerned, never has been.'

'Aye.'

'And then I sort of met Alison and well, it was amazing like.' He saw the foreman's discomfort and decided to change tack. 'But now, Marie's a great woman and all that, you know what I'm sayin'? And I treat her well, you see that, don't you?'

'I do.'

'Wants for nothin'. House is immaculate. Sure that extension is the third we've done since we bought the gaff. Unrecognizable as a council house it is now.' He gave a satisfied nod. 'We have at least two holidays a year and she has a shopping spree in New York with her pals every Christmas. I don't begrudge her, mind.'

'No.' Eugene was a man of few words.

'I idolize the ground she walks on. I do, really. And this way, it means I'm not troublin' her, you know?'

'Sure what would I know.' Eugene fiddled uncomfortably with his beer mat.

'Why? Are you and your missus at it like rabbits?'

Eugene thought of his wife Marge at home in their three-bedroomed semi a few miles from Killeshandra with six kids and two cats. He reckoned they'd had sex in total about ten times in twenty-odd years of marriage. Every time Marge got pregnant she turned her back on him and

97

when she had the baby she was too exhausted for months. It wasn't something he thought about any more.

'What's it like to have an affair?' he asked now, knowing the opportunity would never present itself.

'Great sex, no strings.' Dave liked the older man thinking he was experienced.

'And what about Christmas, birthdays, that class of stuff?'

'Doesn't arise.'

'You must meet women who are quare accommodatin' then.' His Cavan accent was thick and flat.

Dave smiled. 'I make it worth their while.' He winked.

Eugene nodded. With Dave, he knew it always came down to money.

They talked for a while and got back on safe ground and somewhere between the second and third pint Dave decided he was going to make contact with Lily. The thought of seeing her again excited him and he could never resist a challenge.

11

LILY

THE FUNERAL WAS HARD. IT WAS MY FIRST TASTE OF WHAT a broken heart must feel like – strange to think that this one had nothing to do with a man. I felt hollow, as if my insides had been scraped out. The ritual helped: all the people and the nice things said and the hugs did comfort me, but then I'd catch sight of Charlie and I'd find myself praying that it was all a dream. I kept hoping that she'd rush into the church, blonde hair flying, eyes crinkling, and take over like she always did. Now her picture stared up at me from the top of a blond wooden box. It was one of her favourites of the two of us, taken when we were teenagers. I looked mortified and she looked so alive – impossible to get my head around the fact that underneath that picture lay her dead body.

I spoke after Communion because I knew it was what she would have done. The prospect terrified me. I was sure my legs were about to give way as I walked to the pulpit, and when I got there my hands were shaking so badly that I had to abandon the notes Aunt Milly had made me jot down the night before. So I simply told them what a lovely, decent human being she was, one of the nicest, kindest people. I reminded everyone how well she'd looked after me all these years. How she'd always say 'good girl' to me – especially when I'd done what she wanted – as if I was her baby. And now she'd left me her real baby to mind. I told them I was scared without her. Asked them how I'd ever manage, as if they might know some answers, things I hadn't thought of. Then, once I knew I was on the verge of breaking down I wrapped it all up as quickly as I could by asking them to pray for me and Charlie – Alison's good girl and beautiful boy.

Somehow, over the following days, I began to formulate a plan in my head. It wasn't much, but it was a start. I knew I had no choice but to take control of things for the first time in my life. Well, my friend Orla really decided for me. She came home as soon as she got that hysterical phone call from me, leaving her boss at the hotel in Brighton 'gobsmacked'.

'Actually, I think I've reached the end of the road in hotel management,' she told me a day or two after the funeral. 'It's wrecking my head. I'm so glad to be home.' We were in the flat, trying out a new recipe for pizza base at her insistence. Orla reckoned there was no ill that couldn't be cured by cooking.

'I'll never be able to thank you enough for coming so quickly,' I told her as I sifted flour.

'Snow.' Charlie looked up at the flour raining through

the sieve. Our kitchen was tiny, as in most modern apartments, and the three of us were on top of each other – or underneath, in Charlie's case.

'Yes, look, it's snowing.' I tapped the sieve over Charlie's head and he ran off screaming. He came back minutes later with his little umbrella and had us showering him with flour for ages. The three of us ended up covered in the stuff and the kitchen was in chaos as we ducked and dived about the small space.

'Enough,' I called eventually and gave Charlie a small ball of dough to play with. He loved helping me in the kitchen and I knew he'd amuse himself for hours with the stuff, making shapes and sticking them on the fridge door.

'So, have you decided what you want to do?' Orla asked gently.

'I've started to think.'

'Thinking's good.' She smiled.

'I feel like one of those *Big Brother* contestants who've just come out of the house,' I told her. 'I can't get used to making decisions for myself. It's as if the words "I want" or "I don't want" didn't exist in my vocabulary up to now. Ali made most of the decisions for both of us.' I looked over at Charlie barking at a dog made from dough. 'I miss her so much. It's like part of me has been disconnected or something.'

'I know.'

'She always seemed to have some scheme or other on the go and I just sort of ambled along doing whatever she wanted to do.'

'She had a strong personality. It was hard to say no to her.'

'I didn't really think about it much, d'ya know? I've always liked the easy life, you know that.'

'I do, but you're tougher than you seem. It's just, you sometimes . . .' She grinned as she chopped some herbs and the sweet smell of basil filled the kitchen. 'You have that "couldn't really be arsed" air about you that makes everyone, men especially, want to sort it all out for you.'

'I do care, it's not that . . .' I started to argue then realized she was partly right. 'Ali always wanted to sort things out for both of us. I think she liked being in control.'

'I know that.' Orla sighed. 'But you're good too and I believe you'll be well able to cope. You practically run that place where you work single-handed and look at you with Charlie . . . Who would have thought it, eh? I'm really proud of the way you're managing—'

'I haven't done anything yet,' I interrupted. 'At the moment all I'm doing is getting out of bed each morning and trying to remember to breathe.'

'Well, I think you're amazing.' She squeezed my hand.

'I couldn't really get any worse than I was, now could I? Remember the day after it happened, when I rang you back late at night screaming my head off? Not making a word of sense?'

Orla nodded and looked sad. 'I was at the airport and couldn't hear you properly. I didn't know what to say to comfort you . . .'

'You didn't need to say anything. Just getting it off my

chest was enough. God, Orla, even thinking about not having her around . . .'

Orla simply nodded again and continued weighing out stuff.

'I still wake up and think of things I need to tell her.'

'I know you do.'

'Aunt Milly arriving so soon saved my life. And so did you. I'll never forget that.'

'Your aunt is a dote.'

'She's so brilliant with Charlie. It's taken an enormous amount of pressure off me. There's just so much to think about.'

'I wish I didn't have to go back in a few days.' Orla made a face. 'I think I want to come home.'

'For good?' I was surprised.

'Yes, this management lark is not for me, as I said. Handling staff is a nightmare. I'm a cook, like you. It's what I do best.'

'Chef,' I corrected her. 'You're properly trained. I'm a cook.' I turned on the mixer. 'But Orla, I thought you said the hours were crazy and you couldn't take the heat and the tempers . . .' I shouted over the noise.

'You do it.'

'Yes, but I'm my own boss, more or less. And besides, I'm kind of a hostess really. The cooking I do wouldn't kill anyone. But you were working in high-pressure kitchens, sure Gordon Ramsay is a pussycat compared with your last boss or have you forgotten?'

'No, and I'm glad I'm learning the trade. It'll stand to

me, or so everyone keeps telling me.' Orla drained her cup. 'Anyway, let's see how my boss is when I get back. Another snide remark and I'll sock him one, I swear.' She looked at me. 'This week has put a lot of things into perspective for me.'

'Yeah. I know it has. And you were right, I will manage.' I wiped my hands on my apron. 'I feel better even saying the words. Anyway, I need to start by going to see Ali's solicitor.'

'Are you OK for money?'

'He seems to think so, yeah. I know she had some savings, but as far as I was concerned she'd used every penny to open the salon. Perhaps he's taking the value of that into account? I guess I'll find that out when we talk. But he's told me not to worry, which is just as well.' I grinned at her. 'All my spare cash went on handbags, you know that.'

'Yes, let's not discuss your fetish. It's cost you a fortune over the years.'

'No, not really, I don't earn as much as you. Besides, I quite like cheap bags and I love searching around for a decent copy of a designer look. See?' I picked up my latest, which was now covered in specks of flour. 'Looks like a Chloé but it's not.'

'Doesn't have the padlock,' Orla chipped in immediately. 'What am I saying?' she laughed. 'You've almost got me hooked as well.'

'Ali always saved for the one she wanted. Not me, I'm too impatient. I do love e-Bay, though . . .'

'You really were chalk and cheese, weren't you?' Orla looked thoughtful.

'What, you mean she was classy and smart and sophisticated?' I smiled.

'Yes, she was all of those things. But you're sexy and streetwise and . . .'

'And a bit of an eejit,' I added, throwing her some tomatoes so that she could start on the topping.

'Not true, you're just laid-back, that's all. You've a great head on your shoulders, my mother always said so.' She looked around. 'Red onions or shallots?'

'Red onions. Well, I've no head for money, that's for sure.'

'Was money very tight?'

'Since Charlie came . . .' I glanced over at him, now making a bandage for his soldier with the dough. 'Things were tight, but all I did was transfer an amount to Ali's account each month. The rest was mine to fritter away as I wanted. Even looking at the bills that have come in this week . . . I don't know how she managed. The salon wasn't breaking even yet, as far as I know. Sure, I bought food a good bit and I brought home things for the baby all the time, but I couldn't tell you how much is owing on my credit cards, that's for certain.'

'OK, I'll admit it, finance would be your weak point if you ever opened your own restaurant . . .'

'We haven't done that particular daydream in ages, have we?' I smiled at my friend. 'Sally and I went through such a phase of talking about it that she claimed *my* business

105

plan was making *her* insolvent – reckoned her phone bill had gone to four figures.'

'Well, long phone calls from Oz tend to do that all right.'

It was so good being able to talk to Orla like this. I missed Sally so much since she'd moved to Sydney and emailing just wasn't the same.

I hugged Orla. 'Thanks. You've helped me enormously,' I told her.

'You're welcome,' she said, wiping flour off my nose with her tea towel. 'I was talking to Sally last night, as it happens. She's devastated that she can't get home.'

'I know, I keep telling her I'll probably need her more later on, when all the fuss dies down and I'm really alone. She's saving like mad so that she can get here soon.'

'Apparently her folks have offered to pay half her fare,' Orla told me.

'No way! She never said. God, it would be great to see her.'

'Oops, perhaps I shouldn't have told you. I think she was saving that bit of news for later.'

We put the bases in the oven, topped up on coffee and talked away the afternoon, then fed Charlie pizza, which he loved. It was exactly what I needed that day.

Aunt Milly offered to take Charlie back home with her for a while and I resisted at first. But then seeing him kept reminding me of how inadequate I was on my own, and how much our little family had depended on Ali for stability.

Alone in bed at night, thinking about all she'd done for us, I wanted my sister – wherever she was now – to be proud of me and making things perfect for her child seemed to be as good a place as any to start. I knew that not having to worry about him for the immediate future while I sorted things out would help a lot, and he already appeared besotted with Aunt Milly, who was so confident with him.

'Now, love, are you sure you'll manage?' she asked as they got ready to board the train to Cork a day or two later.

'Why does no one have any confidence that I can cope on my own?' I asked her.

'Och no, it's not that.' She had a Scottish pal in Cork and it sometimes rubbed off on her. 'It's just that I know your friend leaves tomorrow and, with me going and all, I'm just afraid you'll have too much time on your own.'

I hugged her. 'I'll be fine, don't worry. You've been a brick. And there's just so much to do over the next few weeks. Will you be able to cope?' I knew she wasn't getting any younger.

'No problem. You leave the little fellow with me for as long as you like.' She adjusted the collar of her coat. 'I'll be glad of the company, to tell you the truth. I never know what to do with myself when I haven't got someone to fuss over.' She smiled and we embraced again, then I quickly gave Charlie a kiss, afraid that I was going to slobber all over him. 'I'll miss you so much, buster.' I crouched down beside him and zipped up his red jacket. He was part of my sister and that made him part of me, and now he was all I had.

'I'm not Buster, I'm Charlie.'

'Well, whoever you are, I love you.' I tried to smile.

'Bye-bye.' He wriggled out of my embrace. 'Choo-choo.' He indicated the train and strained to get on with the adventure, clutching his Thomas the Tank Engine book I'd bought him 'cause it had lots of engines in it.

'I'll call you later, Aunt Milly, and thanks.' I hugged her again. 'Thanks for everything.'

'Sure what are family for?' She ruffled Charlie's hair and smiled at me fondly. 'Call me any time, do you hear?'

'I'll call you every evening and speak to the monster.' I tried to smile as I waved them off and then went home and bawled my eyes out.

That afternoon I called Brian Daly, mainly because I'd promised my friends – including Sally by email – that I'd make a start. Besides, I felt I owed it to Milly, who was putting her whole life on hold in order to help me out. Orla had made me prioritize things and we'd spent hours writing stuff down that I needed to do. Alison had always told me that the trick with a list was to tackle the nastiest job first, thereby ensuring you felt so virtuous that you ploughed through everything else with little or no effort. While calling Brian didn't quite fit into the nasty category, I was sort of dreading it.

As soon as he came on the line I didn't know what to say.

'How are you?' he asked. It was what everyone wanted to know.

'I don't . . . I'm not sure what to do,' I blurted out, immediately annoyed with myself. 'What I mean is, I'm not sure where to start, the business and all . . .' I was waffling: men in suits with authority always had that effect on me.

'Don't worry, that's what I'm paid for.' I could hear him flipping pages. 'Why don't you come in and see me?'

'You did say we needed to talk?' I said hesitantly. I'd no idea when he'd said it; everything about those first few days was a jumbled mess in my brain.

'Yes, that's right. When would suit?'

'This afternoon?' I suggested hopefully.

'I've a lot on today, I'm afraid. How about early next week?'

'Oh.' All the wind went out of my sails. Doing things would keep me sane, I'd decided, and until I talked to him I didn't know what else to do with myself, especially now that Charlie was gone. The flat was so quiet without him.

He must have sensed something. 'I could see you for a quick chat at the end of today, say around five thirty?' he suggested. 'It would just be an informal meeting. We'd still need to sit down properly next week and . . . go through stuff.'

'Great, thanks.' I seized the opportunity.

He rattled off directions. 'And we can schedule a longer, more formal meeting while you're here. There are papers I need you to sign, but I don't have them prepared yet,' he explained.

'Fine.' I got off the phone as quickly as I could, in case

he changed his mind. All I knew was that I needed to keep moving forward and not spend too much time thinking. Otherwise I got a sick feeling in my stomach that threatened to overwhelm me, rendering even the smallest task too much.

'How do you eat an elephant?' was one of Ali's favourite phrases. I could see her laughing as she said it.

'Bit by fucking bit.' I used to stick out my tongue at her in reply.

'But what do you do when you're choking on every bite?' I wanted to know now.

'Keep chewing.' I could hear her as clearly as if she was standing in front of me in the empty kitchen. 'After a while, you'll be taking bigger bites and you won't even notice.'

The offices of Brian Daly and Co. were at the top of Francis Street in the heart of the Liberties in inner-city Dublin. I'd expected something much more posh. One of Dublin's oldest indoor markets, the Iveagh Market, was nearby and I recognized the smell of old clothes and leather shoes that lingered even though it had been closed for years. Women with headscarves still sold fish from wooden bread van boards on top of old prams, so that they could make a quick getaway if the coppers arrived, EU red tape having put paid to this type of casual trading.

Brian came out to greet me almost immediately and when he smiled I instantly felt less nervous. I'd put on my one decent trouser suit and tied my hair back in an effort to look like I imagined his other clients did. Although we were twins, Alison had been the more confident one, at home in any situation. Me, I'd always waited until she'd got the conversation going before I joined in, although Stephen Pritchard, my boss, had told me more than once that I could charm the birds off the trees when I wanted to. Sometimes I got bolshy in an effort to hide my insecurities, of which there were too many to keep secret for long anyway. And I was a bit clumsy too, when I was nervous, which was often.

'Come in.' Brian ushered me into a large room stuffed with metal filing cabinets and dusty books. 'Coffee?'

'No, thanks.' I tried to sound nonchalant. I'd have loved one but felt I'd probably slop it all over the place.

'Sit down, please.' He indicated a worn brown chair. 'How are you doing?' he asked as he sauntered round the desk. He was so laid-back, it helped put me at ease.

'Fine, I guess.' I fidgeted with the strap of my lime-green tweedy handbag, which had been Ali's. I'd borrowed it to give me confidence. It was an Orla Kiely and I remembered wondering how she could afford it at the time. She said someone had given it to her as a present, one of her regular clients, I think. Seemed like an expensive thank-you-for-the-facial to me, but then what did I know?

'I made a list, see.' I held it up like a child who'd just coloured in her first picture and waited for him to acknowledge my masterpiece. Instead he was looking at me intently, watching for signs of a nervous breakdown, I imagined. Last time he'd seen me I'd been raw with grief. I was still mortified about the way I'd spoken to him.

'Ali always made lists,' I said quietly. 'I'm hoping a bit of her organizational skills will have rubbed off on me.'

'She did, didn't she.' He smiled gently. 'So does my mother. It must be a female thing.'

'Well, not this female, at least not until now.' I sighed. 'Suddenly there's so much to do and I'm not sure how to . . . go about most of it, to tell you the truth.'

'This must be hard on you.'

I shrugged. 'Ali was more like a mother, really, even though we're . . . were . . . exactly the same age. I never had to worry about anything . . . She just took care of things.'

'I know.'

'Without her, I feel so helpless.' I was afraid to cry so I bit the inside of my cheek. 'There was nothing much on the list, really,' I admitted. 'Just to call you and Aunt Milly and then try and find her keys to the salon. My friend Orla made me write down every little thing that was on my mind initially. But then I lost that list.' I threw my eyes up to heaven.

'Calling me was a good place to start.'

'I'm worried about money.' God, I hoped he didn't think I was looking for a loan, or worse, trying to get out of paying his fee. 'I'm not . . . skint or anything. I have some money. It's just Ali took care of all the bills and I know we were always broke at the end of the month.'

'Lily, there's no problem with regard to money.' He

rubbed his forehead as if trying to decide where to start. 'I hope I managed to convince you of that the day I came to see you.' He looked worried that I was worried.

'I know, you said. It's just that . . . I don't understand. The business wasn't making money, as far as I'm aware. I mean, I don't have a clue about the actual figures or anything, but from what Ali said I knew it was a struggle . . .' Oh God, I was waffling like mad. I coughed and started again. 'What I mean is, she can't have saved much, really, even though she was always so . . .' I was going to say tight, but that was entirely the wrong word, '. . . careful,' I ventured. 'She never let any bills get out of hand, and always paid off her credit card each month. And any spare cash she had went on Charlie—'

'Lily, your father left money, rather a lot,' he said as soon as I paused for breath.

'Yeah, to his charities. We know all about those.' No matter how hard I tried to be professional and businesslike with Brian, I couldn't seem to keep my lip from curling each time my father's name was mentioned.

'No, not only to those.' He opened a file but I sensed he didn't need to look inside. 'He left a large amount of money for his grandchildren, for instance.'

It took a moment for that to sink in. 'But there weren't any when he died,' I said, completely at a loss. 'And what about his children?'

Brian spoke quietly. 'There was no direct provision for either of you, I'm afraid. But he did want to provide for future generations. And there were conditions attached,' he added quickly. 'He set it all out long before he died.'

'What sort of conditions?' I sighed, but I wasn't really surprised. But why the grandchildren he didn't have and not the kids he did? Even as I tried to figure it out I knew it was typical of him.

'Mr Daly, excuse me.' A gangly blonde put her head round the door just as Brian opened his mouth to say something. 'I'm really sorry to disturb you but you asked me to let you know if Mr Proctor phoned and he's on the line now . . .'

'Oh, right. Thanks, Maeve, I'll take it.' He stood up. 'Will you excuse me, Lily? I've been waiting for this all day.'

'Sure, no worries.'

'Won't be long.' He disappeared. Talking about my father's money made me remember how tight he'd been when we were kids.

'I'm not spending any more money on clothes. It's boarding school, you'll be wearing a uniform most of the time,' my father insisted. 'And if you want to go at all there are rules to be adhered to.'

'I need new clothes,' I said sullenly, ignoring Ali's warning look.

'Your aunt Rose went through all your stuff and said you had plenty.'

'Everyone gets new clothes when they start a new school.'

'If you want anything else you can get a part-time job, and any more cheek from you and you'll spend the weekend in the house studying.' He went out and banged the door.

'Lily, I warned you not to annoy him.' Ali looked anxious again. 'Once we get away it'll be better, you'll see.'

'I'm not wearing those brown trousers for another day, never mind a whole term.' I wanted to cut them up into tiny pieces. 'Why does he always tell Aunt Rose to buy us dark grey and brown stuff anyway?' I was thinking aloud.

'I've no idea but don't worry, we'll manage.'

'It's 'cause he wishes we were boys,' I said sullenly. '"Less trouble".' I mimicked his voice. 'He said it again the other day to Mrs Nolan.'

'Anyway, I'm going to sell my silver watch without telling him.' Ali smiled and winked. 'That way we'll have a secret stash.'

Even then she'd been protecting me, making sure I didn't go without. Remembering made me want her back so badly I almost threw up again.

'Sorry, that was unavoidable,' Brian apologized. 'Now, where were we?' He sat down quickly with a rush of cold air.

I didn't have to think for long. 'Conditions,' I prompted.

'Yes, that's right. Well, in relation to Alison, if she'd been married, it was to be put in a trust fund for any child's – or children's – education.'

'And if she wasn't?'

'Then it became more complicated. If she had a baby outside of . . . wedlock, as he put it, no money was to be paid until the child was three years of age, and then only provided she kept the child.'

'He actually thought either of us would abandon a baby?' I asked, shocked, but only a bit. 'I suppose that's because he didn't really know us at all,' I said, more to myself than to him. 'When my mother died he sort of abandoned us.' I saw Brian Daly's eyebrows knit together and only then realized I was saying it aloud.

'Oh, not literally, we never went hungry or anything. It's just that he never really spent time with us. He couldn't cope with little girls, that's what everyone said.' I thought of all the times I'd missed my mother when I was growing up and how badly I'd needed my father to give me a hug and tell me things would be OK. 'That's why my sister was so important,' I told Brian sadly. 'She was the only person in my life who was always there.'

'Lily, I'm not trying to justify what he did or any-thing . . .' he said quietly. 'My job is simply to carry out—'

'Ali and I had to endure years of scrimping and saving because he thought it would make us better adults.' I could feel the heat rising under my shirt collar. 'And it didn't matter one bit that there was no shortage of money in our family.' I suddenly thought of something. 'Did Ali know about this, I mean is that why she got pregnant?' I was trying to look horrified but was secretly hopeful.

'No, no, she knew nothing about it.'

'Then, if she didn't know anything, why wouldn't he have just made the money available immediately?' Even as I asked I knew that it was typical of my father's controlling nature. Christ, maybe that was where Ali got it from? I felt disloyal even thinking it. My sister was nothing like my father and thankfully I was even less so.

'I imagine it was just an added precaution . . .' Brian trailed off.

'So, provided she kept the baby, when was she to be told?'

'On the baby's third birthday.'

'But that was only a few weeks . . .' I tried to think of the exact date but my brain was as addled as the rest of me.

'Yes.'

'But why make her wait? Suppose she'd given the baby up for adoption or something? I mean, she might have . . .' But I knew she wouldn't. 'Christ, Brian, we've been really struggling for the past few years. If it hadn't been for the business . . .' I shook my head. 'I don't understand it.'

'I can't really speculate, I'm afraid. All I know is that those were his instructions.'

Well, it certainly explained Ali's lightness in recent weeks, her almost carefree attitude, her constant insistence that everything was going to be fine. I suddenly remembered the two expensive purses she'd bought us for no reason.

'So, when did she get the money?' I was amazed at the brazen way I was talking to a man I'd been apprehensive about meeting only hours earlier.

His eyes remained steady but his voice sounded sad. 'The first payment was transferred to her account on the day of her death.'

12

LILY

I SUCKED IN MY BREATH. 'YOU'RE KIDDING, RIGHT?'

Do solicitors ever joke? This one didn't, it seemed.

'No. Would you like a glass of water?' I must have turned a yucky green or something because he quickly made to get up.

I shook my head. 'Oh God.' It all felt too much to take in. 'You mean she'd only just found out . . . ?' I closed my eyes and tried to imagine how she must have felt. It made what happened to her the very same day seem a million times worse.

'I knew there was something,' I said softly. 'She sounded so excited when she phoned at lunchtime.' Neither of us spoke for a second or two.

'She had so much to live for . . . Charlie, the business . . . and finally an inheritance.' I stared at the wall. 'It would have been a dream come true for us.' Right then, sitting in that stuffy brown office, I'd have given anything I owned for things to have been different.

'How much money are we talking about?' I didn't really want to know and yet I desperately did.

'A hundred thousand euro.'

'No.' And I'd thought that nothing else he said could surprise me. 'She actually had it in her hands?'

'Yes. Well, in her account.'

'On the day she died?' I stared at Brian but really I was talking to myself. 'And she knew, in advance . . . that it was going to be that amount?'

He nodded.

'No wonder she seemed so happy these last few weeks.' I swallowed, remembering her humming to herself one night as she fed Charlie, and me teasing her about having a new boyfriend. 'Was she . . . ecstatic?'

He looked at me for a long moment. 'I think she was more excited for you.'

I closed my eyes and nodded. That made sense only to me, I imagined.

'She kept talking about how some of the money would go to you, how she wanted you to start your own business, open a deli or something similar.'

'Ah yes, that old chestnut.' I smiled at him. 'I only ever talk about that particular fantasy when I'm pis— eh, had too much to drink.'

Brian grinned. 'She did mention that you always got very animated about starting your own business when you came home late at night, normally when she was fast asleep.'

'Usually after about twenty Bacardi Breezers. I always

119

woke her up and no matter how many times she heard it she never once told me to sod off.' I laughed. 'Thankfully, it didn't happen often. I couldn't afford it most of the time.'

He didn't say anything and I was lost in thoughts of her for a moment.

'Could she have done that, given me some money, I mean?' I asked him.

'Yes, we'd talked about it but hadn't quite worked out the details. The money was hers to do with as she pleased, basically, as long as it also benefited Charlie. She maintained that you working for yourself would mean that you'd have more freedom to play a bigger role in Charlie's upbringing – she knew that you loved spending time with him. But her primary motivation was you realizing your dream, I suspect. I remember she said you'd been playing at owning a coffee shop since you were a small girl. Claimed you used to pour her cups of water and make her pretend to be having afternoon tea.'

'Dirty water at that. With cucumber sandwiches made out of cardboard with green crêpe paper for the filling.' I smiled. 'As we got older our fantasies became more sophisticated, but only just.'

In fact, we'd daydreamed all the way through our teens, only by then we'd discovered boys so those dreams invariably involved rock stars and stretch limos. Finally, in our twenties we had it all sussed, and on a much more realistic level too. Ali would work during the day and I'd be in my restaurant at night: that way we'd share Charlie.

She used to laugh and promise to pamper my rough hands and achy feet, as long as I kept her supplied with pies and tarts. We reckoned that Charlie would be permanently covered in either body lotion or flour.

'Isn't it just such an awful tragedy then,' I was trying hard not to get emotional, 'that she died on the day when suddenly she had everything to live for? I mean never, even in my wildest dreams, did I think this would happen . . . and courtesy of my father. Christ, how much money did he have?'

'A lot,' Brian said quietly. 'Or at least a lot of land.'

'I knew he was well off, but surely all that land he owned wasn't worth much. Not in Sligo?'

'A huge portion of it was rezoned for development a few years before he died. And some of it bordered that castle, what was it called? I don't know if you remember?'

I shook my head.

'Suddenly he was in a very powerful position. The castle had planning permission for around forty luxury homes in the grounds and they wanted his land badly.' He smiled at me. 'Your father drove a hard bargain. He made a lot of money out of that deal.'

I bet he did. 'So Ali got one hundred thousand in a lump sum?' I said after a moment or two, aware that he was watching me again.

'That's right. And there's more.'

I assumed he meant more conditions attached. 'More?' I still felt my father just might take it all back. Even from where he was now.

'More money. There are scheduled payments to come, every year, on Charlie's birthday. Money for other . . . expenses, as well.'

'How much?' I hated myself for sounding so eager and I hated my father more for turning me into the kind of gloating gold-digger normally only seen in old American westerns.

'It's to be paid in various stages, as I said, but nearly a million overall until his twenty-first birthday.'

'And who decides? I mean, can it be used for anything, or must it be spent on Charlie?' I could feel my heart thumping.

'Well, a good portion of it is tied up in a trust specifically for his education and some goes directly to Alison . . . or you, now. It's administered by myself and Paul Cleary, an accountant attached to this practice, and overseen by our senior partner here, but basically your father wanted his grandson to have a certain standard in life, a good home, etc., and responsibility for that fell to his mother.'

The questions were racing through my mind but I didn't know where to start and I was afraid I'd forget something, then go home and not be able to sleep. 'I still don't quite believe it' was the only thing I could think of saying. I stared at Brian. 'There must be a catch.'

Even as I said the words I thought of one. 'What about now?' I asked in what I hoped was a calm tone. 'Now that Ali's dead? You mentioned me . . .' I tried to keep my voice even, although I felt waves of slight hysteria wash over me, but that was only because I'd just realized it would be the ultimate irony if all this money died with her. Ali had always been my father's favourite – if he had one at all. I was sure he wouldn't have wanted his fortune to end up with me, the child who never let him forget what he was doing to us.

I felt Brian sensed something of what I was thinking. 'It's OK,' he said quickly. 'Alison had made a will.'

'When? How? She only got the money on the day—'

'We'd talked about it in advance. As soon as she heard, she instructed me to draw up a will. I had all the necessary papers prepared. She signed everything on the one day.' He shook his head. 'Lily, I know this is a lot for you to take in.' He shrugged. 'It even seems a bit unreal to me – her death on that exact day.' He consulted his papers again.

'Normally people take ages to get round to even thinking about a will, much less deciding what to do. But Alison was very definite. The minute I told her about the money she gave me instructions. Even if she hadn't signed the papers her intentions were clear.'

'And what were her intentions?' I was half afraid asking.

'She gave custody of Charlie to you.' He paused and rooted around in the file again, more to give me time, I think. 'She also made you the beneficiary of all her assets.'

'Everything?'

'Yes.'

'Even the apartment?'

'Of course.' He was trying to reassure me. 'It was your home too.'

'I know, but she put up the deposit, and because I was

. . . between jobs at the time, she was the only one who could apply for a mortgage.'

'Well, it now belongs to you and . . .' He flicked through another pile of papers. 'She had mortgage protection insurance for you both, as far as I remember . . . Yes, I see a note of that here, and the flat is in your joint names, so the loan will be paid off.'

'You mean I won't even have to pay the mortgage each month?'

'Not a penny. It's what these policies are for.'

For the first time since her death I actually thought I might be able to manage financially, something that had been keeping me awake at night. Yet now I no longer had to worry about being able to afford to look after Charlie properly, or anything else I'd been fretting about. It was mad.

'And my father's will can't change anything?' I came back down to earth with a bang.

'No.' Brian emphasized the word. 'Not a thing.'

'Are you sure? There's not a sneaky clause 14d in there? My father would've wanted the donkey sanctuary to have carrots for the next billion years, you know, sooner than leave all of his money to me – whatever he might have felt about Ali.'

'I'm certain,' Brian said.

'I was the cheeky one, you see. His whole life was about how hard he'd had to work and how much my mother had cosseted us.' I thought about it for a minute. 'And I reminded him too much of her. He wouldn't have given it to me,' I told Brian quietly. 'Because I never let him forget what he was doing to us by being so strict and never being around, pawning us off on relatives, insisting we go to boarding school.'

'No, there's nothing sinister in the will.' He smiled at me sadly and shook his head. 'A few more conditions, but they relate to the child mainly. Nothing that affects your situation. I don't think any of us, least of all your father, would have envisaged this happening.' He looked through me. 'She was so young,' he said quietly. Something in the way he said it made me think that he might have been a little bit in love with her.

'And beautiful.' I always said it as if we weren't related, let alone twins.

'Yes,' he agreed, with a half-smile. 'She was beautiful.' He flicked through his file again. 'Actually, you look very like her today,' he added as an afterthought.

'Not really.' I smiled. 'I never quite had her film star appeal. I just clean up well.'

I must have flagged a bit because he looked all concerned again. 'Perhaps we should leave it there for now. I hadn't really intended to get into so much detail with you. It's still early days.'

'Yes.' I stood up and so did he. 'You know what, I can't believe that Ali was so forward thinking, so organized.' I shook my head as if to clear it. 'Imagine putting all that into place so quickly. If it was me, I don't think I'd even have taken out mortgage protection – or whatever you called it – in the first place.'

'It's what happens when you have a child, I suspect.'

'Do you have children?' I realized I knew absolutely nothing about him.

'No.' He came around the desk. 'Sure you wouldn't like that cup of coffee after all?'

'No, thanks.' I grinned at him. 'I didn't take it earlier 'cause I was so nervous I was afraid I'd spill it. Now I know for certain I couldn't hold a cup to save my life. Look, I'm still shaking.'

'Something stronger, perhaps? I can offer you a small brandy or port?' It sounded like something your grandad would produce in an emergency.

'Got any tequila?' I enquired. 'Joke,' I said quickly as I watched his brows crease.

'Not much call for tequila in this office.' He smiled.

'Actually, I'd murder a drink but I'd better not. I think I need a clear head to sort out all you've just told me.'

'We could go across to the pub and have a glass of wine? That shouldn't harm any of your brain cells.'

'I won't, thanks, I'm actually exhausted and I know I'll have a list of questions for you once I've had time to myself. Is it OK if I call you?'

'Of course, that's what I'm here for. We will need to meet again anyway, as I said earlier. I'll have my secretary call you tomorrow and schedule a more formal meeting.' He smiled tiredly. 'This was supposed to be just a chat . . .' His voice trailed off.

'I know.' I was aware that I'd sort of forced myself on

him. 'And I really appreciate you seeing me today. I didn't know where to start, as I said.'

'Pleasure.' He was being a solicitor again. I held out my hand as an afterthought. He took it and his grasp was firm. 'Mind yourself.' He smiled and was back to being the Brian I could identify with once more.

'I will.'

'I'll see you out. The place might be locked up by now.' He held the door open for me and I realized I'd been there for nearly two hours. What would a 'proper' meeting entail? I was shattered.

We were at the main entrance in no time. As I turned to say a final goodbye another thought struck me. 'What if my sister had had a baby girl?' I asked him. Ali always said my father would have treated us differently if we'd been boys.

Brian looked uncomfortable to be talking in an open space, even though the place was empty as far as I could see.

'Would that have made any difference?' I asked, more out of curiosity.

'Yes.'

'How?'

'There was no provision made for a female child,' he said softly. 'This only applied in the event of Alison giving birth to a boy.'

13

LILY

'IT WOULD HAVE BEEN FAIRER IF IT HAD BEEN ME,' I TOLD
my aunt later that night, after I'd sat for hours thinking
about how happy Ali must have been on the day she
died.

'Shush, child, don't say such a thing. There's a plan for
all of us, I'm certain of it.'

'But she had a child to look after . . . and me, a big baby
– that's what my father always called me.'

'Your father had his own demons.' Aunt Milly never
said a bad word about anyone. 'His own mother left when
he was a child, too, remember. He had little or no contact
with the female sex until he met your mother.'

'Why did she marry him?' Tonight I wanted answers to
all the questions.

'She loved him,' my aunt said simply. 'I think she was
the only one who ever tried to understand him. And he
loved her too, in his own way. He softened up a lot when
he met her.'

'Then why did he ignore us when she died?'

'The way he saw it, she'd abandoned him as well. And I think you two reminded him of all he'd lost.' My aunt sounded as bad as I felt. 'I blame myself, to tell you the truth. I should have fought harder to take you to live with me.'

'Don't say that.' I felt even worse. 'You were always so good to us. And you had Granny and Grandad to look after.'

I tried to reassure her as best I could. We spoke for ages. Hearing about Charlie cheered me up and when he came on the line to talk to me I felt a surge of love for him that took me by surprise and made me silently thank God that he was safe.

Two days later I returned to work, afraid that if I left it any longer I'd never go back. Dreams of owning my own business were beginning to keep me awake, ever since Brian had told me what Ali had been thinking. My boss was surprised and happy to have me back so soon. 'We've been lost without you,' Stephen told me as he greeted me with a hug that nearly strangled me.

'Yeah, right.' I knew he was just saying it. 'Who's been covering?'

'Corporate Catering. It's been fine except we've had someone different almost every day.'

'They're good.' I wasn't about to bad-mouth Audrey and Robert O'Neill, I'd known them for years and they'd been kind to me when I knew nothing. 'I'd love to have the sort of set-up they have.' I glanced out the window.

'They're terrific, but they lack your personal touch.' He noticed everything.

I was thinking about when I'd started cooking and imagining what the future might bring, but even without looking at him I could tell he was watching me.

'You OK, honey child?' He slipped into what I always called his 'deep throat' accent. His mother had been born in one of the southern states of America – Georgia, I think, or Alabama – and he'd lived there for a few years as a child.

'I'm fine.' His pet name always made me smile. He was a bear of a man and I'd have loved him for a father. 'I should warn you that I keep bursting into tears for no reason though. So maybe keep me away from the top brass for a day or two, OK?'

'No problem. And I'd be more worried if you didn't. You've been through a helluva lot.'

'So, what's been happening?'

'Why don't you grab yourself a coffee and we'll go through a few things? Oh, and I'll have a strong one if you're asking.'

'Yes, boss.' I clutched the hem of my linen pinafore and curtsied as I backed out. It was a game we played sometimes to amuse ourselves. I grinned and knew he was relieved as I disappeared into the kitchen and rustled up elevenses at nine thirty.

My job was fairly straightforward. Boring even. I was employed by a large law firm as a hostess cum cook cum waitress cum anything else to do with food. They didn't really need a full-time chef, but they liked having an in-house caterer to impress their clients. Mostly it was lunch for a couple of the partners, drinks parties in the boardroom or keep-them-going snacks for a late night meeting, of which there were many. The only problem was that while I'm a great cook – even if I say so myself – I'm a lousy hostess and I've lost count of the number of Waterford glass bowls and Wedgwood cups and saucers I've elbowed into smithereens. Still, it was handy money that suited the slob I was at heart, even though my taking the easy way out meant I yearned for a challenge a good bit of the time.

As I made my way back to Stephen I passed one of the partners. I kept my head down and moved as fast as I could with a tray in my hands. Paul Canavan reminded me of a businessman who used to visit my father. Ali had always made me be nice to him.

'Now, Lily, promise me you'll be polite and charming to Mr Donaldson. That way we can make our own tea once they're in Dad's study, and guess what? Aunt Milly left us a tuck box hidden up high in the pantry.'

'Ali, why do we have to pretend all the time?'

'Because we're girls and Dad says girls are much more trouble and cost more money.' Ali put her finger to her lips. *'Shush now, I hear him coming. He's in good form tonight so don't say anything, OK? Leave the talking to me.'*

'Can we have coffee instead of milk when we sneak down-stairs later?' I asked hopefully. I'd always loved the smell of coffee.

'Yes, but only if you smile and say hello nicely.'

'I get fed up always being quiet, or polite, or no trouble.'

'I know, love, but it won't always be like this. It'll get easier.'

Every time that poor Mr Canavan spoke to me I thought of how much I hated my father's business cronies because he was only ever nice to us when they were around.

'So, what's cookin' this week?' I handed boss man a steaming cafetière and took out my diary.

'Not much. I just wish everyone I managed was as easy as you.' Stephen Pritchard was a sort of elevated dogsbody – Head of Administrative Services was his official title. He made sure the place ran like clockwork and organized everything from the flowers to the toilet cleaners. His job was a nightmare, I'd always thought, and he got no thanks. Nobody noticed his efforts – unless there was a problem.

'I keep telling you, you need to go sick for a month, only way they're going to realize what they've got.'

'Not my style, honey child. Now, tell me, how are you really?'

'I'm fine.' He was giving me one of his looks. 'Honest,' I told him.

'What about the little fella?'

'He's down in the country with my aunt Milly for the moment.' Thinking about him made me long for our little family to be back to the way it used to be.

'How'll you manage?' He knew there was no one else.

'No idea. Childminder ... eventually, I suppose.' I didn't want to think about that yet.

'Will you be able to afford it?'

'Yep, courtesy of my late father.' I knew he wouldn't miss my sarcastic tone; he knew a good bit about my background. 'Although he never thought I'd get control of his money, that's for sure. I'll tell you all one of these days. Just as soon as I've figured it out myself.'

'No pressure. I didn't mean to pry.'

'I know.' I swallowed my espresso. 'Now, down to business. And please tell me I've no late nights for a day or two.'

'None this week, as far as I remember. Anyway, hire in whatever help you need. Ease yourself back in.' He was looking at me in a pitying sort of way that I wasn't sure I liked. 'OK, honey child? That's an order.'

'Yes, boss.' I sighed and decided I was just being paranoid. Stephen Pritchard was a gem and I was lucky to have him as my manager. 'Thanks. I'll probably need an odd few hours off here and there. Solicitors and all that.' I hoped it sounded casual.

'Take whatever time you need.'

I loved that man.

Later I tore the flat apart, looking for Alison's keys to the salon. I knew she had a spare set somewhere. At first I thought she might have had them with her at the time of the accident, but her belongings had eventually been returned to me – spotted by the rescue services when they'd combed the area looking for her – and only her hall door key was in her purse. She was always separating stuff – make-up, the contents of her handbag, etc. Like me she hated carrying a big satchel – 'at least until I can afford a really soft leather one,' she used to tell me – so I knew there had to be bits around the place. I just hadn't had the courage to have a proper look in her bedroom so far.

I opened the door warily, not wanting to disturb her things, and was unprepared for the smell that greeted me. Her scent was everywhere in this room, the spicy, floral fragrances that she loved to slap on morning and evening. I stood at the door and immediately pictured Charlie playing on the well-worn rug and me sitting swinging my legs on the bed, as we'd done so many evenings. I pushed myself inside, knowing it was now or maybe never. The first thing I saw was another print of her favourite picture, of the two of us when we were about nine. I might have put it on her coffin but it always made me think about the day it had been taken.

'That's lovely, Alison. Lily, smile, for goodness' sake,' Aunt Rose said sourly. 'Isn't it wonderful of your father to let you have a birthday party this year?'

'Yes, Aunt Rose. Thank you, Father,' Ali smiled, always wanting to please.

'We got no presents from Dad,' I told Aunt Milly later as I stuffed a packet of sweets into my pocket. 'And he won't let us keep that picture – the one that Aunt Rose took. He says pictures like that are frivolous. What's frivolous?'

'He's very unhappy, child.' She ignored me. 'He misses your mother a lot and he finds two girls a handful.'

'But we're really quiet, Aunt Milly. Ali makes me do the right thing all the time.'

'That's a good girl, you do as Ali tells you.'

'I hate him.'

'Lily, be careful. Someone will hear you.' Ali was back. 'Aren't we having a great day?'

'Only because of Aunt Milly. Once she goes it'll be back to spending all the evenings in our room and being quiet all the time.'

'I'll come as often as I can then, Lily. And don't you worry, I'll get you a copy of that picture and you can keep it somewhere safe.'

And she had, although it had been Ali who kept it safe.

I spotted the keys I wanted on her bedside table, along with another purse and her Filofax. I grabbed the bunch and closed the door quickly. The rest could wait for another time.

The drive to Wicklow took just under an hour and even in the dark the Sugar Loaf mountain made for a dramatic skyline as soon as I swung off the roundabout at Loughlinstown. When I opened the car window a mile or two outside Ashford I could taste the salt in the air and just before Rathnew I was so close that I reckoned I could hear the faint slosh of the waves. It was funny, because I'd never had any *grá* – as they say in Irish – for rural life but somehow this evening I found myself wondering how the countryside would look in the papery thin autumn sunlight. Not for nothing was Wicklow known as the garden county of Ireland.

When I got to the salon it was back-lit in a mustardy yellow glow and looked warm and inviting in the near-winter damp. Violet had returned to open up a few days previously and fresh lilies and the scent of candles filled the air as I let myself in. So many memories of my sister were connected to smell. She'd always said the same about me, but whereas mine were the comforting aromas of cinnamon, cloves and coffee, hers were the seductive ylang-ylang and eucalyptus and frankincense – the oils she used every day. For the first time I realized our scents didn't really match our personalities – she was the home-maker and I was the flighty one. Although she'd had a couple of relationships, I had never really relaxed around men: a party girl who always went home alone. 'All talk,' Sally used to say about me when we went to the Grange disco years ago.

I was breathing in the smell of Alison and feeling very close to her when my mobile rang.

'Hey, where are you? I've been ringing you at home.' It was Sally on a dodgy mobile line from Sydney.

'Hey, babe, I was just thinking about you.' I was thrilled she'd called. 'It's so nice to hear you, I was just getting maudlin. I'm at the salon.'

'Are you OK?'

'I dunno really. I miss her so much, Sal. I was just

thinking about how she always smelt seductive and I smelt of coffee, and in reality—'

'In reality she was all home comforts and you were all cleavage,' Sally cut across me. I knew she was remembering too.

'So I'm a bit of a slut, is that what you're trying to say?'

'A slut, no, but you are a bit of a temptress . . .'

'Sally Fielding, how long is it since you've seen me? You're thinking of when we were at school.'

'Yeah, you used to hitch up your pleated skirt, finger your damp hair and open your white shirt down to your navel.'

'Don't remind me. It was just a reaction to being away from my father. I knew he'd hate it.' I was so glad she'd phoned. 'That wasn't seductive though, it was desperation.' I laughed at the picture she painted. 'Remember how Alison always looked older because she was so much more sophisticated?' I asked Sally.

'I sure do. All the guys wanted her 'cause they reckoned she was more experienced, whereas in reality you were much more likely to go down the back of the bike shed . . .'

'Shut up, bitch,' I screamed and we were fifteen again.

'Mind you, once you got them there you'd steal their bike and run away.' Sally laughed. 'All talk and—'

'—no action. That's amazing, it's exactly what I was thinking when my phone rang.' Suddenly I felt better able to cope. 'Thanks, Sal. Talking to you always helps. You know me so well.'

137

'I should hope so, after all we've shared.'

After a few minutes she had to go because the call was costing her a fortune, so I promised to ring her back at the weekend. She signed off, telling me she was very relieved to hear me laughing.

I wandered around, in and out of the treatment rooms. Places like this always made me feel inadequate. All those perfectly made-up faces waffling on about seaweed and cocoa butter and rosewater. I was never sure whether to swallow those things or pucker up and slap them on. Still, it was a great space in what was fast becoming quite a trendy town. Very cosmopolitan, I'd heard Alison telling Orla one day when she phoned the flat.

'Cosmopolitan my arse,' Orla confided in me as soon as Ali handed over the telephone. 'Last time I was in Brittas Bay two guys who were chatting me up at the bar in McDaniel's left on a tractor.' We'd fallen about laughing but I hadn't told Ali what we were on about, afraid of shattering her illusions.

'The next big thing. Give it five years,' Alison kept repeating, mantra-like, when everyone told her she was mad trying to start a business 'in the sticks'. It was all she could afford at the time.

There was a decent-sized kitchen out the back – and Violet had it spotless – complete with industrial washing machine and tumble dryer for all the towels and robes and flannels, a pile of which were stacked neatly on the counter top. They felt warm and comforting as I smoothed out non-existent creases the way I'd seen my sister do with Charlie's clothes many times. We both loved touching – another of our similarities – but give me warm, sticky dough over just-dry, fluffy towels any day. I opened presses and found half-full packets of vermicelli and a few tins of tomatoes and jars of spices that I'd used on the odd occasions I'd visited Ali. That was well before the flat upstairs was fitted out and I remembered rustling up a plate of pasta for her, all the time wishing I owned the place, or that she'd opened a café instead. Then I would have been in heaven and she wouldn't have been able to keep me away. So much of her time had been spent nurturing the business over the last few years and even though we lived together in Dublin, any time she was here I was either working or minding Charlie, so I felt now that I'd largely missed out on this part of her life. I often wondered why she didn't invite me down to Wicklow more, but it was probably because I was always slagging her about becoming a culchie.

I wasn't sure I had a key for the flat upstairs, but the first one I tried fitted the lock. I'd never been up here before, except when she was showing me around after she'd first bought the place. In the beginning it was used as a stockroom but then Alison had arranged for it to be cleaned and decorated.

'Whatever for?' I'd asked at the time.

'I dunno, I might have to stay over occasionally,' she'd said with a shrug.

'And leave Charlie with a minder? Or worse, me? I don't think so,' I remember teasing her. 'You'd be afraid I'd have him in some greasy spoon, or force-feed him those lime-green jelly snakes you hate.'

'E numbers are not good for children.' She'd wagged her finger at me. 'Anyway, Mrs Rafter loves having him and she needs the few bob,' she'd reminded me, referring to one of our neighbours, a well-kept sixty-something widow. She was anxious not to make me feel I had to mind Charlie all the time. 'You never know, I might even rent it out.' She'd been vague, but then I hadn't really been interested.

Now, as I opened the door I was surprised to see it was quite beautiful. A few lamps had been left on a timer, for security reasons, I imagined, and the place was filled with plush fabrics and what looked like expensive pieces of furniture. It was a compact flat: just one bedroom, a living room with a galley kitchen off it, a bathroom and a small utility room – more like a closet really, into which was crammed all her stock, I saw as I opened the door. Typical of my sister, though, everything was on shelves, labelled and probably in alphabetical order.

The bathroom was very posh, all white and chrome with thick towels and gorgeous accessories, way too flash for a smelly Wicklow tenant, I decided uncharitably. The bedroom housed an oversized bed with a luscious velvet throw and supersoft sheets with a thread count up in the thousands, I suspected. I only knew about thread count because Alison always made me check when we were look-ing for sheets in Arnotts' sale – the higher the better, apparently.

There was also a delicate Victorian chair which she'd obviously had re-upholstered and her desk, a piece she'd picked up in an antique shop ages ago and which I knew was her pride and joy. I opened an inlaid wardrobe and was surprised to discover some wispy, slip-type things in bridal colours with matching silk wraps. In a drawer I found a selection of pricey-looking underwear, some with the tags still on. Not Alison's, I decided; neither of us could afford this type of thing. And besides, Ali wasn't the kind of girl who wore red-and-black-satin French knickers or virginal white, lacy thongs. I giggled at the thought. She must have had someone staying, or maybe they belonged to demure-looking Violet.

God, perhaps Violet was using this place for illicit sex with that boyfriend of hers? What was his name? I'd met him once at a party in our flat. All I could remember was that he had yellow teeth and a pockmarked face. What a waste of fab underwear. I shuddered as I thought of his lank hair and piggy little eyes.

I sat down at the desk and switched on a lamp and ran my hand over the smooth, warm wood. As with her closet, I felt like an intruder, so I contented myself with a cursory glance. There was nothing much to see except a couple of accounts ledgers and a few bits of stationery. One drawer was locked and none of the keys fitted. I was just about to give up when I came across a key in a small padded pill-box. It fitted. Inside all I could find were some photos and another appointments book, along with a very snazzy mobile phone. Must have been left behind by one of her clients, I decided, coveting it. The book was for the current year and seemed to contain only a few names, as far as I could tell. They all had regular appointments, too, except for someone called Richard, who seemed to come any time he wanted. Maybe they rented out the apartment, a sort of short-term corporate let? That would explain the sumptuous surroundings, although not the crotchless knickers.

Suddenly, I began to enjoy the mystery. I wandered around, checking out the fridge in the kitchen for a soft drink. It was well stocked – wine bottles with gold thread, champagne in wooden casks, you name it. When I looked for a glass I found a press full of crystal and another drinks cabinet containing what looked like expensive cognacs and single malts. This was definitely odd. Alison would never have drunk this kind of stuff and it was hardly the sort of thing you left for tenants. Corporate clients then. Definitely.

Getting into the sophisticated mood that had nothing to do with the way I looked and everything to do with the surroundings I found myself in, I poured myself an ice-cold beer and swanned around, deciding that I could live here very easily. I sat back down at the desk and found another book, an expensive, leather tome. Inside, it contained notes about various people. There were no names, or at least none that I could easily identify, just the odd badly written line here and there. *Smokes cigars, likes Scotch on the rocks*, that sort of thing. There were lots of little squiggles and initials. They must be important, I decided. Maybe it was a secret code? The thought plunged me straight back to my Famous Five days.

I took the book and my drink over to the bed and settled myself comfortably to read more. All I was short of doing was getting under the covers with a torch. I had the same sense of being up to something bold.

The notes looked like a sort of résumé of several people. One was listed as W a few times – Will, it looked like further on, and he had something to do with the theatre. God, maybe he was a celebrity and came here with his girlfriends – or boyfriends even? The tabloid press had never been further south than the M50, I felt sure, so his secret was safe. He'd never be rumbled in sleepy old Wicklow. Maybe he was a cross-dresser? That would explain the underwear. Perhaps he was a movie star and guarded his privacy – wanted his chest waxed in secret. I laughed at myself, enjoying the ridiculous notions. There were more notes on R – maybe the Richard I'd read about earlier. I wondered if they were clients she didn't declare to the taxman, but dismissed the notion immediately. Alison was too straight.

No, these people came here regularly, and were important enough that she wanted everything to be just right for them. I closed my eyes and started to imagine that this was the meeting place of some kind of secret society. Later I began to fantasize that Alison was in a relationship with a woman – or could she be having an affair with a married man? It was a bit of a shock at first, even thinking about it. It just wasn't like my sister. As I lay on the decadent bed in the sumptuous room, a number of things fell into place – like the way Ali sometimes had a last-minute appointment in the evening and needed me to babysit. I remembered grumbling that her clients should schedule their treatments during her normal hours of business, like ordinary mortals.

My God! I sat up in bed as another thought popped uninvited into my head: maybe she did topless massages or lapdancing or something. I started to giggle then because I knew none of this was really possible with Ali, of all people. I had a sudden impulse to ring Sally back and tell her about my detective work. But Sally would say that there was more chance of Camilla Parker Bowles cheating on Prince Charles than Ali lapdancing for wealthy men. No, there had to be a simpler explanation for it all, like why she seemed to be a wizard with money when things were really tight. Whoever they were, these clients must have paid her well and given her expensive presents – hence the endless supply of designer handbags. Perhaps she'd thought I wouldn't understand, especially if they were married. But then we told each other everything – always had. That thought made me sad, until I realized that of the two of us, I was the non-judgemental one, so Ali wouldn't have worried about me thinking badly of her, would she?

And then there was the biggest question of all, which I have to admit had been nagging at the back of my mind for weeks now – why she'd always been so reluctant to tell me who Charlie's father was. God knows I'd brought it up often enough, but somehow she usually managed to make me feel it was none of my business without saying anything of the sort. It wasn't like it was a big deal or anything, not these days in Ireland anyway. Half our friends brought their children to their weddings, for God's sake.

One night when we'd shared a bottle of wine she said that Daddy would have killed her if he'd been alive, which I thought at the time was odd. From then on, I hadn't pursued it really, in case it upset her. I knew she'd tell me one day when she was ready.

Now I needed to know, and I had a hunch that one of these men had answers to at least some of the questions. I lay there for ages until the flat felt cold and less inviting and decided that I was going to try to find out a bit more about the people who visited Ali here. I needed to know if one of them could possibly be Charlie's father – that way I could learn more about what kind of battle I might have on my hands if any of them tried to take him away from me.

I drove home in a bit of a daze. Next morning the whole thing seemed ridiculous. I rang Violet and tried to pump her for information but all I found out was that she was no longer dating the Ali G lookalike. When I casually mentioned how great the flat upstairs was, Violet simply agreed with me. All in all, I got nowhere.

I'd taken home the ultra-cool mobile phone and Ali's appointments book, but my beer-fuelled courage seemed to have deserted me today. I knew I couldn't possibly make contact with these men – never mind meet them.

Later I phoned my aunt, intending to tell her all about my ludicrous notion, but then at the last minute I was afraid she might think badly of Ali. I was only half listening to her because I was imagining she'd be so shocked by even the mention of 'private clients' that she'd insist on talking to the authorities – ridiculous, but that was how big the whole thing had become in my head.

'Are you OK, love?' she asked when I'd said 'yes' or 'no' once too often. 'You sound tired.'

'I am a bit. I went down to the salon last night. It was tough.'

'Oh Lily, don't be putting yourself through all that just yet,' she advised. 'Maybe I could go with you.'

'I've done it now,' I told her. 'The flat upstairs is beautiful, I was surprised.'

'Oh yes, I know all about it,' my aunt said. 'Ali spent a lot of money on it. She had a number of private clients who didn't want to be seen. One was an actress who used to come for Botox injections, I think.'

'Ali didn't do Botox.' I couldn't believe my ears.

'Well, maybe not, but they all came for non-surgical facelifts, that collagen stuff, you know the sort of thing. Ali told me. I thought it was very exciting. Men too, would you believe. I'd say they were worse than the women.'

'Do you know how many clients she had?'

'Not many. Ali told me they liked to relax afterwards. I imagine she had a juice bar and all that. Wheatgrass

146

they're all into now, isn't it?' my aunt wanted to know while I tried to stave off a fit of coughing. 'Are you OK, love?' she asked.

'Yes, sorry about that.'

'Anyway, she was very discreet, that I do know.'

'She never mentioned it to me. Isn't that funny?'

'Well, she only told me because I was in Wicklow one day with my ICA group and I dropped in to the salon unexpectedly. I hadn't phoned because I thought we were only going up as far as Gorey, to see the ostrich farm. Anyway, Alison was all dressed up and she was very apologetic that she couldn't give us the grand tour because she had a client waiting upstairs. Nora Mooney swore she saw Gay Byrne at the window, but then he was on telly later that night so we knew it couldn't have been him. We talked about it all the way back on the bus and from then on I used to try and get regular updates for the Monday meeting.'

'So what was the juiciest bit?'

'Oh, nothing really.' My aunt sounded disappointed. 'As I said, Ali was very discreet. She only ever answered my questions and even then she changed the subject as quickly as she could. I didn't like to pry, that's not my style.' Milly sighed. 'But the ICA ladies still talk about it. Apparently there's some actor on *Fair City* who lives in Wicklow and has definitely had an eye job. Mary Curran is convinced he's a client.'

I had a terrible headache by the time we'd finished our chat. But talking to Charlie and hearing him say how much he loved me gave me the added courage I knew I'd need – because I decided I was going to meet at least a couple of the men who were my sister's secret clients. That way I reckoned I'd have a head start on any problems that might arise in relation to Charlie. He was mine now, all I had left of Ali, and no one was going to take him away from me.

14

WILLIAM

WILLIAM ALWAYS FOUND TUESDAYS TOUGH GOING. THEY usually involved a stint in the public hospital, followed by a couple of hours in theatre, then ward rounds and finally a spell in the private clinic, which was where he was headed now.

He normally went for an early morning run to get the long day off to a good start. That way he was alert and focused and felt he looked the part, which he definitely didn't feel today as he strode through the half-full waiting room without glancing at anyone. His handmade suit and ghost-white shirt helped his image, he knew, as did the slipper-soft shoes.

This day had not gone well, so far. His first patient had been irritable to the point of aggression, he'd had several calls from home, despite the fact that Beth knew he hated being disturbed unless it was an emergency – which Harry crying over a puppy on TV clearly was not – and finally the garage had called to say his new Mercedes had arrived in the country at last, but it was diesel and not the petrol model he'd ordered.

'Sounds like you need a good lay,' John O'Meara, a cheeky new anaesthetist, had told him earlier, after he'd overheard William recounting a long list of gripes to one of the radiologists. William didn't like the latest 'bright young thing' – as he'd heard O'Meara described – so he killed any further conversation with a disparaging look, but not before he'd noticed one of the new theatre nurses giggling coquettishly at the younger man.

'Here's the list, sir.' Adele, his inherited secretary, fussed around as soon as he arrived, tidying his already clear desk. She was forty-five going on seventy and whereas normally he liked her air of deference, today it annoyed him and he wanted to swat her away like a fly.

'Shall I get you a glass of water?' she asked as she always did, despite the fact that he'd never once said yes in the eight years she'd been with him. He bit his tongue for the umpteenth time that day, muttered a curt 'no', then added a grumpy 'thank you', and dismissed her with a slight wave.

'Wheel them in.'

'Certainly, sir.' She was gone with a swish of her pleated tartan skirt.

'Good afternoon,' he said, barely raising his head when he heard the soft click of the door a few moments later. He was not in his normal 'charm the private patients, especially the pretty ones' mood. 'Miss, eh, Ormond.' He glanced at his list. 'Do sit' – he saw her for the first time

150

and hoped he didn't look as shocked as he felt – 'down.'

'Thank you.' She took off her coat and placed it carefully on the back of the chair, which gave him a couple of seconds to study her. This woman was the spit of Alison, who'd been his 'paramour' – as he liked to think of her – for the last few years. He knew it was impossible.

William realized he was staring. 'I'm sorry, do we . . . have we met before?' He was not used to being flummoxed.

'No.' She was looking at him very carefully and he noticed her hands were shaking slightly. 'But I believe you may have known my sister.' It wasn't a question, which was just as well because he wasn't ready to admit to anything.

She waited. 'Alison,' she said unnecessarily. She looked as uncomfortable as he felt.

'I'm really not sure I do . . .' He was playing for time.

'Did.' She never took her eyes off him this time. 'She died recently. Perhaps you read about it in the papers?'

If she hadn't told him what he already knew he'd have been convinced it was Alison playing some sort of trick on him, yet when he thought about it later he knew Alison would never have called to see him at the hospital, not under any circumstances.

He nodded in response to her question and waited for her to continue.

'I'm Lily. I'm not sure if Alison ever mentioned me?'

She smiled and he was transported back to the many

nights Alison had opened the door to the flat in Wicklow wearing that very same look.

William shook his head.

'I'm sorry to have popped up out of the blue like this but I wasn't sure of the best way to make contact.' She twisted slightly in her seat. 'I dialled your mobile number several times but then I hung up before I'd finished. And I rang you at the hospital one day but your secretary said I needed a referral.' She grinned at him nervously. 'I'm afraid I wasn't even sure what should have been wrong with me, because I don't know what you . . . what your specialty is . . .' She trailed off.

William felt less apprehensive now, for some reason. She looked terrified, he decided. He was curious.

'Mr Hammond, my sister's death was a huge shock for . . . the family. We were twins, as you've probably realized . . . so we were incredibly close.' She looked away and fidgeted with her pristine white blouse.

William went round to her side of the desk immediately. 'I'm very sorry. Your sudden appearance here caused me quite a shock. Please forgive me if I appeared . . . rude in any way.' She looked like she might burst into tears at any second and he could have kicked himself for his initial frosty reception. 'Can I get you anything?' he asked anxiously. 'A drink of water, perhaps?'

'No, thank you . . . I'm fine.' She lifted her head and her vulnerability gave William the beginnings of an erection. He moved away slightly and leaned against the edge of his desk, caught off guard for the second time.

'I was very sorry to read about her . . . death.' He searched her face for a moment, wondering why she'd come. His antennae shot up. 'All of this must be very hard on the family?' he ventured, anxious to find out more.

'There's only me,' she said quietly. 'And I'm just beginning to sort out her affairs, so I wanted to introduce myself and let you know that I'll have to start making plans for the business shortly. I'm afraid I'm no beautician.' Lily smiled. 'I'm much less glamorous . . . a cook, actually . . . so I'm looking at the option of turning the salon into a café. And I'm sure you're wondering what on earth all this has to do with you . . .'

William felt excited by her. It must be the startling resemblance to Alison, he decided. He gave her one of his most charming smiles. 'I'm delighted to meet you.' He saw her questioning look. 'You gave me quite a shock at the beginning, that's all, and I'm just sorry our first meeting had to be under these circumstances. Are you certain I can't get you a coffee?'

She shook her head. 'I only came because it wasn't clear if you had any further appointments scheduled and I'm not sure if Violet can be of any help . . .'

'Violet?' He wondered what was coming.

'The other beautician in the salon.' She looked flustered again. 'I'm not sure you've even met her? I'm afraid I didn't really know anything about Alison's private clients, in fact I knew very little about her business really.' She shrugged. 'I was always too busy having fun, I have to admit.' She smiled. 'Or just being lazy.'

She looked far younger than her sister and William relaxed. It was clear she knew nothing about his relationship with her twin. He was anxious not to frighten her off. On the contrary, he wanted her to think well of him.

'I don't want to offend you in any way, Miss Ormond, so I hope you'll understand what I'm about to say next. It's just that I'd . . . hate to think of you as being vulnerable in any way because of your sister's death.' William was comfortable again, playing the role of benefactor. His power was restored. 'Therefore, I feel I have to ask you if money is an issue for you now?'

Lily shook her head quickly. 'Oh Lord, no, that's not why I came . . .' She stood up immediately.

He put his hand on her arm. 'Please, let me say this. Your sister was a very . . . dear friend to me.' He saw her slightly questioning look. 'As well as a . . . business contact, of course. And now, I suppose I feel a certain responsibility towards you, in a way. So,' he paused, 'if there's anything you need, financially or otherwise, I would be only too happy to help.' He liked playing God; it was what he did all day. And he was surprised how protective this woman made him feel. Alison had never had quite that effect on him. Initially, once he'd realized who she was, William had been convinced that this girl was out to cause him trouble, but now he was equally convinced she was what she said she was.

'I don't need money . . . honestly.' Her tone was soft. 'But thank you, anyway.' She smiled up at him. 'Alison left me very well provided for,' she told him as she reached for

154

her coat. 'I simply wanted to make sure you knew about what happened and . . .' She looked a bit lost. '. . . And introduce myself, basically. Actually, I hadn't realized I'd be this nervous. I feel a bit foolish coming here, to tell you the truth.'

'Please don't.' He moved closer. 'I'm very glad you came to see me.' It wasn't quite true. 'I'm so pleased to have met you.' He held out his hand. 'In a funny way I feel it's what she would have wanted.'

'Well, I really don't want to take up any more of your time. You seem like a very important man, judging by the number of people out there.' She indicated over her shoulder. 'I'm sure you're extremely busy.'

William nodded, happy to wallow in his own power for a moment.

'Anyway, I'm glad we met face to face.' She picked up her bag. 'And you have the salon number if there's anything we can do for you in the future. For the moment it's business as usual.' She seemed to be struggling again. 'Violet is there all the time, is what I mean.'

William was very moved by her, and physically excited at what was already happening between them in his head. 'Thank you.' He took the hand she offered. 'And once again I'm very sorry for your loss.'

Lily extracted her hand gently, just as he realized he was still holding it. 'It was nice to meet you,' she said shyly.

'You too.'

'Goodbye.'

He watched as she strode from the room. She had a

155

different walk, but the same long legs and swinging hair. He thought she was thinner, almost boyish, and that made her seem more childlike. He was definitely aroused by her.

William moved quickly towards the door then, aware that his secretary might be trying to charge her for a first visit. He shook his head silently in the direction of her office. Adele followed him inside immediately. 'I'm sorry about that, sir. I'd no idea she'd take so long. She insisted that you knew her family and that her sister was a friend of yours.' His secretary was rambling on. 'I thought it was tomorrow she was due in. I should have warned you in advance.' William saw she was flustered. 'Shall I bring in—'

'Give me a minute, please. I'll buzz you.' He didn't look up. He knew from her voice that she was annoyed with everyone, him included. And he was already running late, which seemed to upset her much more than it did him. As soon as he heard the door close he relaxed back in his chair.

What an extraordinary turn-up, he thought, going over it again in his head. It seemed incredible that she didn't know anything, but then Alison had always been very discreet. It was one of the reasons he'd gotten involved in the first place. William had too much to lose otherwise. As for Lily, she certainly wasn't the type of woman who'd have had any trouble getting a man. But then neither was Alison. William had to admit he'd been picturing them having sex almost from the moment Lily had identified herself. Maybe it had something to do with the fact that she looked younger and fresher than Alison, or perhaps it was just the idea of starting something new, with a complete stranger.

He knew he had to tread very carefully. Alison had come highly recommended and William had no intention of putting himself in a compromising position. Still, it could be exciting: Lily was a different prospect altogether, he'd bet money on it.

He jumped up and strode towards the waiting room, feeling vigorous and energetic and important. Suddenly this day felt much less stressful.

15

DAVE

DAVE'S RESOLVE WAS GOING BACK AND FORTH LIKE A yo-yo. Despite the fact that he had no idea whether she knew anything about him or not, he simply couldn't get Lily Ormond out of his mind. He was dying for a good shag anyway, which didn't help. He kept telling himself it was just that she looked so like her dead sister. Christ, he was even beginning to fantasize about the threesomes they could have had, which was a bit sick given that he had twin girls himself and he'd knife anyone who even looked at them crooked.

He knew it didn't make sense, but he missed Alison. It wasn't just the sex, although that had been fantastic. It was the whole package, especially the fact that she always made him feel like a stud each time he saw her. And she seemed genuinely interested in his views and, what was more, she really listened.

He loved going to the flat. Even though he didn't need to, he took extra care with his appearance, and as soon as he got in the car and headed for Wicklow he felt brilliant.

Having Pink Floyd pumping out on the CD player was part of the ritual. Got him in the mood.

Dave loved his car anyway. It was his one indulgence – well, his one serious one, apart from clothes. Everything else went on Marie and the girls. He begrudged them nothing. Kirstin and Lola – the twins – were nearly nineteen and going to college. Dave was very proud of that. Kirstin was studying journalism and Lola, the really brainy one, was a first-year pharmacy student. They were the only kids for miles around who had stayed in school past second level. But then Dave had made it easy for them, done deals with them even. They got their first independent holiday, all expenses paid, when they passed their junior cert and two spanking new Mini convertibles when they got their points for college.

They were both lookers, too, and were always bringing home boyfriends with smart cars and even smarter addresses. No worries there: Dave could hold his own with any of them.

Marie, on the other hand, often felt intimidated. She was always giving guests tea in real china cups and making sure everything on the table was matching; a total giveaway of their working-class roots, Dave felt. That and the fact that she'd refused to move from the council house they'd bought nearly thirty years ago, hence the three extensions – and that didn't include the double-glazed porch, another of Marie's attempts to keep up with the Joneses. Never mind that some of the Joneses on this particular road were well known to the Gardai. Marie felt insecure with everybody, even the local drug barons.

That was one of the reasons he'd been attracted to Alison. She was different to any other woman he knew. Alison had class. And money couldn't buy that. Dave had watched her over the years and learned a lot. Like how rich people don't care if the cups are chipped or the cutlery doesn't match. Not that Alison was rich; he knew she wasn't. But she came from money and Dave knew you could smell that a mile away. He kept thinking about their nights together. He'd always brought a bottle of champagne. Good stuff, not that Buck's Fizz shite that Marie thought was posh. And Alison really made an effort from her shiny hair to her polished nails. Also she never seemed to be in a rush, usually suggested a drink afterwards, although mostly he drank and talked and she listened and laughed.

They'd met by accident. He'd been working on a big project in Rathnew just after she'd opened the salon a few miles away. He used to see her coming and going to the salon when he went into Wicklow town to meet the architect he was working with. One day he followed her as she came out, and admired her voluptuousness as well as her confident stride. As soon as he saw her go into the smart Italian coffee shop he started going there too. She always ordered the same thing, a double espresso and a side order of hot milk. Right from the beginning he'd been attracted to her, even before he heard her voice. It was almost as if she had a sore throat and when she laughed with the guy at the counter Dave thought it sounded deep and dirty. He started making special visits to the salon, usually towards the end of the day when she was more likely to be alone. He guessed she must be the owner, so he called in once or twice and bought gift vouchers he didn't want, just so they'd get chatting. Eventually he told her he wanted her advice on a Christmas present for a client, and she agreed to have coffee with him.

Then he asked if the salon ever did treatments for men. She told him they did, so he had manicures and pedicures and facials to beat the band, just to be near her.

Months after their first meeting he told her about his marriage. Dave remembered it well. It was during his first-ever back massage. He was so horny he had to keep thinking about his wife walking in on them, just so he could turn over on to his back when asked – without her seeing the state he was in.

When she told him that she sometimes made special appointments in the evening for one or two of her male clients he couldn't believe his luck. In fact, that first night he called to the flat at the appointed time Dave wasn't at all sure he was going to get anything other than a back rub.

Afterwards he was in heaven. The two hours with Alison had been one of the highlights of his life and Dave wasn't going to stop for love nor money. Sometimes he was scared she'd end it, decide she didn't need the money or something, so he bought her expensive presents in an attempt to keep her. A couple of months ago he'd spent a fortune on a big leather handbag that he'd seen her gazing at in a magazine. He'd watched the way she'd run her fingers over the glossy advert and he casually asked her about it. She told him all about her handbag fetish and he carefully noted the make and tried to remember the exact model. He wasn't sure he'd gotten it right until she'd screamed with pleasure when he gave it to her, then told him it was too expensive. He'd laughed and said she was worth it, just like that TV ad kept telling women. And so it had continued right up until a week before her death.

Eventually, Dave decided he had to do something. He dithered for days and then left a voice message on Alison's mobile number, the one he knew she reserved for special clients.

'Hi, eh, I don't know if this is the number for Lily, Alison's sister, but my name is Dave. I, em, met you at the funeral. I was a . . . friend of Alison's and I, eh . . . just wondered how you're doin' like? I hope things are working out OK for you and if you want you could give me a ring some time.' He left his mobile number and hung up, red-faced.

A couple of hours later his phone rang, signalled by one of those top-twenty rappers cursing and generally being obscene. The twins were always changing his ringtones and it drove him bonkers. The incoming number was withheld. Normally he'd let an unknown caller go to voicemail but he was picking up everything today, just in case.

'Dave speakin'.'

'Hello, Dave, this is Lily Ormond, Alison's sister. I just got your message.'

Dave couldn't believe his luck. 'Oh, hello there, how are

you?' His accent changed as he immediately moved out of the office and headed towards his car for some privacy.

'I'm fine, thanks, Dave, how are you?'

'Great, great. Listen, I hope you didn't mind me ringing. It's just that, well, we met at the funeral and I was wondering how you're gettin' on, like?'

'I'm coping. It's been tough, but I have some good friends. And I'm keeping myself busy, which always helps, or so they keep telling me.' He could hear the tiredness in her voice and he wanted to make it better for her, although he sensed a leather handbag wouldn't do it.

'Yeah, it's what they say all right, time heals and all that.' He was waffling. 'I suppose you have to start somewhere.' Dave had no idea what to ask her then and it had been him who'd rung her in the first place. Luckily, she saved him the trouble.

'Dave, I hope you'll forgive me if I mentioned this already when I met you at the funeral, but how well did you know my sister? How did you two meet?'

There was a pause and Dave sensed she wasn't finished so he waited, trying to decide what to say.

'It's just that I'm still trying to piece everything together,' Lily continued. 'Because she worked in Wicklow she had a whole network of friends that I didn't really know . . .' Her voice trailed off.

'Well, eh, I met her in the salon, actually. I was working on a big building project locally.' He rabbited on for ages and she asked him a couple of questions. Eventually, desperate to find out if she knew about him, he

163

added, 'I used to visit her . . . in the flat . . . sometimes.'

'I see.' From her voice, it sounded as if she didn't know what to make of that.

'Yes, well, she often helped me with gift vouchers – presents for clients, that sort of thing.' Dave hadn't a clue what to say next. 'I was . . . eh . . . very fond of her. Very fond indeed. She was very good to me over the years.' Christ, it sounded like Lily hadn't a clue what had been going on.

'Dave, would you like to drop down . . . to the flat, I mean . . . some evening?'

He couldn't believe his ears. 'Do you mean for a visit, like?'

'Yes, perhaps we could have a coffee . . . and a chat?'

It wasn't quite what he had in mind but it was a good place to start, find out a bit more about her. 'Yes, I'd, eh, like that very much actually. When?' He winced because he sounded so eager.

'Why don't I call you in a day or two, now that we've made contact? Is it OK to use this number?'

'Yes, certainly. If I, eh, can't talk I'll call you straight back.' He hoped he didn't come across like a lovesick schoolboy.

'Fine. Well, it was nice to speak to you, Dave.'

'Yes, you too, Lily. You too.'

'Goodbye for now. I'll be in touch.'

'Great, bye for now.' Dave hung up and rubbed his crotch. Christ, just the thought of her had given him one hell of a hard-on.

164

16

RICHARD

'YOU'RE A LOVELY FELLA.' THE GLAMOROUS GRANNY WITH the dyed yellow hair and gold hoopy earrings tweaked Richard's cheek as if he was a podgy nine-year-old.

'Get outta here, Alice, or I'll have to bar you for sexual harassment.' Richard opened the door for her. She was one of their regulars.

'Jaysus, that'd give the girls at bingo something to talk about all right.' Alice manoeuvred her tartan shopping bag on wheels. 'See you tomorrow, love.'

'Mind yourself, you're lethal with that weapon.' He picked up a plastic bag that had lodged in the doorway, just in case she got caught – and as he stood up he came face to face with Alison, except he knew that wasn't possible.

'Sorry, excuse me.' She glanced at him and stood back until the granny was safely on her way.

'Thanks, love, mind your feet there. Richard's lost a few toenails with me trolley over the years.' The pensioner cackled her way down the street.

Richard stared at the new arrival until she'd walked past and then realized he was holding the door for nobody.

When he turned round, the girl was seated in one of the booths facing the counter. He went behind the coffee machine and tried to get a good look at her. If he hadn't read the papers himself he'd have sworn it was Alison. He picked up a menu and strolled over to her table.

'Hello.' He hoped he sounded laid-back. 'Would you like to see a menu?' His heart was thumping like a school-boy's on a first date.

'I think I'll just have a skinny latte.' She smiled and looked directly at him but made no effort to take the laminated card which he'd thrust in her direction.

'Regular or large?'

'Large please, I need the caffeine.' Her smile was different – sort of lopsided – and he felt slightly relieved. 'Actually, on second thoughts I'll have a look.' She held out her hand and Richard was confused all over again. If this wasn't Ali it was her double. Her eyes were exactly the same and so was the way she looked at him under her lashes. Her voice wasn't as gravelly though.

'Why don't I bring your coffee and give you a chance to decide?' He needed to escape and get another look at her from a safe distance.

'Thank you.' She was fishing in her handbag. 'I always come into places just for coffee and end up ordering half the menu.'

'Well, take your time and let me know if you'd like me to check what specials are left.'

'Sure.'

Richard watched her as he worked. Everything about her screamed Alison. The colour of her hair – although he couldn't see that much of it – and the long legs he'd caught a glimpse of earlier. The likeness was uncanny. He knew he had to find out.

'One latte.' He was at her table before he knew it and hadn't a clue what to say to find out more about her.

'Thanks.' She looked unsure, nervous even, and he was under her spell immediately.

'I made it extra strong.' She didn't react so he continued, 'You said you needed the hit . . .'

'That's great, cheers.'

Richard made to walk away then turned abruptly. 'Excuse me, forgive me please for interrupting your break but . . . have we met before? It's just that you're awfully like a . . . girl . . . I used to know.'

'I don't think so, no.' She paused for a split second. 'Unless you knew my sister?' Another hesitation. 'People always mix us up.'

'Alison?' He felt his eyebrow up around his hairline. Damn, he'd meant to work up to it.

'Yes,' she said quietly.

'You're Alison's' – his voice was as high as a Welsh choirboy's – 'sister?' He coughed and tried again. 'God, you're the image of her. I knew you had to be related.'

'I'm her twin.'

'Alison has a twin?'

'Had.' She lowered her eyes and stirred her coffee, then quickly looked up at him again as if checking something. 'I presume you heard . . . or read about her death?'

'Christ, yes, I'm so sorry.' He ran his fingers through his hair. 'It's just that this is so surreal . . .' He hadn't a clue how to handle this. 'I did hear, I read about it in the papers. I'm very sorry.' He knew he was repeating himself. 'It was such a shock.'

'Yes, it was very sudden.' She looked around. 'Have you time to sit down for a moment? Or perhaps you're busy.'

'No. I mean yes, I've time.' He slid into the seat opposite and stood up again immediately, almost dislocating his knee under the table. 'Actually, I'll just grab a coffee myself, if that's all right?' He suddenly thought she might be waiting for someone. 'I'm not interrupting or anything, am I?'

'Not at all.'

'And can I get you anything else while I'm up?' Richard felt at a serious disadvantage here.

'No, thanks, I'm fine for now. My appetite's pretty much gone at the moment anyway, to tell you the truth.'

'Yes.' He could only imagine.

'This will do the trick nicely.' She unbuttoned her coat and stood up to slip it off her shoulders. 'Unless you have a minimum charge?'

'No, no.' He noticed now that her hair was in a thick plait. Also, she wasn't wearing much make-up, he realized as he grabbed a double espresso. Alison had always been impeccably groomed; part of the business she was in, she'd once told him. This girl seemed more relaxed about herself.

Richard smiled at her as he returned to the booth. 'I'm sorry ... again. I never introduced myself, I'm Richard Kearney.' He held out his hand.

'I'm Lily.' Her grip was firm but cold. Ali's hands had always been warm, a result of the constant massage and use of warming oils, she'd told him once. This was one of the oddest experiences of his life, Richard thought as he sat down.

'I hope I didn't give you too much of a shock then? Was this one of Alison's regular haunts?'

'No, no, she was only here once, as far as I remember.' Richard took a gulp of his coffee and burned his mouth. 'Sorry.' He tried not to splutter.

'I hope you don't mind me asking, but how did you know my sister?'

'Gosh, how did we first meet? Let me think.' It sounded incredibly false as he tried to buy time. 'It was a good few years ago.' He pretended to search his memory. 'Oh yes, through a workmate ... I used to be in the corporate sector.' He glanced around him. 'I wasn't always a sloppy waiter.' He grinned as he wiped coffee splashes from his chin. 'He, my colleague – ex – introduced us.' Richard decided to keep talking, in case she asked too many questions. 'I'm sorry I wasn't at the funeral.' The lie came easily. 'I only heard about it afterwards.' He took a more leisurely sip. 'It must have been a huge shock to your family?'

'It was.'

'And how's . . . the baby?' He couldn't remember what the little fella was called, although he'd read the name more than once in the paper.

'Charlie's fine, he's so young still. You've met him?'

'Only once or twice.' Shit, he didn't know why he'd said that. He wouldn't recognize the child if he parachuted into the café right now. He'd never even known of his existence. 'Is he . . . with you?' Keep talking, you idiot, he chided himself.

'He's with my aunt in Cork for the moment.' She cradled the warm mug. 'There's been so much to sort out . . .'

'I can imagine. I know she had her business and all that.'

'Yeah. It's doing well, which is something, although I have no idea about the beauty industry.' Lily smiled at him and he felt awkward about deceiving her like this. He tried to think of a way out.

'Did you ever visit the salon?' she asked.

The question jolted him back to normal. 'No, I kept meaning to.' He wasn't sure why he was lying like this but he just had a feeling she knew nothing about Alison's 'clients'. 'God knows, I could do with a facial or whatever you call it. And all those dishes are murder on the hands.' It was a feeble joke.

'So how come you switched career?' She looked around her, interested. 'This must be quite a change from being a businessman?'

'Got fired.' He grinned at her. 'Only joking. I'd had enough, I guess.' He thought about it for a second. 'I was always moaning to Alison about it. In fact' – he drained his cup – 'she helped me make up my mind to buy this place. She was a very good listener.'

'That's what everyone says.' Lily looked sad. 'I miss her so much.' She didn't seem embarrassed to be telling this to a stranger. 'Even though we were the same age, she was like a mother to me.'

Richard looked at her and saw a very young girl. 'I'm so sorry.' He started to stretch out his hand to her in a gesture of comfort. It was the oddest thing, but he really wanted to touch her.

'Richard, Daisy's on the phone.' Lucy was beside him so he rubbed an imaginary fly off his nose instead. 'Tell her I'll ring her back, Lucy, thanks.'

Lily said nothing for a moment. 'Everyone's been so kind,' she told him eventually. 'I've met lots of people I never knew existed . . . Friends of hers. It's odd really because we were very close.'

'Sorry again, she says it's urgent and your mobile is off.' Lucy was back.

'Actually, I have to go.' Lily stood up as the waitress wandered off. 'It was nice to meet you . . .'

'Please, wait, let me get you another coffee.' Richard jumped up. 'I'll just get rid of this, don't go . . . I'll only be a minute.' He backed into a customer. 'Sorry, sorry.' He smiled at the woman and as he turned back to Lily he saw she'd sat down again. She seemed to him to be in a bit of

171

a daze. 'Stay, please,' he urged. 'I won't be a mo . . . really.'

He headed for the phone, not quite sure why talking to Lily was so important. It was unnerving, having her here, even though he'd nothing to hide. It wasn't as if he was married or anything, although he wryly supposed that going to a prostitute wasn't the sort of thing your average middle-class guy in the street did on a regular basis. Still, he knew he wasn't going to tell her about his relationship with Alison unless he was absolutely sure she already had an inkling.

He got rid of Daisy in double-quick time and fidgeted about for a few moments, watching Lily studying the menu. He was excited by her. She was the same as her sister yet completely different, he felt, even from their brief encounter. He needed to know more, a lot more, about her but he'd no idea how much longer he could keep up the pretence. Surely she had to know something?

17

JAMES

'HELLO, I'M SORRY TO BOTHER YOU.' HE WAS businesslike. 'MY name is James Weldon and I'm trying to get in touch with Alison's sister. I wonder if you can help me?'

'I'm afraid she's not here at the moment. She's gone to get some stock from the wholesalers.' Violet wasn't sure how much to say. There had been one or two tabloid reporters lurking around a while back and it had made Lily nervous.

'And, eh, what time do you expect her back?' He wished he knew the sister's name.

'About four, I think.' Violet came to a decision. 'Can I take your name and number and ask her to call you?'

'Actually, if you don't mind I'll . . . em, call her later.'

'OK so.' Violet did mind, actually, and he sensed it.

'Thanks very much for your help.' James said goodbye quickly and considered what he'd just this second decided to do.

* * *

At about a quarter to four he stood outside the salon. Main Street in Wicklow on a rainy day was depressing; funny how he'd never noticed that before. There was litter about and a lot of the shopfronts seemed tired and a bit dated. The tiers of iced cakes in the neon-lit bakery opposite looked like they'd seen better days and someone had left sacks of clothing outside the charity shop, despite the large red notice urging people not to do so. The wind had blown a couple of them open and they looked set to take off down the street any second. James walked over and pushed some baby clothes back into the bag and tied a knot on anything he could. It was the sort of thing he did.

As he walked back towards the salon he remembered the nights he'd spent with Alison in the flat upstairs. They'd laughed a lot, and talked only a little at first, which for him was quite a relief. Mostly it had just been great, uncomplicated sex – the sort that had left him feeling like he could conquer the world. The idea now filled him with a mixture of desire and guilt. The guilt quickly began to win out so he pushed open the door before he changed his mind.

'Can I help you?'

'Hello, I think I may have spoken to you earlier. I rang looking for Alison's sister?' He noticed the young woman was frowning. 'I hope I'm not disturbing you, it's just . . . you said you were expecting her back around four, so I thought I'd . . . drop in.'

Her look told him she was very unsure. 'That was a

guess, it all depends on the traffic. I'm afraid you might have had a wasted journey, Mr—'

'Weldon, James Weldon.' He stuck out his hand. 'And you are . . . ?'

'Violet.' It was hesitant.

'Don't worry, I'm happy to wait.' She looked like she was about to kick him out, James thought. 'I promise not to disturb you in any way.' He held up his newspaper and gave her what he hoped was a friendly grin. 'You won't even know I'm here.'

James wasn't sure why he was being so apologetic. After all, this girl had no idea who he was or what he wanted. He just wished he could remember what Alison's sister was called, he'd definitely read the name in one or two of the papers, but he'd been so paranoid that he'd thrown them all away immediately. 'Perhaps you could let her know I'm here as soon as she returns?' He tried to be assertive but it came out as a plea. James was too soft – always had been – and it meant he got passed over in life occasionally. Most people underestimated him as well though, which some-times worked to his advantage.

'Are you a reporter?' Violet asked tentatively a moment or two later.

'God, no.' James was shocked. Christ, that was all he needed right now, to end up on the front page of one of the tabloids.

'I knew Alison,' he spluttered, anxious to reassure the girl. 'For years,' he added. 'I just wanted to extend my condolences to her sister and I thought it would be easier to do it in person.' Thank God he had a face you could trust, because he felt she believed him.

'OK.' She nodded and seemed to relax.

He tried not to keep looking at the door but within ten minutes he'd read the same paragraph three times, so he mentally slapped himself and turned to the sports section. He was just managing to keep his interest in rugby going when he heard her voice.

'Violet, sorry, the traffic's mad.' He glanced up, shocked even though he was expecting a twin.

'Oh, Lily, hi . . .'

Violet looked like she didn't know how to explain his presence, James thought, getting his first glimpse of the woman who had come rushing in, hair flying and smelling of flowers and traffic fumes. Lily, thank God she'd said it.

'There's a gentleman . . . Mr, eh, Weldon, to see you. He called earlier to speak to you and, em, he was in the area.' It was clear to all three of them that the last part was a lie.

'Hello.' He was staring openly. 'I'm James. I just wondered if I might have a word with you?'

'As long as you're not selling anything?'

He sensed she said it to cover her nerves. James shook his head immediately.

'I'm afraid I've had a glut of people calling lately, mostly salesmen, and I've discovered it takes up a lot of time. I'm new to this business. It belongs . . . used to belong to my sister.'

'Actually, that's what I wanted to talk to you about—' He stopped in mid-sentence, watching her face for signs of apprehension, but she continued to smile pleasantly. 'I was a friend of Alison's and I was very upset to hear about her death.'

'Thank you, Mr Weldon, that's very nice of you.' She glanced around. 'Would you like to go for coffee?' She shrugged off her coat as James nodded quickly. 'Sorry, I feel very warm all of a sudden,' she apologized. 'I'm afraid our kitchen's not big enough for guests but there's a little Italian down the road and the latte is excellent.'

'Great.' James was on his feet in an instant.

'Violet, is that OK with you?' Lily turned towards the other girl. 'I won't be long.' She flung her coat over her arm and picked up her handbag.

'Fine, no problem.' Violet seemed relieved that she'd done the right thing.

'Want me to bring you back something?'

'No, thanks, I'll make myself a cup of tea here.'

'Grand.' Lily turned towards James. 'Shall we go? I'm afraid I don't have that much time.' She checked her phone. 'I have an appointment here later.'

Once they were settled with their drinks she cradled hers and watched the steam escape, as if enjoying the moment.

'So, Mr Weldon . . .' she said as she came back to earth.

'James, please.' He was nervous and as usual he pushed his wedding ring up and down his finger.

'James,' she amended. 'What brings you to Wicklow? It's not an obvious stopping-off point.'

'Well, I . . . I don't know where to start, to tell you the truth.' He couldn't take his eyes off her. Seated this close, and even in the unkind neon light that streaked the walls, he realized how alike they were. 'My goodness, you are identical to Alison, it's frightening.' He found himself examining her face with a frown on his own.

'We were twins.' When she got no reaction she continued, 'I presumed you knew . . .'

'Yes,' James said quickly. 'She told me she had a twin but never mentioned you were identical.'

'Funny, I don't see it.' She smiled. 'I always thought Ali was much better-looking.' She seemed to get lost again for a second or two. 'Were you close?' She sipped her drink. 'I'm just wondering if you're the same man she mentioned, the architect . . .' She blushed as she spoke and James had the distinct impression she was lying.

'Yes, actually, I am an architect.' He was still convinced that Alison would never have discussed him with anyone. Maybe it's a genuine mistake, he thought.

'And your wife? Is she a counsellor, or . . . ?' She looked so uncomfortable he knew she was feeling her way. But where had she got the information, if not from her sister?

'Psychologist.' He stared at her, still unsure. 'I can't believe she talked to you about me . . .' He didn't know what to say next. 'It's just that she was a very private person . . . I knew very little about . . . certain parts of her life.'

178

'Actually, I don't know much about you at all,' she admitted after a second or two, 'although I thought Ali and I had no secrets from each other.'

Bloody hell, that could have been dangerous, James thought, and took a gulp of the hot liquid to buy a few seconds. 'I was . . . very fond of her. She was incredibly good to me.' He felt sad talking about Alison, and a bit disloyal, which seemed absurd given the circumstances of their friendship.

'Don't tell me – a great listener.' Lily kept her eyes fixed on his. 'Or so everyone keeps telling me.' Her voice was slightly sarcastic, he thought for a second, but then decided he'd imagined it. 'Sorry, forgive me.' She lowered her head. 'It's just that I've a lot on my plate at the moment. I didn't mean anything by that remark.' She looked like a lost child. 'I loved her very much. She was my hero,' she said quietly.

James watched her fidget with the sugar sachets. 'She was one of the best.' He meant it.

'It was nice of you to come all this way to pay your respects. Thank you.'

'It was all . . . such a shock. I got an awful fright when I heard.' He spoke almost to himself. 'I miss her terribly.' He felt guilty speaking about someone other than his wife in this way. As soon as he'd said it he felt like he'd confessed.

He felt her eyes on him and stirred his coffee for ages.

'I hope you won't take offence at this.' She bit her lip

and swallowed. 'But I feel I have to ask. Were you in love with Ali?'

James was many things but not a liar. 'I think I . . . I'm not really . . .' He struggled with it himself. 'I'm married, you know,' he said needlessly.

'Yes.'

He sighed. 'I suppose I was . . . a bit,' he admitted. 'Yes, I was in love with her, incredible and all as that feels, saying it out loud like this . . . and to you.'

'And you were having a relationship with her,' she asked after an awfully long pause, although it wasn't really a question. She sounded as if she was talking to herself.

'Yes,' he said gently.

She seemed to come to a decision. 'James, can we meet again? Properly, I mean?' He knew she was thrown by his admission, even though at first he had thought she knew all about it.

'Of course, if it'll help?'

'It will, yes. It's just that now I have to go. I'm sorry.' He saw that she was fighting back tears.

'No, it's me who should be sorry for arriving un-announced like this.' He stood up. 'Let me give you my number.' He reached in his pocket and took out his wallet. 'Here's my card.' He handed it to her. 'Call me when you're ready. I can come down here again . . . any time.'

'Thank you.'

'Pleasure.' He smiled and debated whether to say any-thing else. 'Are you OK? I haven't upset you or anything?'

She shook her head but it was as if a veil had been

drawn over the subject. Clearly she wasn't prepared to talk any more about it for the moment.

'Goodbye.' She shook his hand and went quietly, leaving him with all the emotions he'd buried since he'd found out about Alison. He ordered another coffee and let the feelings of lust and loss and guilt wash over him.

18

LILY

I DON'T KNOW WHY I FELT SO UPSET, SO COMPLETELY thrown, but I was. As soon as I reached the salon I changed my mind and went upstairs to the flat. There wasn't much time: I had to meet a bride-to-be in less than an hour, to discuss the hen party she wanted to have in the place. Apparently, it was all the rage. A group of girls arrived and drank champagne while they detoxed. A waste of money on both counts, I would have thought, but then what did I know?

Still, I was enjoying my time in Wicklow. I'd finally given in my notice to Stephen Pritchard and I was only helping them out a couple of mornings a week, otherwise my days were spent here.

I threw myself on the bed. So, it was out: Ali was having an affair with a married man. I felt incredibly stupid because even though I'd known, deep down, that something was going on, it had still come as a shock. And I couldn't understand why. Christ, I wasn't a prude and this was 2006, not 1966. It was just that Ali had always been the sensible one, my guardian angel, the one I looked to for guidance. What the fuck were you thinking of, putting yourself through all that? I wanted to ask her, really angry for the first time since the death of my twin. I paced the room.

'We always said that only idiots got involved with married men.' I started talking to her as if she were standing in front of me. 'Or was that just me?' I wondered aloud. 'Were you that desperate for sex?' I demanded, flinging my coat on the bed.

'Remember the old chestnut about some men wanting it both ways?' I realized it was Aunt Rose who'd drummed that particular one into our heads when we were teenagers. 'All that shite about men not respecting you in the morning.' That one smacked of our father.

Christ, that's it. I sat down again on the edge of the bed. She probably did it to get back at him.

'You two had better not give me any cause for concern now that you're off to that fancy boarding school.' My father was lecturing us again. 'Remember what I told you: all men are the same. You keep that in mind and talk to your aunt Rose if you need to know anything.'

'I'd get more information out of Sister Imelda, and she's about ninety,' I'd giggled to Ali when we'd been sent up to our rooms. 'Oh Ali, I can't wait to get free of this house, can you?'

'Just promise me you'll always come to me if you're ever in trouble?'

'I promise. Sure we'll always be together anyway.'

'And be careful if I'm not around, won't you? Not all men can be trusted, you know.'

'I know that, I'm not stupid.' I was mortified.

'And think before you make any decisions, Lily. Don't always rush straight in, sure you won't?'

'No, Ali,' I told her. *'I'll be good.'* It was my mantra by this stage.

'And always remember that there's nothing you can't tell me, ever. OK?'

'So why didn't *you* tell *me*, eh?' I finally said out loud what was really bothering me in all of this. 'I could have helped, even if only to listen.' I sat there for ages in the cold room. Eventually I knew I had to tell somebody.

'Are you OK? You sound a bit flat,' Sally said after we'd made small talk for a bit.

'Ali was having an affair.'

'Hang on, Lily, say that again, will you? I don't think I heard you properly.' Sally cursed the phone line and the time delay and everything else that was getting in the way of having a proper conversation when you were more than four thousand miles apart.

'Oh yes, you heard right.' This would have been the most incredibly juicy chunk of gossip to tell had it not involved my sister. Ali just wasn't the type of woman who had an affair; up until now I'd have bet my life on it.

'Did you say she was having an affair?' Sally laughed but it was slightly nervous.

'Yes.'

'Hang on, let me close the window,' Sally yelled as static drowned her out. 'On second thoughts, I'll ring you straight back. The noise here is deafening.'

'No, I'll ring you. This is going to take a while,' I shouted back. 'Hang up, I'll call you straight away.'

I dialled again and Sally answered immediately.

'That's a bit better, although I hate being so far away when there're things going on.' Sally tried to sound matter-of-fact. 'Now, start again, tell me all.'

I told her everything I knew.

'OK, so she had a lover,' Sally said eventually. 'I'm a bit surprised but, let's face it, it wouldn't even make *Oprah*.'

I laughed in spite of myself. 'I think it wasn't the first relationship she kept secret, either.' I told her about the notes and bits and pieces I'd found written down. 'Do you know something, Sal? I'm so angry with those fuckers that for a split second before I rang you I even considered having sex with them myself, just so I could totally ruin their lives.' I had to say it out loud, that way I knew for definite it wouldn't happen. For one thing, I'd never have the balls; and for another, Sal wouldn't let me.

'How?' Sally didn't seem shocked. 'How were you going to ruin their lives, I mean, as opposed to how were you planning to ride them all?'

'I was going to record it and then post it to their wives.'

'They're all married then, I take it?'

'Well, one of them certainly is. Wears a nice shiny wedding ring. Actually,' I took a gulp of the stewed tea I'd brewed when I came in, 'he's the one I liked the most. He said he was in love with her.'

'You've met them?' That got her attention. 'This is a joke, right? You're winding me up?'

'I wish I was. It's freaking me out. Jesus, Sally, we were so close and she was always so . . .'

'Perfect.' Sally sighed. 'And you looked up to her. Lily, are you absolutely sure this is not your imagination running riot?'

'There were at least four men in her life at one point or another and she was having a relationship with one of them when she died. He admitted it.'

'Maybe he was the only one. The rest could have just been, I dunno . . . massages or something. Anything.' I sensed Sally felt disloyal even talking about it. Ali always had that effect on us all. She was always banging on about morals and doing the right thing.

'Jesus, what were they like? Did they make your skin crawl?' Sally continued, sounding fascinated.

'One of them did, definitely. Dr William.' I laughed. 'But one I liked in spite of myself. And then there's a guy who owns a restaurant, he's cute. Christ, does that sound weird?'

'No. How cute?' Typical Sal, can't put anything past her.

'I haven't decided yet. Anyway, the other one I met is a bit . . . I dunno. He sort of looks like Tom Jones.'

We talked for another half-hour and then Sally had to go.

186

'Listen, I'll ring you tomorrow. Meanwhile, promise me you've abandoned that insane notion of sleeping with them for revenge, or whatever it was you said?'

'I promise,' I told her. 'I don't have the balls for it anyway, Sal.' I said aloud what I'd been thinking. 'You know me. Christ, I was mortified even talking to them.'

'Good, keep it that way. Otherwise I'll come straight home and drag you to a shrink. Failing that we'll have a gang bang – you and me and the four you've discovered, OK?' She was trying to snap me out of it, and her way was always to be a bit outrageous.

'It is odd, though, isn't it? I mean, she was the last person you'd expect to have a married lover.'

'I told you, it's no big deal. It's just a lot for you to take in right now, with all you're dealing with. If this had happened when she was alive, we wouldn't even be talking about it.'

'Listen, gotta go,' I sighed, glancing at my watch. It all felt much less dramatic now. 'Thanks, babe, I was going bonkers here, thinking about it. By the way, ring me in Cork tomorrow night, will you? At Aunt Milly's. I'm going down to see Charlie. I can't wait.'

'Will you tell her?'

'Are you mad? Christ, she'd have a fit. She idolized Ali.'

'So did you,' Sally said in a quiet voice. 'That's why this is all so hard. But it doesn't change anything, you know that.'

'I know.' Suddenly I was all teary again.

'Remember me, Lil? Your best friend – the one who

offered her very married boss a blow job at the Christmas party a few years ago. Christ, thank God I left Dublin, I couldn't have faced him leering at me every day. I was soooo drunk that night.'

'But that's you, Sally. And if I heard anything like this about you after you died, I wouldn't be at all surprised,' I told her and laughed as she snorted all the way from Oz. 'But this madness . . .' I scratched my head. 'This wasn't Ali.'

'Well, she must have had her reasons. And whatever they were, you can bet she wanted to protect you and Charlie as well, so maybe that's why she kept it all so secret.'

'I guess.'

'Listen to me,' Sally said. 'Will you talk to Orla about all this? I don't want you shouldering it on your own. You have enough pressure at the moment.'

'No.' I was adamant. 'The only reason I told you is because you're away. I don't want anyone around me knowing. It's . . . I dunno, a bit gross, I guess. I have to deal with it myself first. Can you understand that? And you have to swear on your mother's life that you won't breathe a word to anyone.'

'You don't have to ask.' Sally sighed.

'Swear.'

'I swear.'

'OK, I'll talk to you tomorrow, so.'

'Yeah, and Lily, try to remember not all men are like, you know . . .'

'What?'

'I dunno what I'm trying to say, actually. Don't mind me. You take care.'

'Yes, you too. Bye.' I hung up slowly. My father again, that was what she meant. Why did it always come back to him? I thought as I wandered downstairs to meet the head hen.

I spotted them as soon as the train pulled in. My aunt was waving madly and holding Charlie up on a low wall so he could see. I saw him first and my heart skipped a beat as I watched him anxiously scanning the faces. Christ, I should never have let him go away, I thought now. What was I thinking of? I pushed my way out and ran towards them.

'Mammy Lily,' he screamed the second he saw me. His face broke into a huge smile and he practically flung himself off the wall, almost toppling my aunt in the process.

'Lily, I mist you,' he said as Milly struggled to keep a hold of his hood.

'Oh Charlie, I missed you too.' I grabbed him and he flung his arms around my neck and I swung him round, kissing him on the head and trying to get a good look at him. My aunt smiled and told me we were a picture.

'Lily, you came on the train to see me.' His eyes were huge. 'Choo-choo.' He blew steam and tried to whistle. 'I want to go home. With you. Now.' He got straight to the point.

189

'No, love, not today. All the trains have stopped for the night.' My heart turned over as I realized that I meant home to him now. 'Hi, Aunt Milly, how are you?' I stood up and hugged her in an effort not to get upset.

'Grand, love, just fine.' She tried to help with my bags but I shooed her away. 'Honestly, I can manage.' I felt guilty. Coping with a small child was more than enough for her. 'He's grown so big, have you been managing OK?'

'Och yes, he's a dote.' Milly dismissed my worries with a smile. 'Come on, I've got the car parked illegally right outside the door. I know Tom Dunne, the stationmaster. He always lets me park there.'

'I have a lollipop.' Charlie produced a bright orange circle with a face on it. 'And I'm going to eat it.'

'Not yet, love, once you've had your dinner,' Milly told him. 'Tom gave it to him as we came in,' my aunt apologized. 'I do try not to give him too many sweet things, but he's such an adorable little chap, it's hard to resist him at all.'

'You're a rogue.' I ruffled his hair, which had grown longer and even curlier.

'Doggie, I love doggies,' he changed tack suddenly, making a run for a rather sullen-looking mongrel. I followed and grabbed his hood.

'Woof-woof!' He laughed and tried to pet it.

'Be careful,' I urged as Charlie went for his tail. 'We don't know him and he might be grumpy.'

'He might bite me.' Charlie looked like he'd welcome any contact with the animal and I eventually had to drag him away with the promise of more doggies and trains around the corner.

We spent a very enjoyable weekend at the movies and in the park, and when we were at home I threw together a huge shepherd's pie and made lasagne and soup for Milly's freezer. It helped ease my guilt. My aunt, meanwhile, churned out endless batches of scones and two of her neighbours called in because they knew there would be rhubarb tart on the go – but also to inspect the visitor, I suspected. I made real custard using organic cream and vanilla pods I'd picked up at the incredible English Market in Cork city. It was declared 'better than Bird's' – the ultimate custard compliment in Ireland.

We went to town on the train and Charlie was ecstatic and insisted on waving to everyone he met. I bought him a station-master's cap in a toy shop in the city centre and he wouldn't take it off, so Milly took photos of the two of us in the bath together, naked except for that cap. I wasn't sure if my aunt would be embarrassed when she saw that I had stripped off and climbed in opposite Charlie. In fact the older woman didn't seem one bit put out about it, so I took my cue from her, although she ran out laughing when Charlie urged her to 'Get in, Milly, get in and play.'

Over dinner and a glass of wine I told her about my fledgling plans to turn the salon into a café or deli of some sort.

'I think that's a wonderful idea, love.' Her eyes were

shining. 'I just wish I was ten years younger and I'd come up and give you a hand.'

'Slow down, I haven't made any decisions yet. I'm not even sure I can afford it.' I laughed, delighted with her enthusiasm. 'But if I do go ahead, you'd better get in training,' I told her, 'because I don't care how old you are, I'll need you.'

'It's a deal.' The older woman beamed at me.

'Aunt Milly, did Ali ever mention anything to you about Charlie's father?' It was all I could think about since discovering her secret.

'No, love, she didn't.' She took a sip of her drink and watched me for a second or two. 'Are you concerned at all about that?'

I shrugged, not sure how to answer. 'I suppose I am. It's funny, initially all I worried about was how I'd cope with Charlie and the effect it would have on my life.' The wine had loosened my tongue. 'Does that sound awful?'

'No, child, it's perfectly normal.' She rubbed the back of my hand the way I vaguely remembered my mother used to.

'Anyway, in all this madness I think I've learned that the only thing that really matters is the bond between us. When I saw him as I was getting off the train this weekend, looking so like her and straining to catch a glimpse of me, my heart did a sort of flip.' I smiled at her. 'And I want so much to take care of him, wrap him up and protect him from everything bad in the world. Does that make sense?'

'Yes, and do you know something?'

'What?' I asked her.

'I think he'll take care of you too.' I could see she was near to tears. 'In fact I'm certain of it.'

'My father left money . . . a lot of money, for a grand-child – a male grandchild, surprise surprise.' We'd skirted the issue a few times on the phone and I knew she must be wondering, but she'd never pushed it with me. 'It came through on the day of Alison's death.' I waited for a reaction, but none came. It wasn't her style to judge.

'I knew that something had happened, from what you told me' was all she said. Neither of us spoke then.

'I'm so glad you'll be looked after,' she said eventually, breaking the silence.

'Milly, why did he push us away all the time? I hated him for all those years after Mum died. If it hadn't been for you . . .' I trailed off, determined not to cry. I had been so weepy these past few days, I was afraid that if I started I'd never stop.

'It was all he knew, love. His own life was terribly strict. He always felt your mother spoilt the two of you, and most people fussed over you because you were twins.'

'But we were so small when Mum died and he was so cold . . .' I didn't want anyone taking his part, especially not her. 'Because of him, I'm suspicious of all men. Most of them give me the creeps.'

'I just wish I could have done more for you. I should have made him listen to reason . . .' Now it was her turn to look upset. 'I tried, love, but with Mother and Father . . .'

'I know you did.' I went over to her. 'We'd have been much worse off if it hadn't been for you.'

'He never . . . hit you or anything, did he?' I saw the worry in her face.

'No,' I told her. 'He just ignored us mostly. Made us be quiet, sent us to our rooms all the time. And packed us off to boarding school as soon as he could.'

'Well, I thanked God for that at the time. It meant I got to see you a bit more. I was always afraid for the two of you, just in case there was any violence at home, although I didn't think so. He was very wrong to treat you as he did, but I didn't think he had any brutality in him.'

'No,' I said quietly. 'But he scarred us for life anyway, that's for sure. Now, will I let the dog out for a last run before bed?' I needed to lighten the moment. 'I think Charlie's been giving him Coca-Cola to drink, so he might need to chew on some grass or whatever it is they do when they feel sick.'

As we headed back to catch the train on Sunday, I broached the subject of taking Charlie back to Dublin.

'Why don't you wait and see what your plans are for the salon first?' Milly suggested.

'I feel guilty leaving him with you for so long. Besides, as you rightly said last night, we'll take care of each other.' I watched him waving at people on the buses. 'I have no one else.'

'You have me.'

'Of course I do.' I could have kicked myself for being so

insensitive. I put my hand over hers as she drove, by way of an apology. 'What I mean is that he's all I have of her and that makes him very precious indeed.'

'I know, love, but give yourself time. I'm fine, I really enjoy having him so don't worry on that score. He's here, safe and sound for you.' She patted my arm. 'He adores you, you know. Talks about you all the time.'

'Thanks.' The waterworks were threatening again and I quickly rubbed my eyes.

'I'm so glad he's yours now.' She smiled sadly.

'So am I,' I told her. 'And nobody's going to take him away from me, ever.'

19

DAVE

DAVE WAS GIVING IT HIS ALL IN THE SHOWER, HUMMING
about getting his rocks off. He was strutting around his
tiny – one metre square to be exact – stage. The perform-
ance was tuneless but supremely confident. He was in
excellent form and the reason was simple. He expected to
be getting his Nat (King Cole) again in Wicklow any day
soon and he was as excited as a schoolboy watching the
Miss World bathing-costume section. OK, it was his first
real meeting with Lily this evening and all she was offering was coffee, but Dave was nothing if not an optimist.

At eight o'clock he cupped his hand to his mouth then
blew and sniffed, just to give a final check to his breath as
he rang the bell of the flat over the salon. Looking down,
he decided to close one of his shirt buttons. He didn't
want to seem like he was trying too hard to impress her.

When the buzzer went he gave what he hoped was a
breezy 'Dave here' and was smiling broadly as he got to
the top of the stairs.

'Hello.' She opened the front door just as he put out his hand to ring the bell and he almost pressed her nipple.

Embarrassing, but the lads would love it, not that he'd be admitting it had happened to him. He'd really have to be careful, though. Sometimes, with a couple of pints on board, he couldn't resist the temptation to gloat a bit about his love life.

'Oh, I . . . eh, hi, how are ye?' His voice had developed a new high pitch all of its own, making him sound like a Corkonian instead of the true Dub that he was.

'I'm very well, Dave, and how are you?' She appeared to lean towards him slightly, so he went straight in for a peck on the cheek. He thought she looked taken aback, but she recovered quickly and smiled brightly at him.

'Great, thanks,' he said in an ultra-cheery voice. 'That's a cold night out there, balls off brass monkeys an' all, what?' He handed her an ice-cold bottle with a foil top.

'Champers,' he said unnecessarily. 'Mo-et, actually. Chilled an' ready.'

'Oh, thank you.' She seemed embarrassed then. 'Actually, I'd just made some coffee, but perhaps you'd like something stronger?'

'JD and Coke if you have any?' Dave looked at her admiringly. She was a corker, that was for sure. If he played his cards right he'd be on to a winner in no time, he could feel it in his waters. 'The bubbles are for you. Alison always loved a glass or two . . .' He trailed off, a bit uncertain, but she seemed relaxed enough so he ploughed on. 'Always got her . . . eh, helped her unwind . . . after a

197

hard day, like.' He'd been going to say 'in the mood', but thought better of it, ditto with the broad wink he'd been about to give her. He quickly pretended to have something in his eye.

'So, how have you been keeping?' he asked as he flicked away an imaginary speck of dust. He thought he smelt food; must be that chipper next door.

'Fine, thanks. Busy.' She poured a generous measure of Jack Daniel's into a tumbler and added ice without asking. Dave watched her and thought she looked very fragile.

'I'll leave you to dilute it to your own taste.' She smiled as she passed him the Coke. He noticed the lamps were on and there was stuff strewn around, not like when Alison was here. It looked as if she hadn't made any special effort, he thought, a bit disappointed. The cushions weren't arranged and the flowers were messy, yet it all worked. Shame about the shite orchestral noise in the background, though. Must be that James Last guy. Dave hated instrumental music with a passion, despite Marie's best efforts. His wife was big into Richard Clayderman – had been for years. Dave himself preferred Tony Christie or Tom Jones. He added a splash of Coke to his drink and took a big gulp. 'Aaah, that's better. Do you mind if I smoke?'

'No,' she said but he sensed she did. Dave needed a fag badly otherwise he wouldn't have suggested it. Lily was looking around, uncertain where to find an ashtray.

'Don't move,' he ordered. 'You just relax. I know where she kept them.' He headed towards a cupboard. 'If that's

OK?' He stopped and turned to check with her. 'I can stand over here by the window if you like?'

'No, please, make yourself at home.' She waved her free hand in the air and watched him. He noticed that she sat on the edge of the couch and crossed her long legs, so he decided to take things a step further. This was all progressing nicely.

'Thanks. In that case,' he lifted out an ashtray and placed it on the table, 'I'll just change the music.' He grinned at her, then saw that she looked uncomfortable. 'Not exactly my cup of tea,' he offered by way of explanation. 'What is it, anyway?' He was rooting around in another cupboard.

'Handel.' She sipped her coffee and Dave knew he shouldn't have been so forward. He wanted her so badly, and the last thing he needed was to be thrown out on his ear.

'Well, the only handles I know are luuuv handles and I ain't got none of those.' He pivoted around and decided to back off bigtime and concentrate on getting to know her better. In typical Dave fashion, he tried to lighten things by making her smile. 'I'm a bit of a John Travolta fan myself.' He found what he was looking for and treated her to one of his moves on the way to the stereo. He liked the way she laughed. Women generally responded when he did his impersonations and Dave had enough self-confidence not to mind making a fool of himself. 'Or maybe Patrick Swayze.' He held his arm out in front of him and circled his finger in a twirl with an imaginary partner. 'I was good in me day, I'll have you know,' he told her as he bowed. He liked flirting with her. 'And I can still give those Westlife guys a run for their money when I do me karaoke in the club.' He winked at her.

The funny-guy routine worked, because her smile was instantly more relaxed. 'I've no doubt about it, in fact I'd say you can still turn a few heads on the dance floor.'

'Yep, I'm well fit.' He sauntered towards her, thinking that now might be the perfect time to tell her about him and Alison. It was only then that he noticed a table set for dinner.

'What's this?' he asked, disconcerted.

'Oh, I'm sorry, I should have explained.' She walked over and smoothed an imaginary crease from the snow-white cloth. 'I'd nowhere else to put it, there's so little space here' – she played with her hair and it drove him mad – 'and my sister didn't really cook much.' She blushed. 'I'm making supper for us. I'm a chef. . . that's my job.'

'I see.' He didn't.

'I hope that's OK? You are hungry?'

'Oh yeah, absolutely,' he lied.

'It seemed like the best way to thank you for all your kindness, coming to the funeral, ringing to enquire how I was getting on.' Her smile was a bit childlike and he felt a rumble in the jungle. Jaysus, Dave thought, I was hoping more for dessert.

'Great.' He gulped down his drink.

'Please, sit down, it's all ready.' She led the way to the

table. 'It's mostly cold, anyway. I wanted to give us time to talk.'

'Great' seemed all he was capable of saying.

'Do you like eel?'

'Slippery little suckers, but yeah . . . great,' he repeated, cursing his stupidity for not noticing what she'd planned.

She laughed, took his glass from him and returned a few moments later with platters of food, most of which he'd never seen before.

'So, tell me,' Lily said as she served him a little of everything. 'How did you meet my sister?'

He was very nervous at first so he skirted round the details. She seemed content to let him talk.

'And are you married, Dave?' She slipped it in while refilling his glass for the second time.

'Oh, eh, well, I am and I amn't.' He choked. 'My wife and I, well, we sort of have an arrangement, like.' He gave Lily a knowing look but she said nothing.

'Yeah, she does her stuff and I do mine, you know, that class of thing?'

'And children?' she enquired.

Dave was happy to tell her all about them and she seemed interested.

'Light of my life, the twins,' he finished as he mopped up with bread.

'It's a special bond,' she told him softly, but it went over his head.

'Great girls, great girls, sure they have me wrapped round their little fingers.'

'So, you and your wife, you lead . . . separate lives, as it were?'

'Oh totally, yeah. Absolutely. Own rooms and all that, you know how it is.'

'No, actually. I'm sorry but I don't,' she said and it sounded innocent.

'Well, to tell you the truth, it's bloody lonely at times.' The drink had loosened his tongue. 'My missus, she sort of went off that side of it, like, after the kids were born. Don't get me wrong now, I idolize her, it's just that she made it clear, well, you know . . .'

'That must be hard on you?'

'It is, yeah.' He sensed she knew exactly how he was feeling so he shovelled it on, hoping for the sympathy vote. As he talked he realized that he really resented Marie sometimes, for not wanting him that way. It was hard on a man's ego, he told Lily, although not in those words exactly.

Dave noticed she asked a lot of questions about him and Alison, but luckily he had his story ready. He'd rehearsed a couple of scenarios on the way down in the car, just in case. As they talked Dave knew she didn't have a clue about her sister's life. He tried to hide his disappointment as he realized it might take a while to get her into the sack.

Still, maybe this is the way in, he thought happily, as he pretended the eel was delicious. He relaxed after a while. What the hell, he could wait for it.

20

WILLIAM

WICKLOW TOWN WAS BUZZING WHEN HE ASKED HIS DRIVER to drop him outside the courthouse and wait. William was glad he'd rung and suggested they meet and slightly surprised that Lily had immediately invited him here, to the apartment. She intrigued him and William was keen to know more. He stepped out of the shiny black Mercedes and adjusted his jacket. Unusually for him, he was out to impress.

Two hoodies ambled by with their fists dug into brown paper bags and he could almost taste the fat and the vinegar. A couple of smokers outside Ernie's pub nodded to him as he passed and he inhaled their fumes without asking, which annoyed him slightly, though not for long.

'Hi there,' Lily greeted him. 'You made it.' He'd telephoned her earlier to say he was running slightly late because of a problem with an MRI scan. 'So, you survived the madness?' she said casually. 'You mentioned that it had all gone pear-shaped?'

'That's not quite how I put it,' he laughed, 'although we had a few problems early on with some test results.' He loved talking about his work. 'And then it just seemed to get worse as the day progressed. Sorry about that.' He smiled, taking in her fitted white blouse and short grey pinafore. He didn't tell her that nothing could have put him in a bad mood today. He'd been on top of his game and enjoyed the surge of adrenalin that coursed through his veins when he felt untouchable.

'You look lovely, may I say,' he told her and saw that she looked a bit uncomfortable. 'You are so like your sister,' he added for good measure, but didn't include the words 'younger and fresher and deliciously alluring', which was what he was thinking.

'Thank you.' She blushed and he loved it. 'Make yourself at home, please.' She disappeared into the kitchen and William glanced around the apartment as he shrugged off his overcoat. There was a new scent in the room and the lighting appeared warmer and a bowl teeming with what looked like overblown roses lent the place an air of opulence. He savoured the gentle piano sound of Rachmaninov for a moment, enjoying the atmosphere of tranquillity. It seemed very seductive, William thought, and wondered if that had been her intention.

'Sorry, I was trying out some new lamps.' Lily returned and switched on the main light, putting paid to his theory. 'I've been looking at lighting – for the café I'm thinking of turning this place into,' she said when he raised an eyebrow. 'Although that's still a bit of a question mark at the moment so I won't bore you with the details.' She had a bottle of wine in one hand and two glasses in the other. The wine was not one of his favourites – which Alison had kept a stock of for his visits. 'Drink?' she asked.

'Thank you, that would be lovely. Here, let me do that.' He took the bottle and corkscrew out of her hand without waiting for a reply. William wanted to look after her although he sensed she didn't need it. From what he'd seen of her so far, she was very different to her sister.

'I can open wine, you know. I use it a lot.' She grinned and he felt old-fashioned and didn't like it.

'My apologies.' He handed it back.

'Cheers, what is it?' William asked when she handed him a half-full glass moments later. He twirled the stem and sniffed appreciatively.

'Guess.' Her grin was cheeky as she turned away and switched off the music. 'I'll bet you're an expert.' He liked her slightly bold approach. Alison had always been more circumspect, he remembered. Most people were where he was concerned. It excited him that this girl didn't seem to care what he thought about her. She fiddled with her hair, a long plait that had swished around her shoulder as she turned back towards him.

'No idea, but ten out of ten.' He grinned, playing along. 'It's cold and wet and that's all I need this evening,' he said truthfully.

'Phew, that's a relief,' she said flippantly. 'Food's my thing, as I said, and while I do know a good bit about wine I'm not an expert.'

'Speaking of food, I wondered if you'd like to have dinner with me? I booked us a table, but I can easily cancel if you have other plans?'

'Eh, that would be nice.' He knew she was surprised – that had been his intention. 'Although if you'd prefer, I did get some bits and pieces in, just in case you were famished and only had an hour to spare?'

He shook his head. 'I did my homework and discovered a great new place a few miles out towards Roundwood. It's supposed to be excellent.'

'Isn't that rather a long way for you to drive?'

'I have a driver waiting downstairs, if that's OK?'

'Fine, yes.' She hopped up. 'I'll just get my coat.'

'Take your time.' William smiled nonchalantly. Round two to me, he thought, watching her disappear into the bedroom.

'So, you mentioned earlier that you know your food.' William helped her off with her coat. 'I'll be interested to hear what you think of this place. One of my colleagues reckons it's the best for miles around. People travel from as far afield as Wexford, apparently.'

'Yes, I know the chef,' Lily told him. 'He's excellent.'

'Really, how come?'

'It's what I do for a living, did I mention that before? I make it my business to know. In fact, I had intended to check this place out, so I'm delighted to be here . . .' She smiled, a bit nervously, he thought.

'You're a chef?'

'Well, I'm self-taught, but yes, I cook for a living. You sound surprised?'

'You don't look old enough.'

'I'm the same age as Alison,' she said quietly.

'What I mean is' – he was slightly disconcerted – 'I always think of chefs as overweight, middle-aged men who go around playing God and terrifying people.'

'That's doctors you're thinking of.' She didn't miss a beat and he laughed out loud.

'Touché!' He liked her style. This was turning out to be a very interesting evening.

Lily asked him about his work but he sensed she wasn't that impressed. She had many questions about his relationship with Alison, which didn't throw him one bit. William found her to be an interesting dinner companion, intelligent and funny, and he really enjoyed her company. He in turn wanted to know all about the café thing she'd mentioned earlier. When he thought about the evening on the way home, William realized she'd actually said very little.

'Have you children?' she enquired during a gap in the conversation.

'One of each. Monsters.' William smiled.

'I'm sure they're not. How old?'

He told her. 'No, they're great really. Beth, my wife, does a marvellous job with them.'

He asked her a bit about Alison's child, out of politeness really. William had no worries on that score; he'd always been careful and Alison had been on the pill – he'd seen her supply in a drawer several times.

Lily declared the dinner excellent. At his insistence they shared a velvety chocolate concoction with their coffee.

'I can't, honestly.' Lily laughed as he picked up her spoon and tried to force-feed her a last morsel. William saw some of the other diners looking at them – enviously, he imagined – and it gave him a hard-on. They had a connection, he decided then. But he wanted it to be different to what he'd had with her sister. He planned to take her to Paris and New York with him. Looking at her as she recounted a story about a temperamental chef, she seemed to glow. He'd met and been attracted to many women over the years. But this one was different and William decided he wanted her.

21

JAMES

JAMES WAS NERVOUS AND IT SHOWED. HE TAPPED HIS FOOT anxiously and took a quick swig of his gin and tonic. It tasted warm and lacked the sophistication that a slice of lemon brought but it hit the spot regardless. He took a deep breath. 'I'm afraid I only have about an hour,' he said apologetically as Lily returned and handed him a glass of ice.

'No problem.' He thought she looked relieved. 'I'm under a bit of pressure myself.'

Lily sat down opposite him and tucked her legs under her. He noticed she was wearing black patterned lacy tights and high boots. She looked young and trendy. James felt old and tired beside her.

'I'm racked with guilt about coming here tonight,' he said straight away. 'Even though it's just a chat . . .' He turned crimson.

'If it's any consolation I'm nervous too.' She smiled at him. 'This is not the sort of thing I do every night of the week – meet someone with whom my sister had a secret relationship, that is.'

'Why, then?'

Lily sighed. 'Curiosity, I suppose.' She sipped her drink. 'I felt we made a connection that day you called to the salon and I know that you must have been very important to my sister, so . . . here we are.'

He looked troubled. 'When we talked that day, I hoped we'd meet again. You remind me so much of her.' James wasn't sure what he was saying.

'I guess I need to piece her life together as best I can.' Lily looked far away for a moment. 'I never knew about . . . you two . . . you know.' Lily sighed. 'She kept you a secret and it's kinda hard, to be honest.'

'She was lovely,' he said softly. 'And she became very important to me.' He seemed to be talking to himself. 'And I've really no idea why.' He realized that he had tears in his eyes. Christ, she'd think he was a complete looper.

'James, perhaps by talking about it – we can help each other.' She sounded very young.

'I love my wife. Does that seem strange?'

'No.'

'I mean really love her. I'm not just saying it.' He gave a little laugh. 'This is not one of those my-wife-doesn't-understand-me conversations, I promise. She's my soulmate.'

'You're lucky then.' It was an odd thing for her to say, he thought. He didn't feel lucky.

'Alison was marvellous. Being here with her was so . . . so liberating, I guess is the word.' James saw she looked like she wasn't sure about hearing this. 'She made me feel very special,' he added quickly.

Lily nodded and she reminded him so much of Alison that James suddenly felt like a teenager again. He also felt comfortable with her, which loosened his tongue. 'Things have been so strained at home where sex is concerned.' He told her a bit about their attempts to have a child. 'I get the call, she's ready, it's all about precision timing.' He hoped he didn't sound as bitter as he felt. 'Sometimes, I can't even . . . get an erection.' He buried his face in his hands. 'I don't know why I'm telling you all this. I suppose it's that I feel I know you, in a way.'

'Have you told your wife how you feel?'

'Yes. Although not in those words. We talk about everything, of course. Well, almost everything.' James laughed sarcastically. 'But any time I tried to explain about how it wasn't really working for me, how having to do it on command all the time wasn't easy . . . and her making no real effort . . . to turn me on, that is . . . at least, not like she used to . . . she'd just get upset and then I'd feel like a monster or something.' It all came tumbling out. James looked intently at Lily, as if working it out for himself. 'Can you understand what I'm saying?'

'Yes, I think so.'

'I suppose it would have all been worth it if she'd conceived, but we're one of many "unexplained infertility" cases, although apparently I've got a low sperm count anyway . . .' James laughed. 'Great catch, eh? And now . . . it's all been for nothing and I've got this huge guilt thing going

211

on.' He stared straight ahead, not really seeing her. 'If Alison hadn't died,' he said eventually, 'I don't think I would have been able to give her up.'

'I'm sure once you got through this patch . . .'

'Lily, it had been going on for years,' James told her.

'Really?' The thought hurt.

'I'd become addicted to her.' James didn't seem to hear her. 'She was . . . magic.'

'Yes, she was,' Lily agreed, even though they meant it in completely different ways.

22

LILY

STRINGING THEM ALONG WAS GOING TO BE MUCH HARDER than I'd originally thought, I decided over the next few days. William Hammond sent the biggest bouquet of flowers I'd ever seen to the salon. The note simply said, 'Thank you for the pleasure of your company.' It was unsigned. Dave left a couple of 'hey, babe'-type messages that might have sounded cool if he'd been a nineteen-year-old black rapper and James kept texting me to tell me what he was doing, as if I was his new best friend. What surprised me most was how much I liked the feeling of power I imagined I now had over them. In my head it compensated for the feeling I had that somehow they'd been responsible for Ali not telling me about them. I'd concluded that they'd called all the shots and she'd simply played whatever role they wanted. Well, not any more, boys, I told them over and over again in my mind as I worked out my frustration by cooking up a storm.

Soon the freezer was groaning under the extra weight and I still had no answers. In bed at night I had weird dreams about having sex with all four of them together and each one telling me they were Charlie's father.

Sally had rung a few times and I was avoiding her calls, not wanting to talk to her until I'd worked it all out a bit more. When sleep wouldn't come I tore the flat apart looking for clues. In the process I found out quite a bit more about Alison's secret life, but the more I learned, the more confused I became. And not in any drawer or cupboard could I find the answer to another question that now haunted me. And it was a much less complicated one, really. Why?

I made another appointment to see Brian Daly and we went through Alison's affairs in detail. At least here I felt I could get some results.

'Brian, what if Alison had had more than one child?'

'There was a certain amount set out for each . . . male child,' he told me, 'but the main funds were to be paid once the firstborn turned three.'

'And would she have known that there was . . . more?'

'No. I wasn't at liberty to tell her.'

'I see.' But I didn't really. 'So how come you're telling me now?'

'Because it doesn't apply any more now that Alison's dead.'

'So what happens to the money that might have been hers if she'd had more children?'

'I'm sorry, Lily, I can't really go into . . . details of your father's will that don't directly concern you.'

'Right.' I sighed. It was all so complicated. My father shot up to number one on my hit list again. 'But apart from that, the money that was meant for Alison up to now goes to me?' I blurted out. 'Sorry, that came out all wrong,' I said quickly. 'It's just that every time I think about him ... I turn into another person entirely.' I glanced at him. 'I'm afraid he always had that effect on me.'

'Yes, it all goes to you, and you're quite right to ask,' Brian said matter-of-factly.

'Provided I keep Charlie, of course?' I'd no idea where that came from except it seemed like the sort of thing my father would have thought.

It was the only time I'd seen him look perplexed. 'Is that an issue?'

'No, no, of course not.' How could I tell him that I was worried about who might be the father? I didn't know what I'd do if any one of the men I'd met tried to claim him, although what was left of the rational side of my brain told me that that was highly unlikely. 'It's just that ...' I could see he was watching me closely. 'I ... really don't know how I'm going to cope without her,' I told him. 'She was an amazing mother too, you know that. I'm a very poor substitute for Charlie. Not many maternal instincts, I'm afraid.' That part wasn't really true; I just didn't seem to trust my instincts – maternal or otherwise – any more.

'He's a lovely little fella.' It sounded unusually soft coming from a man. 'How are you getting on with him so far?'

215

'Great, actually. I saw him last weekend.' Brian looked confused. 'I did tell you that he's in Cork with Aunt Milly, didn't I?' I watched his face. 'That is OK, isn't it? I mean it's not a problem as far as . . . ?'

He shook his head. 'No. Lily, Alison left everything to you, the money, the business, the flat. It wasn't conditional on you . . . keeping him with you all the time.' His face softened. 'I know how hard this must be for you.' He sighed. 'From what you've told me, having a child of your own wasn't on the cards right now.'

'No, and not many candidates queuing up even if I had wanted one,' I told him. 'But I love Charlie to bits, you know . . . just in case you have any doubts.'

'I know that.'

'Sometimes, though, I feel so guilty that I didn't pay more attention when she was with him. I'd know much more about what to do now that she's gone. I got all the good bits of him.' I smiled. 'Ali got all the broken nights, the heat rashes, the teething.' I grinned, remembering. 'Sometimes, we'd hide on her, the two of us. Under the bed. Especially when she was trying to feed him parsnips, or make me go through the bank statements.' I closed my eyes and thought about all we'd shared. Everything except the things that were tearing me apart right now, that is.

'She loved him so, so much, you know.' I jolted myself back to the present just as an image of my sister swinging Charlie in the air one day in the park flashed through my mind. I remembered the look of pure, unconditional love I'd seen on her face. 'Anyway' – I tried to shut it out immediately, because it was too painful – 'the Aunt Milly thing is just to give me time to get my head around all this. As far as I'm concerned, Charlie's my number one priority now.' Then I asked the question I'd been wanting to ask all the time. 'Unless you're going to tell me anything about anyone else who might have a claim on him?'

'What do you mean?' His face was straight out of solicitor training school.

'His father?'

'No.' He shifted in his seat. 'Actually, that was one thing Alison never discussed with me. I do know that she was adamant that no DNA tests or anything would ever be carried out on the child.'

'Why?' It seemed an odd thing to have discussed with your solicitor.

'I've no idea. We only ever talked about it briefly, when she was making her will.'

'DNA tests came up in her will?'

'Not quite as baldly as that, no.' He smiled. 'But we discussed the possibility of his father coming forward some time in the future.'

'And?' My heart was thumping.

'She said it wasn't a possibility.'

'Is he dead?' I asked hopefully. That would explain why she'd never talked about it.

'I've told you all I know.' He seemed uncomfortable.

'But what if someone came forward now?' It was my worst nightmare. 'Say if the person got to know about the money, for instance?'

'That's highly unlikely, I think.' I could see he didn't know what I was getting at. 'Are you worried about it?'

'I . . . think about it, yes.' I wished I could just tell him everything, but I couldn't do that to her, even after what she'd left me to find out for myself. It seemed wrong, somehow.

'Lily, the only two people who know about your father's will are me and you, unless Alison told somebody, which I doubt. You were the only one she wanted to tell, as far as I'm aware. And obviously, I won't be telling anybody . . .'

'I know, you're right, of course.' I sighed. 'It's just, this is all so complicated.'

'We'll work it out, don't worry. Let's just take it one step at a time.' He paused and then said quietly, 'I should tell you that Alison did leave a letter.' He seemed a bit distant, and for the first time since we'd been thrown into all this he looked unsure of himself. 'But it is only to be opened in the event of someone trying to claim rights in relation to Charlie.'

'What?' I was thrown. 'So he is still alive?' That one faint hope vanished into thin air.

'I've no idea,' he said. 'But she made it crystal clear that it was extremely unlikely to happen. She was adamant.' He must have seen my face. 'I don't know what the letter contains,' he added quickly. 'My instructions were that the letter was only to be given to you if you presented me with proof that some individual was claiming to be the child's father.'

'Given to me? I don't understand . . .'

218

'The letter is addressed to you.'

It was all too much for me to get my head around. My mind was completely addled. 'Brian, I think I need to see that letter.' I tried to sound calm and reasonable. I couldn't explain to him that it might just answer all my questions.

'That's not possible, Lily, please understand.' He looked put out. 'I probably shouldn't even have said anything to you at this time. It was just that you seemed . . . upset about the child and I thought it might help you to know that this was here in the event of anything . . . arising.'

'OK, I understand, I think.' I tried to think logically again and then sighed. There was nothing logical about any of this. 'I'm not really happy about it but I guess there's nothing I can do, is there?'

'No,' he said quietly and that seemed to be the end of it.

After that we went on to more mundane matters such as funeral expenses and the transfer of the business, which left me totally brain-dead. I said goodbye to him after another hour, feeling more confused than ever.

'By the way, Brian, what about if I have a baby?' I asked him as I walked ahead of him to the door. 'Is there any provision in his will for my children?'

'I'm sorry, Lily, I'm not at liberty to discuss that with you unless the situation arises.'

'I should have known, I suppose.' I turned back to give him my regular sardonic grin. 'It's just that *me* having a baby would have been his very worst nightmare. In my case, he'd have had the local wino down as a potential father. I was always the wild one, as far as he could see. I regularly got the dire warnings, never Ali.' I looked at him. 'Funny that it turned out the other way . . . Ali having the baby, I mean.'

He nodded and looked a bit uncomfortable again. I guess I was giving him a very hard time at these meetings.

'I'm sorry, you must think I'm particularly bitter and twisted. It's just that my father tried to control us – me especially – for years. So it's ironic that of the three of us, I'm the one left sorting all this out . . .' And the only one who's emerged whiter than snow, I didn't add.

'Please, don't apologize, you've been through an awful lot these past weeks. I'll arrange to have the money we discussed transferred to your account immediately, to tide you over until everything is finalized.' He held out his hand. 'And Lily, don't hesitate to call if you need me.'

'Thanks,' I told him. 'I just wish I wasn't on my own. I need her, you see. She'd have told me what to do next.'

23

LILY

'HELLO,' I SAID ABSENT-MINDEDLY, MY MOUTH FULL OF butterscotch sauce.

'You've been avoiding me,' Sally said.

'Not really. Well, sort of.' There was no point in lying.

'What are you eating?'

'A toffee concoction that I've obviously got wrong because it's sort of glued itself to my teeth.' I was running my tongue around my mouth, hoping to rid myself of the sticky brown substance that was threatening to dislodge one of my molars, never mind half my fillings.

'Right, so tell me all.'

'Well, I've talked at length with each of them,' I said, gulping water straight from the bottle.

'What? Lily, are you mad? Alone? Where?'

'Yep. I could hardly have brought Aunt Milly, could I? In the flat in Wicklow.'

'For God's sake, that's the most stupid thing I've ever heard!'

'You read too many Real Life Murders, or whatever

they're called,' I told her. 'Anyway, one of them took me out to dinner in a chauffeur-driven limo, another was in tears half the time and the third one was too busy doing John Travolta impressions.' I heard her familiar dirty laugh and realized how much I missed her. 'The stink of his aftershave is still all over my clothes.' I wrinkled my nose as I spoke.

'Ugh, well, that's it, she couldn't have had an affair with him.'

'That's exactly what I thought as soon as I opened the door to him. It would have been like having sex with a member of a boy band, all carefully styled and everything co-ordinating. Like a cardboard cut-out. In fact, I just know he'd have been worried about tossing his hair.'

'Right, I get the picture. Was he young, even?'

'No,' I told her. 'He was Tom Selleck without the class.'

'Does Tom Selleck have class?' She laughed doubtfully. 'I suppose he did, sort of, in *Friends*. One of our garbage collectors looks just like that, come to think of it. Leathery skin from too much sun. Gold chain nestling underneath his luminous yellow jacket.'

'That's Dave.' I filled her in a bit more.

'So tell me about the surgeon? How did you know where to contact any of them, by the way?'

'Well, I had all their mobile numbers, but with William I made an appointment at the hospital where he works. It wasn't difficult to find out which one – there aren't that many private hospitals in Dublin. Still, I was terrified, to be honest.'

'So how did you end up going to dinner with him?'

'He had it all arranged the night he came to the flat,' I told her. 'Christ, I'd say he's the one who bought Ali that expensive handbag, now that I think about it.'

'Is he loaded? What does he look like?'

'Yeah, he's worth a few bob. He's smooth, well groomed – though not to within an inch of his life, like Dave. You know the type, Sal, they're in every boardroom in the country.'

'Yeah, I've even had a few come on to me and they were married too,' Sally said. 'Clean nails, I'll bet? Manicured.'

'Clean everything. And the only thing he smells of is money. I'd say he likes his girls young,' I told her, thinking about him now.

'Lily, that's obscene.' Sally sounded agitated now.

'I don't mean children or anything,' I said quickly before she hopped on the next flight home. 'I'm making it up,' I told her. 'It's just that I was wearing a pinafore and white blouse and I plaited my hair – you know, the way I do sometimes. He commented on how different I looked, that's all.'

'Christ, Lily, be careful.'

'I was. I am. All I did was have dinner with him, remember? Cost a fortune too, I'd say. I think he liked being seen with me, though. I reckon his ego is bigger than his car engine. The only thing I'm surprised about is why doesn't he just find a new girlfriend, if that's what Ali was? Surely powerful men like him simply move on when they get tired?'

'Listen, Lily, mistresses become just like wives, eventually.' Sally sounded very knowledgeable all of a sudden so I teased her for a bit. 'So . . . James, anything new there?' she said after we'd exhausted the subject of two of her single friends dating married men.

'I really liked him, for some reason, just as I did the first time. Happily married, as I told you . . . loves his wife to bits.'

'Now where have I heard that before?' Sally wanted to know. 'And don't tell me, she just doesn't understand him?'

'No, on the contrary,' I told her. 'They're soulmates.' I explained about the infertility thing. 'He was fantastic to talk to, Sal. You know, like having a gay friend? Or a night in with you?'

'Is he gay?'

'No, but the way he understands women you'd swear he was. Not a bit effeminate or anything, mind.' I tried to think of how to describe him. 'Ordinary,' I said at last. 'Boy-next-door material. Clean-living.'

'God, I wish I was at home. I could talk to you about this all night.' She sounded a bit lonely. 'And tell me briefly, when are you meeting the fourth guy?'

'I've met him once. He's single, did I tell you that last time? He and Ali seem to have been just good friends, as far as I can tell. He met Charlie once. I wonder why she never mentioned him?' Questions like that were keeping me awake at night.

'Maybe they were having kinky sex or something.' We

laughed together at the thought, neither of us able to imagine it.

'Listen, if most of my friends – such as you – are anything to go by, kinky sex is not a novelty any more.' I giggled.

'Run of the mill.' She laughed. 'On TV over here on a daily basis. One guy even brought in his favourite sheep on *Sleepless in Sydney* on the talk show channel last week.'

'Ugh. I am not even going there, Sal, it's gross. So, come up with something else . . .'

'Commitment phobia? Now that I do know something about.' She went on to tell me the story of some man in her office – single – who refused to commit to anything more than two days in advance. He liked to keep his girlfriends guessing, apparently.

'Maybe, although I couldn't see Ali putting up with that sort of shite, could you?' I asked. 'No, for some reason it suited her to have it all casual. Oh, I dunno any more, it's wrecking my brain,' I said tiredly. 'Anyway, I haven't found out much about Richard yet, although someone called Daisy rang in the middle of our chat. I told you he owns a café, yeah? So I'll want him for his brains rather than his body if my plans ever come off.'

'What does he look like?'

'Gangly, thin. Hair like Jonathan Ross.'

'Lily.' I could feel the warning all the way from Oz. 'Don't go falling for him. I'm suspicious, you sounded all soft there.'

'Don't worry, I'm not that much of an eejit, I promise.'

'Tell me honestly, why are you doing this?' Sally's tone changed.

'I'm not sure. Mostly to try and find out why she hid that side of her life, I suppose . . . and to see if I can—'

'I'm just worried about you, that's all,' Sally interrupted. 'I don't want you getting fixated by this because I don't think you're ever going to find all the answers. It's just too complicated, Lily . . . and in real life the ends don't get tied up neatly. That's the movies, remember?'

'Yeah, I know that.' I sighed. 'Anyway, I'm more worried about someone completely new turning up out of the blue and claiming to be Charlie's father. What would I do then?'

'What's brought this on again?'

'I haven't a clue,' I told her honestly. 'But she didn't really have a boyfriend at the time she became pregnant, remember? I tried to talk to her about it but she hinted it was a one-night stand.' I wished I'd probed a bit more at the time. 'Anyway, I want to be prepared if someone tries to take him away from me.'

'Lily, listen to me. That is *not* going to happen. I'd say they'd run a mile, all of them.'

'What about James, though? He's been having problems in that department.' I filled her in on the bits she didn't know.

'I'd bet his wife would leave him if she even got a hint of it.' Sally sounded definite. 'Her soulmate having an affair? Come on . . .'

'That's true. Anyway, I'm not going to think about it

226

any more.' I felt nervous even 'supposing' with her, so I changed the subject to the café idea.

'Lily, are you sure this is what you want?'

'You know it is. You've heard me talk about it for years.'

'Yes, but it was a pipe dream, that's all.'

'Why are you throwing cold water on it all of a sudden?' I asked.

'I just don't want you getting out of your depth, that's all. Finance was never your strong point and you're not trained as a chef or anything. I mean your job is more a hostess thing, isn't it?'

'Was. I've more or less resigned. I'm just helping them out at the moment. Anyway what has that got to do with it? I can cook, you know that. *And* I love it. Look at Nigella, I don't think she had formal training either.' I was a bit pissed off with her. 'And I'm learning to be good with money, it's just that I've never had—'

'You're right, I'm sorry,' Sally interjected. 'Hell, I'm probably just jealous, ignore me.'

'You could come home and run it with me?'

'Have you been listening to a word I've said?' Sally demanded. 'I'm trying to put you off, not encourage you.' She laughed. 'Anyway, I'd say Orla would be a much better bet. We're a bit too close, you and me.'

'Well, think about it, Sally, because I definitely am doing something. It's now or never.'

We chatted for a while longer and when I hung up I was feeling more excited and less worried.

24

RICHARD AND DAISY

'DAISY, LOOK, I'M SORRY BUT I CAN'T TAKE TIME OFF JUST now. I told you I have to meet someone.'

The young woman pushed back her dark hair. 'Please, just an hour?' She sensed he was hesitating. 'My car's outside, I'll have you back in no time, I promise.'

'No can do.' He moved away from her. 'Talk to you later, OK?'

'No, it's not OK.' She tried another tack. 'Richard, I told you about this last week and you promised. Can't you put your meeting off? The sale ends today and I don't want to spend all that money without your approval.'

Richard shook his head. 'No, and I'm not wasting any more time discussing it.' He was getting irritated and she sensed it. 'Now go.' He guided her towards the exit. 'Look. Order. Pay. It's simple and besides, you've had loads of practice.' He was trying to cajole her and was opening the door and reminding her that it was only a sofa when Lily walked in.

'Hi.' She smiled at them both.

'Lily, hello.' He stepped back quickly and hoped she'd pass through.

'Don't worry, I can wait,' she apologized, sensing his discomfort. 'I think I'm early anyway.'

'Eh no, it's fine. This is Daisy, by the way.' Richard hoped he didn't look as nervous as he felt. 'My girlfriend,' he added when neither of the women spoke for what seemed like a full minute.

'Fiancée.' Daisy kissed him lightly on the lips. 'Hi, how are you?'

'Hello.' Lily held out her hand.

'This is Lily,' he said, trying to usher Daisy out. 'The meeting I told you about?' he added when she didn't move.

'Oh, sure. Nice to meet you, Lily.' Her smile was warm. 'Ciao, babe. Talk later and you'd better be very nice to me this evening to make up for shoving me out on my own to buy "our" sofa.' She rubbed his arm and disappeared in a whiff of something toxic, Richard thought, sniffing her latest perfume.

'Sounds like you're in trouble.' Lily laughed at his discomfort.

'I'm always in trouble with Daisy.' Richard ran his hands through his hair. 'Although to be fair, it's mostly my own fault. I've a head like a sieve. Please, sit down.' He indicated a quiet table which was already set up. He was really glad she'd phoned and suggested they meet again. There was definitely something about her, he decided.

'Can I offer you a glass of wine?' he asked quickly as soon as he realized he was staring.

'No, thanks. It's a bit too early,' Lily told him. 'Just some sparkling water, please.'

'Right, coming up.' He moved away and decided he needed a drink himself. The brief meeting of the two women had made him edgy.

'Nice menu.' Lily looked up as he appeared again a few minutes later.

'Thanks. We've a good chef, so it changes regularly.'

'And are your clientele mostly regulars?'

'Yeah, a lot of office workers at lunchtime. There are two big firms nearby.' He indicated with his head. 'It helps.'

'And I suppose you get support from locals as well?'

'Yep. Mass-goers and yummy mummies in the morning, mostly. Afternoons can be quiet, although we still get guys who have meetings on the way home. They stop in here for informal chats rather than go to a noisy pub.'

'So how many would you cater for in a day?' She couldn't help herself. The whole business fascinated her.

'We do about a hundred and twenty covers between twelve and three,' he told her.

'Do you open in the evenings?'

'Nope. I'm too lazy, I also want a life.' He sipped his wine. 'You sound interested, or are you just being nice to me?' It was an effort at teasing, but she seemed not to notice.

'Actually, I'm trying to get into the business. Though not near here, obviously,' Lily felt obliged to add.

'What do you do for a living?'

'I'm a chef, sort of.' She was still smarting a bit from what Sally had said.

'Really?' He was amazed. She was so demure, he'd decided she worked in a bank or something. 'You don't look crazy enough.'

'You've read *Kitchen Confidential* too?' She laughed.

'Sure have. So, where do you work?'

'I'm in the corporate end. I've been working for a law firm up to now.'

That explained her tailored outfit. 'You look like a lawyer.' He was teasing again. 'Do you cook at all, really?' he asked, smiling at her and sniffing loudly in her general direction. She smelt of baby powder. Chefs generally smelt of yeast and grease.

'Yes, of course,' she laughed, 'although not as much as I'd like. I'm not formally trained or anything,' she felt she should add. 'A lot of the time I've been on hostess duty, actually.'

That made sense. He guessed she was quite an asset. They talked more about the business and she told him that she was considering turning the salon into a café. As she chatted he watched her closely and had to remind himself that he was not supposed to have seen the place. Several times he almost put his foot in it. Fuck it, he thought, I'm a terrible liar, I can never remember what I've said. That's how Daisy's always catching me out.

231

'Well, maybe I can help you?' he offered quickly as he realized she'd finished speaking. She fascinated him and he wanted to see her again, and unknowingly she'd just given him the perfect opening. 'Perhaps I could come down and look at the place?'

'Would you?' She sounded delighted. 'That'd be great – although you know it's in Wicklow?' she added. 'It's a bit of a trek.'

'No problem, I could do it on Saturday after we finish here. Then you could introduce me to the culinary delights of the east coast, maybe?'

'Or I could cook something for you, if you'd prefer?' Lily looked really pleased at his offer. My God, she's so like Alison, Richard thought again. It unnerved him. 'There's a small apartment – flat – over the salon and Alison used it often to . . . meet people.'

'Sounds splendid. I'll bring some wine . . . and I have some literature – information packs from banks, that sort of thing. I'll dig them out for you. They might come in handy. I also have my original business plan for this place somewhere, too. Might be useful to glance at . . .' He knew he sounded way too eager.

'Thank you, that's really nice of you.' She beamed at him.

'Pleasure.' He was going to have to be careful: she was way too fanciable, in a totally different way from Alison.

'Would you like to bring your girlfriend?' He was jolted back to reality.

No, he certainly would not, he told her, but not in those

words. She didn't seem to care, one way or the other. Her air of slight detachment was a real turn-on.

He decided to change the subject. 'Now, what would you like to eat? I've gone all nervous now that I know you're a chef.'

'Cook,' she corrected. 'Surprise me.'

'OK.' He was definitely not going to pass that on to the kitchen, he decided. She obviously hadn't much experience. Most people in the trade would stir-fry their own testicles rather than risk another chef grasping an opportunity to use up the leftovers from the previous day the moment someone said, 'Surprise me.'

'Give me one minute.' He was back in two. 'On the way.' He eased himself back into the chair. 'Although it'll probably take a while. All of our food is cooked to order.' It was a bit of a porky, but Richard was enjoying chatting to her and wanted a bit more time. 'Sure I can't offer you a drink? Small one, even?'

'Go on then, I'll have a half-glass of white. And I'd love to talk to you some more about my sister.' He thought she looked a bit tentative. 'I'm afraid I'm still trying to put bits of her life together.'

'Well, she was a remarkable woman, and great fun to boot.' Richard felt like a hypocrite not telling her everything. 'I was very fond of her,' he told Lily truthfully as he made to get up.

'Were you close?' she asked unexpectedly.

'Eh, yes, we were.' Fuck it, don't go there, Kearney, he warned himself.

'Did your girlfriend – fiancée, I mean – ever get to meet her?'

'No, actually. Daisy and me, now that's another tale altogether.' Richard grinned at her. 'Definitely for when I've had a couple of drinks.' He winked and tried to keep it light.

Lily raised her eyebrows. 'It sounds like an interesting story.'

'That's the understatement of the year. There's a book in it, or so my mates tell me.' He left to check on the food before he said too much.

Ten minutes later Richard presented her with a frittata – an Italian omelette heaving with bacon, cheese and herbs. He watched Lily's face and saw her pick at the food nervously.

'You don't like it?' He was on his feet within seconds.

'No, on the contrary, it's delicious. Anyway, I'm no expert. I haven't any formal training, as I told you, so I don't think . . .'

'That's it. I'll sack the chef. Bring in some new blood.'

They were suddenly wrestling with the plate. She looked mortified.

'Give it back to me, please, it's lovely.' It was only when Richard saw she was really embarrassed that he sat back down.

'OK, listen, now I need your help too,' he told her, anxious all over again. 'I'm going to take you to several really trendy places in Dublin and I want your honest opinion.' He warmed to his plan. It was a great way to get to know her better, way ahead of just visiting her in Wicklow. Oh, he'd do that too, but this gave him the opportunity he'd been looking for. And he could even tell Daisy about it.

25

LILY

APART FROM RICHARD, WITH WHOM I FELT A CONNECTION, I'd made no real progress with the new men in my life. William had been playing golf in the exclusive Druids Glen nearby in Newtownmountkennedy and had asked me to join him for lunch afterwards, but I was too nervous. All James seemed to want to do was talk about Alison any time he phoned, and Dave – well, basically Dave just wanted me to get my kit off, as far as I could make out. The thought made me retch. So, with all this stuff turning my brain to mush, I decided to concentrate on making my dream of owning my own café a reality. First thing I did was ring Aunt Milly.

'Help,' I said as soon as she answered. 'I need you.'

'Lily.' She didn't seem at all put out by my plea. 'Charlie, it's Lily,' she called and immediately I could hear him shouting my name.

'How is he? I miss him.' It still surprised me, the bitter-sweet tug I felt every time I heard his laugh or saw a photo of him even.

'Fine, as you can hear.'

'Can I say hello to him?'

'I'd say we won't be able to chat until you do.' She laughed. 'Each time the phone rings he screams your name and won't stop until he's said hello to whoever it is, just to check that it's definitely not you.' My heart skipped a beat. 'He thinks I'm hiding you, he told me last night.'

'I'm too big to hide, tell him.'

'Here he is, love.'

'Hi, gorgeous, how are you?' I asked him.

'Lily, when are you coming to see me? Come to Cork. *Now*,' he shouted.

'I will, love. I'll be down soon, on the train. Will you come to meet me like you did before?'

'Yes, I will.' He sounded all grown up. 'Choo-choo,' he sang, putting paid to that idea.

'Do you miss me?' What a ridiculous question to ask a child.

'Bye bye.' He was gone with a clatter of the phone.

'So, what's up with you, child?' Milly wanted to know.

'I've decided to go for it.'

'The café, do you mean?'

'Yes,' I told her uneasily. 'Am I mad?'

'No, I think it's just what you need.'

'Will you come up and talk to me about it?' I hadn't intended to say it. 'God, Aunt Milly, all I seem to do is ask you for favours.'

'When?'

'I dunno, this week?'

'I could come on Wednesday, I suppose. But I'd have to be back on Friday for my novena.'

'Great.' I was suddenly excited. 'Will you bring Charlie?'

'If you want. I'm sure I can manage him, even though he'll be a bit of a handful on the train.'

'Are you OK?' I tried to think of a way I could help her. 'I could come down, if you'd prefer? It's just that, well, I'd like to show you Wicklow and bring you for a walk on the beach in Brittas Bay, let you see where I'm looking for a house, that sort of thing.'

'That's it so. I'll be there.'

'I'll meet you off the train and we could stay in the flat in Dublin. Then we could go down to Wicklow on Thursday for the day.'

'Sounds good.'

'Will you bring your cookbook, the one your mother wrote all those recipes into?'

'Yes, if you think it will help.'

'It will, definitely, it's just what I need.' I realized I was smiling to myself. 'I can't believe it, I'm so excited,' I told my aunt and I knew she was pleased.

Violet was upset initially when I told her my plan, but came around to the idea once I'd offered her a job in the new venture, something I wasn't at all sure about. Her background wasn't in food, but she was very good with people and a hard worker, as far as I could tell. Also, I knew she wanted to stay in Wicklow because she'd told me all about her new boyfriend – Shane the barber – over a coffee one day.

'What's it going to be called?' she wanted to know as soon as she'd warmed up a bit. It had been a frosty start.

'No idea yet,' I told her cheerfully. 'But it's going to be old-fashioned, although not in décor. No gingham-covered wicker baskets for the scones or anything,' I said quickly. 'No tea cosies. But the food is going to be a return to home cooking, not a panini or a wrap in sight.'

'Oh.' She sounded disappointed but I had done my homework, which was just as well because Brian Daly had done his too and he did his best to dissuade me when I met him the following day.

'Wicklow's full of coffee shops,' he told me over lunch. 'I spoke to the Enterprise Board and what they're looking for is ideas on the manufacturing end, or ones with export potential.'

'But I've no experience in that area. Besides, this is something I've always wanted to do and if I'm to make a move to the country I need to do it before Charlie starts school.' I was trying hard to convince him because in my head I needed him on side. We'd become friends since Alison's death and he knew more about me than any other man.

'You'd move permanently to Wicklow?'

'Yes, I'm already looking for a house close to Brittas Bay. It's beautiful.' I couldn't hide my enthusiasm. 'Miles of sandy beach, hills to the west, and so much space. Nothing else, really – one pub, one shop, no traffic jams.' I laughed nervously, hoping he wasn't going to send too much sense my way. 'Do you know that there's not a moment's silence in the city, at least not where I live? I'm fed up of house alarms rocking me to sleep at night and car horns waking me up every morning. I haven't set a clock in years. I judge the time by the traffic.'

'I know the feeling,' he admitted grudgingly.

'Anyway, my aunt is coming up on the train tomorrow – with Charlie – and we're going to look at a few cottages. Imagine being able to walk in the fields every morning with Charlie and the dog?' I was excited all over again.

'What dog?'

'The one I'm going to rescue from PAWS.'

He tried his best but really he didn't stand a chance. This new venture was the only thing keeping me going.

Charlie's welcome next day helped reinforce it all in my head. He practically knocked me over when he saw me.

'Mammy,' he kept shouting and my stomach did a somersault.

Aunt Milly loved Wicklow and, as soon as Charlie was asleep, we spent the time poring over cookbooks and arguing about the best way to make dumplings. I was in heaven. Brittas Bay looked magical, all those bluey-grey tones along the sea road and masses of purple tinging the mountains. We parked in the almost empty South Beach car park – the main one – where in July and August you'd have to queue and possibly even fight for a space. I could almost smell the fat from the closed-up chip van still sitting in the corner, looking tatty and grimy.

'Nothing beats the taste of chip butties laced with vinegar and sand, does it?' I asked my aunt.

'No, except maybe the first drop of hot tea with milk and sugar when you're parched and miles from civilization,' she said with a smile. 'I think it's the fresh air that makes everything taste so good.'

'Ice cream!' Charlie pointed at the colourful chart still stuck to the front panel of the van, faded now after the months of summer sun and grubby, kiddy hands. I was nervous showing Charlie the beach. He seemed fine, even when he saw the sea, but then a huge wave crashed in and he panicked.

'Mammy,' he cried and clung to me. I burst into tears.

'It's all right, love, I'm here,' I kept repeating as I held him tight and tried to console him.

'That was really stupid of me,' I told my aunt. 'I should never have brought him here.'

'Let's just try and get him interested in something,' she said. 'Not here, but further back, maybe.' I could see she was struggling too.

So the two of us sat sheltered in the sand dunes where he couldn't see the sea and told him that it was OK over and over again.

'You not to go near the sea,' he kept saying, looking frightened.

'No, love, I won't go near it, I promise.'

'Bad sea,' he said quietly. 'Very bold.'

'Look, Charlie, there's a big red kite over near the picnic

area. Will we go see? You can hold both our hands and we won't let you go, ever. Lily, come and look.' Aunt Milly strolled casually towards the only other people we'd seen – a hardy family playing games – and eventually Charlie couldn't resist taking a peek.

'Thank you.' I hugged her once I knew he'd recovered. 'I'd never have managed that on my own.'

'He's fine now, love. Don't worry,' she reassured me and soon Charlie was talking to any dog we met along the path. I had to stop myself taking him to get one there and then, just to make it up to him.

'Woof-woof,' he shouted for the rest of the day. 'Choo-choo,' he waved at every tractor we met on the road.

That weekend I simply closed the salon. Alison hadn't built up many regulars – most of the trendy Wicklow set preferred to go to Dublin for their facials – and the few chatty locals who came in seemed to understand that I needed a change. Her main business had been during the summer months and they were mostly the yummy mummies of South Dublin who decamped to Brittas Bay in their 70,000-euro Volvo and Mercedes jeeps as soon as the schools closed, and didn't care how much a facial or manicure cost. Wicklow town during the tourist season was a different place to the one I saw now on my visits. Most of the locals avoided coming into town during high summer because of not being able to park in the main street, or having to queue for their fish, or being made to wait for a table in any of the popular places they patronized all year.

Early the following week I met with an architect who was willing to oversee the transformation of the salon. Maureen Stanley was a local girl who'd trained in London and returned to live in the area the previous year when her mother was widowed.

'I'm a country girl at heart,' she told me cheerfully, looking anything but. 'Actually, I hope it won't put you off but this is my first project in Ireland' – she must have seen my face because she continued quickly – 'but I've done loads of work in the UK, so don't worry. Here's my portfolio.' She reached for a leather satchel. 'And since our telephone calls I've been pulling stuff out of magazines to do a kind of mood board, just to give us a starting point.' She was trying hard. As I hadn't a clue what I was doing, I really needed an experienced professional, and I was a bit anxious, to say the least. However, as soon as I saw her work I knew she was perfect.

Structurally the place was almost ideal. We already had the toilets and by knocking down two walls at the back we could greatly expand the food preparation area. Here I was in my element. For the first time in my life I was able to design my dream kitchen, albeit on an industrial scale. I let my imagination run riot while Maureen concentrated on the café proper. It was all starting to take shape.

My one slight concern was that the local traders weren't exactly friendly, and as I'd need to apply to the planning department of the County Council for change of use, I hoped I wasn't going to encounter any opposition. Wicklow people, it seemed, treated 'blow-ins' with a certain amount of suspicion. It was amazing how often they answered a question with another one, thus avoiding giving away too much.

Maureen cheerfully assured me that they'd still be treating me as an outsider in twenty years' time and I was wasting my brain cells worrying. She'd already had a word with the authorities and they seemed to be on side. I told her I'd enough on my plate without giving the competition much thought. My only concern was the planners.

In the meantime, Richard Kearney insisted on taking me on a culinary tour of Dublin on several evenings and lunchtimes over the next few weeks. God knows what his staff thought when he disappeared at the busiest time of day. I didn't object because I was learning loads. He certainly had a finger on the pulse where trendy eateries were concerned, and as a result of massive exposure to every 'fusion' combination known to man I was slowly but surely refining my own tastes.

The only slight problem was that during our many jaunts he never gave me any information about his friendship with my sister. Oh, he was completely self-deprecating, very funny and a bit of an old-fashioned, anorak type and the combination was really attractive, but the whole Alison thing was a major complicating factor that I needed to sort out, in order to save my sanity. No matter how much I prodded and prompted, he still hadn't told me any details about why he'd been so chummy with my sister, especially when he had a stunning girlfriend tucked up at home.

We never made it to the apartment in Wicklow that first time, when it had been my intention to really try to draw him out. Daisy had been involved in a minor accident – broken nail, Sally suggested uncharitably when I rang her to moan, but Richard had assured me it involved a car and a very irritable pensioner on his way to mass – so he'd had to cancel. Now, three weeks later, having been to restaurants as far afield as Drogheda to the north and Dungarvan to the south, I'd finally plucked up the courage to invite him back to the flat, hoping the familiar surroundings might relax him enough to loosen his tongue.

'That was fantastic. You sure can cook!' He'd just cleared his plate and my wild mushroom risotto had obviously impressed.

'Thank you.' I was aware that my drinking the white wine as well as using it to cook with had rendered me slightly tipsy and more relaxed than usual. We'd gotten to know each other a good bit over the shared lunches and dinners, and in bed the previous night I'd begun to fantasize that he'd actually turn out to be Charlie's father. What happened next was that Daisy would discover the truth, wallop him, then conveniently disappear with a Jude Law type and finally me and this endearingly attractive nerd would open a string of restaurants and live happily ever after.

I dragged myself back to earth as I realized he was topping up my glass again.

'No more, please, or I might say something I'll regret.'
I regretted that one as soon as I heard myself. The last
thing I wanted was an intimate conversation I wouldn't be
able to remember half of in the morning. 'Strawberries
with some cracked black pepper or a bit of smelly cheese?'
I asked as I hurriedly cleared away the plates in an effort
to avoid his grin.

'I don't think I could manage either.' He immediately
got up to help. 'Lily, I . . . we need to talk.'

I was already in the kitchen before I realized he just
might be about to tell me something I wasn't entirely sure
I was ready to hear, like how in love with my sister he'd
been. The truth was I'd been thinking over dinner that I
sort of fancied him myself, and having come to that con-
clusion I desperately didn't want him to say anything that
might spoil it. Dumping the plates, I came to an alcohol-
fuelled decision, so I checked my face in the stainless steel
hood then turned to find him standing behind me.

'There are some things I . . .' His face had a pink tinge
and his eyes were darting all over the place. His 'I wish I
was anywhere but here' air was endearing and he was very
close in the small kitchen and I liked the normally rather
off-putting smell of tobacco and sweat I sniffed as he ran
his hands through his hair. Clean sweat, I decided.

'You are so . . .' He gulped. 'Sweet . . . and . . . innocent.
And . . . gorgeous. To tell you the truth, I'm a little bit
afraid of my feelings for you.'

I don't know who made the first move but suddenly we
were kissing and it wasn't the usual. It was the gentlest

exploration of my mouth and it went on and on and on.

'Oh God, Lily, this is not meant to happen. I—' He pulled away.

'I know.' I couldn't look at him.

He continued his investigation of my mouth, and this time there was no doubting his interest.

'Listen.' He pulled back from me and cupped my face in his hands. 'I'm not sure I can do this.'

'Is it Daisy?'

He shook his head. 'It would be much simpler if it was.' He looked away.

I reached up and touched his cheek. It was meant to soothe him. Almost immediately I had a vision of my sister doing the exact same thing, here in this apartment. Two sneaky thoughts crept in then, in rapid succession. The first was to wonder what if Alison really had been in love with him but he refused to give up Daisy, and the second was Christ, just supposing we have a relationship and I get pregnant and he turns out to be Charlie's father as well. It was so real that I could see the headlines on *Oprah*.

Suddenly, just as he seemed to have put whatever doubts he had to the back of his mind, all I could think of was that I didn't want to be intimate with him here, like this, and I wasn't even sure I wanted to have anything at all to do with him any more, so I said the only thing I could think of.

'Richard, I'm sorry, I shouldn't have let it go this far.' I felt slightly out of breath but I guessed it was probably just a minor panic attack. 'The thing is, I know about you and Alison.'

247

26

LILY

'WHAT DID YOU SAY?' HE LOOKED AT ME AS IF HE WAS trying to figure out something. 'Exactly what do you know?'

'Enough.'

'I see.' He seemed to come to a decision. 'Lily, I think we need to talk.' He moved further away and I mumbled, 'Excuse me,' as I headed for the bathroom, afraid I was going to throw up.

When I came back he was filling the kettle.

'Coffee?' He was avoiding looking at me.

'There's some made already.' I indicated the pot. 'It's been keeping warm so it should be OK.'

'Black or white?' He was also playing for time, apparently.

'Black.' I reached for two mugs and went ahead of him into the sitting room. I knew I looked a mess but glancing at his face I reckoned it was no longer an issue.

'So, what's this all about?' he asked as he poured.

'How do you mean?'

'I mean what are you trying to tell me?'

'I'm not sure, really.'

'Lily.' This time he tilted my head up to look at him. 'I haven't a clue what's going on here. You need to fill me in.'

'You lied to me.' I was immediately on the defensive.

'Yes, I probably did lie by omission, but I would have told you.' He looked like he'd rather not be having this conversation.

'When?' I asked baldly.

'I never intended this to happen. Jesus, my life is complicated enough.' He said nothing for a second. 'But what I don't understand is where you're coming from? Tell me, please.'

'I don't know. In the beginning, I wanted to see what you were like . . .' It was out before I realized it.

'That first day, when you came into the restaurant, it wasn't a coincidence?' He sounded like he'd only just thought about it.

'No.'

'I see.' He hesitated for a moment. 'I suppose it was natural, wanting to know more about me. What had Alison told you?'

'Absolutely nothing.'

'Nothing?' He digested this. 'But you said . . .?' I could see he was confused. 'So, how come you knew about me . . . in the first place?'

'Actually, I think I'd like you to go now.' I got up and grabbed my mug and started tidying up.

'I can't go until you tell me what this is all about.'

'Please . . .' I felt like crying, but maybe that was just the drink.

'You did . . . know about me and her though?'

'Not really,' I said truthfully, and it hurt to admit it. 'Just a few things I found out . . . afterwards. Did she talk about me, or her baby, even?' I needed to know.

'Not much.' He looked upset for me. 'She was very private. I really liked her, she was great fun to be with. And as for her family, I knew she had a sister, although not that you were twins – that's why I got such a shock when I saw you that day. And no, I never knew she had a baby. She talked very little about her life outside . . . of here.'

'You said you'd met him?' I was surprised.

'I lied, you caught me off guard.' He looked a bit shamefaced and I was glad. I could see the creases on his forehead. 'Is that what this is about?' He looked even more perturbed. 'You think that maybe I'm the father?'

'You tell me.'

'No, I'm not, Lily. Definitely not. Not possible, in fact. I had the snip a few years ago.' He shrugged. 'If I'm honest, I never really wanted kids.'

'As simple as that?' He sounded just like me – before I inherited Charlie, that is – and came across as selfish and self-absorbed, I realized. Not to mention immature. 'And what about Daisy?'

'Daisy will go along with me.' It sounded false.

'That's what she says now . . .' I wondered why I was bothered about his girlfriend.

'Well, she's known about the operation from the start,'

250

he told me. 'I've always been upfront about having no real interest in fatherhood.' He looked a bit lost. 'Can't even blame my parents.' He smiled. 'I had an idyllic childhood, actually. Big country house, plenty of money about, lots of love and attention.'

It was the direct opposite to what I'd known and talking to him in this matter-of-fact way made me understand – a little bit, at least – that the whole Charlie thing was perhaps much bigger in my head than it was in anyone else's.

'Can I ask you something?' I didn't wait for a reply. 'Why would someone like you – single, man about town, everything going for you, lovely girlfriend, all that – why would you be seeing my sister . . . on the side? At least, I take it you weren't open about it?'

'No.' He thought for a moment. 'I dunno really. Excitement, the feeling that you're playing with fire. I can't explain it. It's like asking why do people take drugs? Because they can? Search me,' he said.

'So it wasn't because your life at home . . . with Daisy, was' – I couldn't think of the word – 'dull?'

'Hell, no. Daisy is many things but she's never dull.' He looked uncomfortable talking like this. 'Besides, I played around . . . occasionally. It was probably something to do with no strings attached – you know, no pretence, no having to meet the folks on Sunday afternoons, that sort of thing. And most men my age have issues with commit-ment, even though some of them, like me, are making plans to get married.' He must have seen my face. 'Sorry,

251

Lily, you may not like hearing it but it's true, I swear. And it suited Alison as well . . .' He trailed off, unsure how much more to tell me, I sensed.

'Listen.' I came to a decision. 'I need to be on my own, to think . . .'

'That mightn't be such a good idea. Are you staying here tonight?'

I nodded.

'Look, why don't I stay? I could sleep on the couch.'

'No, I'm fine, there's no need.'

'Sure?' He couldn't quite hide his relief.

'Yes, honestly.'

'OK. Look, I don't want to leave it like this. How about if I come back in the morning? For breakfast, if that's acceptable to you?' He was treating me with kid gloves.

'Fine.'

'Promise me you'll still be here?'

'Yes.'

'Good. About ten?'

I nodded.

He gathered his stuff without speaking. 'Are you sure you'll be all right?' He was heading for the door and then seemed to think better of it. 'On your own? Tonight?'

'Yes.'

'You're not nervous?'

That was a laugh. Alison had obviously never told him about how much time we were left alone as small kids, when we really were frightened.

'No, I'll be fine.'

'Right, then. I'll pick up a cab on the main street.'

I nodded. 'Goodnight.' I didn't move.

'You have my mobile, just in case?'

'Yes.' I didn't know what else to say. 'Thank you,' I added as an afterthought.

Later, I tried to doze but the fact that I was more confused than ever about Alison, combined with having to face Richard again in the morning with our relationship – if you could call it that – on a different footing, meant that sleep did not come easily. There was no escape route.

27

JAMES AND TAMSIN

JAMES DIDN'T KNOW WHETHER IT WAS THE SMELL OR THE sound that tickled his senses as he closed the front door, but the first thing that registered was the sound. There was music playing and Tamsin was laughing. He sniffed. And cooking something spicy. The absence of silence in the house surprised and pleased him at the same time.

His wife and her best friend were in the kitchen and Tamsin was already at the door when he pushed it open.

'Hello, darling. How are you?' He liked it that she usually left whatever she was doing to come and greet him as soon as he arrived in the door.

'Fine.'

He kissed her and looked over her shoulder. 'Hi, Maria, what are you doing here?' It was unusual to see her at this time of day, when normally her brood were at their most demanding.

'Had a row with Dan and decided I needed a drink and a shrink.' She grinned. 'Came here and got both for nothing.'

'Cheapskate.' He kissed her on both cheeks. 'How's Dan?'

'Driving me mad. You won't believe what he's—?'

'Stop right there.' James poured himself a glass from the half-empty bottle and knew the girls thought he was settling in for a natter, as he normally would. 'Your husband is a mate.' He saw Maria's nose twitch. 'I refuse to bitch about him.' He pulled her hair. 'So there.'

'Bastard,' but he knew she didn't mind really. Maria and Dan fought like cats and dogs. He'd long since given up getting in the ring, as had most of their friends.

'You look nice.' He noticed that Tamsin was wearing new jeans and a pretty smock top. It was a while since she'd made any effort at home. 'And you're cooking. How come?' he asked absently as he threw the ball for Levi, who had dropped it at his feet and was circling him, eyes bulging and tail threatening whiplash.

'I decided it was time to look after my husband again.' She came up behind him and put her arms around him. 'I've been neglecting you lately.' She kissed his back.

'Well, you won't hear me complaining about being looked after, you know that, don't you?' He turned to her and pulled her close, kissing the tip of her nose. He winked at Maria over her shoulder.

'Ugh, that's enough, leave her alone.' The other woman was smiling as she pushed back her chair. 'Christ, it's bad enough hating my own husband. Please don't treat me to a display of how it could be.' Maria drained her glass. 'I'd better face the music.'

'Stay for dinner,' Tamsin suggested.

'Yes, do,' James added. He noticed the tired look in her eyes. 'Please?' he asked.

'I'd love to but I'd better not.' She took her jacket from the arm of the chair. 'Anyway, I'm driving and if I stay here any longer I'll have drunk the bottle I brought.'

'I'll run you home later,' James offered.

'You're a dote, but no, thanks. I'll leave you two love-birds to your fragrant green curry and pristine house.' It was said without a hint of envy. 'Call you tomorrow.' Maria picked up her bag.

'Sure you won't stay? You're not disturbing us in the slightest,' James said, but secretly he was glad when Maria shook her head. He wanted to try and talk to Tamsin about the future, now that she seemed to be coming back to her normal self again.

'But thanks for asking.' She touched James's arm as they walked her to her car. 'You always make me feel so welcome.' She hugged her pal. 'You take care.'

They said their goodbyes and waved her off.

'You look great. Are you feeling good?' James asked as they stood watching the tail-lights disappear, arms wrapped around each other.

'Yes.' Tamsin smiled. 'I am. Now come indoors and finish your drink. Dinner's almost ready. I've got rice in the oven and all the bits are already on the table.'

'Sounds perfect. Marks and Spencer?' he teased.

'Tesco Finest. But I did add a few extras myself, the way all good cheats do.'

They had an enjoyable meal and then sat on the couch in front of a blazing fire and watched TV. After the news headlines Tamsin reached for the remote and turned to him. 'I've been thinking.'

'Uh-oh.' He kissed her nose. 'What about?'

She hardly missed a beat. 'I'd like us to try and adopt a baby.' It was typical of Tamsin, straight in as usual.

James was taken aback. It was something she'd always refused to consider when he'd suggested it in the past. Now he wasn't sure he wanted to any more. It had been said simply to take her mind off things during the worst of the IVF. A sort of 'don't worry, there's always fostering or adoption to consider'-type conversation. It had helped keep them going during the many long waiting periods, which they both dreaded.

'Are you surprised?'

'I guess I am.'

'But it was something *you* brought up in the past.' Now she looked taken aback.

'I know. But that was because I thought it might be easier . . . on us, on our relationship. Things were pretty tough going there for a while,' he reminded her gently.

'I know. And you were absolutely incredible to me during all that time—'

'No, that's not what I meant.' James dismissed the compliment, feeling guilty. 'I meant that for a while we seemed to have no . . . excitement. No spontaneity. Sexually, that is. It was all about dates and times and charts and temperatures. I remember thinking that if we decided to adopt we could go back to how we used to be . . . before all this got in the way.'

'James.' She moved closer to him. 'I know this was harder on you, much harder than maybe I originally guessed.' She looked deflated just thinking about it and he hated himself.

'No, it wasn't,' he insisted now. 'It was equally hard on both of us.' He felt he had to be fair to her.

'You missed the sexual freedom more than me. I know how important that side of things is for a man.'

'Not only for a man,' he said quickly, feeling a bit miffed. 'You were always into it too . . . before.'

She reached out and rubbed the back of his neck: it was what she always did when she wanted him on side. 'I know I was.'

'You haven't done that in ages.' He arched his back in pleasure.

'I haven't, have I. I'm sorry.' She knew how much he adored being touched.

'No . . .' He felt guilty again. 'It's me, I've—'

'James, hear me out. In many ways I've been very selfish in all of this.' He tried to interrupt her again but she put her finger on his lips. 'No, let me finish, please. I didn't really think about what I know is vital for you.' She looked at him as if she was only just considering it all. 'I know how important spontaneity and passion and . . . excitement are to you.'

'They're essential if a relationship is to thrive, I would have thought.' Jesus Christ, what are you saying? James asked himself. You were getting all that somewhere else and now you're taking the moral high ground with your wife. 'What I meant was . . .' He tried to backtrack.

'Remember the nights when we'd have showers and I'd put on the sexiest new thing I'd bought and you'd pour us drinks and light the candles in the bedroom?'

'I remember.' He swallowed hard.

'Well, I bet you can't remember the last time, it's been so long.'

'No, I can't.' He wished she'd stop being so nice to him. It made the whole thing harder to bear, especially when he'd been talking to Lily only a few hours ago.

'Oh James, I've been a selfish cow.' She threw herself at him. 'I knew how hard it was on you, but I thought it would be OK to make it up to you once I got pregnant.' There were tears in her eyes. 'Please forgive me.'

'Don't be silly.' He pulled a tissue from the box on the console table and wiped her eyes. 'There's nothing to forgive. We've always been in this together.'

'But it's been me leading the campaign,' she said quietly.

'Tamsin, I wanted a child of my own just as much as you did, don't forget that.' He was getting irritated again. 'Maybe I just accepted earlier than you that it might not happen.' He paused. 'I wasn't wearing rose-coloured specs the whole time.'

'James, that's cruel, how can you say that to me?' She blew her nose.

He didn't know what had come over him, except that he

wished she would stop living in this fantasy world where everything went according to plan and they all lived happily ever after. He wanted her to at least consider the possibility that it might have forced him into the arms of another woman, but that was just his ego. He knew she'd never guess, not in a million years.

'I'm sorry,' he said weakly. 'I didn't mean to upset you. You know I wouldn't hurt you for the world.'

'I know you wouldn't.'

'Will we go to bed?' He was exhausted.

She didn't hear him, it seemed. 'And now here I am, babbling on about adoption, putting you in second place again . . .'

'You're not.'

'It's just I . . . have this desperate ache . . . right here.' She took his hand and placed it low down on her stomach. 'It's like a hole, like something's gnawing away at it.' She looked like a child herself.

'I never want you to feel lonely.' He tucked her hair behind her ear. 'I'm always here for you, you know that.'

'Yes, James. I know that.'

They were both silent for a bit. 'If you really want to consider adoption, I'm willing to talk about it.' He knew he'd do anything for her. Even give up the double life you've been leading? a voice in his head asked. He sighed. 'Just give me a little time to get used to the idea.'

'Thank you.' She kissed him, their first real kiss in a while.

260

'I've missed you.' He smiled at his wife. 'I've been lonely too, you know.'

'I know you have, James. I know you have.'

They held each other for ages, not saying anything. He kissed her this time and she kissed him back as if she meant it. It had been a long time since he'd felt this close to her. Before either of them realized, they were a jumble of arms and legs and wet kisses and they made love on the rug in front of the fire the way they used to in the old days.

Afterwards, her kiss was lingering, all urgency gone. 'I love you so much.' Her face was damp. So was his.

'Let's not lose each other again.' He took her face in his hands. 'I'm not . . . right without you, somehow.'

'We never lost each other, darling. We, I . . . just lost my mind for a bit.'

'Me too.' Absently he shoved a few briquettes on the fire.

'What do you mean?'

'Nothing.' He smiled at her. 'Nothing at all.' But he felt horribly guilty. They used to have no secrets.

'James . . .' Tamsin sat up. 'Hang on, let me get my robe.' She moved away. 'Back in a jif, hold that thought.' She kissed his head.

'That's better.' She was tying the belt as she sat back down and he was pulling on his shirt. 'Now I can relax. James, I know there's something on your mind. I see you looking pensive when you don't know I'm watching.' She tilted his face up. 'I can see it now, in your eyes.' She smiled at him. 'It worries me.'

'There's nothing to worry about.' He'd long ago decided he could never do that to her. Now he abandoned all thoughts of going to bed, as he had wanted. 'I'm getting another drink. Can I get you a cup of tea or something?'

'No, thanks.' She followed him into the kitchen. 'James, come back inside.'

'OK.' He refilled his glass and let her lead him back to the couch.

'I know there's something worrying you.'

'No, there isn't.' He sipped his wine.

'Don't hide behind alcohol.'

'I'm not.' He hated it when she went on about his drinking. 'This is only my third glass, I'm hardly on a bender.'

She ignored that. 'James, I'm so glad we had tonight and I'm so sorry for not . . . seeing things clearly before. I want to make it up to you. But I know you. I know there's been something troubling you for a long time. It comes and goes, but every now and then I see the anguish in your eyes.' It wasn't the first time she'd said that to him but he'd always managed to brush it aside. 'I can't ignore it any more, James. Or maybe I don't want to. Please.' She took his hand. 'I'm your best friend, remember? I'm sorry I've been so self-absorbed for such a long time. Please tell me what's wrong?'

'No.' He shook his head. 'I'm too tired to talk any more.'

'So there is something.' Tamsin was in interrogating mode and just for once he wished she'd put him first. 'Please, James, I won't be able to sleep now.'

He just kept shaking his head. 'I can't.'

'You can. You can tell me anything.'

'You'll hate me.'

She knelt in front of him. 'James, I could never hate you.'

He saw surprise and worry in her face. 'I'm sorry' was the best he could manage.

'I'm begging you, James. Please, tell me what's on your mind. Whatever it is, we can handle it together.'

'It'll drive us apart.' His voice cracked. He knew it was now or never.

Tamsin looked shocked. 'What are you saying?' She searched his face. 'You're my whole life. Nothing in this world could ever drive us apart.'

He bowed his head then and started to cry as he prepared to tell the woman he loved the one thing he knew would break her heart.

28

WILLIAM AND BETH

THE PARTY WAS IN FULL SWING WHEN WILLIAM TURNED the key in the lock.

'Daddy, you're home.' Winnie threw herself at him and William realized that his daughter was becoming more like Beth every day. He was surprised that he hadn't noticed it in ages. 'You're missing it, it's the best party ever.' She twirled so he could see her dress and the eyes that sparkled up at him were exactly like her mother's. 'Do you love it?' She had the same energy too, William realized, as he watched her dance around him.

'Yes, I do indeed. You look terrific, darling, and I promise I'll be at the best party ever in just a few minutes.' He kissed the top of her head. 'Have you been drinking?' He pretended to smell her breath. 'Is that why you're spinning around so much?'

'No, silly,' she giggled adoringly at her daddy.

'Good, now go find Mummy while I leave my briefcase in the study.' He needed to shower before he greeted anyone.

'Hi, Dad. How come you're so late?'

'Hi, Harry. I got caught up at the hospital.' He dumped his stuff and quickly flicked through the post which Beth had stacked neatly on his desk.

'As usual.' The little boy sighed.

'Don't be cheeky.' William was only half listening. 'Your sister says I'm missing the best party ever, so how come you're not in the thick of it?'

'It's OK, I suppose.' Harry was not that easily impressed.

'There you are, I thought you'd never get here.' Beth put her flushed face around the door. 'The place is heaving and you'll never believe what happened to Audrey—'

'Sorry, sorry, I know I'm late.' He came to meet her halfway. 'Who's Audrey? Hey, you look great. New dress?' He kissed her absently and took a mouthful of her champagne.

'Yes.' She too did a twirl, momentarily distracted. 'What do you think? It cost a fortune.'

'Worth every penny.' He looked at her admiringly. She was a good-looking woman and tonight she positively sparkled. Beth liked it when he thought she looked good. He knew it mattered. Sometimes, if she put on a few pounds, it made her look older than him, even though she was two years younger. He remembered how depressed she'd been when a colleague of his had seemed surprised that she was the younger one. 'He's drunk, darling.' William had smiled at her fury. 'Ignore him.'

Looking closely at her now, he saw that she was wearing

more make-up and her hair was different. 'What have you done to yourself?'

'Like it?' She pouted.

'Love it.' He slapped her bottom. 'Keep it up and don't go dipping into the cookie jar,' he said, only half in jest.

She didn't appear to hear him. 'I thought I'd better try to compete with all those young nurses.' She grinned.

'No worries there, my love,' he told her truthfully. 'Now, I need a shower and a drink, in that order. Give me fifteen minutes and I'm at your disposal for the entire evening.'

'OK. Now don't get upset but we're a bit behind with the food. Audrey had an accident.' She followed him up the stairs.

'But it's sorted, right? We do have food?' He searched for his favourite shirt; it was important he looked extra good tonight. 'Have you seen my blue Armani shirt? You did remember to collect it from the laundry?'

'Yes.' She pulled it down from the cupboard in the dressing room. 'There.' She smiled at him. 'And of course we have food, but there was a bit of a panic earlier, I can tell you.'

'So who'd you get?'

'She organized it all, can you believe that? While she was waiting in A&E. Some of her staff. They're working frantically in the kitchen as we speak.'

'Great, well done.'

'Only thing is, we could do with another pair of hands. I'm trying to supervise it all and I really need to be out there.' She thought for a moment. 'I don't suppose you could pull a few strings with any of your corporate caterers? Get someone over, even for the next two hours?'

'Are you mad? It's Friday night.'

'I suppose . . . anyway,' she turned away, 'gotta go. Don't be long.' She disappeared with an animated Harry in hot pursuit. He'd come back to find his parents, impatient as always.

'Actually, I just might be able to help.' William had the most bizarre idea. He wanted to see her again and his wife had just given him an unexpected opportunity. 'I'll make a call or two,' he told Beth, who'd popped her head back round the door. 'Remember, Harry, bed by ten,' he called after the child, who promptly let his pink tongue be seen by everyone except his father.

Twenty minutes later William was immersed in the crowd, glass in hand, feeling very pleased with himself. He'd rung Lily and persuaded her to help them out. She was on her way over. William had a cock as hard as a conker just thinking about his wife and his potential mistress at the same party. And Beth had engineered it really, he convinced himself as soon as a doubt crept in. Besides, he'd scored a few Brownie points there as well. She was very impressed when he told her.

William loved their annual autumn bash. It got the party season off to a good start – even though Christmas was over two months away – and gave them a chance to catch up with friends, some of whom they hadn't seen since the summer holidays. Beth always had the house and gardens looking fantastic and tonight was no exception. She'd had a new lighting system installed outside and there were hundreds of candles in all the windows. It looked magical. William approved.

They mingled effortlessly for an hour, then Beth grabbed some food and they surveyed the crowd. 'Here, try this, it's absolutely delicious.' She smiled as she handed him his plate.

'You know I detest coleslaw.' William wrinkled his nose.

'No onions and it's homemade, you don't often get that with caterers.' Beth smiled at him with her fork halfway to her mouth. 'Anyway, it goes beautifully with that rare beef. It's got a bit of horseradish in it, I think. Try it, you'll like it.'

'Thanks.' He tasted it and she was right. 'That beef is very good, what's that on the outside?' He poked it with his fork.

'A mushroom pâté thing – sort of like beef Wellington without the pastry.' She kissed his cheek. 'That caterer of yours is a genius, by the way. She walked in and had the kitchen organized within minutes. Even brought some stuff with her.'

'Lily's here? Already?'

'Don't look so surprised, you rang her, remember?' his wife teased.

'Sorry,' he backtracked. 'You know all this last-minute stuff always makes me a bit grumpy.' He kissed her cheek. 'I hate us not being prepared.'

'I was prepared. The caterer had an accident, remember?' Beth sounded annoyed at him, the last thing he needed right now. What he needed was to see Lily, who was only metres away, in his kitchen. Earlier in the week she hadn't returned his call and he didn't like it. William was used to being in control, and besides, he'd been feeling particularly horny these last few days.

'Oh, I forgot – or at least didn't have time to tell you – Noel and Triona have split up,' Beth whispered in his ear just as he was about to make his escape. 'Act normal, here she comes.'

'Hello, William, avoiding me as usual.' He saw Triona Ashurst's breasts way before he saw her face. They were coffee-icing smooth, beautifully moulded and made of plastic.

'Hi, Triona, nice to see you. How've you been?'

'Not bad, considering my husband has just left me. I suppose you heard?'

I'd have never married you in the first place, William thought. 'Triona, I'm very sorry to hear that.' He listened – attentively, he thought, considering her monotonous tone – for a minute or two, then glanced over her shoulder at a new arrival.

'She's older than me, can you believe it? A widow with two kids.'

William noticed that Triona was slightly slurring her words. He nodded absently and was frantically trying to work out how to get away. Her next sentence brought him sharply back to the present.

'Beth, darling, what would you do if you discovered William was having an affair?' she asked.

'He hasn't time.' Beth laughed. 'The hospital is his mistress.'

'What about one of his patients?'

'He wouldn't risk it, would you?' She was surveying him with a contented, bordering on complacent smile. It was most unlike her, William thought now; she was the least smug person he knew. He shot her what he hoped was a warning look: there was no way he wanted to aggravate this woman with the mad eyes any further. He'd never liked her, even when she was sober.

'You're a fool if that's what you think.' Triona was leaning towards him. 'William is a very attractive man. He must have women throwing themselves at him every day of the week.'

'Chance would be a fine thing.' William tried to humour her. 'So, Triona, when did all this happen?' He couldn't have cared less but she launched into a rambling tirade and William nodded occasionally and scanned the room every few seconds, hoping to catch a glimpse of Lily.

'Why don't I get you some food?' Beth interrupted as soon as her friend paused for breath.

William sighed with relief. The woman really was a gigantic pain in the butt, he didn't know why his wife was so fond of her.

'See you later.' Beth linked her arm through her friend's and guided her gently towards the buffet in the next room.

William was then forced to be charming to the daughter

of one of their oldest friends as he made his way to the kitchen. Mind you, this time it was no hardship. Isabel Harpur was like a sparkler in a field full of soggy fireworks. She fizzled away and outshone every other woman, even though she wasn't particularly beautiful. It was her youth, William knew at once, and the thought only irritated him further. There was nothing good about getting older, he decided, signalling a passing waiter to refill his glass.

'I saw you looking at my breasts earlier.' Triona was back.

'Hard not to.' William's heart sank. He tapped her nose in a playful gesture and tried to be charming. 'You look lovely, Triona.'

'How lovely?'

'Gorgeous.' He wasn't going to waste much more time on this.

'I'd like to fuck you, William Hammond.'

He glanced around nervously and laughed to show he wasn't taking her seriously.

'You're always so in control, I'd like you to dominate me for a night and give me a good seeing-to.'

William hoped he didn't look as nauseous as he felt. The woman had simply no idea. He'd rather service their fifty-nine-year-old cleaning lady with the moustache.

'How about it, big boy? Wouldn't you like it too?'

'Frankly, no.' He'd had enough. He didn't know which offended him more, the fact that she thought so little of Beth or the fact that she thought so little of him. 'Excuse me, Triona, I see someone I need to talk to.' He turned and almost collided with a young woman wearing a simple black dress and her hair in a pony tail.

'Hello,' she said shyly.

'Lily.' She had caught him off guard, even though he was en route to see her. 'I was just on my way to find you.' He glanced around quickly to check on his wife, then on Triona. It was just the sort of thing that bitch would latch on to in a second.

'Well, here I am.' She grinned up at him.

'And you may just have saved my life,' he teased, trying hard not to appear overexcited at her being here, in his house.

'Actually, you won't believe this, but Audrey and I fill in for each other all the time. She was my replacement when Alison died. She covered for me for two weeks at very short notice so I've been trying to repay her anyway.' She looked around. 'So, how was the food?'

'Hello there.' Beth was back. 'I see you two have met?' She beamed at Lily. 'Of course you know each other already. Hospital parties, I presume?' She was completely relaxed.

'Yes, and . . . through my sister,' Lily explained. 'She was one of his . . . patients.' She smiled at Beth and William hoped she wasn't going to say too much.

'Oh, I'm sorry to hear that. I hope it wasn't serious.' Beth didn't wait for a reply, which was unlike her. 'By the way, the food was divine, I really must get your number.'

'I did nothing, honestly. I'll give you my card, of course,

but I don't want to muscle in on Audrey's territory . . .'

'Nonsense. You arrived at exactly the right moment. And you brought food, I saw it.'

'Just a few bits I always have in my store cupboard. We didn't even need them, Audrey had everything organized.'

'And I must sort out money with you.' William decided to take control at last. 'Perhaps if you leave your card with me?'

'Yes, certainly. And don't worry about money tonight, I'll send you a bill.'

'I wouldn't hear of it,' Beth told her. 'You saved our lives.'

Lily tried to object again, William noticed, but his wife was on a high.

'The least we can do is pay you immediately,' she insisted.

'So, can I get you a glass of champagne to say thanks?' William tried to steer her away.

'No, I'm driving and I never drink when I'm working, but thank you anyway. It seems like a great party. The house is beautiful.'

'Thank you, Lily, it's very nice of you to say so.' Beth was delighted. She turned to her husband. 'William, why don't I look after Lily? My cheque book is in the study. There's Andrew Haslam, darling, he's asked me twice where you were and I think he's about to leave. Now, if you'll come with me, Lily, and don't let me forget your card.' Beth turned away.

'Goodnight.' Lily smiled at him.

'Goodnight and thank you again.' It was not what William wanted to say to her. Damn Beth anyway, she never normally bothered about this sort of thing. He could have persuaded Lily to have one glass and kept her chatting and found out a bit more about what was happening in her life. Still, the last thing he wanted was his wife getting suspicious so he gave in gracefully, but he couldn't shake the vague, uneasy feeling that followed him around afterwards. Having her here, out of the blue – and after he'd been thinking so much about her – made him want her even more than before.

He watched the door until his wife reappeared and was disappointed to see her come back alone.

'Nice girl and her organizational skills are very impressive. Did you know she's catered for the Taoiseach?'

'Darling, I've only met her twice, I think. I just happened to have her number handy when you mentioned our dilemma, that's all.' The last thing William wanted was his wife becoming friendly with his soon-to-be mistress. 'Now, let's dance.' He didn't want to, but he didn't want to talk either. What William really wanted was to rush out the door and see if Lily was still around.

For the first time in years he didn't get his usual buzz from comparing cars and holidays and finding out what the next big thing was, just so he could decide if it was worth getting before everyone else he knew. Much to his annoyance, he found himself comparing all the women here tonight with Lily, who'd looked chic and understated and very sexy with her cute hairstyle.

It was two o'clock before the last of the guests left. Beth was tipsy and he was well on.

'Leave everything, that's what we're paying for,' he commanded as his wife swanned about chatting to the staff.

'Oh, you're so bossy. I like it,' she teased in response to his slight rebuke. 'Speaking of paying, did you fix them all up?'

'I sorted it with Christy.' He indicated the head barman they'd had for years. 'Come on, let's go to bed. Christy'll look after it from here and lock up. He has my keys. He'll drop them back in the morning and I'll go through everything with him then. I gave him a blank cheque the other day to cover all expenses.'

'Great, I approve.' She linked her arm through his. 'You looked gorgeous tonight, William. Everyone commented on it.'

He was relieved that she seemed so relaxed. He'd been afraid she'd guessed something when she spotted him chatting to Lily. Beth was usually razor-sharp.

'Really? Like who?'

'Yes, really.' She reached up and kissed him lightly. 'Tom Arnold said you were getting younger-looking and Scott asked me how much time you spend in the gym.'

William liked being envied. He could feel the stress beginning to leave his neck and shoulders. 'Actually, let's have one for the road. We can bring it upstairs with us.'

'You wild and crazy thing.' Beth laughed as they walked

over to the bar. Christy was there before them and almost had their drinks poured as they arrived.

'Thank you, Christy, that's lovely, but only a half-glass.' She smiled at the slightly bloated man on the other side of the counter. 'I'll have bubbles coming out of my ears,' she giggled. 'Oh and could I have a glass of water as well, please?'

'Certainly. Ice and lemon?'

'Not necessary,' Beth told him. 'It's for when I wake up in the morning. I think I'm going to need it.'

'Thanks.' William accepted the tumbler of Scotch and took a mouthful.

'Pleasure.' Christy was all business.

'Goodnight,' his wife called to no one in particular and the remaining staff responded easily. Everyone liked Beth.

'Oh, and Triona told me I'd better watch myself or I'd have trouble holding on to you.' Beth was giggling again as she took off her clothes in their dressing room. 'Anne Mason was all ears.'

William liked Anne, one of their oldest friends. He played golf with her husband Trevor. 'Well, that new suit I bought in Paris worked wonders so.' William was used to people noticing him, but it never hurt to hear it.

'Or maybe it was the hair?' Beth made a face. William's hairdresser had recently suggested he might consider having some colour put in. He'd made the mistake of asking Beth's opinion and she'd been slagging him about it ever since.

'I have not, repeat *not*, had my hair dyed.' William laughed in spite of himself.

'But you're considering it. I keep catching you running your fingers through it in the morning when you're shaving.' Beth thought it was hilarious. 'I know you're checking for grey.'

'Watch it, woman, or I'll make you pay.' William came up behind her and tapped her bottom with his suit hanger.

'You wouldn't dare.' She turned to face him and he saw that she was wearing a white lace one-piece with a push-up bra as part of it. It had little pearl buttons all down the front and he reached over and pulled her to him, kissing her hard on the mouth. When he let her go her hair was tossed and her lips looked purple. He liked the sudden rush of power he got.

'Watch me.' He grabbed her arm and led her towards the bed in the other room. He sat down first and pulled her to him, in between his legs. Without looking at her he tore open her lacy body and exposed her breasts. He heard a slight gasp, so he reached up and bit her nipples. They were rock hard.

The sex was raw and a new experience for Beth. He suspected that she enjoyed it because he'd never been quite that rough with her before. As for himself, he kept thinking of Triona wanting it so badly and the way Alison had always made him feel so powerful by being submissive, but mostly he enjoyed it because he imagined he was making love to Lily and she was teasing him about

277

forcing her to turn up at his party, just so they could sneak off and have sex in his bed.

'You owe me three hundred and fifty euro by the way.' Beth was smiling broadly when he looked up from pouring himself some very strong coffee next morning.

'Why, did he steal it?' Harry asked, wolfing his Coco Pops.

'Let's just say he damaged something belonging to me.' Beth kissed her son on the head and touched her daughter's hair as she passed.

'Although I'm sure he didn't mean it, did you, darling?' She was holding her cup out.

'Of course not.' He winked at her. Apart from the beginning of a nasty ache at the back of his head he was in great form.

'Did Christy call?' Beth wanted to know.

'Yep, all sorted. They drank a lot of champagne, judging by the bill.' He glanced at the paper on the table.

'Daddy, you say that every year,' Winnie gave out to him.

'Well, this year I mean it. So no Christmas presents for anyone.'

'Not even for your loving wife?' Beth asked him above the howls of protest. 'How about a weekend away? Didn't you say you have to go to Paris in a couple of weeks?' She sidled up to him. 'We could ruin a lot more of my outfits,' she whispered.

William was just about to reply when a thought came to

278

him, so his wife had to make do with a pat on the backside. He mulled it over as he finished his coffee. 'Right, I'm off to shower. Then who's for a walk and a lazy lunch?'

'Me.'

'Not me.'

'Sorry, didn't I say? You've no choice.' He grinned at his children and headed upstairs. As he pottered about in the dressing room he made a decision. He was going to invite Lily to come to Paris with him. She could stay in a different hotel and he'd make it a good one. Maybe even the George V. He'd offer it as a way of cheering her up after all she'd been through. It gave him an excuse to ring her later, although he'd been going to anyway, to thank her for her help last night. He liked the idea of being seen out and about with her. He'd even buy her some clothes – pretty, trendy short skirts and high boots. He resolved to leave her a voice message later in the day once he'd done a bit of research on hotels on the net.

William was so pleased with this idea that he decided to cancel his shower and make a quick visit to the gym first. He'd need to be in good shape for the trip.

29

DAVE AND MARIE

DAVE WAS SEXUALLY FRUSTRATED AND WANKING WASN'T helping. He even tried doing it while watching some serious porn that would have horrified his wife – as far as he knew she'd never even glanced at the magazines he kept under his side of the mattress – and although it had offered some relief it wasn't in the least bit satisfying.

'What's up?' Marie asked over her shoulder as she sat watching *Coronation Street* while he made a lot of noise stacking the dishwasher.

'Nothing.' He clattered a few pots and noticed she looked a bit annoyed. He knew it was her favourite half-hour of the day when the *Street* was on. When it wasn't, she tutted and fidgeted and couldn't get comfortable. That she would even speak to him while there was a row going on in the Rovers suggested she'd really noticed he was off form.

'Sorry, love, I'm just a bit fed up, that's all.' He patted her on the knee. 'Will I make you a cup of tea?'

'D'ya know, I'll maybe have a Bacardi and Coke.'

'Who do you think ye are, Deirdre Barlow?' He indicated the screen. 'Better increase the size of your specs, so.'

She laughed. 'Go on, spoil me.' He shook his head and sauntered towards the kitchen. 'And join me,' she called after him. 'Live dangerously.'

Dave didn't feel like one, but then he thought what the heck. It was so unlike them, they never drank at home. He brought in her drink and a long necked beer for himself and plonked down beside Marie again. They watched in silence. When the soap was over he flicked around but all he could find was some yuppie DIY thing on Channel 4. His wife switched almost immediately back to *The Bill*. Dave had had enough.

'Listen, love, I think I'll go down the local for a pint. Would you mind?' He indicated his bottle. 'This just doesn't taste the same.'

'Sure, go ahead. I'm off to bed soon anyway.' She reached up and kissed him on the cheek. 'See you in the morning, so.'

'Yeah, grand.' He sighed but she didn't seem to notice. Dave wished she'd at least offered to go with him for a few scoops. But he knew she was already thinking that she'd missed a crucial bit of *The Bill* while he'd been flicking channels. Marie hated getting distracted for even a second during the first ten minutes. According to her, it meant you never really caught up with the plot.

The pub was buzzing and Dave joined in a darts match,

which meant he downed beer faster than usual because he was in a round with some serious drinkers. Later he stood by the bar and chatted to his mates. A group of women were laughing uproariously in the corner opposite. Dave watched them and knew that if he was even ten years younger he'd be in like Flynn.

'Hiya.' It was the dark-haired one he'd noticed earlier, all fake tan and costume jewellery.

'OK, you?' He drained his drink and decided he'd better make a move. He shouldn't be driving as it was.

'Great, yeah. D'ya fancy joining us?'

'Not tonight, maybe another time, eh? Gotta go.' He picked up his keys and made for the door.

She was behind him in a second. 'Would you mind givin' me a lift, so?' She indicated her mates. 'They're all pissed and I have to be up for work in the mornin'.'

Dave was about to make an excuse.

'I only live round the corner but you know yerself, can't take chances these days.' She indicated her lime-green strappy sandals. 'Anyway, me feet are killin' me.'

'OK, come on.' What the hell, he thought, at least his conscience would be clear. He'd like someone to give one of his daughters a lift if they were a bit pissed. Still, if they ever got into a car with a stranger he'd murder them. There were a lot of weirdos around, and drunken broads with everything on display like this one were easy prey. Thank God his two had more sense.

'I've seen you in there before, haven't I?' she asked once she'd settled in and given him directions.

'Yeah, possibly. Marie – my, eh, wife,' he said pointedly, 'and I go in there fairly regularly.'

'I only noticed 'cause you're like, very attractive.' She chewed on her gum and looked him up and down.

Dave grinned at her cheeky manner. 'What's a young one like you doin' flatterin' an oulfella like me?' he asked in a fatherly manner. 'I bet half the gougers in there would love to be takin' you home.'

She shrugged. 'They're kids, mostly. I like men who are more sophisticated. And experienced.'

Dave threw back his head and laughed. At least she hadn't said mature.

He'd pulled up where she'd told him, at the edge of a waste patch with trees in front. 'Where to from here?'

'This'll do, I live just over there.' She pointed towards a nearby council estate that even in the darkness Dave could see was littered with debris.

'OK, so. I'd best get home.' He smiled at her. 'See you around some time.' Marie would laugh when he told her about this.

She reached for the door handle and then turned back to him and pulled his mouth down on hers without saying a word. Before he knew what he was doing he found himself kissing her back. Within seconds she'd pulled him over to her seat and was straddling him. She pushed her tits into his face and buried his head in them. Dave decided it was just a drunken snog, but he was vain enough to be flattered so he cupped her tight bum and began stroking her thighs. She whooshed herself up and knelt in front of him, then she deftly unhooked her bra and offered him a mouthful. It was a complete turn-on and as his hands wandered up and down her legs she reached down and unzipped him. With her hands guiding him he quickly discovered she wasn't wearing any knickers and within seconds he'd entered her and she was rocking backwards and forwards. It was all over in less than a minute.

She kissed him once more, smiled coyly and got out of the car. He sank back in the seat and closed his eyes, savouring the release and unable to believe his luck, when he realized he was sitting there, fully exposed. After he'd quickly tidied himself he looked up and she was waving at him over her shoulder as she waddled across the waste ground.

He drove off immediately but once he got home he sat in the car for ages. The initial elation had worn off. 'You stupid cunt.' He banged on the steering wheel. 'What the fuck were you thinking of?' But even going over it in his mind got him hard again and he had to admit it was one of the most exciting things to have happened to him in a while.

Once inside, he poured himself a large Scotch and spent an hour flicking channels in peace. Eventually he calmed down, and decided it had been a very pleasant payment for the lift home. No need to feel guilty, he reassured himself. Still, he resolved not to go near the pub for at least a week – a promise he knew he'd never keep – and spent a restless night dreaming of being arrested for having sex with a minor.

* * *

Next morning he thought about it again while trying to shower with a humdinger of a hangover. It was completely out of character, he justified it to himself. She was a slapper, not his type at all, even for a quick shag. Dave liked to think he had more class than that. So when was the last time a nineteen-year-old – he was guessing – fucked you in the front seat of your car? he asked himself. Grow up, he chided, men half your age would be queuing around the block for it.

About noon he got a text saying thanks for the lift home. At first he couldn't figure out where she'd gotten hold of his number. A casual visit to the pub at lunchtime for a coffee and a few enquiries solved that. She'd been in asking about him, Damien the barman confirmed.

'Yeah, said she wanted you to do a job for her,' he slagged Dave. 'I'd say you'd do a job on her more like.'

'Would ya fuck off, I'm old enough to be her father. What would ya say she was, eighteen, nineteen?'

'Bit older than that, I'd say.' Damien was losing interest. 'Christ, she looked dog rough though, even for you.' He winked.

Dave was relieved. The age thing had bothered him a bit; you never knew these days. Sounded like he'd had a lucky escape, though. He swallowed his coffee. 'Listen, do me a favour. Don't give her any more info.'

The barman raised his eyebrows.

'Just, I, eh, did a job for a mate of hers and she left me

short a few bob. Her brother threatened me when I went lookin'. You know what I mean?'

'Sound as a pound.' Damien went back to the racing pages.

That evening Dave got another text. This time she wanted to know if he fancied meeting her for a jar. She signed it 'Kylie' with two x's after her name.

No, thank you. He pressed delete. Jaysus, he thought, I bet she has a mate called Britney. He was just about to turn off his phone when he got a text from Lily: **Wd u b free 2 mt 4 drink 2nite in CLEARVIEW htl? Bout 8?**

Dave couldn't believe his luck. He'd been convinced she was avoiding him. He got up – casually, he thought, until he realized he'd knocked Marie's crumpet off the arm of the sofa and into her lap. 'Sorry, hon.' He apologized by planting a kiss on her head. 'That was a plumber about a job. OK if I go out for an hour?'

'As if my permission mattered,' said his wife, laughing. Dave headed for the shower pronto.

At exactly ten to eight he was poised – nonchalantly, he hoped – on a bar stool with a good view of the door. He'd gone over it all in his head. At best she would invite him upstairs to a room she'd already booked – although he'd insist on paying; at worst she'd tell him it was over.

As soon as he saw her he knew it wasn't the latter. She looked absolutely amazing in tight black jeans and high boots. She was wearing a fitted top and a long, oversized lacy cardigan. Dave felt sure she wouldn't have gone to all that trouble unless she fancied him. As she waved and walked towards him with her shiny blonde hair and fresh face, Dave wanted to fuck her so badly that he shifted in his seat several times as he tried to appear casual.

'Hello.' He managed to wait until she was almost beside him before jumping up to kiss her on both cheeks.

'How are you, Dave? You're looking very smart,' she greeted him and he felt ten feet tall.

'I'm grand.' He smiled and indicated a quiet table. 'What can I get you to drink? Champagne, maybe?'

'A glass of white wine would be lovely.'

Dave looked around and signalled a waiter with a click of his fingers. He noticed several people glancing in their direction.

'What white wines do you have by the glass?' he asked and then couldn't understand a word the Polish waiter said.

'Chablis?' he asked hopefully and the waiter nodded and disappeared.

'So, tell me, how are you?' he asked as he settled back in his chair to get a better look at her.

'Good, thanks. I was in town for a meeting with my solicitor, and I thought this would be a handy place for us to meet.' She thanked the waiter and took a sip of the wine.

'Great, yeah. I come here all the time, actually.'

'Do you? It's very posh, isn't it? They took my car keys at the entrance and offered to bring it around when I was leaving. How American is that?'

'Well, they, eh, sort of know me here.' Dave shrugged.

'I mentioned that I was meeting you so that might have had something to do with it.'

'I see. Well, I'm impressed.' They chatted for a while and Dave's hopes were dashed again when all she wanted to talk about was a quote for some work she was doing on the salon. Still, he reasoned with himself as he headed for his local an hour and a half later, it was better than nothing. He'd offered to call down and give her a quote, and maybe working closely with her would move things on between them. He'd already decided that he wanted more than an odd night here and there with Lily. As he waited for his pint he fantasized about explaining to Marie that he had to leave, how neither of them had intended it to happen but they'd fallen in love. Dave and Lily, it had a nice ring.

'How'ya?' Kylie interrupted his daydream.

'Oh, hello,' he said as she sidled on to the next barstool.

'Did ye get my texts?'

'Oh yeah, been busy all day. I've just come from a meeting in the Clearview Hotel, actually.'

'Very snazzy.' She eyed him up. 'You look bleedin' great. Smell all right too,' she told him. 'Want to buy me a drink?'

'Actually, I'm only having the one . . . but yes, of course.'

'So am I. Double vodka and Coke, Damien. I'm parched.' She winked at the barman who gave a thumbs-up to Dave.

Christ, Dave thought, Damien was right. She's dog

rough. He didn't want to offend her though, so he made small talk for ages and listened to her innuendos and gave as good as he got, all the while thinking of Lily and how she'd rubbed up against him as they'd prepared to go.

'I'd better head,' he told Kylie as he drained his glass twenty minutes later. 'I'll see you around, yeah.'

'Want to give me a lift home, like last night?' She had unbuttoned her jacket to reveal her huge breasts only partially hidden by a red, shiny top with black lace edging that looked way too tight for her.

Why not, he thought now, deciding that this time they'd go to a quieter spot he knew. He'd quite like to get her on the back seat on all fours, he decided. This time he'd show her who was boss, all in a playful fashion, of course. Dave was not a man to be rough with women.

'Nite, Dave.' The barman's grin was very broad as Dave picked up his keys. Hell, he thought, it's a far cry from walking upstairs in the hotel with Lily the way I imagined, but what the heck, my gearstick is throbbing.

Kylie put her hand on his crotch as soon as she'd closed the car door. 'Where to, big boy?' She grinned, feeling his cock.

'Wait and see.' Dave drove past her estate around the corner to a small wooded area and pulled in facing a wall. It was pitch black.

'Now, you bold girl, you've given me a hard-on and I am going to have to make you pay.' He got out, opened her door and pulled her out, then opened the back door and helped her inside. 'Bend over, you naughty hussie,' he instructed, shoving her black Lycra skirt up around her waist.

'Yes, sir!' She laughed and turned to show him her breasts, now on full view below her T-shirt, which she'd yanked up.

Dave reached over and got on top of her, pulling down her knickers. Suddenly, he felt a sharp pain in his chest. He leaned back and tried to breathe.

'Give it to me, big boy' was the last thing he heard.

30

LILY

FOR SOMEONE WHO'D SPENT MOST OF HER ADULT YEARS plodding along, avoiding decisions and happy to be led, it was a radical departure. I'd never realized there was such a high to be had from taking control. I wondered how many days – weeks even – I'd wasted sitting around watching TV, waiting for Alison to tell me what we were going to do next. Since Charlie had arrived and Sally had moved away, I'd even given up partying the way I used to. My life became one long round of reality shows and Maltesers. I'd taken the term couch potato to a whole new level. Now, I was buzzing. The café had taken shape, in the space of a few weeks. All the hard graft and relentless haggling had kept my mind occupied as well, which had helped me enormously.

It was a beautiful space, I decided as the cleaners buzzed around me, plenty of natural light and much roomier than I'd first imagined. Maureen Stanley had done a great job with the design. There was lots of wood, polished to look like chocolate, and a wonderful granite counter top that

291

resembled broken biscuits. The chairs were so comfortable they made you want to sit and relax, and instead of flowers there were tiny pots of growing herbs on each table and window boxes on the inside low ledges, full of tomatoes and chillies, all thriving – for the moment, at least – and enjoying the south-facing aspect.

But it was the food I was most excited about. Orla, Sally and I had spent hours on the phone over the past few weeks, and emailing recipes or faxing articles from magazines. I was up to my neck in the latest food trends, most of which I was determined to ignore. Orla had come over twice: flying visits, mind you, but her presence had helped me hugely and it was her idea to go for what she called 'home-baking colours' – caramels and creams with splashes of raspberry on the herb pots. She and Maureen got on like a house on fire and Sally was constantly wailing because she couldn't be here.

No drug I'd experimented with had ever given me this kind of buzz. Champagne didn't even come close, I decided as I stood in the middle of the café on the day of the launch – having had only four hours' sleep – and revelled in it all as if I'd built it myself, brick by brick. It was called The Confident Kitchen, a play on the title of the book I'd so much enjoyed. Richard had scoffed at my ingenuity but I'd laughed at his sarcasm. Aunt Milly had suggested Cheeky Charlie's, after the boy who tugged at my heartstrings every time I heard his voice on the phone, especially with the cute Cork accent he was rapidly acquiring. Sally had emailed from Sydney to suggest Serious about Food, which I'd discarded on the basis that she must have been either drunk or stoned or both when she thought of it. The locals had already named it the Con Shop.

'This café is based on being confident about what we serve instead of being dictated to by trends,' I told anyone who asked, and the *Wicklow People* even picked up on it and requested an interview with me. I nearly had a heart attack when they rang, but only after I'd convinced myself it wasn't someone I knew pretending to be a reporter. Sally thought it was all a hoot.

'Morning, chef.' I turned to find Orla beaming in the doorway.

'Oh my God, you made it.' I still couldn't believe she was here.

'Of course I did. Didn't we speak on the phone last night from my mother's?'

'Oh, you know what I mean.' I crossed the floor in double-quick time.

She produced a big bunch of flowers. 'Lilies for Lily.' It was her customary declaration – on even the most piddling occasion – and I loved her for it.

'Idiot!' I hugged her and she smelt of yeast. 'Am I glad you're here,' I told her, grinning from ear to ear. 'Can you believe it? I'm so excited that I'm afraid for what little sanity I have left.' I pinched her and she yelped. 'Are you really here – home, I mean? For good?'

'As long as you'll have me, boss.' Her eyes darted around. 'God, it looks brilliant. Even though it's only two weeks since I've seen it it's changed so much.' She did a little dance. 'And I'm warning you, Sally is saving like mad. She doesn't like the thought of the two of us being in this without her. Jealous bitch,' she said mischievously.

'I meant to email her earlier, just to let her know we're missing her.' I grinned. 'Although we did talk briefly a couple of times yesterday. Anyway, I'll ring her tonight with all the gossip.'

'She'd love that, she's dying to know how it goes. Come on, show me around, quick.' Orla was excited.

'Let's grab a coffee.' I moved over to the machine. 'I want you to try it anyway 'cause I'm no expert. Then I'll give you the grand tour, so you can see all the finishing touches. Should take fifteen seconds, twenty if you need to pee.'

'Listen, babe, I'm impressed already. Even from the outside it looks different from anything else on the street. And you've added loads of little personal touches since last time, I can see that already.' She glanced around. 'I like the signs.'

'Thanks. Maureen found a local artist only last week and he did them for me. I wanted them incorporated into the tiles.'

'*All of our poultry is free-range and local*,' she read. 'Sounds good.'

'*Tell us if you have any food allergy and we'll prepare your meal in a separate area of the kitchen*,' she quoted as I handed her a coffee. 'That could be a lot of trouble,' she warned. 'And it's not really practical.'

'I know, but we can just about do it. I'll show you in a sec. Besides, it's important. I've done my research. Apparently, it rarely happens but it's very reassuring to people, especially those who have children with nut allergies, that sort of thing.'

'I like this one.' She was smiling at a sign that said '*This week's main supplier of fruit and vegetables is . . .*' It was a tile that looked like a picture frame. Underneath there was a photo of a bunch of nuns holding carrots and massive marrows. 'Someone should tell the farmers of Wicklow that they shouldn't expose the general public to their cross-dressing fetishes,' she said with a grin.

'The local nuns are the best farmers for miles around,' I told her. 'Wait till you see their farm shop. I was very excited the day I found them.'

'That is seriously anal,' Orla teased. 'So, show me the rest of the changes then put me to work.'

'I have to bring you over to your new flat after we're done here,' I reminded her. 'Christ, even the mention of the word flat makes me realize how much work I've still to do sorting things out in Dublin.'

'Are you OK? You've a lot on.' She looked worried.

'Yeah, just logistically it's tough at the moment: flat in Dublin, flat and shop here, Charlie in Cork.' I sighed. 'But *your* flat, madam, is gorgeous.' I'd only found it the day before, which was cutting it fine. 'You're going to love it.'

She screamed. It was a jagged sound, like those electric shocks that cartoon characters get. I'd forgotten that one annoying habit of hers. Still, today it seemed perfectly normal so I joined in and we danced around, which is what we were at when Violet and her friend Naomi – new recruit – arrived.

The day was as demanding as a newborn baby after that. Orla settled in quickly, which was great, and she really did seem to love the flat in a converted stable block on the Marlton Road, fifteen minutes' walk from the café. In the afternoon she set to work on the food for the party that evening. I'd made all the breads the night before and left them ready for the ovens. We were doing a variety of seafood from nearby Kilmore Quay in Wexford as well as homemade bangers and mash, and there was a big beef and Guinness casserole simmering on the stove. For dessert a local woman had made the most divine rhubarb crumble. She was to be one of our regular suppliers and offered to call in today with a big jug of her 'proper' custard, brimming with organic eggs and 'cream from grass-fed cows'. We also had a drizzled lemon cake – my speciality – with a tangy icing, to be served warm and runny with home-made vanilla crème anglaise. Orla was impressed with how organized it all was. 'Hardly any need for me.' She grinned and I swatted her with a slotted spoon.

'Get outta here, I just wanted to ease you in.' I laughed and we worked in the comfortable silence of friends who know each other's ways. 'Anyway, as you and Sally keep telling me, I'm not a chef.'

'Only joking, chef.'

'No, I'm a cook, self-taught. From tomorrow you're the boss in the kitchen,' I warned her.

'So, what are you wearing tonight?' Orla asked as she made a tempura batter with ice-cold sparkling mineral water and munched some of the vegetables waiting patiently to be coated.

'I bought an amazing dress. It's sort of, I dunno, all colours really.'

'You, in a dress?'

'Yeah, gas, isn't it? Who'd have thought it, eh? Still, you can take the girl out of the tomboy but you can't—'

'You look great at the moment, actually. I noticed it the minute I arrived.' She was watching me. 'I expected you to be . . .'

'In tatters?'

'I was going to say in mourning . . . I know,' she held up her hand as I was about to interject, 'you are still in mourning but, well, you've changed these last few weeks. Last time I was over you were, I dunno, haunted-looking but now you're blooming and I'm delighted. I know how difficult it's been.'

'Yeah.' I felt the memories creep up my back. 'But having Charlie's kept me going,' I told her. 'He'll be moving up any day, as soon as I find a house. I can't wait. And having this,' I looked around with delight, 'has been my saviour, actually.' I smiled at my old friend. 'All the hard work's meant I'd no time to think. Now, well, it's a dream come true.' As I said it I felt a wave of guilt wash over me as I remembered that it had taken my sister's death to fulfil this particular dream.

'I'm sorry I wasn't around much at the time.' Orla

picked at her bottom lip with her teeth. 'What with Mum ill and the job and everything . . .'

'I know.' I went over and hugged her. 'Your phone calls helped – a lot – and you came when I really needed you. Having you here for the funeral saved my life.' I shrugged. 'It was just bad luck that my two closest friends were living out of the country at the time. But even the few short trips you made during the planning stage here helped me loads.'

'By the way, Sally says I'm to make you talk to me.'

'About what?' I was wary.

'She wouldn't say. But she said you'd know.'

'Don't mind her, she's barking.'

'She is. Still, losing Ali like that . . .' Her voice trailed off.

'That's one of the hardest things. No time to say all you should have said in the past to someone you love, and no future to make up for lost opportunities . . .' It was out before I realized it.

'Yeah . . . I can imagine,' she said quietly. 'And Lily, I won't put any pressure on but you know where I am . . .'

'Yes, right here in my kitchen.' I couldn't help smiling.

'Or in my new flat a few minutes down the road.' She came over and danced me round the room again and we laughed about it all.

As we worked in comfortable silence I thought more about what she'd said. Actually, there wasn't that much to tell her. Progress was slow. I'd had a message from William inviting me to Paris for the weekend. I'd no idea what that was about. Judging by his voice, he was on the weirdest master-of-the-universe trip at the time. There was a missed call from him as well. I was astounded by his cheek. Just a day or two after I'd met his wife he was casually inviting me to Paris to 'savour the culinary delights of the most romantic city in the world', according to his message. Yeah, right, mister.

Dave was a bit of a mystery at the moment. After our meeting in the hotel when he'd practically thrown himself on top of me, I hadn't heard any more from him. He was supposed to come down to look at the shop conversion and even though I'd left a few voice messages and sent him a text, he'd never responded. Maybe he was sulking, I thought, which was a bit uncharitable of me. Still, it was odd. He'd been all over me like a rash last time I saw him.

James sent me a text saying simply **I've told Tamsin about us**. That had made me very uneasy for a while, but then I realized there was no 'us'. He was referring to him and Alison, and really, at the end of the day, it had nothing to do with me. I was a bit surprised not to have heard anything further, but then I'd been too busy to give it much thought.

Richard was my only success story in that department to date, after the near-disaster that night in the flat. He'd called the next morning, all fidgety and with darting eyes. I was very businesslike and told him I valued the tenuous friendship I believed we had struck up – which was true. Then I threw myself on his mercy and asked for his help. He was as generous as I'd first found him to be and, as a large portion of my happy-ever-after fantasy had deflated once I knew he couldn't have been Charlie's father, this seemed to work. So we decided – without talking about it – to become mates. This mostly involved him helping me sort out the café and me buying him the occasional pint in order to pick his brains even further. So far so good.

Later that afternoon I went all out and got my hair blow-dried and Violet did my make-up. It was so late by then that I threw on my dress and went to check on all the last-minute details downstairs.

The place was magical in the half-dark of a November afternoon. The darkness was something else I was looking forward to in the country. It was solid, no street lamps or car lights to break up the inkiness once you got off the main roads.

I adjusted the wall lights several times and lit the candles. It looked perfect: in fact it would have been, if only my sister had been there to share it all. I had a lump the size of a gobstopper in my throat as I thought how proud she would have been, so I walked outside quickly in my flimsy dress and never felt the bite of the wind as I surveyed my kingdom from the opposite side of the road. Crossing back again I was bathed in a shaft of pale pink light that seemed to fill the entire street during the blue hour of that particular mid-winter afternoon.

'Alison?' I heard the voice but didn't immediately turn around. In Dublin I was used to people confusing us, but not here. Besides, the details of the accident were well known and now I found my heart thumping when I realized that someone still thought she was alive.

'Ali, is that you?' The voice was closer now, and softer, and I thought I detected a slight Australian twang.

'No.' I hadn't a clue what to say next. 'Actually I'm—'

'Oh sorry, I could have sworn you were Al—' He was staring, as if unsure. 'Then you must be Lily?' His smile was lopsided and I noticed he was tall, and his face was open and friendly. 'Well, she wasn't lying when she said you were very alike.' He laughed. 'You're the spit of her.'

'Yes, hello.' I was thrown.

'I'm Daniel Williams, a friend of Alison's.' He held out his hand and something happened when he touched me. My stomach went plop, for a start.

'Bloody hell, I knew you were twins, but you're identical. I'm not sure I could tell you two apart.' He searched my face.

Stop looking at me like that, I wanted to say. It's unnerving.

'I don't suppose she's mentioned me?' he asked when it was clear I wasn't saying anything.

'Eh, no, she didn't actually.' Oh God, not another man from her past was my next thought.

'That's OK, I wasn't expecting that she had. Don't look so worried. Is she around, by any chance?' He waited, looking up and down at the building.

'No, eh, I . . .'

'It's just we have a date.' He grinned. I noticed his teeth were white and even. He was dressed casually and he carried a leather satchel on his shoulder. Not your typical Irishman.

'A date? When?' This had to be some kind of joke.

'Tonight at seven.' He laughed at the look on my face.

31

LILY

I WAS LOST FOR WORDS, MOST UNUSUAL FOR ME, AND HE appeared to be waiting for an answer, so we simply looked at each other for what seemed like ages.

'What is it?' he said eventually. 'You're giving me an awfully funny look and it's making me nervous.'

'I, eh . . . I'm sorry, would you like to come upstairs for a moment?'

'Sure, to the flat? She told me about it.' He glanced around again. 'Where's the salon? I thought it was part of the same building.' He seemed confused. 'It's just, I used to know this area very well. I was born in Wicklow, Mum lives just a few miles out the coast road.'

Thankfully, I had keys in my hand so I was able to lead him up the stairs without having to say anything.

'Please, sit down. Sorry it's all a bit of a mess.' It was the understatement of the year.

'It's fine.' He was watching me, waiting for me to tell him what was going on. I noticed him properly then for the first time. He was a big man, big as in broad, not fat.

His skin was olive and he seemed charged with energy. I wanted to touch him and grab some of it for myself, because all of a sudden the adrenalin that had kept me going all day evaporated.

'The salon isn't open any longer.' I wasn't sure where to start. 'It's now a café, actually, and we're about to have our launch in' – I glanced at my phone – 'less than an hour.'

'I see. Well, that's a change.' He smiled at me in an encouraging way and waited.

'Eh, Damien, this is—' I felt like I was going to throw up all over my new dress.

'Daniel,' he corrected me with a grin. 'But I've been called worse.' My stomach flipped again. 'Is something wrong? You look awfully pale.'

'Yes, I'm afraid it is.' I took a deep breath. 'I'm sorry, there's no easy way to tell you this but my . . . Alison . . . She died a few months ago.' I saw his body stiffen, so I looked away, just to give him a moment.

'You're joking?' he said quietly and all I could do was shake my head. 'How? Where?'

I told him the details and he just kept nodding. I wasn't even sure he was taking it in.

'Would you like a drink? Brandy maybe, or coffee?' I got up.

'No, thank you.' He still looked confused.

'Are you OK?'

He nodded. 'Yes, I'm fine. Sorry.' He seemed to snap out of it. 'It's just been a bit of a shock, that's all. I lost my father recently as well, and that was sudden too. Heart attack.'

'I'm really sorry, this must be awful for you.' After a few seconds, when he didn't say anything else, I went on. 'I hope you don't mind me asking, but how could you have been meeting her here, tonight?'

'We arranged it a year ago,' he told me. 'Ah, it was a joke really, I suppose.'

'I don't understand?'

'No, you couldn't,' he said quickly. 'This must be a shock for you, too, meeting me like this.'

'How well did you know her?'

'Not well at all, really. Where do I start?' He scratched his head. 'I met her in London last year. I'd been living in Sydney for a few years and was on my way home, via practically every capital city in the world.' He laughed but it seemed forced. 'She was in London at some health and beauty thing . . . in Earl's Court.'

'Yes,' I remembered.

'She, eh . . . We hit it off, spent a couple of evenings together, talked a lot. I really liked her and I think she felt the same way. She told me that she had a lot of things going on in her life that she needed to sort out.' He paused, as if remembering too. 'I was in a relationship back home . . . in Sydney, I mean. I had sort of decided on the trip that I didn't really want to settle down . . . or at least that the relationship wasn't going anywhere . . . so I laughingly suggested that we meet up again when we'd both sorted out our lives. She seemed really taken with the idea.' He smiled. 'She'd seen some old black-and-white movie, apparently.'

'*An Affair to Remember*.' I bit my lip and smiled at him. 'It was one of our favourites.'

He nodded absently. 'Some broad with broken legs, I think.'

'Paralysed, actually,' I told him and we both laughed, to ease the tension, I suspected. I liked his smile and there was something about the way he looked at me, as if he was really taking it all in. It was disconcerting.

'Right. So, we agreed to meet in exactly one year – today – in Wicklow, to see if we'd both sorted out our lives. So here I am.' He shrugged.

'It was six months in the movie,' I told him. 'And what a stupid conversation to be having after the shock you've just had.' I tried to pull myself together. 'Are you sure you're OK?'

'Yeah, I'm fine. We weren't an item or anything . . . It was just a bit of fun, really.' He seemed miles away for a moment or two and then he smiled that smile at me again. 'She was quite a girl, though. A looker, and a nice person as well.'

'Yes, she was.' I bit the inside of my cheek.

'You're the image of her.'

'I'll take that as a compliment.' I tried to grin and he seemed to relax a bit. 'Christ, I've just realized!' I nearly had a heart attack. 'The café . . . downstairs. We're opening . . . launching . . . whatever you call it, in less than half an hour.' I jumped up. 'I'm really sorry but I have to—'

'Go, please.' He got up with me.

306

'Will you be OK? You can stay here as long as you like, it's just . . . oh God, Orla's going to kill me.'

'Can I do anything to help?'

'No, not at all.' I grabbed my keys. 'Unless you'd like to come?'

'Oh no, thanks. Anyway, I should be—'

'Why? You've nothing better to do now . . .' I winced at my lack of cop on. 'Sorry, that came out all wrong.' I was mortified. 'It's just that it would give us a chance to chat a bit more, later on.'

He seemed to come to a decision then. 'Well, if you're sure, that'd be great. But put me to work, please?'

'Terrific.' Neither of us knew what to say then.

'Are you certain you're up to it?' I felt terribly responsible for him all of a sudden.

'Yes.'

'OK then, come on, or we'll be skinned alive.'

I needed a drink and a soluble headache tablet, preferably in the same glass, I thought as soon as I was downstairs. I knew that neither was a possibility until I'd finished a few bits and pieces.

'Hell, Lily, where've you been?' Orla pounced. 'I need you to taste something in the kitchen, I think it's too salty.'

'OK, let's go.' I sprang into action.

'Give me something to do,' Daniel Williams reminded me.

'Chairs need to be moved . . . and that corner needs to be swept, oh, and those boxes need to go to the back room.' I indicated over my shoulder, heart pounding as panic set in. I noticed Orla looking at him.

'Orla, this is Daniel Williams. He's . . . was . . . a friend of Alison's.' I smiled at him. 'He's from Sydney,' I said, as if that explained everything.

'Blainroe, actually, three miles out the road.' He held out his hand.

'Hi.' Orla sounded as panicky as I felt. 'I used to live in Sydney. You'll be sorry you came, by the way,' she told him as they shook hands.

Within an hour the place was hopping. Most of the invited locals had turned up, which pleased me, even though I knew they were only having a nose around. My friends and family were a paltry lot. Milly had cancelled at the last minute, which left me feeling even more like an orphan. I wanted to see Charlie so badly and I needed Milly's approval too. Aunt Rose had come though, and she was trying hard not to be impressed.

Brian Daly arrived bang on time with his brother Kevin, who was 'a bit of all right', according to Violet, after she told me that every single Wicklow woman had casually enquired who he was and if he was available.

'You look familiar,' I said hesitantly as soon as we were introduced. 'Have we met somewhere?'

Orla, who had magically appeared from nowhere, gave me a look that said, 'you wish'.

'No, I wouldn't have forgotten.' His grin said he knew it was the worst cliché in the world and didn't care. He had the most incredible purply-blue eyes and hair that looked as if it had been buffed up with black polish. 'A looker', as Daniel had described Ali.

'I would.' I knew I was trying a bit too hard to be witty. 'I have a terrible memory.'

'Can't have everything, I guess,' he retorted just a little too smoothly, which put me off slightly. I didn't know whether I fancied him or wanted to slap him, but my chef clearly approved.

'Hi, I'm Orla Parker. I work with Lily, just moved back from the UK.' She grinned. 'Before that I was in Sydney.' I wanted to tell her she was gushing.

'Well, Orla Parker, your mother shouldn't let you out in public.' He wiped a speck of flour off her nose.

'What is it?' She was horrified.

'Nothing green and slimy, don't worry.' He winked at me, seemingly enjoying the attention. 'That's gross,' I gave him a withering look. There was something about him, I decided then. He was completely over the top but in a very funny way. I knew I could fall for him big-time if I wasn't careful. My father would have hated him, that's for sure.

His brother looked a bit uncomfortable.

'Brian, have you met Orla?' I enquired, practically shoving them together. 'And let me get you a drink.'

'No, no, we're not staying. I just popped in to wish you all the best.' He produced a small box from his pocket. 'It's from the angel shop.' He grimaced. 'The girls in the office seemed to think it was appropriate. It's for luck in a new venture apparently.'

'Well, bro, you're becoming a noughties man, that's all I can say. I can't imagine a lawyer in an angel shop. Where is it anyway, Paradise Road?'

It wasn't remotely funny but Orla laughed like a hyena and eased back into a threesome with the brothers as I turned to greet some new arrivals. Kevin Daly could easily spell trouble for me, I decided.

Richard and Daisy had arrived just as I'd finished speaking, for which I was truly thankful. I hadn't intended saying anything at all, it's not my style, but people insisted and eventually I caved in and mumbled a few sentences that I'd half rehearsed just in case. Being in the spotlight didn't come easily to me. I felt hot and sticky, whereas Ali would have glowed. I was missing her all over again that night, I realized as I listened to the applause. Under normal circumstances we'd have headed home to discuss every aspect of the evening over tea and toasted cheese sandwiches, or hot crumpets if I was feeling energetic enough to whip up a quick batter. I was happier than I'd been in ages, but still it felt like a little bit of me was missing, which of course it was. I had so much to tell her, that was the problem. And I always would have.

'Congratulations, the place looks amazing.' Richard leaned over to kiss me. We were both awkward so he ended up brushing my ear with his lips.

'Yes, well done.' Daisy smiled.

Kevin was over in an instant. I kind of liked the way he stood so close to me; it helped fill the void. 'Kevin Daly.' He shook hands with Richard but his eyes were on Daisy.

Within seconds she was lapping up the attention.

'Let me get you both a drink,' I said, smiling, needing to escape.

'I'll come with you,' Richard offered, but got side-tracked by two admiring yummy mummies. Kevin and Daisy didn't seem to notice either of us go.

'Can I do anything to help?' Daniel Williams appeared from nowhere.

'No, I just needed an excuse to catch my breath,' I told him. 'Do you think it's going OK?' I'd no idea why, but his opinion was important.

'Yes, I do. Everyone's talking about the food.'

'Really?'

'Really. Are you happy with the turnout?' He glanced around as he sipped his drink.

'Yes, I think I am. I'm very excited.'

'Good. You should be. And proud.' That look was there again. 'From what you told me earlier, it's been quite a year.'

'It has. Thank God my speech is over, at least.' I laugh-ingly explained that I'd been pushed into it. 'And thank you so much. I saw you clapping very enthusiastically at one point.'

'Pleasure.' He seemed quietly pleased.

'Lily, you look great by the way.' Richard flicked my hair as he passed. 'Very sophisticated and—'

'Not like me at all,' I interrupted, feeling the heat spread down my throat.

'I was going to say . . . and very like your sister,' he said gently, then went to answer Daisy's call.

'You must miss her a lot?' Daniel looked cautious, as if he was afraid of upsetting me.

'I do, yes. She was a special person anyway, as you said earlier, but on nights like this . . .' I looked around and Kevin Daly winked at me. 'Tonight it feels like the hole in my heart is massive.' I was staring but not really seeing him.

He reached out and pulled me close. It was an oddly intimate gesture and I didn't want to move. I felt safe with him, although my heart clearly didn't. It was bashing around again. I sensed Daniel was about to say something just as the door opened and Aunt Milly flung herself inside. When she saw the party in full swing she beamed.

'How did you get here?' I broke away and hugged her, still with tears in my eyes. She smelt of laundry.

'Don't ask. There is no easy way to get from Cork to Wicklow by public transport,' she told me, her eyes shining. 'But I made it.'

'This means so much to me.' A weight was lifted as I took her hand and introduced her to everyone. Daniel got her a drink and a plate of beef in Guinness, which she pronounced 'just like good, old-fashioned stew used to taste'. I was delighted.

'I'd hoped to bring Charlie,' she said, matter-of-factly, 'but he didn't want to leave his friends.'

'That's OK.' Selfishly I hoped he wasn't having too much fun without me in Cork. 'I miss him a lot more than I thought I would, it's just incredible,' I told her, half sad, half in awe.

'I know, love. Anyway, here's your present instead.' She pointed to where Orla was pushing a big square box out from the kitchen. It was enormous, covered in bright red wrapping paper.

'It's too heavy to lift,' Orla apologized.

'What is it, a dishwasher?' I said, laughing. Aunt Milly had told me I needed one last time she'd been up, after we were left with a shedload of pots and pans one night following a marathon cooking session.

'Looks like it,' Daniel said smiling as he moved to help Orla push it towards me. By now everyone had stopped talking and people were straining to see.

'Christ, it's wriggling.' I nearly jumped out of my skin, then looked horrified. 'It's a dog, isn't it?' I wasn't sure I was ready for this.

'Don't be silly, the ISPCA would have you up on charges.' Orla laughed.

I started to tear away the paper, a bit gingerly at first. Then all of a sudden the whole thing burst open and I panicked and screamed, almost knocking a drink out of someone's hand.

'It's me, Charlie!' said a small but very loud voice unnecessarily.

'*Charlie!*' I screamed even louder. 'Oh my God, how did you get in there? You could have suffocated.'

'Don't be so melodramatic.' Orla laughed. 'Your aunt and I planned it between us. He only went in ten seconds ago in the kitchen and we had holes in the sides of the box, look.'

'I climbed in the box myself,' Charlie said helpfully, smiling shyly at me. 'And I saw the choo–choo.'

'You came on the train.' I grabbed him and hugged him to death. 'Thank you so much,' I said to my aunt. 'You've no idea how much this all means to me.'

'This is Charlie, everyone.' I showed him off. 'My sister Alison's little boy . . . and mine too.' I kissed him and he struggled to get away. I glanced quickly at Daniel, wondering if he knew, but he smiled and nodded at me.

'Don't cry, love.' My aunt hugged me again.

'I'd give anything for her to be here.' I blew my nose for the tenth time.

'I know you would.'

'Still, at least I have him.' I nodded to where Charlie was, jumping in and out of the box while everyone clapped.

'He didn't want to leave Squirt,' my aunt told us.

'Squirt eats dandelions.' Charlie was back and crawling around on all fours. 'He looks like this.' He weaved about on the floor. 'He has a shell, it's his house.' He patted his back.

'Squirt?' I didn't like the sound of him.

'His pet tortoise,' Aunt Milly said apologetically.

'*Finding Nemo*,' Daniel said with confidence.

'Exactly – not that I'd know – but he and Thomas agonized about it for hours.' Aunt Milly smiled at him, trying to win his support, I suspected. 'I hope you don't mind, dear. He wanted it so badly. Apparently Alison had

314

promised him one and the Exotic Pet Centre in Douglas gave us a great discount . . .'

'They're not cheap . . . but great for a little boy,' Daniel added encouragingly.

'How much is she paying you?' I laughed, sensing they were ganging up on me.

'Did you get a vivarium?' he asked Milly after giving me a knowing wink.

'Oh yes, and a heated pad and two lamps.' Since when had my aunt become the local reptile expert, I wondered.

'I'll pay you for it.' I gave in. 'I am so happy, this has made my night.' I hugged her. 'How on earth did you manage to get it all organized?'

'I had a bit of help.' Now it was her turn to wink at me. 'This is all fantastic, love. I want to see everything.'

'My God, where are you staying?' I just remembered I'd no spare bed in the flat upstairs.

'I booked a B&B just down the road, walking distance. The lady knew all about you.' Milly was clearly impressed. 'I didn't want to ask you for names. It would have ruined the surprise.'

'You're amazing.' I was so glad to have her in my life.

'And I brought you up some of my mother's old recipe books.' She looked really pleased with herself.

'I can see you two are getting all geared up to talk shop.' Daniel smiled. 'I should go. Nice to meet you.' He kissed Aunt Milly on the cheek, then turned to me. 'I had a good time. Totally unexpected, but just what I needed.'

'Are you sure you're OK?' I was flustered. Hell, I'd just

told him his date had died and then abandoned him in a room full of strangers.

'Yes, I am, honestly. I'll drop in and see you – tomorrow or the next day, when things have calmed down a bit.'

'Yes, please do.' We shook hands awkwardly and then he leaned in and kissed my cheek and it tingled. I had a sudden urge to turn slightly and kiss him back.

'She would have been very proud . . . of you both.' He fluffed Charlie's hair but the child had his face in a piece of lemon cake and never even noticed.

'Don't forget to call in,' I told him.

'I won't,' he promised and disappeared as quickly as he'd arrived.

'I'm just glad this place isn't any competition for me.' Richard was back. 'You and your aunt, you're a formidable pair.' He drained his glass. 'I'd better find Daisy. I promised her we'd get back early.'

'Thanks, you helped me a lot,' I told him, feeling very confused about the evening. First Daniel, then Charlie appearing, the speeches, everything. I wanted to talk to Richard, ask him what he really thought, but he was here with his girlfriend.

'Hey.' Daisy appeared, as if I needed reminding.

'I was just coming to find you. Ready to go?'

'Sure.' Daisy reached over and almost kissed me. 'Thanks for inviting us. Sorry we're rushing. Wedding plans.' Her eyes danced.

'Oh?' I hoped it was bright and breezy.

316

'Yes, we've finally set a date. They had a cancellation at Kinnity Castle. Somebody died apparently,' she said without a trace of sympathy. 'So, December the thirty-first it is.'

'This year?' I looked at Richard. Somehow I'd felt he'd never get round to it.

'Yep, provided I can find someone who's very friendly with Vera Wang,' she giggled. I'd no idea what she was talking about.

'Dress,' she said helpfully, noticing my raised eyebrow.

'I'd no idea either,' Richard told me. 'Now, mention Elizabeth David to one of us . . .' He looked at me expectantly.

'No idea,' I joked.

'Is she like, one of those Delia types?' Daisy was losing the will to live, I could tell. 'Anyway, let's go, big boy.'

Richard coughed. 'Pet names, don't you just love 'em,' he apologized.

'More than life itself.' I grinned at him.

'Anyway, hope you can come,' Daisy said generously, while Richard stood there wishing she wasn't saying it, I suspected. 'I can't wait to hook this guy.' She blew him a kiss. 'He's quite a catch.'

'Lucky you,' I said and I think I meant it.

32

LILY

WHEN THE REMAINING HANGERS-ON HAD FINALLY legged it Orla and I sat down for a last-minute run-through. At least that was the intention. There was some wine open so we poured ourselves a generous glass each and settled at one of the tables that faced the main street. Within minutes a drunk was trying to get in to order a kebab. Reluctantly I pulled down the blinds and turned up the dimmer on the lamps.

'So, are you happy?' Orla wanted to know.

'Yes, I think so. As happy as I can be.' I smiled, knowing she'd understand. 'I'm exhausted, though,' I told her. 'All those nerves finally caught up with me.'

'You sure hide it well.' Orla laughed. 'I've never seen anyone look so relaxed.'

'It's called internalizing.'

'Yes, you do that a lot.'

'You know, if Alison had been here she'd have organized everything and I would have just chilled. This is really the first thing I've ever had to do on my own.'

Orla reached out and rubbed my leg. 'Well, I know it's probably not the right thing to say but I think you've blossomed. You wouldn't have had the courage to do this before, I bet.'

'Or the money . . .'

'Yes, you never did tell me that story.' Orla sipped her wine. 'Not that I'm prying or anything.'

'I know.' But I knew she was curious. 'It's complicated and I will tell you, but not tonight.' I raised my glass. 'Let's get tomorrow over with first.'

'Cheers,' she clinked, 'and well done. I think it was a huge success. You got a great turnout and there were even a few cute guys.' She grinned at me. 'Top of the pile was Kevin Daly.' She fanned herself. 'I'm coming over all warm just thinking about him. He fancied you, though. I saw him watching you a few times.'

'No comment.' I grinned, but I was pleased.

'OK, I get the message. Now, what do we need to do?' Orla was all business.

Within half an hour we had it sorted. We finished our drinks and I saw her to the door.

'Your aunt left early,' she remarked.

'Yes, Charlie was wrecked. I wanted to keep him with me but because of the four a.m. start we decided it was better if he stayed with her tonight in the B&B. It's a farmhouse, apparently, and he's all excited about feeding the chickens in the morning. Wasn't it great of Aunt Milly to come, though? She's getting on and it can't have been an easy journey with a three-year-old in tow. I told her to have a lie-in in the morning but I suspect she'll be over first thing.' I wagged my finger at Orla. 'Just watch yourself. She'll be in that kitchen giving instructions, I can tell.'

'I liked her.'

'Isn't she a dote? She's a great cook too, always was.'

'How long will Charlie stay with her?'

It was the question I asked myself every day. It was getting harder to be without him.

'I don't know, we agreed to think about it again once the café was up and running. I really miss him, though. Imagine,' I laughed, 'me, the least maternal person you've ever met, slobbering over a three-year-old? I nearly choked when I saw him in that box.'

'He's gorgeous, sure you couldn't not fall in love with him. Those eyes.' Orla rolled her own. 'I was so happy to be part of tonight, Lily, it feels like a turning point for all of us.'

'Thanks for everything.' I gave her a hug. 'I'm glad you're here too.'

'Well, gotta go.' She stood up. 'Early start and the boss is a cow.' She made a face and we hugged again.

I thrashed around in bed that night, my dreams a major blockbuster starring Alison, Charlie, James and his wife, Daniel, Richard and Daisy, William, Dave and my father. I was exhausted and it took a very strong power shower to revive me before dawn. It was blue-black outside when I was ready to go downstairs.

I dressed carefully in a long grey linen pinafore with a

320

white T-shirt underneath. I'd bought a couple of things specially. It was important to create the right image, I'd decided, so I tied my hair back in a plait and put on a little make-up. It felt exactly like it used to all those years ago when I'd secretly tried on Alison's clothes and pretended to be her.

Even though it was still the middle of the night as far as I was concerned, Orla and Violet were wasp-like as they buzzed about the place. I slotted in easily and even Aunt Milly, who arrived shortly afterwards, didn't put us out too much. I was surprised to see her so early.

'Where's Charlie?' I asked, disappointed. 'Still snoring after all the excitement?'

'Don't be ridiculous, he's been up for hours.' My aunt smiled. 'Couldn't wait to see the moo cows. He refused to come with me, even the promise of a brownie couldn't shift him.' She took off her coat. 'Hazel, the owner of the B&B, insisted I leave him with her. She's got a young 'un of her own, anyway. Said it would give her a good excuse to drop in later for a coffee. Now, where do you want me?' she asked.

'Are you sure he'll be OK?' I wasn't entirely convinced.

'Yes, I'm sure, love. Don't worry. I left her the number here, just in case. He's going to help feed all the animals. Can you think of anything nicer for a three-year-old boy?'

'No, I suppose not,' I said reluctantly.

Soon she'd busied herself polishing mirrors and adjusting bits and pieces and it was lovely to have her around. She was content in silence, too, which I liked.

321

At eight o'clock I turned over the sign for the first time and declared the place open, without breaking a bottle. Once again I walked outside to look in. It was a picture I never tired of. In the early grey winter light with only the odd streak of pink in the sky, most of the locals were still snoozing, and I liked the fact that my little haven was the only warmth in an otherwise chilly-looking street. It was a funny old town, a curious mixture of old-fashioned drapers' shops side by side with mobile phone cubby holes and trendy pubs. I wished there wasn't as much litter though, I thought as I picked up a chip bag, and made a mental note to ring the county council and complain about the lack of bins up this end of the street.

'Do you do takeaway coffee?' A voice behind took me by surprise.

'Yes, of course.' I must have looked startled.

'Sorry, I didn't mean to frighten you.' The young woman in the business suit smiled. 'It's great you're open early. No one in this town moves before nine thirty. They still haven't copped on to the fact that most of the population commute to Dublin and leave at the crack of dawn. You have to go through Bray to get a coffee – and no one in their right mind does – except for one trucker pit stop near Ashford.' She raised her eyes. 'And the coffee there is . . . well, let's just say it's an acquired taste.'

I beamed at her. She couldn't have known it, but she'd said exactly the right thing.

She ordered coffee like an American, and then started texting while I got out the paper cups.

'I don't suppose you'd consider stocking soya milk?' she asked without looking up. 'I have an allergy to dairy and I'm going to suffer for this one all day.' She indicated the milk I was just about to pour into the jug for steaming.

'We already do.' I reached for a carton. 'Is this one OK? It's organic.' I made a mental note to make sure it was on the board so that customers knew they had a choice. 'We also have rice milk if you'd prefer?'

She was completely taken aback and I was ridiculously pleased. 'Jesus, the locals are going to hate you.' She stopped mid-text. 'I've been asking them in Romano's to do that for months. I'd given up trying. Soya's fine.' She indicated the carton.

'I'm glad we can help.'

'I'm going to be your best customer.' She looked around. 'Actually, can I book now for lunch for two on Saturday? About twelve thirty? I'd better introduce my husband to this place fast.'

'Certainly. And please, do tell us if there's anything we're not doing.' I was on a roll. 'I promise we'll act on it if we can, and if we can't I'll tell you why.'

'Better and better.' She beamed at me.

'There you go.' I handed over the coffee. 'Now, as you're our first customer, can I offer you a muffin on the house?'

'I'd better not, I'm—'

'They're still warm, just out of the oven, and we've raspberry or white chocolate?'

'Go on then.'

323

'I'll tell you what, try one of each and let me know what you think. They're actually mini muffins, hardly a calorie in sight.'

'Thanks very much. I hope you get lots of customers.'

'Well, you can thank me by spreading the word.'

The morning passed in a flash. We had quite a few customers and Aunt Milly proved a great self-appointed front-of-house person.

'Mrs Pearson doesn't get out much with her arthritis,' she told me as she arranged a plate with two warm sultana scones and a little dish of homemade strawberry jam.

'Who's she?' I asked.

'Table eight.' She was busy doing butter curls.

'Do you know her?' I wasn't even aware we had a table eight.

'No, but I knew what was wrong the minute she walked in. Poor love, her hands are all swollen.'

'You're amazing.' I'd never have picked that up in a million years.

'We should be serving fresh juices, do her the power of good.' She bustled about.

'I purposely decided not to. I don't want to get too trendy,' I replied, considering what she'd said.

'Well, I think you should try a few – especially the green juices, using all fresh ingredients. People are really copping on to the health benefits associated with spinach, for instance.'

'How would you know?' I grinned. 'The only thing you drink is Winter's Tale Sherry or Barry's Tea.'

'We have books in Cork, you know.' She gave me one of her withering looks. 'I'll send you something in the post.'

'Yes, ma'am!' I saluted. The woman was a marvel.

We weren't as rushed off our feet at lunchtime as I'd hoped after our busy morning, but all the plates seemed to be coming back empty. One man even asked for the recipe for our casserole – not a local, I decided.

Charlie didn't appear till almost two o'clock and he couldn't stop talking, words I didn't even know he knew. Hazel Sinclair declared him to be the brightest child she'd come across in a long time and Milly and I turned pink with pleasure. He'd been milking cows, apparently, so he had a white, frothy moustache and went around trying to get milk from the legs of the chairs, which had all the customers in stitches.

Aunt Milly cleaned him up and we left to catch the Cork train less than an hour later. She was hugged to death and made to promise to come back soon. I, on the other hand, was practically flung out of the place. 'If you rub down that counter once more you're going to change the colour of the granite,' Violet said, only half joking.

'Thanks for covering for me,' I told them, knowing I was abandoning ship. It was messy, but the only way to get a direct train to Cork was from Hueston station in Dublin, and the hour-long car journey there meant that taking a taxi was ridiculously expensive.

I was quiet on the journey, thinking again about being separated from Charlie. Aunt Milly kept asking if I was tired. Once satisfied on that score she chatted away for the entire trip, making suggestions gently and offering to help out any time.

'You've been amazing.' I hugged her for ages at the station, not keen for her to see my watery eyes. 'And you mind Aunt Milly, won't you, Charlie?' I knelt down and buttoned up his coat, just to get to eye level with him. I noticed he'd gone all quiet and had been watching me for ages.

'Don't go to work,' he said now, throwing his arms around me. 'I love you, Mammy.'

'Oh Charlie, darling, I love you so much.' I kissed him all over his face. 'I have to go to work now, but I'll be down to see you soon – and Squirt too,' I added quickly. 'And don't forget you'll be coming to live with me before long.' I brushed his hair out of his eyes.

'Aunt Milly too?' he asked in wonder.

'Yes, if she wants,' I told him, kissing him again. 'And Squirt of course. And we'll be getting a new dog.'

'Woof-woof,' he said, happy again.

'I guess I'd better speed up my plans.' I stood up and spoke to my aunt.

'There's no hurry, child. You take all the time you need.' She tilted up my face. 'You've done an incredible job to get as far as you have since your sister died.' She kissed my head like she used to when we were kids. It was

326

such a motherly gesture that it made me want to cry, especially after what Charlie had said.

'Mind yourself now and don't do too much. And call me and keep me up to date. I already love that little place.'

'I know you do. And the customers adore you, from what I saw.' I threw my arms around her. 'I'll never be able to pay you back.' I buried my head in her cardigan. This time she smelt of vanilla.

'What are family for?' She stroked my hair as if I were a baby and gently untangled me. 'I'd better go, otherwise I'll never get a seat.' We were at the final carriage.

'Safe journey.' I tried to get one last sniff of Charlie but he was having none of it.

'Choo-choo!' he roared and blew on the toy whistle that Orla had nipped out and bought him just before we left.

'Ring me later and let me know how the day finished.' Aunt Milly blew a kiss and waved frantically as soon as she'd climbed on board.

'Thanks for everything.' With one final wave I strolled away, trying to look nonchalant, afraid the parting would overwhelm me.

When I got back to Wicklow the girls were cleaning up, getting ready to close the café. They were all on a high.

'It's been really good, I think.' Orla came out of the kitchen and wiped her forehead. 'Hot but good.'

'Everyone's been very complimentary about the food,' Violet said, in an uncharacteristic flush of praise.

'Well, I think we should celebrate,' I announced just as the front door opened.

'Hi there, any chance of a coffee?' It was Kevin Daly.

'What are you doing here?' I asked, my heart speeding up. Orla whipped off her apron, I noticed.

'Had to come and support you on your first day.' He smiled and handed me a huge bunch of flowers.

'Wow!' I was surprised. 'Thanks, they're lovely.'

'I'll get you a coffee.' Violet had noticed him as well, it appeared.

'Sit down, please.' I indicated a table.

'Sure I'm not too late?'

'Not at all, we're not closing for another fifteen minutes.'

'Will you join me?'

'Yes, I will. I'd murder a strong latte,' I told Violet, who was definitely giving him the once-over.

We chatted about the previous night and he said all the right things and I found myself giggling up at him, most unlike me. He certainly knew how to make a girl feel good.

'Let me take you out to dinner,' he suggested lazily, as we finished up.

'Me?' I looked around, pretending to be shocked.

'Yes, you.' He brushed the tip of my nose with his finger. 'Who else?'

'Actually, I've just . . . sort of invited the girls for a drink,' I apologized, surprised to find that I was disappointed.

'OK . . . then I'll take you all out. If that's all right with you?'

'Yes, great. Give me ten minutes.' I stood up. 'Let me

328

just tell the girls and nip upstairs and change.' I smiled at him.

'You look lovely, Lily, you don't need to do anything to yourself.' He smiled a slow smile and my heart sort of missed a beat. Maybe he was just what I needed in my life right now, to banish any lingering foolish thoughts about Richard and me.

33

WILLIAM AND BETH

WILLIAM HAD HAD BETTER DAYS. FOR A START THE hospital resembled a war zone and you'd have needed a 4x4 to negotiate A&E, which unfortunately was right beside one of his rooms. Then a patient who'd undergone routine surgery two days previously had developed a complication and had to be rushed back into theatre. That meant the staff there were grumpy because it was Friday and they now had an unscheduled late finish.

'You'd think it was my fault,' he mumbled to the little Vietnamese nurse who'd paged him initially about the problem. She ignored him. This only served to irritate him further. She was young and 'hot', according to the junior doctors, which was the only reason he'd deigned to make small talk in the first place.

Another patient, a big burly man in the public hospital, was irritating William that day as well, asking too many questions and querying the need for the course of treatment he was prescribing. Damn the internet, William thought as he listened with a glazed expression to the

330

man's inner-city monotone voice. William treated him to a barrage of medical jargon, silenced the intern who was trying not to guffaw with a killer look, and hot-footed it to the consultants' private quarters for a strong cup of coffee. Under normal circumstances William didn't do caffeine.

When he made his way into the hospital's new wing afterwards, it resembled Grafton Street as he knew it on any pre-Christmas weekend. The place was thronged with people of all ages, the only difference being that this crowd were in various stages of undress and a higher percentage were using crutches or wheelchairs. The coffee shops along the main route were full to bursting and the magazine and sweet stalls were under siege as well. William usually loved the buzz, but today he failed to notice the sense of camaraderie that made people here smile more, hold doors open and generally nod encouragingly at complete strangers wheeling drips or clutching plastic bottles of urine disguised as handbags. He knew he had to hang around to check on the patient they'd just opened up for a second time, so he changed and decided to go for a run to work off some of the tension that was building up in his neck and shoulders. Dressed in pristine white to emphasize his tan, he jogged confidently out through the main car park and headed for the coast road. It was a murky November afternoon. A car sailed past, spraying him with dirty water. Two student nurses nearby giggled. William pretended not to notice but all the good was gone out of the run for him. He cut his route short and spent the rest of the time drinking even more coffee, which didn't help his headache.

Leaving the hospital several hours later he checked his messages, hoping for a response from Lily. Nothing. She'd told him about the opening of the café when they'd spoken a while back, using it as an excuse not to take him up on his offer of an all-expenses-paid trip to France. She was always pleasant but a bit aloof when they spoke, which meant his plan of making her his mistress was going nowhere fast. Maybe I'm being too subtle, he thought as he purred out into the traffic. When he'd mentioned the trip initially he'd been casual, telling her that it was something Alison had always wanted to do and now he felt that she might enjoy the rest and relaxation, but she'd said straight away that she couldn't possibly accept such a generous offer. William began by being ultra-cautious – in his position he had to be – but then he'd told her it was a freebie from one of the pharmaceutical companies, lust overriding discretion. That didn't work either: she simply said she was sure Beth would be thrilled, and thanked him for thinking of her.

Sighing, he resolved to drop in to the café in Wicklow over the coming weekend. Maybe he'd even bring her champagne to wish her luck. Yes, that was a good plan – he could say he was in the area checking out a site for a new clinic. Turning on Lyric FM and then flicking to Drivetime for the news, William felt in control again. He needed sex, that was it, he thought, becoming aroused while listening to a report on a lapdancing club that had been raided the previous night, releasing a number of near-naked girls on to the streets, according to the outraged resident now being interviewed. Definitely a night for a shower and a large whiskey, he decided as he zapped the electric gates to his home almost an hour later. Maybe sex with Beth too, he thought, fantasizing about the lapdancers.

William checked his post and wondered why his wife didn't come to greet him as usual.

'Hello, anyone home?' he enquired in the general direction of the kitchen as he poured himself a generous measure of Crested Ten.

His heart sank as he recognized the voice of the Swedish au pair from down the road calling out a greeting in response to his own.

'Oh, hello, Brigitta.' He headed straight for the ice as he entered the kitchen. 'What are you doing here?'

'Mrs Hammond had to go out.' The blonde student smiled at him as she stirred something that didn't smell at all appetizing. 'Would you like some meatballs? I make plenty, to leave some for the children's lunch tomorrow.'

'No, thanks.' He gulped some of the whiskey, feeling his mood nosedive. 'Did my wife say where she was going?'

'I think she left you message on your mobile. Out for a Chinese with her girlfriend, I can't remember name now.'

'Fine, I'll call her.'

'I'm afraid she forgot her phone.' Brigitta indicated the gleaming silver object lounging uselessly on the worktop.

'Did she leave any food?' William was trying hard not to take his irritation out on the young woman.

'Yes, in the bottom oven.'

He extracted a large plate covered in tinfoil. Underneath the shiny exterior was a congealed mass of food that had been there way too long, if the colour of the broccoli was anything to go by.

'Are the children in bed?' William tipped the plate into the bin.

'Yes, of course.' She sounded surprised that he would ask. 'The food is not good?' she enquired needlessly as she watched him.

'I'm not hungry.' He picked up his glass and headed for the comparative safety of the sitting room. His chair was full of newspapers, including today's *Irish Times*, with holes in them – Beth was always cutting things out.

Abruptly, he stood up and headed for the stairs.

'Mr Hammond, now that you are home, it is OK if I leave?' Brigitta appeared with her plate half empty.

'Actually, I'd rather you stayed in case the children need anything.' He didn't even glance in her direction. 'I'm going to relax in my bedroom.' He topped up his glass en route.

An hour later he'd mellowed considerably. On the spur of the moment he dialled Lily's mobile.

'Hello.' She sounded like she was in a pub.

'Hi there, it's William.'

'Oh hello, how are you?' Was it his imagination or did

she sound sorry she'd answered? 'Just let me move outside, I can hardly hear you,' she said, cheerfully enough he thought.

'Where are you?'

'I'm having a drink . . . with a friend of mine – Kevin. The café opened today, it went really well.'

'That's why I was ringing you,' he said smoothly.

'Why thank you, that's sweet.' She sounded young and excited and talking to her while lying on his bed made William horny.

'So, what are your plans for the evening?' he asked casually.

'We're going to dinner later. Kevin is insisting I don't cook,' she said laughing.

'Great,' he said falsely. 'Where?'

'Oh, nowhere special, just a little Italian about a mile outside the town. Have to keep checking the competition, you see.'

'Yes, well, that's also why I was ringing you.' William immediately wanted to do better. 'There's a new Vietnamese restaurant just opened in the IFSC. Supposed to be amazing. I was just wondering if you'd like to have dinner there next week?' To hell with the champagne and the casual visit. He wanted to move this relationship on – he'd been lusting after her for long enough.

'What's the IFSC?' She sounded hesitant.

'The Financial Services Centre. You know? Along the Liffey near the Customs House?'

'Right, yeah.'

'I'll ask my driver to collect you, that way you can relax on the journey up.'

'Not at all, don't be silly . . .'

'I insist,' he told her. 'So, just name your night.'

'Em, can I text you? It's just that . . . my aunt might be coming up and I need to call her first.'

'Fine.' Now it was his turn to sound distant. 'I'll wait to hear from you then.'

'Great. Thanks for the call. I'd better get back inside . . .'

'Enjoy your evening. Bye.' He clicked off before she could say anything. Time for a new plan, he decided.

34

RICHARD AND DAISY

'DAISY, ARE YOU SURE YOU WOULDN'T RATHER WAIT UNTIL the spring?' Richard asked his girlfriend, who was getting her knickers in a twist because the invitations were going to be late.

'Richard Kearney, are you trying to avoid getting married?'

Daisy was smiling but not friendly.

'No, I'm not, but you seem to have been in bad form ever since we fixed the date.' Richard knew he sounded defensive.

'Well, if you'd help out a bit, I wouldn't be.' She flounced out of the room. 'Please OK the wording and the design tonight,' she called over her shoulder. 'The printer starts work in the morning. Oh, and have a look at the first draft of the invite list and see what you think.'

'Where did you get these names?' He glanced at a roll call of every relation he wasn't even sure he still had, along with a shedload of people he'd never heard of.

'I had lunch with your mother and now I'm meeting

Trudy to discuss her dress,' she called. He only knew she was gone when he heard the door slam.

'Look, mate, you know I'll be your bleedin' best man.' Tom Dalton, fresh from his radio show, plopped two pints down on the counter in Ryan's a couple of hours later. 'But, never mind Daisy, are you sure you're up to having a trouble and strife living with you twenty-four/seven?'

'Don't be daft. Daisy and I, well, we're good together.' Richard scratched his head. 'Or at least we were.' He downed a third of the glass in one. 'But all this is beginning to do my head in. We haven't even had sex for a week.'

'Well, there's always whatshername.' Tom winked. 'Or is she more choosy than her sister?' He elbowed his mate in the ribs. 'Have you seen her at all?'

'Yep, but that never got started, I told you. I was at the opening of her café the other night and I'm calling in for lunch on Saturday but we're just mates.'

'You've never been just mates with a woman under forty in your life.' Tom diverted a call from his mobile. 'So when are you going to pick up from where you left off in her flat that night?'

'We're not. I'm not even sure I want to any more.'

They both knew it was a porker. Tom guffawed.

'Seriously, there's something going on there that I'm a bit nervous about. Besides, we're sort of skirtin' round each other at the moment . . .'

'It's called sexual chemistry,' Tom said sarcastically.

'No, she has some agenda, and I haven't a clue what it is.'

Tom downed most of the rest of the glass of beer. 'So what are you doing still seeing her if that's the case?'

'I'm not "seeing her" in that sense. I'm just giving her a bit of advice, until she gets the place up and running.' Richard shrugged. 'Maybe out of loyalty to Alison, maybe 'cause I feel sorry for her, I'm not sure.'

'Or maybe 'cause you'd really like to give her one.'

Tom was all 'nudge nudge, wink wink' and it irritated Richard, but then everything did these days, it seemed.

'Twin sisters an' all that.' Tom sucked in his breath.

'Jesus, one's dead.' Richard laughed. 'And while the other one is very attractive, I'll admit—'

'That's it. Call the fucking wedding off until you've had time to think, mate. Same again?'

'No, it's my twist.' Richard signalled the barman for two replacements. 'The thing is, I do love Daisy, she's a great girl. And besides, I've never been good at fucking around, not like you, you stallion.'

Tom pretended to choke on his pint. 'So what was the thing with the hooker then?'

'You know what I mean.' Richard was pissed off with the turn this was taking.

'Besides, if you do get married, what about kids? Are you absolutely sure she's not gonna want them in a year or two?'

'We've never really discussed it in detail.' Richard only

realized it as he said it out loud. 'But Daisy will go along with whatever I want.'

'She does know, doesn't she?' Tom was incredulous.

'Of course she bleedin' well knows.' Richard stood up and fished out a twenty from his jeans pocket. 'So she's definitely not envisaging *The Brady Bunch*.'

'You never know, she could be thinking of a reversal . . .' Tom made a scissors motion with his fingers.

'Listen, let's talk about something else, OK? I've had enough bleedin' chat about women and weddings to last me a lifetime. Just keep New Year's Eve free and give me your measurements for the suit.' He plonked back down and grinned. 'And when Daisy phones you tomorrow for a rant about what an arsehole I am, put in a good word for me, eh?'

'Will do.'

Richard was in bed when Daisy came home. 'Are you awake?' She ran her hand up the outside of his thigh.

'I thought you were staying at your own house tonight?' He twisted himself around to face her sleepily.

'I thought you might miss me.' She kissed him hungrily. 'You were so grumpy earlier that I suspected you might need to do some unwinding.' She climbed on top of him and he could see she was wearing a black lace plunge bra and matching thong.

'I was grumpy?' He flicked her over and began to kiss her neck and shoulders. 'I don't think so.'

'Yes, you were, admit it.'

'Was not.' He moved his tongue down slowly.

'Did you do the invites thing?'

'Hmmm?' He pretended not to hear. 'Relax, babe, you're too uptight. I intend taking your mind off everything except me for the next half-hour.'

'I am not uptight.' She yanked herself into a sitting position and nearly broke his nose in the process. 'That's typical of you to blame me. I'm the one putting all the effort into this wedding, you know.'

'Fucking hell, Daisy, relax, will you?' Richard could feel a headache coming on. He knew he shouldn't have had that whiskey at the end of the night.

'No, I will not relax.' She jumped out of bed. 'I'm sick of you telling me to relax, chill out, stay cool. And as for you, any more laid-back and you'd be laid out – in a coffin.' She grabbed her robe. 'I'm sleeping in the spare room until you apologize. And if you're not careful there won't be any wedding.'

35

LILY

I FELT AS IF I'D NEVER GET A PROPER NIGHT'S SLEEP AGAIN and the fact that it was all down to too much sex was of little comfort when my alarm went off each morning at five thirty.

'Come back to bed, let the girls do the work for once,' a sleepy voice pleaded from under the duvet.

'I wish I could.'

'You can, you're the boss,' Kevin Daly said sleepily. 'I'll make it worth your while.'

'Haven't you got work to go to?' I threw my pillow at him.

'Not at this hour. Jesus, what time did we get in at?'

'One thirty, I think. You'd better get a move on. The traffic starts building in Wicklow from six thirty.'

'This place really is the sticks, isn't it? Listen, take the morning off, stay in bed with me and then we'll go out somewhere for a leisurely breakfast, my treat.'

'Kevin, I provide other people with leisurely breakfasts.' I yawned. 'Call in for a coffee and a muffin on your way.'

'No, I won't,' he said, sounding miffed.

'Gotta go, Orla will kill me.' I blew him a kiss and headed for the bathroom.

My eyes had grit behind the lids and my face the sort of pallor usually only seen in hospitals. I threw myself under a scalding shower and prepared to face another long day. In the end, I hadn't even tried to resist Kevin's charms. After that first day I was on such a high that I drank a bit too much and Kevin and I sort of drifted away from the gang and the flirting started in earnest. Orla had left shortly afterwards and I'd been feeling guilty ever since. When I'd woken up in bed beside him next morning I wasn't at all sure I'd done the right thing. One-night stands never happened to me – I was too insecure to cope with the fallout – and besides, casual relationships just weren't my thing, never had been. And the fact that Orla was even mildly interested would normally have sent me scurrying in the opposite direction. But that night it was like I was finally getting rid of the old Lily and ushering in a new, sophisticated, grown-up businesswoman – all the things I wasn't. Next morning, of course, I was back to being good old insecure me.

'Hi.' I was all smiles as I trundled into the café, anxious to placate them. I was very late.

'Hi,' Orla said quietly.

I started into making bread immediately. It was the only thing guaranteed to soothe my aching muscles, even though most people found it hard work. Kneading had the same effect on me as a hot port at the end of a winter walk did on most of my friends.

'How's the form?' I asked Orla as soon as we had a quiet moment to ourselves.

'Fine. You?'

'I'm grand, but then I didn't take the head off Violet and almost decapitate Naomi with a bread knife yesterday,' I said with a smile.

'If you're trying to cheer me up then I should tell you that your bedside manner is seriously lacking.'

I sighed and set out some seeds to give the bread a bit of crunch. 'Want to tell me what's wrong?' I asked Orla gently.

'Nothing.'

'Something's happened. You were in flying form in the pub the other night.' I wasn't sure how to proceed.

'Yeah, well.'

'That bread'll be like glue if you keep going much longer.' Violet was becoming quite the expert as she put down a coffee beside each of us.

'Thanks, V.' I picked up the cup and waited until she'd gone out again. 'Is this about me and Kevin?'

'Well, you jumped in there fairly quick,' she said in a couldn't-care-less voice. 'One minute we were chatting, the next he had his tongue down your throat.'

'I know.' I gulped, preparing to take it on the chin. 'I've no excuse. I was a bit drunk and on a high and things like that never happen to me, you know that. I lost the run of myself.'

'Yeah, well, shame it had to happen with a guy I spotted first.' Orla didn't look at me.

'Orla, I'm really, really sorry. It was wrong of me, I knew it the minute I woke up next day, in fact I knew it the minute you left early, if I'm honest. I guess I was just . . . I dunno . . . flattered by his attention. It was completely unexpected and I . . . I've been so lonely these past few months. It was stupid and thoughtless, especially after all you've done for me.'

'I wouldn't have done it to you,' she said.

'I know that. Mind you, you did end up with the cheeky pharmacist in Galway that August bank holiday weekend, remember? Exactly two hours after I told you I thought he was cute.'

'Bitch!' she said but her mouth was turned upwards. 'Nah, it's OK, I wouldn't have been able to hold on to him anyway. He's far too good-looking for me. What really annoyed me was that you just drifted away from us – one minute we were having a laugh and—'

'Don't remind me.' I felt terrible. 'I'm such a dork. I just got carried away with . . . power or something equally stupid. The café opening made me feel ten feet tall. And the bloody champagne had me thinking I was Anna Kournikova or something. 'Are we OK?' I asked gingerly.

'Yes.'

'Thanks.' I meant it. 'You saved my life, coming home like this, and I'm truly sorry that I was such an idiot. I'll open up,' I told her, glancing at the clock as I untied my apron and flung off my hairnet. 'God, I look wrecked.'

'Be careful you don't frighten the customers so.' She grinned her forgiveness at me and I stuck out my tongue as I passed.

'Still better than your ugly mug,' I told her, two fingers raised.

'Hello again,' I greeted my soya-drinking only regular so far. 'How's your week been?'

'Terrible, but at least it's Friday. By the way, those muffins were amazing. I'll take one of each if you have them.'

'Blueberry and custard today, I think, and . . . some nice ones just out of the oven made with organic raspberries and vanilla,' I told her, checking the tray that had arrived. 'Is that OK?'

'Perfect. Do you really make them yourself?'

'Of course. We make practically all our cakes, and where we do buy in they're from "real" bakers – local women I've sourced personally.'

'Well, I've been singing your praises all over town, so expect a few Dubs in over the weekend, I'd say.'

'Thank you, that's great. I don't even know your name?' I told her apologetically.

'Sandra Horlicks.' She held out her hand. 'Actually, here's my business card, just in case.'

After that it was all go and we had quite a few phone orders as well, another encouraging sign, and one of the after-massers declared our organic porridge with honey and berries 'the best healthy breakfast I've ever had, apart from the cream'. It was all looking very promising.

346

Daniel Williams dropped in around eleven. I was glad because I'd been thinking about him on and off since the opening night.

'How's it going?' He smiled in a lazy fashion and I was thrown by the tingle I felt on seeing him again.

'Those teeth must be false, they're way too white and straight.' I said it simply to hide my nerves and he looked a bit taken aback.

'Thanks, I think. Do you always get so personal with your customers?'

'Sorry.' I laughed. 'I do that sometimes. It goes straight from my brain to my mouth without any editing. Coffee and a muffin on the house to make up for it?' I wanted him to hang around.

'Not good commercial sense.' He wagged a finger at me. 'Too many freebies could put you out of business in the first year.'

'Right so. In that case let's start over.' I cleared my throat. 'Good morning, Daniel, nice to see you again. What can I get you?' I liked teasing him, I decided.

'I think I'll try your . . . Let's see.' He glanced at the specials board. '*Scrambled orange eggs with wild Kinvara smoked salmon on a toasted bagel*,' he read aloud. 'What's an orange egg?'

'A real egg, proper orange yolk, none of that pale yellow watery stuff,' I said proudly.

'Might be a tad too obscure for us culchies, that one.' He winked and I laughed.

'Coffee or tea to go with it?'

'Double espresso, I need the hit.' He yawned. 'Have you time for one yourself?'

'I have. But peppermint tea for me, I think. I'm wired enough as it is. I'll just put your order in and join you with your coffee in a mo.'

'Gimme one of those things with the berries sticking out of them while I'm waiting. I'm famished, I've been up since seven.'

'Try five if you want an early start.' I tonged a muffin on to a plate. 'Actually on second thoughts I do need a coffee.' I handed him the cake and he settled at a table by the window and stretched out like a cat in the sun. Two girls going by nudged each other and giggled and I knew he wouldn't stay single around here for long.

'Sorry about that.' He'd almost finished his breakfast by the time I finally got a chance to sit down beside him. He'd rolled up his sleeves and I smelt cut grass and fresh air and I found myself wondering what he'd be like naked. I blushed.

'Bit of a rush, eh? That's good.' He mopped up the last of his runny egg. 'How's business?'

'Great, yeah. Children's allowance today so the lady in the shop next door warned me what to expect.' I was relieved he hadn't copped my red face. 'I'm glad you called in actually, because after you'd gone I realized I had no contact number for you and I've been wondering if you really were OK – after what I told you?'

'Yeah, I am. It was a shock, naturally. I suppose I'd built

up our meeting in my head. I was definitely looking forward to seeing her again but we were only getting to know each other really, although we'd talked a lot.'

I wondered if he knew anything about her life. 'How many times did you meet?'

'We spent a couple of days together. I don't know what it was. Maybe it was because we were both away from home – a bit more carefree, you know? Then we discovered we had Wicklow in common . . .' He drained the last of his coffee. 'I liked her a lot but I hadn't any great expectations coming here the other night, though it sure was fun thinking about it.' I liked the way he cocked his head to one side when he smiled.

'Did she tell you much – you know, about her life?'

Was it my imagination or did his face change? 'What do you mean?' he said easily.

'Oh, you know, anything really?'

'Nothing I hadn't heard before.'

'Oh.' That was that, so.

'So, tell me about you. Alison did mention you quite a bit. And Charlie. He was so cool the other night.'

'Yes, he was.' I smiled at the memory. 'She left custody of him to me . . . Well, there's only me, we don't know anything about his father.' I watched his face as I spoke. 'So, it's just the two of us now.'

'And he lives with your aunt in Cork?' He didn't take the bait.

'Just for the moment. He'll be coming to live here . . . shortly.'

'I liked your aunt.'

'Isn't she a dote? I must ring her this evening, it's been mad around here and last night by the time I got upstairs it was too late. So, tell me about you? What's in Wicklow for you?'

'Wicklow's home, although I was born in Australia.'

'Really? How come?'

'My mother is Australian.' It explained his ever-so-slight drawl. God, he's attractive, I decided. I must tell Orla.

'We lived there for a few years, but my father had a hankering for the rolling hills of Wicklow.' He laughed. 'Always singing about them, any time he had a drink. My folks own the golf course out the coast road. I'm an engineer by profession. No intention really of settling down here – Dublin maybe, but Wicklow's too small. Then my father died suddenly and my mum needed me, so I'm running the place. We do major golf holidays and tours. We have a big country house, the kind Americans love. It's quite an operation so I'm here for the foreseeable future, I guess.'

'Are you enjoying it?' I hoped he was, I kinda liked knowing he was around.

'I am, actually. I'm surprising myself. The countryside is so beautiful. Jeez, I must be getting old.' He laughed. 'Never thought I'd hear myself saying that.'

'Hey, babe, I'm off.' Kevin appeared out of nowhere.

'Are you still here? I thought you'd an appointment at nine?'

'I cancelled it.'

'Oh sorry, Daniel, this is Kevin Daly, Kevin – Daniel. You probably met the night of the party?' I couldn't remember.

'How's it goin', mate?' Kevin asked.

'Nice to see you again.' Daniel stood up.

'Cheers.' They shook hands. 'Talk to you later.' Kevin kissed me lightly.

'Yes, OK.' I was a bit flustered.

'Boyfriend?' Daniel grinned.

'Sort of.' I was mortified. 'Actually, we only just got together, so who knows?' I hoped I sounded casual enough. I was anxious that he wouldn't think I was 'spoken for' – to use a Wicklow phrase.

'Sure,' he said and got up to go. 'I'd better work off that muffin by walking the course. Thanks for breakfast.'

'Pleasure.'

'You must come and see it some time.'

'I'd love to. Oh,' I looked around for my phone, 'I should take your number, just so I know where to find you.'

'Sure thing, but don't forget, I know where to find you.' He winked.

I had arranged to meet James after work that evening. He'd sent me a text, asking me to meet him in a bar in Ashford, which I found strange. When I asked why, he simply said it was important. I hadn't spoken to him since he'd told his wife the truth, so I wasn't looking forward to tonight. It would be heavy going, I suspected.

I arrived bang on seven but he was nowhere to be seen. I was settling myself in a corner when my phone rang. Just as I was fluttering around my bag looking for it, naturally it stopped. Then a quiet voice in front of me said, 'Hello, you must be Lily?'

'Yes?' I was confused.

'I'm Tamsin, James's wife.'

'Oh.' My heart started beating faster.

'I'm sorry, that was me ringing you just now. I wanted to be sure before I approached you.'

'I see.' I didn't.

'I was the one who wanted the meeting, actually. It was me who sent you the text.'

'Oh.' My vocabulary seemed suddenly limited.

'Can I buy you a drink?' she asked as a waiter hovered.

I could've used one, but sensed I might need my wits about me. 'Black coffee, please,' I said to the waiter.

'Same here, thank you.' She smiled and he disappeared. 'May I sit down?'

'Yes, of course.' I didn't know what else to say. She had obviously come straight from work. I noticed her slate-grey well-cut suit and soft leather shoes and it didn't help my nerves one bit. She was pretty in a well-groomed New York-executive sort of way – the kind you see on *Will and Grace*. I tried to console myself with the fact that she'd orchestrated this meeting and so I'd let her do the talking.

'I'm sure you're wondering why I would want to meet you?' she ventured as soon as we'd had our coffee delivered. It was weak and just about warm and more expensive than ours and I hardly even noticed, never mind gloated.

'Yes,' I said truthfully. 'Does James know?' I'd only just thought about that.

'No. As I said, it was me who sent you the text – on his phone. I did it one night when he was in bed – and then worried that you wouldn't reply until the next morning, when he'd have had his phone with him.'

'And did I?' I couldn't remember.

'Yes, luckily for me you did.' She sipped her coffee and put it down carefully, as if considering where to start. 'I suppose I'm looking to figure the whole thing out,' she said after a short pause. 'All this has been a shock to me, naturally enough, but what's really frightened me is that I never saw it coming.'

'How do you mean?' I was intrigued.

'James and I, we have – had – the perfect marriage. He's my best friend. I love him more than I ever thought it was possible.' Her eyes lit up. 'We talk about everything under the sun.' She sipped her coffee. 'So I have to ask myself, was I so obsessed with trying to get pregnant that I failed to notice what it was doing to him?'

'That sounds very harsh on yourself.' I was a bit afraid of being drawn in but it was out before I could help myself.

'Well, he said he really tried to tell me how he was feeling many times before he . . . actually did anything. And I believe him. He wouldn't lie in order to save his own skin, he's not capable of it.'

Surely he lied to you lots when he was seeing my sister? I didn't say it but she read my mind.

'Oh, he did tell fibs about where he was when it was going on, I know that. But he's never lied to me about anything important . . .' I think I knew what she meant.

'Lily, we have no secrets, I promise you.' She seemed to be forgetting that my sister had been one very big one.

'So why didn't he come with you . . . to meet me?'

'Ah.' She knew I'd caught her out. 'I needed to speak to you alone.'

'About what, exactly? I cannot tell you anything about his relationship with my sister, I'm afraid . . .'

'Why not, if you don't mind my asking?'

'I didn't know anything about it.'

'Nothing at all?' She seemed surprised but I sensed she believed me.

'No.'

'So, when did you find out?'

'After she died.'

'So, why did you . . . How did you contact—'

'It's complicated.' I intervened before she could say any more. I wasn't prepared for her questions in that regard.

'I'm sorry, it must have been a very difficult time for you.' I saw the pain in her eyes. She was nice, the sort of person you'd like to have as a friend, I imagined. I had an urge to tell her everything then and ask her advice. Maybe it was her soft, sympathetic voice. She wasn't in the least bit pissed off with me – or Ali, as far as I could tell – and she wasn't judging either me or my sister.

'It was.'

'Were you very close?'

'Yes, we were twins, did you know that?'

She nodded and her face was sad.

'I told her all my secrets. She was like my mother and my sister and my best friend all rolled into one.' I looked at this stranger and she had tears in her eyes.

'James said your sister was a good person,' she said as if she'd read my thought. 'He also said she was very special to him. It hurt me to hear it, actually.'

'She was special, yes. I miss her a lot.'

'So who's looking after you in all this?' she asked.

'I'm OK.' It was my stock answer.

'Are your parents alive?'

'No.'

'You poor girl. What an extraordinary thing to have to deal with on your own.'

'I have friends.' I didn't want her pity.

'I don't doubt it.' She smiled at me. 'But have you someone you can talk to, tell everything to, I mean?'

I shook my head, not trusting myself to speak.

'I can recommend someone,' she whispered. 'If you ever need help – professional help, I mean.'

Again I shook my head. 'Thanks, but I'm fine. Really.'

'That's a lot to deal with at once.'

We were both lost in thought then. 'More coffee?' I asked eventually. I needed to lighten the mood.

'Yes, please.' She took my cue immediately and I went to the bar. I needed to escape for a bit.

355

'Lily,' she said after I'd settled down again. 'James and I, we have a lot to sort out between us. But we're talking, at least, and now I'm really listening. Even though at times I'm so angry with him I want to . . . oh, I don't know, hurt him the way he's hurt me, I suppose.'

'You wouldn't be normal if you didn't.'

'But I couldn't ever hurt him, not deliberately. I'd rather die myself than cause him pain.' It was a dramatic statement, but it wasn't said with any drama.

'You must love him an awful lot?'

'Yes.'

'Does he love you back? The same way, I mean?'

'Yes, I believe he does.'

'You're lucky, so.'

'I know.' She looked me straight in the eye. 'There's something I need to ask you. The main reason I wanted to talk to you alone this evening. And I don't expect an answer now, all I ask is that you give it some consideration. Would that be OK?'

'OK.' I hoped I didn't sound as apprehensive as I felt.

'It's about your sister's baby.'

'What about him?'

'From what James told me, it appears that there's at least a chance that this child could be his.' She must have seen the question mark go 'ping' on my face as I wondered where this was leading. I sat up straight.

'The dates match.' Her voice was very soft. 'And I understand there was . . . an incident . . . an accident,' she clarified, 'on one occasion.'

This was news to me. My heart started beating wildly. Could this woman have the answer I was searching for?

'I also know the child is living in the country, with your aunt?'

'Only temporarily.' I was immediately on the defensive.

She nodded and leaned in ever so slightly. 'Lily, I'm desperate for a child of my own.' I saw her bottom lip wobble and I watched as she tried to control it, as if she didn't want to play the sympathy card. 'Please just hear me out,' she said, even though I'd made no attempt to do otherwise. 'I'd . . . James and I . . . we'd like to . . . give him a good home. We'd take great care of him. I'd love him as if he was my own.' She couldn't quite control the tremor in her voice. 'Please, would you at least think about letting us adopt him?'

36

JAMES AND TAMSIN

'YOU DID WHAT?'

'I went to see her. I . . . needed to.' She shrugged. 'And I knew if I'd told you you'd have tried to stop me.'

'And you used my phone to set it up?'

'Yes.'

'This is outrageous. I can't believe you would do such a thing. And behind my back . . . Christ, Tamsin, what were you thinking of?'

'You went behind my back in the first place,' she said and he knew he'd asked for that. 'I'm sorry, I didn't mean it the way it sounded,' she said immediately.

'Yes, you did, but I deserved it,' James told her grudgingly.

'I liked her,' Tamsin said.

'So do I.'

'Is she very like her sister?'

'In looks, yes.' He thought about it, not wanting to upset Tamsin any more than he had to. 'In terms of personality they're completely different.'

'She's beautiful. I was jealous,' Tamsin said softly.

'You've no need to be.' He sighed and gave her a hug.

'I spoke to her about the child.' She felt she might as well get it over with.

'You what?' James felt sure he was hearing her wrong.

'I asked if she would consider letting us adopt him.' Tamsin never took her eyes off his face.

'What did she say?' He couldn't quite take it in.

'Not much. Well, she said no, of course, but that doesn't mean she meant it.' Tamsin was matter-of-fact. 'She cried a little. It wasn't me . . . I didn't . . . I mean, I was very gentle in my approach.' She saw his reaction.

'I don't believe what you're telling me.' He backed away from her then as if he'd been scalded. 'Tamsin, no, tell me you didn't?'

'James, I had to.' Her voice was pleading.

'Maybe,' he said after a long time. He was trying hard to see it from her point of view. 'But I can't believe you did it without talking to me about it first.'

'I wasn't even sure I was going to have the courage to do it, until I met her.' Tamsin was staring at him. 'But I sensed something. She was, I don't know – sympathetic, maybe – guilty, vulnerable even, I'm not really sure. But I just felt the moment was right . . .'

'But did it never cross your mind to see how I felt about it first?' James was trying very hard to understand. 'We hadn't even discussed it, Tamsin.'

'We had, in a way.' He waited for her to explain. 'I asked

you if there was any possibility the child could be yours . . .'

'Yes, so?'

'And you told me that you used condoms . . . with her . . . except for that one time . . .'

'When it broke.' He hated her having to hear it again but she'd been adamant about wanting to know every detail, and they'd exhausted the topic many times in the past few weeks.

'Yes, and then I asked you what age he was.'

'I remember, but I was guessing, really.'

'Don't say that.' His wife jumped up. 'You said it was a couple of months after that that she went missing – to look after her aunt, or something. And in the newspapers it said—'

'In the papers it said he was anything from three to five and a half, as I recall,' James told her.

'Please, James, he's the right age . . .'

'It's a million-to-one chance, though. I don't know how many other men she was seeing at the time.' He saw her wince and was sorry. 'Tamsin, we have to be realistic about this.'

'Please don't.' She started to cry. 'Don't kill what little hope I have.'

He was at her side in an instant. 'Oh darling, I'm sorry.' He cradled her in his arms. 'I didn't mean to upset you, I'm so sorry, really I am.'

'James.' She took out a tissue and blew her nose. 'This could be our only chance . . .'

'Tamsin, we can't take a baby out of its home, away from its family, just because . . .'

'He's in the country.' She had a look in her eyes he hadn't seen before. 'With an elderly aunt, you said so yourself. She's young, she doesn't want him ruining her life . . .'

'She's the same age as his mother was,' he said quietly.

'But she can have other children – her own family – in years to come. For now she wants to concentrate on the business, she told me so.'

'I know, I know.' He stroked her hair. 'But listen to me, love. You have to understand, this is not as straightforward as you think, that's all I'm saying. It's a massive gamble. We haven't even seen the child.' He looked at her desperate face and wild eyes and was afraid for them both.

'James, we have to try. He could be your son.' She took his hands in her own. 'And I'd love him as if he were mine, I promise.' She was crying again.

'I know you would.' He started to cry with her. 'I know you'd make a wonderful mother. He'd be the luckiest little boy alive.'

'Then please, I beg you, go with me on this. Our only hope is if we're together on it.'

'Oh God, Tamsin, I'm not sure I can do this. I would do anything, anything in my power to give you the child you so badly want.' He shook his head. 'But not this. It's not right.'

'Please.' She knelt down beside him. 'She didn't say no outright.'

He shook his head.

'Please, James, I'm begging you. I'll do anything.'

'Shush, it'll be OK.' He never could hold out against her. 'Let's just see what she says.'

37

LILY

EVERYONE KNEW I WAS UPSET ABOUT SOMETHING OVER the next few days, they just didn't quite realize how annoyed I was. Years of living with an angry father meant I was used to keeping my temper in check. Ali had taught me well, yet now my anger was on her behalf. It bubbled up each time I thought about Tamsin's 'proposal', which had come as a huge shock, on top of everything else. There was so much to go over in my head, too much actually, so for a while I tried to block it out completely.

My fling with Kevin Daly came to an abrupt end just as I realized it had been a big mistake. The truth was that I was in danger of being bored to death. The man was completely self-absorbed, to the point of obsession. He asked me several times a day what I thought of his hair, clothes, new car. He lived either in the gym or my flat, it seemed, and I was beginning to actually feel like a pig, he called me 'babe' so often.

I found him glancing at the wedding invitation –

adorned with pictures of Richard and Daisy as babies – when I got upstairs to the flat very late for the second night in a row.

'How did you get in?' I asked.

'Violet gave me the key.' He reached out to stroke my leg as he lay on the couch watching sport on TV. 'Are we going, babe?' He held up the invite.

'I don't know.' I was playing for time. 'It only arrived this morning.'

'I've been thinking.' He pulled me down beside him. Now there's a novelty, I thought uncharitably.

'What about?' I smiled sweetly.

'We should think about it – getting hitched, I mean.' He planted a lingering kiss on my open mouth.

'Don't be ridiculous!' I waited for him to shout 'Gotcha' or something, but then saw he wasn't teasing. I closed my mouth – eventually – and did the only thing I could think of. I ignored it completely.

'Have you eaten?' I jumped up, all smiles.

'Yep. Orla rustled me up a plate of something or other. Not bad, but the pastry on the beef was a bit dry.'

It was the final straw, I later realized, but my brain hadn't quite registered that yet.

'Where was I?' I asked, amazed at his neck.

'Out picking up flowers or something, Violet said. Anyway I was ravenous, so it plugged a hole.' He got up. 'Glass of wine?' he drawled, strolling over to *my* wine rack and taking out *my* crystal glasses. 'So, what do you think?' he asked as he fiddled about looking for a corkscrew.

'You're not serious?' I had hoped to avoid this for now, at least. My mind was too full of James and Tamsin and my latest fear of losing Charlie to them. This was all getting so complicated that I needed a shrink, not a husband.

'Yeah, why not?' He pulled the cork without even looking at the label. 'We make a great team.' He glanced at himself in the mirror as he walked over to where I had plopped back down on the couch before I fainted. 'And you're a tiger in the sack.' He kissed me again. 'Grrrr,' he growled, stroking my thigh after handing me a glass of wine, which at this point I practically downed in one.

'Kevin.' I choked. 'I think we need to talk . . .'

'Later maybe?' He was groping me again and I wondered what on earth I'd ever seen in him.

'Kevin, I . . . eh, perhaps you'd better go' was what came out of my mouth then, but all I could think of was How did I get myself into this? Imagine, to think I could have seriously damaged my relationship with Orla over him. I was a plonker, that's what I was.

'Hey, babe, chill, come on. Let's go to bed.' He got up and tried to take my glass, but I was clutching it very hard. 'We can talk about this later.' He treated me to a lazy grin.

'No.' It was the first sensible thing I'd said. 'Kevin, I'm sorry, it's been fun, really . . . but . . . I think we've reached the end of the road.' And a very short road it was too.

'Don't be silly, we haven't even started,' he said but I think the penny had finally dropped.

'I'm sorry, it's not you, it's me.' I delivered the classic

line. 'After all that's happened I think I may have rushed into a relationship and—'

He must have seen something in my face and decided I was deadly serious. 'Fuck you.' He put down his glass. It was the first time I'd seen him angry.

'Kevin, I'm sorry . . . It's just that, with Charlie and everything, I'm not really ready right now.'

'Hey, listen, it's been fun.' He completely changed tack. 'I understand.' He looked around for his car keys and bent to pick them up off the floor.

'No hard feelings then?' I asked tentatively.

'Nope,' he said casually without looking at me. 'So, I guess I'll see you around?' He picked up his gym bag.

Not if I see you first, was what Sally would have said. 'Sure,' I said trying to smile.

'Anyway, you know what I said earlier about you being good in the sack.' He leaned over and kissed me lightly before heading for the door.

I sensed I wasn't meant to answer that one.

'Well.' He paused with his hand on the doorknob and turned to face me. 'You're not as good as your sister.'

Next morning I was up even before what birds were left about the place started singing for their winter breakfast. The ovens were on and coffee was bubbling long before Orla and Violet staggered in around seven. This morning I even had the first batch of cherry scones and crumpets baking by six thirty and the sesame bagels were standing by.

My anger was directed at everyone I knew, except, of course, Charlie, and the girls and Aunt Milly. Oh and Daniel Williams. He and I had become friends and if he hadn't been involved with Ali first I'd have been more encouraging. As it was, I had to fight against the growing attraction I felt each time I saw him.

He on the other hand was showing no signs of regarding me as anything other than a good pal. In some ways we were very alike: both engrossed in new projects, both very driven. For him his father's death had been the catalyst, for me Alison's. And I now had a child to consider. Daniel was the only one who seemed to understand the enormity of that.

Sometimes we had soup with warm bread and cheese and a glass of red when the café closed; other times we went out to the myriad new eating places that had sprung up all over the south-east of Ireland. He never once mentioned Kevin, and neither did the girls, following one fleeting comment from Orla the day after the fiasco in my flat, which almost resulted in her finger being severed on my chopping board. She had obviously told Sally too, because she was leaving 'Has Kevin "the body" Daly finally bitten the dust'-type messages on my mobile.

In some respects Daniel had replaced Richard in my life, and funnily enough I'd no regrets where he was concerned. Thinking of Richard now, even in passing, focused the anger that had been bubbling under the surface since my conversation with Tamsin – and which had reached boiling point when Kevin Daly had delivered his parting shot. All these men with their perfect lives. Had Alison meant anything to any of them? I wondered again and again.

The aforementioned Richard had his model girlfriend who was so carefree she made me feel old just being in the same room as her. All that and a fairytale winter wedding to look forward to.

I was also pissed off with James, for wanting the gorgeous little boy, all that I had left of my sister. And I envied James and Tamsin because of the invisible bond that held them together even in the midst of a crisis like this. It was yet another perfect relationship haunting me. I was annoyed at Dave Madden too, for dropping me completely after having promised to help with the café. I'd never heard a word from him after that night in the hotel, when he as good as asked me to go to bed with him. Probably too busy with his wife and his very own twin daughters. And then there was William, who seemed to believe he could buy me with trips to Paris – a sort of instant replacement for my dead sister. And as for Kevin Daly, well, he'd just waltzed straight into my life and my bed on the same night. All pretty sussed lives, I couldn't help thinking.

'I forgot to tell you,' Violet said the following morning as she hung up her coat after collecting the papers, 'your aunt Milly called yesterday. Orla spoke to her.'

'Who's taking my name in vain?' Orla was helped inside by an icy gust and shook herself like a puppy after a bath.

'Have you noticed the hills today? They look all sparkly with frost,' she said, bursting with the energy that walking to work brings.

'What news from Cork?' I asked as Violet headed out front to polish the tables and set up.

'Well, your aunt wanted to know everything.' Orla poured herself coffee and got to work. 'Said she'd put stuff in the post for both of us. Suggested we put real cod and chips on the specials board on Fridays. With mushy peas.' Orla wrinkled her nose. 'Apparently, there's a return to tradition among the young people in Cork. No meat on Friday – wasn't it a mortal sin or something?'

'Not that anyone who comes in here remembers.' I laughed. 'Although spanking fresh fish and thick, home-made chips does sound good.'

'Not the peas though. Proper tartare sauce, maybe?'

'Yeah, let's try it.' I liked the idea. 'Did she say anything else?'

'Only that Charlie was asking after you.' She was tying her apron. 'He wants to come and visit you again.'

'When?' My heart skipped a beat. I was thinking about him so much these days and since my meeting with Tamsin he seemed safer tucked away in Cork. And besides, I was still no nearer to finding a house. I knew I needed to do something positive on that front, instead of always thinking that I couldn't afford anything on the coast. Aunt Milly had sent photos of him and Squirt the other day and I wanted to burst into tears when I saw them. He was getting so big and I was missing it.

'She didn't say when,' Orla told me. 'I said you'd call her today though.'

'Great, thanks.' I sighed, desperately wanting to talk to her about everything.

'Are you OK?'

'Yeah, I'm fine.'

'It's just that I haven't seen Kevin around, and you've been sort of edgy lately. Sally said you've been avoiding her calls. She emailed me last night. She's worried about you.'

'I'm sorry, Orla, I've had a lot on my mind.' I had been talking to Sally on email but all I ever spoke about was the café, no matter how many times she asked about other things. I think I was afraid to tell her about Tamsin's offer. It would make it seem more real.

'I need to stop looking for the perfect house with sea views that I can't afford and focus on finding somewhere fast, so that I can have Charlie with me. I miss him so much.' I felt my mood dip even further. 'Now, come and taste these mini pizzas.' I made a supreme effort to shrug it all off. 'I think the tomato base with basil and garlic is yummy. All we need are a few decent toppings – some of those good anchovies, maybe. Or a bit of that chorizo sausage with one or two olives.' I was making notes as I spoke. 'Or what about tuna with red onion?'

'Sounds great, except for the tuna.'

'You could be right. Anyway, taste one with just buffalo mozzarella and some chilli oil and a sprinkle of oregano. It's divine. I think we've a winner on our hands.'

'Any of those lemon and raisin crumpets ready?' Violet popped her head around the door. 'And I need a toasted bagel with cream cheese and salmon, hold the capers.'

'Christ, is it that time already?' We were off.

As soon as I got a break I phoned Cork.

'How's it all going?' I asked my aunt.

'Great, love. You?'

'Mad.' I filled her in on all that was happening. 'How's Charlie?' I was dying to know.

'Terrific, except he's asking about you a lot.'

'Really? Is he OK?'

'Fine, fine, nothing at all to worry about, except that the other day on Sky News he saw a helicopter and ran behind the sofa and hid.'

'What? Oh my God, Milly, why didn't you tell me? He's obviously thinking about the accident again.' I felt sick.

'Listen to me, love, he's forgotten all about it. I did leave you a message at the time but . . .'

'I'm sorry, you did,' I remembered guiltily. 'I thought you were just ringing to say hi and I forgot . . .' I was close to tears now. 'Oh God, Milly, I'm a terrible mother.' It slipped out before I even realized that that was how I saw myself now.

'Lily, I promise you it's OK. I wasn't even going to tell you.'

'I'll come down today— Christ, I can't. Violet asked for tomorrow off . . . Let me think.' I was frantic.

'You'll be down for Christmas. That's all he can talk

about right now, so just concentrate on that.' My aunt eventually calmed me down, as she always did.

As soon as I put the phone down it rang again. 'Hello,' I said in a distracted voice.

'Lily?'

'Yes?'

'It's Daniel.'

'Oh Daniel, hi.'

'How are you?' he wanted to know.

'Grand.' I knew I sounded anything but.

'Is everything all right?'

'No.' It all came pouring out. 'I need to find a house.' All the steam went out of me suddenly.

If he was surprised at my outburst he didn't let on. 'OK, well, tell you what, I'll be in town in the morning and I'll do a quick whip round the auctioneers. Also, have you been on myhome.ie?'

'No, I'm useless,' I told him.

'Stop being so hard on yourself, you've had a lot on your plate. Why don't you do a search tonight? Then I'll drop in tomorrow evening and drag you out for a walk and we can chat. OK?'

'OK. Thank you.' I could have kissed him. In fact I wanted to. It was his voice. I really loved his accent, too. I hung up and smiled to myself.

Richard put his head in later that afternoon, just as I sat down with a juice – one of Aunt Milly's recipes – and my notebook to plan tomorrow's menu and also to make a list of everything I needed to do for myself. I was even more determined now to have Charlie with me as soon as possible, and at least the last few hours had finally made up my mind how to tell James and Tamsin what I knew would hurt them.

'Hi. Am I disturbing you?' Richard looked carefree and chilled and I envied him slightly.

'No, sit down,' I invited. 'Don't tell me, you were just passing?' I joked.

'Not exactly, no.'

'Coffee?'

'No, ta. Actually, I was wondering if I could buy you an early dinner in that new Indian in Arklow?'

'You paying?'

'I thought maybe we could go Dutch?' His grin made him look about twelve.

'Not a hope.'

'OK then, you can pay if you insist.'

'Richard Kearney, you are such a cheapskate.' It was the first time in ages we'd had a bit of banter. 'Anyway, I was in the Indian the other night.'

'Oh. Good?'

'Not bad.'

'Who'd you go with?' He sat down and dumped his keys on the table.

'Brian Daly, not that it's any of your business.'

'Lawyers, don't you just love them. Who paid?'

'He did, of course.'

'Bet it came out of your fee.'

'He's not like that.' I slapped his hand. 'Anyway, if you like, we could try out that new Italian in Rathdrum?'

'Great, yeah. How long will you be?'

'Give me half an hour. And I'll even pay.' I looked at him. 'I'd say you're saving up for the wedding.'

'Did you get the invite?' He was fiddling with his keys.

'Yep, I sure did.' I was remembering the disaster with Kevin.

'Will you come?'

'Do you want me to?'

'Yes.'

'Can I bring a date?' I'd no intention of it.

'Yes.' He looked a teeny bit put out, which was nice.

'Then I wouldn't miss it.' I finished my juice. 'How's Daisy coping?'

He sighed. 'Life is one long list.'

'Are you nervous?'

'I don't know.'

'Excited?'

'I guess so.'

'God, you're a riot.' I poked him in the ribs as I stood up. 'When's the stag?'

'Next week.'

'Do I get to come? One of your mates, like?'

He shuddered. 'Fuck, I dread to think what they've planned. Tom Dalton's waited a long time for this.'

'Let's see, I'd say drunk and naked will feature, anyway. I'd love to see it.'

374

'You'd like to see me naked?' he asked, tongue firmly in cheek.

'Only if I can be the one pouring paint over you and sticking feathers on your private parts.'

We looked at each other for a moment. I laughed first, happy that I'd finally sorted him out in my mind.

38

LILY

FOR THE REST OF THE WEEK I WAS TOO BUSY TO WORRY about anything and spent what little spare time I had shopping for clothes and presents for Charlie and my aunt, and willing the days away until I could get to Cork. Without warning, it snowed and Wicklow – the greenest county in Ireland, according to locals – turned into a giant Christmas cake. It was freezing. Down at the harbour an icy wind propelled the kids who were sliding and skating everywhere while the older people shuffled about on the now highly polished pavements. The purple heathery hills became giant snowmen presiding over the town.

We hired a student and set up a stall outside the café selling hot chocolate with marshmallows and toasted crumpets runny with butter, and the holiday season was suddenly under way and leisurely lunches were the order of the day. Sandra Horlicks hired a coach and brought a group of clients for a long liquid one. They spent a fortune on alcohol and I was grateful we'd been able to secure a wine licence when we opened, even though it had meant a huge amount of paperwork and a lot of help from Brian Daly. Watching Sandra and her gang toast each other, I was glad it had all worked out in our favour. I'd gone to a lot of trouble to keep her happy. We'd planned a special menu – not a slice of turkey in sight – and when I'd faxed it to her she rang immediately to confirm.

'And best of all, I live around the corner,' she told me when she dropped in to order the wine the day before, so that it would be on the table waiting for the revellers. 'I'll go up on the bus in the morning and once I see them off I can walk home. Clever, eh?'

'Very.' I grinned. 'And thank you. It's great business for us.'

'Pleasure.' She beamed. 'But they're noisy, I'm warning you.'

She wasn't joking. A few of the regulars complained. I couldn't see this working for long.

'What do you think?' I asked Orla, as soon as we'd served the main courses.

'It's a disaster.' She didn't mince her words. 'The place is just too small.'

'And the acoustics are brutal.' I hadn't noticed it before. 'I'm going to have to talk to Maureen Stanley after Christmas.'

'She'll be in on Monday. She's bringing four of the Wicklow County Council planning officers here for lunch, along with the senior architect in her office. She dropped in yesterday to see how it was going. Said she hadn't seen you in ages.'

'Yeah, I've no life at the moment.' I was feeling sorry for myself today. 'Anyway she's going to have to come up with something – this is madness. We can't continue or we'll lose all our regulars. I can see Yvonne Treacy and a couple of the ladies who lunch trying to catch my eye and I doubt it's to compliment me on the Thai fishcakes.'

'Why don't you consider clearing out the stock room and putting the stuff upstairs for the moment?' Naomi was cleaning up. 'Then you could use that room for private parties.'

Orla and I looked at each other.

'That's a great idea,' she got in just before me.

'Girl, you're a genius.' I couldn't believe neither of us had thought of it before.

The young girl shrugged. 'And there's a hatch through to the kitchen as well.'

'There'll be a small bonus in your wage packet at the end of the week.' I slapped her on the back. 'You may have just saved our bacon.'

She was delighted, in a teenage mortified way.

Daniel was turning into a frequent visitor. He'd been trawling the local auctioneers but couldn't find a house he thought I'd like. We'd spent an hour in the newly revamped McDaniel's pub in Brittas Bay the previous evening going through another lot of brochures, after he'd dragged me out to his place to admire the vast expanse of freshly ironed white fields.

'Come on, townie,' he'd urged, after I refused to walk another step because my feet were so cold.

'Who d'you think you are, Chris Bonington?' I laughed, pulling off his hat. 'You look like a bounty hunter. It's totally ridiculous.'

'I know, as if my head wasn't big enough without all this fur.' He danced around like a puppy. 'The flaps make me look like Pluto.' He was always so self-effacing. It was one of the many things I liked about him.

'That's it!' I was delighted. 'Pluto, that's spot-on.'

'My mother bought it for me.'

'Well, tell her to stick to socks and jocks.'

I had a phone call from Beth Hammond just after lunch.

'I need your help,' she said cheerfully. 'Could I drop down to see you in Wicklow?' I was surprised she remembered, even though she had been very chatty that night at the party in her house.

'But it's miles away,' I said, trying to put her off.

'Well, I've a friend, Celine, who lives in Avoca, so I thought I could combine the two.'

'Tell you what,' I came to a snap decision, 'I'm coming to Dublin today to visit my solicitor. Why don't I drop by your house?' At least it meant I would be in control and could leave whenever I wanted.

'Would you? That'd be fab. Thanks.'

I hung up wondering if I'd done the right thing.

As it turned out, all she wanted was someone to cater for a very special Christmas Eve dinner she'd planned for

William's family. We had a great chat about the pressures of the season and I noticed she wasn't the bubbly person I'd met the night of the party.

'I can't help you, I'm afraid.' I tried to explain how overworked I was and her face fell as we sat in the warm kitchen on our second cup of coffee. 'Anyway, I'll be firmly tucked up in Cork on Christmas Eve with my family.' I smiled at the pleasure even saying it gave me as I tried to suggest other options for her. The thing was, I really liked Beth Hammond. She was smart and funny and very attractive. What on earth was she doing with William, I asked myself, but I knew really. The Williams of this world always got the girls.

'Oh dear.' She sighed then seemed resigned quite quickly. 'Actually, maybe you've just given me the perfect excuse not to do it this year.'

'Oh yeah?'

'Well, I'm a bit cheesed off with my husband at the moment. He's been totally preoccupied lately. More coffee?' She reached for the pot.

'Thanks.' I held out my china cup.

'And I've hardly seen him. He's always so damn busy. Does that sound incredibly selfish?'

'No.' How come I kept getting pulled into these lives, I wondered.

'Sometimes it's hard when you don't work. So much happens to him whereas every day's the same with me. And lately he hasn't been talking to me all that much.'

I milked my coffee and said nothing, although I was itching to tell her exactly what I'd do with him.

'I'm sorry.' She smiled. 'I think I'm just being paranoid. My friend Triona – whose husband has just left her for an *older* woman, even though she spent a fortune getting her boobs done because he wanted her to – thinks I let William walk all over me.'

I wondered if Triona was the over-made-up, very drunk woman I'd seen clinging to him the night of the party.

'And I've desperate PMT this week and still no sign of my period so that's probably making me madly hormonal anyway. And if all that's not enough another friend of mine has just discovered her husband's been buying expensive presents that have not been finding their way to her.'

'Maybe they're for business clients?' I'd no idea why I was defending the unknown man.

'His customers all have four legs. He's a vet.' She half smiled. 'And he's been to several away conferences as well. D'ya know, I'm not sure what's come over me all of a sudden.' She grinned. 'I don't usually unburden myself like this. And we barely know each other.'

'Well, my sister always said forewarned is forearmed or something like that.' I took a deep breath and decided to plunge right in. 'So what would *you* do if you . . . discovered something about your husband?'

'Oddly enough, that's the thing that's probably bothering me the most. You see, I'm not sure I'd do anything. Does that sound crazy?'

'No.' Surprisingly, I wasn't surprised.

'I love him, you see.' She looked sad. 'And I have a gorgeous life, a house I love, kids I adore and the lifestyle I've always wanted. It sounds silly but I can go anywhere, do anything, buy whatever I want, no questions asked. Also – and you're going to think this is stupid because you're young and single and independent – I like being Mrs William Hammond. I've been his wife for most of my adult life. Can you understand that?'

'Yes, I can, perfectly.' It was the truth. But I had the strongest urge to get back at William somehow.

'What do you think I should do?' She looked like she'd been dying to talk about it to someone. 'You see, I've no one to talk to really. In our circle everyone knows everyone else so I couldn't risk it and, well, my closest friend doesn't really like William . . .' She trailed off. 'This is ridiculous, actually. I don't even know if I need to do anything. I've nothing to go on, not a thing. I'm just another silly, insecure housewife.' Beth looked close to tears.

'Well, I've got a friend in Sydney . . .' I told her about Sally's friend who'd been a mistress for years. Actually I didn't know that much about her, so I improvised a bit and felt extremely guilty afterwards.

'Oh my God, so what did his wife do?' Beth was animated.

'Well, she didn't let on, of course, but essentially what she did was take control. And she reined him in so tightly in such a reasonable way that he'd no choice but to go along with her.'

'I see. What sort of things did she do, exactly?'

'Well, she joined his gym for a start,' I lied, trying to think of all the things William loved. 'And she took a taxi there every evening the same time as him, so they could "have a bit of quality time on the way home, darling" – at least I think that was the way she put it. Oh, and she started going out herself, and suddenly there were no babysitters to be found and so he had to come home early. Lastly, I believe she arranged for his brand new Jag to be stolen and then insisted they could cope with one car to save the environment.' I had a horrible feeling I'd just taken this story a step too far.

'She did not?' Beth's eyes were out on stalks.

'Well now, her family weren't exactly model citizens, it has to be said.' I tried to make it more plausible. 'There were lots of questions about where they got their money, I believe. Apparently, there was a cousin – Vinnie or somebody, who'd done time for theft. He sorted out the car.' Shut up *now*, I warned myself. Quit while you're ahead.

'Well, it serves him bloody well right,' Beth announced.

'I'm sure you'd be a bit more subtle.' I smiled. 'Of course, all this is just supposition on your part . . .'

'Lily, you've helped me a lot.' She patted my hand.

'Really?'

'Yep, you see, even if he's a model husband, I've let him get away with murder for years. For instance, what am I doing *hinting* about going on this upcoming trip to Paris with him? It's what fifteen-year-olds do when they want a boy to ask them out.' She burst out laughing.

'This has actually cheered me up, can you believe it?'

'Me too.' I checked the time on my phone, relieved that my conscience was clear about the Paris thing, at least. 'Now I'd better get going,' I told her.

'Thanks.' She gave me a hug. 'Oh, and Lily, it might be better if we kept this to ourselves – just in case you meet William when, hopefully, you cook for us in the future. In fact I'm not going to even mention you were here, if that's OK?'

'Sure,' I told her and beat a hasty retreat, not feeling very good at all about what I'd done.

I had arranged to call in to Brian Daly's office at five thirty that same afternoon, to go through a few things. We were having dinner afterwards and I was staying over at the flat in Dublin. I was looking forward to it. It was weeks since I'd had a night away from Wicklow and I was enjoying the buzz of Dublin after so long.

'You look well.' Brian seemed pleased as he ushered me into a chair. 'How's it all going?'

'So far so good.' I knew he was still very cautious about the venture.

'Not sorry?'

I shook my head. 'It's the best thing I've ever done,' I told him honestly.

We had just finished going through some papers and had arranged one or two financial matters when there was a tap on the door.

'Sorry to disturb you, I was just— Hey Lily, how are

384

you?' Kevin Daly strolled in, not missing a beat when he saw me. I could smell the cologne before he got to within ten feet of me. He was all dressed up, obviously on the pull, and I had to admit he looked good. All brawn and no brains, I thought, relieved that he appeared so relaxed. While I still hadn't forgiven him for his parting comments that night, right now I was just happy that he wasn't holding a grudge.

'Hi,' I said casually.

'I was just wondering if you fancied a quick drink?' he asked Brian. 'I didn't realize you had company. Your secretary is gone . . .' He smiled at us both and looked straight down my top.

'We were just finishing.' Brian always looked uncomfortable any time his brother was around, I'd noticed. 'Actually, Lily and I are off out to dinner.'

'A date, eh?' He managed to make it sound like a dirty weekend. It was his constant smirk that did it. I wondered how the hell I'd ever dated him, even for a couple of weeks.

'Just dinner,' I told him, smiling, but it had absolutely no effect.

'Well, I won't disturb you two lovebirds so, but how about I buy you a drink across the road beforehand?'

'Fine by me.' I wouldn't give him the satisfaction of making up an excuse.

'Are you sure?' Brian looked a bit put out.

'Yeah, why not? We have time for a quick one, don't we?'

'I suppose so. Give us a minute or two . . .' Brian indicated his papers.

'OK, I'll get them in. What'll it be?'

'Pint of Guinness for me.'

'Pint of Heineken for me,' I told him.

'Pint, eh? Not very ladylike,' he leered. 'And you look so demure.' He winked at his brother.

I noticed Brian looking closely at us.

'What century do you live in?' It was a vain attempt to put him down. He laughed and pulled my hair. With anyone else I could take it. With Kevin Daly I simply wanted to kick him in the goolies.

By the time we joined him in the pub ten minutes later he was chatting up a less well-heeled version of Madonna.

'Don't let us disturb you.' I snatched my pint while Brian signalled to the barman that he was ready for his Guinness.

'Now, now, don't be jealous.' He patted my bottom as I walked away and I swear I had to stop myself flinging my drink all over his moisturized, combed chest. 'You know I only had eyes for you at one time.' He grinned at me and winked at the Madge lookalike, who wouldn't be singing 'Like A Virgin' to him later, I guessed.

Thankfully, it was just one drink, although Kevin dominated the conversation with stories of deals he was about to do and trendy places he'd been to. For brothers they were polar opposites. Luckily for me, Brian seemed as keen to get away as I was and afterwards we had a lovely dinner in Howth.

'I have to tell you something,' I said eventually. 'Kevin and I had a brief – very brief – fling a while back.' I was mortified just thinking about it. 'Madness,' I explained, hoping he wouldn't take offence. 'Sheer madness.'

'I wondered what was going on between the two of you.' He sipped his drink thoughtfully.

'It ended a bit . . . well, badly, I suppose.' It was all I was going to say.

'Were you hurt?' he asked and I almost choked on my prawns.

'No, no,' I said quickly, too quickly. 'Just . . . not suited, I guess.'

'Be careful, Lily.' Brian put down his knife and fork. 'I know he's my brother, but he's not always the most . . . honourable. He's a charmer, too good-looking, really. You wouldn't be the first woman to fall for him. I'd hate it if he . . . left you high and dry.'

I bet I'd be the first woman to puke at the thought of him, though, which was what I was about to do. How could Brian automatically assume that his sleazeball of a brother had dumped me and not the other way round?

'Actually, Brian, I sort of . . . ended it.' I'd had enough of being nice.

'Oh, I see' was all he said.

Later he dropped me back to the old place in a taxi, and walked me to the door while the driver happily let the meter run.

'I had a lovely time. You're a funny girl,' he was laughing at one of my jokes, 'and you're also very good company.'

'So are you.' I knotted my hands through his arm. He felt like the brother I'd always wanted. 'You're so kind to me, I don't know what I'd have done without you these past few months.' I was glad of an opportunity to say it.

'It's a pleasure.' He smiled down at me. 'Any news from Cork, by the way? How's Charlie?'

'He's fine, learning new words every day.' I always worried he thought I wasn't doing enough where Charlie was concerned.

'Will you see him soon?'

'Unfortunately not soon enough.' I sighed. 'We're even open Sundays until Christmas, I'm afraid. It was a tough decision to make, because it means I can't get down to Cork even for one night, but we've been inundated with bookings for lunches and parties and I simply had to do it, just in case January is a dead month.'

'I can see how it might be,' he said.

'Everyone with massive credit card bills, so no one eating out.' I hoped it wouldn't be as bad as I feared. 'My aunt was going to come up to help out for a day or two next week and bring Charlie but she can't face the train journey at this time of year.'

'Would she not drive?'

'I hinted at it but she hasn't made the journey in a car in years, and Charlie's not the best traveller.' I wanted so badly to see him I'd even considered sending a car to pick them up, but the cost was astronomical. 'Anyway, I can't wait for Christmas.' I smiled, determined not to get maudlin.

'Poor little lad, he needs a father figure,' Brian said quietly.

I was a little bit tipsy or I'd never have taken offence. 'We manage,' I said, more sharply than I'd intended.

'I'm sorry, Lily,' he interrupted immediately. 'I didn't mean—'

'No, I'm sorry.' I had an urge to tell him what had been keeping me awake lately. 'I'm a bit sensitive . . . It's just,' I looked at him, 'there's someone I . . . came into contact with recently who . . . might be . . . Charlie's father.' I felt better once it was out.

'What did you say?' Brian's face was chalk-white.

'I met somebody who . . . used to know Alison.' I realized I wasn't prepared for this at all, standing in a draughty hallway with a man I liked a lot and didn't want to upset. 'It's only a vague possibility.' I was backtracking now.

'Who is he?'

'Nobody you know.'

'Lily, this is important. We need to talk about this. I don't want you doing anything foolish.'

That annoyed me. 'I'm responsible for Charlie now.'

'Look, let me get rid of the taxi.' He was already halfway down the stairs. 'Make me a coffee? Please?'

'I've no milk.' I wasn't giving in that easily. 'And besides, the place is freezing. I was planning on going straight to bed.'

'Please,' he repeated. 'I won't be a second.' He disappeared, leaving me with little choice.

* * *

The flat was indeed cold and without my sister's homely touches it looked neglected. A few potted plants had died and there were cobwebs in corners and the windows looked grimy.

'So, why are you so concerned?' I asked him a couple of minutes later as I handed him a mug of vile-looking liquid, made with a jar of instant coffee past its sell-by date.

'You know how fond I was of Alison.' He seemed uncomfortable. 'And I know that she wouldn't want this.'

'How do you know that?'

'She wanted no contact with the father. I got the impression she didn't even like him.' I had the distinct feeling he was talking off the top of his head, which was unusual for him. He was always so considered.

How could anyone dislike James? I wondered. 'Well, this person, he and his wife . . .'

'Wife?'

'Yes, he's married.' I was ashamed of myself when I thought about it later, but I got some sort of perverse pleasure out of letting him know that Alison wasn't a saint, as he thought. 'They can't have children.' I watched him closely. 'His wife recently found out that her husband and my sister had a . . . thing . . .' I wished then I'd never started this conversation.

'So what's this got to do with you?' He looked grim.

I sipped my coffee and played for time. 'They want to . . . have some sort of role in his life,' I muttered.

'That's not possible.'

'I haven't agreed to anything.' I was on the defensive right away. 'And what do you mean, that's not possible?'

'Lily, this is crazy.' He came very close to me and made me look at him. 'Alison wanted *you* to bring up her child. You know how much she loved him . . .' I knew he was genuinely upset, but even so I resented the vague innuendo that I was somehow neglecting Charlie. I wanted to tell him that I wasn't the sort of person who'd ever give him up, not even to his father. But childishly I wanted him to know that without me having to tell him.

'Listen to me, Lily, this is extremely important. I'll help you.' He seemed to be searching for words. 'But he's not Charlie's father.' I had a feeling he was sorry he'd started this too.

'How do you know that?'

'It doesn't matter,' he said too quickly.

'Oh, but it does.' I thought about it for a second. Maybe I was putting two and two together and getting forty-four, but I immediately felt I had to ask.

'Brian.' I stood up. 'Are you Charlie's father?' I knew it was ludicrous the minute I said it, but he'd been acting very strangely ever since I'd mentioned James.

'No,' but he wasn't looking at me.

'You are, aren't you?'

'No, I'm not, Lily.' He looked straight at me and I knew he was telling the truth.

'So why are you so concerned about him?'

He wrestled with something in his head. It was written all over his face.

'Tell me,' I begged him.

'I'm his uncle.' He waited for my reaction.

'His uncle?' I couldn't figure it out. 'I don't understand.'

'He's Kevin's son,' he told me quietly.

39

WILLIAM AND BETH

'HI, GUYS,' WILLIAM CALLED TO NO ONE IN PARTICULAR. He was relieved to see lights on and smell dinner. He'd been deliberately cool with Beth these past few days and it had obviously paid off. After long days in the clinic he didn't deserve her vaguely sarcastic comments and ever-changing moods, he'd decided.

When he went into the kitchen the table was set and there were fresh flowers and candles prettily arranged and even an open bottle of wine.

'What's the occasion?' He smiled at his wife and indicated the setting. He decided to forgive her.

'What do you mean?' From her voice it seemed that she wasn't playing ball.

'Flowers and candles? It's Tuesday. Are we expecting company?'

'No. I just thought we might as well get into the Christmas spirit. Only a little over a week to go.'

'Yes, and normally you're fussing about with lists, on the phone all the time, at your desk after dinner, that sort

393

of thing. Yet you've hardly mentioned it this year.' He accepted the glass of wine she offered. 'Did the tree arrive?' he asked, a bit miffed that he'd had to order it himself.

'Yes, and I'll be organized, don't worry.' Her smile was a touch too bright, he thought.

'Cheers.' He took a sip then set down his glass. 'Actually, let me get changed and say hello to the kids first. What's to eat, anyway?'

'Stuffed pork steak. Tell them it's time for bed while you're there, will you? Harry was up twice last night so he's exhausted.'

'Will do. Back in a minute.' He did as requested and returned to find everything ready and just as he liked it, down to the snow-white napkins and proper cutlery.

'So, tell me what we're doing for the holidays?' William asked his wife as soon as he sat down.

'Well, we're not doing the traditional Christmas Eve thing for your family,' she told him casually. 'Can't get a caterer for any money.'

'Oh, who have you tried?'

'Everyone. Audrey tried to get me somebody, then told me I was wasting my time.'

'What about that girl we used last time?' William had no idea why he was saying it except that he was becoming obsessed with seeing her and she was not playing ball.

'Lily? No, she was the first one Audrey asked, apparently. I think she said she was going away somewhere,' Beth said vaguely.

This was news to William.

'Anyway, unless you want to organize something yourself, William, I'm just too busy at the moment.' Without pausing she regaled him with all the usual stuff – Santa presents ordered by phone from Selfridge's and Hamley's – oh, and she was going to London for the day on Thursday with her friend Shirley, early flight. Could William babysit? The kids loved it when he took care of them.

'Fine.' He decided to humour her. 'How's Shirley?'

Beth looked at him for just a moment too long, he thought, and then said quietly, 'She thinks Martin's having an affair.'

'Don't be ridiculous.' It was out before he realized he didn't need this. He saw his wife's mouth set in one of those 'don't you dare say that to me' looks and decided he'd better be careful.

'What's that supposed to mean?' was all she said.

He took a bite of his food. 'It's just, Martin of all people. Quite frankly I can't see it.'

'I can.'

'He's a vet, for God's sake. He spends all his time with smelly animals.'

'Those smelly animals have owners, you know. Some of them young and attractive.'

William snorted. 'What on earth's put this notion into Shirley's head, anyway?'

'Stuff.' His wife sipped her wine.

'What sort of stuff?'

'He's out a lot . . .'

'Beth, every man I know is out a lot. Come to think of it, you've been missing a bit lately yourself.' He winked at her. 'Anything I should know?' He made an attempt to lighten the mood.

'Very funny.'

'So, is that where you've been? With Shirley?'

'Once or twice, yes.'

'Darling, I don't think you should get too involved,' he said gently. This was definitely not the sort of conversation he wanted to be having with his wife.

'Would you ask him – in a roundabout way? Find out anything you can?'

William was appalled. 'I most certainly will not.' He saw her look. 'Beth, no, I mean it. Leave me out of this.' The very idea made him uneasy. 'Anyway, we're merely social acquaintances, hardly bosom buddies.'

'I suppose he'd deny it, anyway.' She attacked her food again.

'Look, if Martin Henderson, timid, shy Martin who wouldn't say boo to a goose, is having an affair, I'll buy you a diamond bracelet for Christmas, how's that?' He made a face at her and she smiled at him for the first time all evening. 'Now, will you relax, you're all tense.' He got up and went round to her side of the table. 'How about a massage later?'

'Good idea.'

He picked up both their plates and headed for the sink. 'I mean, he doesn't even look the type.' He tried to sound casual, all the while wondering if he could get to Cork immediately after Christmas and surprise Lily. He assumed that's where she was going. He just hoped she wasn't off somewhere with that Kevin guy, since Beth had said she was going away. Cork, barely three hours from Dublin, could hardly be called 'going away'.

'Well, if it is true Shirley will kill him. She'll never forgive him.' Beth looked positively livid, which was unlike her. He wished now he hadn't brought up the subject again.

'What's for pudding?' He opened the fridge.

'I wouldn't either, if I were in her shoes,' his wife muttered, ignoring his question. 'In fact, if you ever did it on me, I'd disconnect your balls with a pair of pliers.'

40

JAMES AND TAMSIN

'ANY NEWS?' TAMSIN WAS AT THE DOOR AS SOON AS SHE heard his key turn.

'No, nothing.' James tried to keep it light. 'We just have to be patient, love.' What he didn't say was that he'd been thinking about it non-stop, wondering if they had, in fact, done the right thing. When his wife had initially suggested that they meet Lily together he'd been completely opposed to the idea, couldn't even get his head around it for ages. But as usual she'd persisted, assuring him that if Lily saw them as the loving couple they were, she just might be tempted to agree to what he had at first considered to be an outrageous idea. Put simply, Tamsin wanted to adopt – or at least share custody of – the child she was sure belonged to him. Mad, James thought, but so mad it just might work, he had eventually privately conceded.

'It's hard. I alternate between being seriously nervous and desperately excited.' She followed him into the kitchen.

'I'm the same. It was all I could think about on my run this morning.' James went straight for a fizzy drink.

'I'm not buying that stuff any more.' Tamsin indicated the bottle. 'Fizzy drinks were number one on Gillian McKeith's top twenty baddies the other night.'

'Listen, we don't smoke, you'll barely let me touch alcohol and we're forever juicing and eating our greens. Leave me something bad, for God's sake, woman.' James slapped her on the bottom as he passed.

'Remember, if we're going to be parents we'll need all our energy.' She wagged her finger at him.

'Please God,' he said quietly. 'But Tamsin, we don't even know if the child is mine.'

'I don't care.' She had an odd look on her face that he'd seen before. 'I want him, James, regardless. I really, really want a baby.'

'I know you do.'

'And you've come round to the idea, haven't you?' Tamsin seemed to relax. She rubbed his back and he wriggled with pleasure, like a dog having his belly stroked.

James nodded. 'Yes, I have.' He turned and grabbed her in a bear hug. 'You've convinced me.' He planted a kiss on her head.

'She likes us too, doesn't she?'

'Definitely. It was worth meeting her together, you were right to make me do it.' He sighed. 'Even though it felt wrong, at first.' James knew he had to be careful. She was still very sensitive about the whole Alison episode.

'I know it did, but it had to be done. It's just, my

instincts are that she might be struggling with the idea of caring for him full time. She didn't say it but . . . why else would he still be in Cork?' Tamsin sighed. 'What we're offering provides her with the perfect solution.'

'Tamsin, she adores that child, it was written all over her face,' James said quietly.

'And as you told her, she can see him whenever she likes,' his wife continued, ignoring his remark.

James pulled out a chair after popping some toast in the machine. He needed carbs after the run. 'Are you having tea?'

'Yes, please. James, did I make it clear that she could have him for holidays, or any time really? That we just wanted to have him live with us some of the time?'

'Yes.' James smiled tiredly. 'Relax.'

'And Christmas, did I mention Christmas?'

He nodded again. 'Tamsin, you're a psychologist, you used every trick in the book.' He heard the pop and went to get the toast. 'All we can do now is wait.'

'James, I'm not . . . I mean . . . I wasn't trying to trick her or anything. She won't think that, will she?'

'No, that's not what I meant and you know it.' He buttered the toast and made two pots of tea, one herbal and the other regular. Then they sat at the table in the streamlined, immaculate kitchen and went over it all again.

'You know, I want this little boy so much it scares me,' she told him. 'I wish we had a picture, even.'

'I know, I know.' He sighed. 'So do I. But Tamsin,' he

took her hand in his, 'we can't get our hopes up too high, just in case.'

'I realize that.' But she seemed to shrug off the notion. 'I'm trying not to, honestly.' She was lost in thought for a moment. 'But,' her face broke into a grin, 'can we go into town and have a look for things, just in case?'

'What sort of things?' He was trying desperately to hold back.

'For him, you know, for his room?' She saw his face. 'Not buy anything,' she said quickly. 'Just look, please?'

'Darling, let's wait a while longer. Just till we hear something concrete . . .'

'Yes, you're right.' She smiled at him. 'As usual.'

'We could go to an early movie, in Stillorgan?'

'OK, but there's that lovely children's shop in the centre. Maybe just a quick look around while we're parking . . .?'

'Tamsin—'

'Please.' She kissed him. 'Not to buy anything, remember?'

James knew when he was beaten. He drained his cup. 'Let me shower and change. And I need to do one or two bits around the place first. I've been neglecting things recently. Say we leave here about two? That should give us plenty of time. Oh, and go check the movie times on Aertel and decide which one you want to see.'

'Will do. And thanks.' She put her head on his shoulder. 'Thanks for understanding.'

'I want this child as much as you do, just remember that. And I pray every day that it happens.'

'Me too. I went to mass this morning.' She gathered up their stuff. 'Oh James, we're so close to having it all.' She sighed. 'I promised that I'd never ask for anything ever again if this happens. When do you think she'll call?'

'I've no idea. But I hope it's soon.'

'Leave your phone on silent during the movie, just in case.'

'Tamsin, we can't let this take over our lives. Anyway, she'll probably text.'

'Whatever you say, husband. You're the boss.'

'And don't you forget it,' James told her with a grin.

They had a very pleasant day, cleaning out the spare room 'just in case' and pottering in the shops as if they were already parents. He had to stop Tamsin buying cute little wellington boots and when they looked in the furniture store she went straight to the stuff for kids' bedrooms. They discussed paint colours and the best schools and had coffee and chocolate cake and generally behaved as if they already had him.

An hour into the movie his phone vibrated. He saw it was Lily. He excused himself and went outside to the car park. After he'd spoken to her James stayed where he was for a long while. It was one of the few times he wished he was a smoker. Standing leaning against the wall, he noticed a woman opposite take a long drag on a fag and visibly relax. James needed something himself right now.

When he turned around to go back in he saw his wife standing at the door to the cinema.

'What is it?' She came towards him. 'James, tell me, please?'

He led her to a graffiti-covered bench at the edge of a green area beside the lower car park.

'Tamsin, darling, you have to be brave . . .'

'What?'

'That was Lily. She's found out some information, from her lawyer.' There was no easy way to break the news. 'It's not going to work out . . .'

'How do you mean?' She looked terrified.

'I'm not Char— the baby's father.'

'That doesn't matter.' She jumped up. 'James, ring her back. Tell her we don't care, we still want him. We'll do anything . . .' Her eyes had that wild look in them again and he was afraid for her.

'Tamsin, darling, listen to me.' He took her by the arm. 'She says she was . . . wrong . . . to give us false hope.' He felt very low, having to tell her all this. 'She said she'd die if she had to give him up . . . even the temporary separation is killing her.'

'No.'

'I'm so sorry.'

'James, please don't give up so easily. I beg you.'

'Shush, Tamsin, listen to me.' He pulled her down beside him and put his arms around her. 'She knew from the start she'd never be able to do it, no matter what. Honestly.' He put his finger over her lips. 'She was upset

403

too, but she said that the child is part of her and all she has left of her sister.' He wished he could change it for her. 'Darling, we were foolish to let ourselves dream . . .'

'No, we can't give up, James, we can't.'

'He's not mine,' James told her softly. 'That was our only hope.'

'No, we'll do tests, it might be a mistake.'

'No, her lawyer told her. When she mentioned us to him—'

'She mentioned us? James, that means she was going to go through with it, don't you see? Call her back. Ask if we can meet her. Now, tonight. James, please . . .' She burst into tears. 'Please, James, don't give up,' she kept repeating.

'Come on, darling.' He put his coat around her and led her to the car. 'Please, don't cry. Please.'

'I want my baby' was all she said, over and over again.

41

RICHARD AND DAISY

'WHAT DO YOU MEAN, YOU'RE GOING AWAY?' RICHARD asked. 'I thought you were going to give me a hand in the café?'

'Are you mad?' Daisy laughed. 'I need my rest. I'm getting married in less than two weeks, or had you forgotten?' She kissed him full on the mouth.

'Fat chance of that.' Richard grimaced. 'Where are you going, so?' They were having a drink while waiting for Tom and Trudy. Another meeting with the best man and bridesmaid. His mate had sounded less than enthusiastic when Richard phoned him earlier.

'The Canaries.' Daisy sipped her water. She hadn't been drinking alcohol for weeks.

'What? I don't believe it.'

'Yep, but I'll be back a couple of days beforehand, don't worry,' she teased.

'You'll be away for Christmas? What am I supposed to do?'

'Go home to Mummy. She can't wait to get her hands

405

on you, she thinks you don't eat properly.'

'But Daisy, I really do need help in the café,' he pleaded.

'I couldn't anyway. My hands and nails would suffer,' Daisy said.

He saw her glance at her perfectly manicured finger-nails and flick away an imaginary speck of dirt from under her thumb and knew she was serious. This was all becoming a bit scary for casual, couldn't-care-less Richard. He had a mad urge to see Lily then. He wanted to spend time with someone who didn't mind getting their hands wet.

Tom arrived. 'What's the story?' He straddled a stool.

'Drink?' Richard asked quickly. He knew it would be a struggle to keep his mate interested for more than two minutes. A creamy pint was his only chance.

'Thanks, mate. So, how's it going, Daisy?'

'She's off to the Canaries.'

Tom laughed. 'You're a scream. What for?'

'A tan, what do you think?' Daisy was rooting in her bag. 'Now . . .'

'Jesus, not another list. You sure know how to delegate.' Tom was only half joking.

'I've a printout for each of us. It's a run-through of the day.' Daisy handed them one each as Richard came back with the drinks.

'She's put times on everything, look . . .' Tom was laughing. 'Eleven ten, give Richard rescue remedy.' He took a swallow. 'What the hell is rescue remedy?'

'I haven't a clue.' Richard looked thrown.

'It's to relax him,' Daisy said indignantly.

'Any more relaxed and he'll be fucking comatose, eh, mate? Sorry, Daisy.' Tom knew she hated bad language. 'Look!' His mouth fell open. 'I've to get a new suitcase.' He handed it to Richard, who already had a copy. 'What do I need a suitcase for in the first place?'

'You'll be carrying stuff for me,' Daisy told him calmly. 'And I've seen that scruffy old thing you drag around with you – it's held together with a belt. I am not having it anywhere near the castle.'

'This is mad.' Tom made a face behind her back and shot his mate a pitying look. 'I'm outta here.'

'Sit.' Daisy pushed him back on to the stool. 'Trudy'll be here in a minute. Now, Tom, here's a separate sheet with what you've to do while I'm away . . .'

'Daisy, I'm a bloke, I don't do lists. Besides, I've a radio show to present every day.' He took another swallow. 'I do work, you know,' he told her, a bit miffed. 'Anyway,' he glanced at the list, 'if anyone heard me ringing a florist, my reputation'd be in shreds.' He winked at Richard.

'I want a report each morning.' Daisy tried to relax. 'And no keeping him out late drinking every night. I want him fresh-faced and energized on the day.' Tom nearly choked.

'Listen, mate,' he whispered as soon as Daisy had gone to the loo. 'It's not too late, honest.' He grinned. 'Just say the word and I'll take a week's holiday starting New Year's Eve. We could go off to Thailand and meet a few babes.'

'Don't tempt me.' Richard finished his drink in one.

'Jesus, I wouldn't even mind if the bridesmaid was a

looker.' Tom waved at Trudy, who was glancing around trying to spot them.

'Ah, she's OK,' Richard sighed, 'although I don't suppose she'd win any beauty contests.'

'Listen, mate, the only competition she'd ever win is best in breed.'

Daisy was back and she decided to ignore their snorting. Trudy was quickly given the job of phoning each of them first thing every morning to go through the list. That'd wipe the smile off their faces.

'Aw, come on, Daisy, lighten up. I've seen military academies with less rules and regulations,' Tom pleaded.

'Tom Dalton.' Daisy leaned in and he decided not to tell her she reeked of garlic. 'This is my wedding day and I will not have anyone – least of all you – spoil it.' She smiled sweetly. 'I'd kill you first with my bare hands.'

42

LILY

BY CHRISTMAS EVE I WAS FINDING IT HARD TO PUT ONE foot in front of the other. It really had been a rollercoaster ride. I was up at five each day, the café seemed to have absolutely no down time and as soon as we'd closed and cleaned up I was almost ready for bed, except that I had a mountain of orders to keep on top of. We were being asked to do more and more catering and my main problem was learning to say no – hard for any new business owner. We'd had at least half a dozen calls from south County Dublin yummy mummies since Beth Hammond's party. At least I was having no trouble refusing those requests. The last thing I needed was to run into William, who was now talking about coming to Cork over Christmas – with absolutely no encouragement from me. The man's ego knew no bounds and, since Brian had dropped the bombshell about Kevin, I had zero interest in keeping him on side.

All that and bills and VAT to keep track of meant I spent several hours on the computer each evening before collapsing into bed around eleven.

I had planned to spend at least part of the days over Christmas sleeping and thinking about Kevin and Brian Daly as well as all the other complications in my life, but Aunt Milly had other ideas. 'All the neighbours want to meet you,' she told me excitedly during one of our nightly chats. 'I've made so many new friends through Charlie. And because I have time on my hands, sure I'm now letting plumbers in and taking deliveries and returning books to libraries. It's a whole new world,' she said happily.

I was too tired to argue intelligently. 'So there's no chance of you coming to me instead?' I asked feebly, thinking of the journey to Cork with a mountain of packages.

'Personally I'd enjoy it, love – all those sales – but I can't do that to the little chap.'

'Why not? He'd love the adventure.'

'He's so excited, you won't know him.' She appeared not to have heard. 'He's gotten so tall, too. Anyway, he has a group of little pals here and there are so many outings and parties planned for them over the few days. I can't just uproot him and bring him to Dublin.'

'But Dublin is his home, he's lived there most of his life, all his things are in the flat . . .' I began to feel a bit panicked that he might not want to come and live with me at all. Wicklow would mean yet another new start for him.

'I know, I know, and of course he will go back there eventually, or hopefully to Wicklow if you find a house. By the way, have you put his name down for the local school yet?' She didn't wait for an answer. 'He really seems to love the country, Lily. He's got a healthy glow about him and he's eating like a horse. And he adores going to the park every day. He's able to feed the ducks now.'

I felt horribly guilty once more as I wondered if I would ever be enough for him, what with working and being a single parent.

'OK, OK, I get the picture.' I tried to laugh away my worries. 'You're right, of course. I'll come down. It makes sense, I don't know what I was thinking. Blame it on lack of sleep. I'm worse than any new mother,' I told her. 'I'll take the early afternoon train on Christmas Eve.'

'That's a good idea, I don't want you to drive. We can pick you up.'

'No worries, I'll take a taxi.'

'I wouldn't hear of it.' She was all business. 'And Lily . . .' She paused.

'Yes?'

'I'm very proud of you, you know that, don't you?'

I felt tears at the back of my eyes. 'Yes,' I muttered.

'You're a remarkable young woman and you've been magnificent since . . . the accident.'

'Thanks.' I got rid of her before I bawled.

Brian Daly offered to drive me to Cork but I refused. I was afraid I'd say something nasty about his brother. The truth was I still couldn't get my head around the Kevin Daly scenario. The more I thought about it, the more unreal it seemed. Alison loved men and enjoyed their company but

I just couldn't imagine her and him together. And worrying about what it might mean for me and Charlie was driving me nuts.

Eventually I decided I had to tell someone. I needed a dose of reality. Orla wasn't the right one: we were living in each other's pockets as it was; besides, I still didn't feel right talking to her about Kevin after what I'd done, so I emailed Sally in Sydney, who soon put me straight.

From: laydownsally@heatmail.com
To: lilyofthevalley@goodoldireland.com
What the hell do you mean, creepy Kevin
might be Charlie's father? Who is this
bloke? All I can remember is that you
stole him off Orla (only joking!) Do I
need to come home? (Actually I can't cause
I'm broke, but I am saving. I thought I
was making the journey to see your new
business venture, now it might be to sort
you and all these men out — I'd like that,
come to think of it.)
Love,
S xx
PS Does Orla know? Can I tell her? I'm a
bit jealous of you two sharing all this.
No I'm not, I'm just a bit drunk. Hic.
PPS Was the sex magic with creepy Kev?

From: lilyofthevalley@goodoldireland.com
To: laydownsally@heatmail.com
Just a quickie — I'm exhausted. I'll phone
you later in the week but pleeeease don't
mention Kevin and me to Orla — I feel
guilty enough already.
L xx
PS Did I tell you about Daniel? He's cool
but I don't really know him. Anyway, I've
just discovered he has a 'friend' coming
home for Christmas and staying with him.
Why are all the nice men taken??
PPS Richard's getting married on New
Year's Eve, but I've finally grown up
where he's concerned. (I think!)

We had several telephone conversations after that where
she was drunk and I was drunk with tiredness, but talking
to her really helped.

Daniel's friend arriving put paid to our meetings and I
missed him. I guess I'd got used to him being around for a
beer or a walk or just to chat to over a coffee in the mornings. He was the only uncomplicated person in my life at
the moment and he seemed never to judge me, or anyone
else for that matter.

He'd been in great form when he appeared in the café
for lunch with Zanna earlier in the week.

'I thought you told me her name was Lucy?' I asked,
confused.

'No, Lucy was my fiancée,' he said. 'Keep up.'

'I'm too tired.'

'It'll all be worth it when you see your profits.' He grinned and took the tray over to where his friend was waiting. They looked very easy together. I knew I was jealous and I'd say I wasn't the only one. Daniel got noticed everywhere he went and I was willing to bet that lots of mothers of fine strapping Wicklow lassies were disappointed when Zanna appeared on the scene. All that land helped, of course. He was seen as quite a catch round these parts.

I was still worried about James. I'd never met a man like James in my life. I thought they only existed in films. Which was why I felt terribly guilty about him and Tamsin. I should have said no the minute she suggested adopting Charlie but I'd been so traumatized that I wasn't thinking straight, and then seeing them together had been pretty stressful too. I'd phoned James a couple of times since, just to make sure they were coping. He was incredibly kind and assured me they were.

Richard phoned on the morning of Christmas Eve.

'Are you OK?'

'So tired I nearly fell asleep on top of the treacle tarts this morning. You?'

'Messy that, very nasty. Yep, I'm wrecked, too. If one more customer complains I'll throw them out.' He laughed. 'Is it me or is everyone grumpy this year?'

'It's not you,' I told him.

'Will you come out with me for a drink before the wedding?'

'Another stag, you mean?'

'No, just you and me.'

I was getting tired of this. It was a conversation we'd been having on and off since a date had been set for the wedding. He was always hinting at things between us, yet he never came straight out and said anything. Not that I wanted him to. I'd begun to understand him in the last while. Richard was a classic case of wanting to have your cake and eat it. I'd actually begun to feel a teensy bit sorry for Daisy – not easy. She was a cool customer, very aloof, hard to warm to.

'Richard Kearney, you're getting married in a week's time. Don't you think you should be concentrating on your wife-to-be?'

'She's gone off and left me,' he whined, sounding like a spoilt nine-year-old.

I laughed at him and I could tell he was miffed.

Daniel put his head into the café early on Christmas Eve.

'Hi there!' He looked so alive, he must have been out in the fresh air for hours. No wonder oxygen facials were the latest beauty must-have. 'Got any breakfast for a starving man?'

'You smell of heather.' I sniffed in his general direction. 'Where've you been?'

'Out walking the course. We've major work starting in the New Year so I'm trying to get on top of it. As it is,

Zanna's keeping me up half the night, so I'm a bit of a zombie most days.'

'Where is she today?' This Zanna was beginning to get on my wick.

'Gone into Waterford with my mother to do some last-minute shopping. Speaking of which, I'm heading to Dublin to do some myself. Do you need a lift to catch the Cork train, by any chance?'

'Really?' I could hardly believe my luck. 'It's such a pain to have to go to Dublin in order to get to Cork, but there you go. If you could drop me anywhere near Hueston Station it would be brilliant.'

'No worries, I'm going out to Chapelizod to collect some stuff for my mum, so it's not out of my way at all. What time?'

'I'd need to be there any time around two, so I suppose we'd need to leave here around twelve thirty in case the traffic is mad. Does that suit?'

'Yep, I told my guy I'd ring him once I got to Dublin. Otherwise, my time's my own. The shops in Dublin never close apparently.' He winked. 'How Ireland's changed.'

'Daniel Williams, I think I want to have your babies.' The lack of sleep was making me say weird things. 'Don't mind me, I'm hallucinating,' I told him honestly. 'It's just that I've got so many packages I'd need a truck anyway, so your big jeep thing would be fantastic. Aunt Milly's been giving me chores to do all week. I had to bribe a customer to go to Smyths Toys in Dublin yesterday for me.'

'Can I do anything else?' He really was a dote.

'A lift to the train would make my year,' I told him.

I fussed about for the rest of the morning and Daniel appeared bang on twelve thirty. Orla, Naomi and Violet whooshed me out the door and promised to lock up later and leave the place tidy. We were closing shortly anyway. We'd had a little present-giving session earlier and I'd handed them all their bonuses – presents really; we'd only been open a few weeks. It gave me such a thrill to be able to do it. I hoped Ali was up there somewhere looking down at me and feeling proud.

'So, how's it all going?' I asked Daniel as soon as we'd set off up the N11. 'Between you and Zanna, I mean?' I still wasn't convinced they were just friends.

'Great, yeah, she's a gas ticket.' He laughed, giving nothing away. 'I don't think she knows quite what to make of this country, though – not to mention my mother, who's treating her like royalty. So how about you?' he asked. 'I feel as if we haven't talked in ages. Are you OK?'

'Wrecked,' I told him truthfully, 'but I can't wait to see Charlie again. I really miss him.'

'Missing's good,' he said softly and I felt the hairs on the back of my neck stand up.

'Yeah, it is,' I told him, dying to feel those chubby little arms around me again. 'So, what are you doing tonight? Will Christmas Eve in Wicklow town be a riot?'

'I'm meeting a couple of mates. And then I promised I'd bring Zanna over to Redcross, where they have some

417

traditional music. Tourists, you know.' He shook his head. 'How about you?'

'Reading a bedtime story to a three-year-old, I imagine, and having a sherry with Aunt Milly.' I grinned. 'And I can't think of anything nicer.'

'You're a right raver.' He winked at me and my stomach lurched. Get a grip, I told myself. You've definitely been working too hard.

'By the way, I think I may have a house for you,' he said casually.

'What?' This time my heart did a major somersault and it was nothing to do with chemistry. 'Tell me quick. We're getting near to Dublin.'

'We have a house – it's nothing special, mind you – on the edge of our land. We've had a tenant living in it for the last ten years but he died suddenly. Heart attack, fifty-nine.' He shook his head. 'Tragedy.'

'And . . . ?' I hoped I didn't sound too grabbing. It was awful that the poor man had died but my own heart wasn't doing so well since he'd mentioned a house. I needed to know more, and fast. This could be the answer to all my prayers.

'And . . . my mother and I were talking about it last night. She thinks we should sell it.'

'Oh my God. Where is it?'

'Just outside Brittas Bay – on the coast road to Arklow. But,' he held up his hand, 'don't get too excited until you've seen it. It's a very basic, modern-ish bungalow. No redeeming features. It's definitely not the cute little cottage you were looking for.'

'What's the view like?'

'I think you might like the view.' He grinned at me.

'How much?' I was trying to get to the catch, because there simply had to be one. This was too good to be true. I'd become a slave to myhome.ie since he'd told me about it, as well as all of the property supplements – but each time I'd enquired about a house the guide price had been a joke, even though interest rates were rising across Europe and the boom was over, according to the economists. I'd seen no evidence of a slump or even a levelling-off of prices in Wicklow, especially. All I'd heard were stories of sellers shouting 'sucker' as they shot off to the bank with a wodge of money in their fists.

'We haven't put a figure on it yet.' Daniel must have noticed my look of dread. 'But don't worry,' he said quickly. 'We won't fall out over it.'

I sat in silence for a few moments as I tried to take in the fact that my search just might be over. 'Oh my God,' I said when eventually I couldn't contain myself any longer. We'd arrived at the station and I hopped out and ran round to his side and practically dragged him out by the scruff of the neck to give him a hug. 'Can I tell my aunt? And Charlie?' I asked as I danced him round in the freezing cold.

'I guess so.'

'Thank you.' I was suffocating him, I could tell. He slowly unwound my arms from around his neck. 'Thank you, thank you, thank you.' I kissed him then, full on the lips, without thinking about it at all. 'You have just given

419

me the best present ever, Daniel Williams. I am so glad you came into my life.'

'Come on, there's your train.' He laughed as we ran to the platform.

'Maybe Ali sent you,' I told him as we clattered along with bags and boxes weighing us down. 'Maybe it was meant to be.'

'You were managing fine on your own,' he smiled as I boarded. 'Happy Christmas, Lily,' he yelled as I hung out the window and blew kisses at him.

'I love you.' I grinned but the wind carried it away, which was just as well because I was feeling slightly delirious when I said it.

When I finally lost sight of him he was still laughing as he waved me off.

43

LILY

EACH TIME I SAW HIM IT SEEMED HE TOOK ANOTHER BIT OF my heart and tore it. This evening a head of corkscrew curls that had grown out of nowhere hurled itself at me and I found myself staring into Ali's eyes. He'd changed so much.

'Mammy, mammy, mammy.' His screams brought smiles to many of the weary travellers as they rushed past and almost smothered us both.

'Who're you?' I asked him.

'Charlie,' he grinned.

'You're not Charlie,' I said.

'I am,' he roared.

'Aunt Milly, where's Charlie?' I looked everywhere but at him while I blinked a few times and swallowed hard.

'Here, I'm here.' He was wrapped around my legs.

'You're not *my* Charlie.' I looked down at him. 'My Charlie is small and has short hair.'

'I am,' he screamed. 'It's me, Charlie.'

'Are you sure? Let me look at you again.' I bent down.

'Well, so it is, you are my Charlie after all.' He almost knocked me over with his hug.

'Have you got my present?' he wanted to know then, wriggling out of my arms as quickly as he'd come in.

'You'll just have to wait and see,' I told him and stood up.

'Hi, love, you must be exhausted.' Aunt Milly gave me a bear hug. 'Let me take your bags.'

'Thanks, that would be great.' I grinned. 'After all, they're mostly yours anyway.'

'Sorry about all that.' She laughed. 'I'll explain later.'

'Carry me, Lily.' Charlie didn't want to be left out.

'You're too big to carry,' I told him. 'Hold my hand instead.'

'OK,' he accepted. 'I'm big,' he told my aunt importantly.

He talked all the way home, and once we got to the house I was able to have a good look at him.

'You're so grown up,' I told him.

'I'm a big boy,' he said proudly.

'Such a big boy.' I kissed him and laughed again at all his curls.

'You and me and Mammy.' He pointed as he took my hand and brought me to the mantelpiece where a picture of Alison and me with Charlie as a baby stood, both of us relaxed and smiling.

'Where did you get this?' I looked at it and then at my aunt. 'It wasn't here any other time I've been.'

'Alison sent it to me. I kept it . . . upstairs, in case it

422

would upset you. But he keeps bringing it everywhere with him so I've lost track of it.' She smiled at Charlie. 'It's his favourite.'

'Well, we'll have to get a new one of the two of us with Aunt Milly. Would you like that?'

'No,' he said adamantly.

'But we can still keep this one, of course.' I'd noticed his face had clouded over.

'That's grand.' He sounded just like my aunt as he toddled off, leaving us in stitches.

'The old range is hanging in there.' I was still smiling as I warmed myself up against it.

'Still going strong, thank God. Dinner's in the bottom.' Aunt Milly was all business. 'Now, you sit down and I'll dish it up. Homemade beef and vegetable pie OK?'

'With your own pastry?'

She nodded.

'And fluffy mash?' I teased. She'd been trying to persuade me to put it on the menu in Wicklow.

'If this doesn't convince you nothing will.' She had the table set and the fire stacked up. 'Would you like a glass of wine, love? I got some in specially.'

'Gosh, that's posh, but no thanks, I'd be asleep in my dinner,' I told her. 'But definitely tomorrow.'

'Lily, come to the tree.' Charlie was back and had me by the hand again. I let him lead me into the front room. Memories of me and Alison playing in this very room, breaking ornaments and trying to glue them back together, hiding from the adults, eating biscuits when we

423

weren't supposed to, all came tumbling back again, only this time they seemed sharper than ever.

'Lily, please don't cry. It's OK.' Ali dried my eyes with the corner of her skirt.

'I want a bike. You said it would happen if I was good and I've been very good. Why is Santa so mean?' I wailed.

'Santa might have left it in Aunt Milly's. We'll ring her later and check, OK? Now, say nothing to Father for the moment. We don't want to spoil the day, do we?'

'I suppose.'

'And you know Aunt Milly will have lots of surprises under the tree for us anyway, so be a good girl now.'

'I can't wait to go to Milly's house. It's always warm and it smells of sausages and gravy.'

'This is mine.' Charlie rattling a big box, just as I used to do, brought me back.

'From who?' I asked. 'Santa hasn't come yet.'

'Tonight.' He ran over and stared at the chimney. 'Hi, Santa,' he yelled and ran away again. 'This is from Thomas.' He pointed to the box.

'Who's Thomas?' I asked him.

'Thomas and Molly and Jack and Anna,' he counted on one hand. 'Three.'

'Four, actually. Are they your friends?'

'Bestest friends.' He was off again, back to the kitchen this time. 'Santa's my friend too,' he told me over his shoulder.

'You're a clever boy, having Santa as your friend.' I laughed at his cheek.

'I was just thinking about the year you bought me a bike, remember?' I asked my aunt later.

'I do indeed. I've never seen anyone so excited.'

'Had Alison anything to do with it?'

'Aye, she rang me on Christmas morning and begged me to get you one. I got it cheap in the sales just in time for your visit.'

The emotion of it all finally got to me and I started to cry softly. 'I want her with us this Christmas. I'd give anything to have her back.'

'I know you would, love, I know.' She held me just like my sister used to.

'Why was my father so mean to us?' I asked her. Being here brought back so many memories of difficult Christmases. 'Why didn't he just love us? We were good kids, weren't we?'

'Yes, you were. And I'm not going to defend him. All I know is that your mother said he was always afraid of letting anyone get too close. She managed to, just barely. And then she died, and I think he retreated further and the two of you just reminded him of her all the time . . .'

'But was that so bad? He loved her, didn't he?'

'Aye, he did in his own way, but he blamed her too, for dying and leaving him to look after you both.'

'And now it's just me, and I have all this money – his money – and I'm going to spend every penny of it on

Charlie, except I'll give some of it to help other kids who aren't loved,' I said and the tears helped wash some of my bitterness away, at last.

'You've come so far, love.' My aunt tilted up my chin. 'Out of this awful tragedy you've grown up.'

'I suppose,' I admitted, knowing it was true. I hardly recognized the old me any more. 'I often wonder how I wasted so much time going nowhere.' I smiled through the tears.

By ten o'clock we were all in bed. I'd given Charlie a bath and we sang his favourite song, 'Jingle Bells', as we splashed about covered in suds. It was the most I'd done for him in ages and I thoroughly enjoyed it and his happiness helped restore mine. I was sleeping in his room and after I'd tucked him in and helped clear up, I returned to find him thrashing about and calling out 'Rudolph' and 'Prancer' in his sleep, a mass of limbs and curls. I settled him, cleaned my teeth and lay awake listening to him snoring and wondering what the future held for both of us. My prayers that night were for a long and healthy life for the two of us in our little house in Wicklow, with regular visits from Milly.

Next morning was hectic. Charlie woke me from a dead sleep at six thirty – later than usual, according to Aunt Milly. He didn't really understand about Santa but his face was a picture when he discovered the carrot half eaten and the juice glass empty. I saw my aunt was close to tears and I hugged her and thanked her as I too watched his eyes light up when he discovered the shiny red bus and the train set. He was happier than I'd ever have believed possible a few months ago. For some reason I thought of James and Tamsin then, and afterwards, when we went to mass in the tiny church I'd explored as a child, I lit a candle for both of them. Everyone stopped us on the way in and I was glad I'd worn my new coat and boots and some people called me Alison and didn't notice their mistake.

'It's OK,' I assured my aunt, who was worried that I'd get upset. 'Life moves on, people forget, I know that.'

Charlie ran off to play with Thomas and the gang and Aunt Milly and I sang hymns and then went for strong tea and cake laced with porter in the convent next door with the nuns and Father Bertie. The smell of polish and soda bread remained and the women still glided around effortlessly and hadn't aged at all, it seemed.

The day flew by and the house was filled with neighbours and friends, most of whom called to thank Aunt Milly for some small kindness – and have a proper look at me, I suspected. Chocolates and puddings were exchanged and I poured sweet sherry and bottles of frothy stout and I could see my aunt was in her element. She beamed at me and looked so proud of us both as she introduced me to the parents of Charlie's friends. I whizzed around fetching ashtrays and adding logs to the already blazing fire and opening biscuit tins that contained slabs of richly scented cakes groaning with fruit, all to try and help the woman who had given so much to me these past few months. And everyone said it was lovely to see me after all these years and wasn't I the lucky girl owning my own home in Dublin and having a café in cosmopolitan Wicklow. It was small town rural Ireland at its very best.

Our days were taken up with walks and visits to friends and we even springcleaned the house in December, which gave my aunt a boost. I told her more about Daniel's cottage as we sat dozing by the fire one night. It was our first real chat because life had been so full over the days of Christmas. We were eating the last of the pudding and drinking gallons of tea. We agreed that Charlie should move as soon as the house was habitable and I knew she had very mixed feelings about him going.

'It's the right thing, though. I know that.' She smiled but her lined face was sad for a split second. 'For you both.' She patted my knee. 'Although there's no hurry, you know that, love, don't you?'

'That's what you always say.' I smiled back at her. 'Will you come and visit us often? In fact will you come and stay for a while at the beginning?' She nodded happily and I admitted that I was a bit scared of having him, in case I did anything wrong. 'I'm not as good as you are with children. I wasn't even very good as one,' I told her and meant it, but for the first time I was confident that what I lacked in practicalities I'd make up for with love.

'You'll be fine. I've watched you these last few days.' She looked at me. 'I think you make a great mother. He's a lucky boy. And I'll still be here as a fallback if you can't cope. You know that, Lily.'

'I know.' But I could see she was tired. The last few months had taken their toll. 'Maybe the three of us could go off on a week's holiday. Get some sun on our backs.' I wished I'd thought of it earlier: it would have made a nice surprise present for her and relieved my conscience somewhat.

'I'd like that,' she beamed.

All too soon it was the day before New Year's Eve and I was on the train again, although this time much more able to handle the crowds. Charlie clung to me and I prayed that the house worked out, so that I could have him for good soon.

'Don't go. I want you here,' he cried. Even my promise of a dog met with a very muted response. 'I'm sad,' he told me.

'So am I, but it's not for long, I promise.' I kept a smile pasted firmly on my face. 'Be good.' I wished I hadn't said it as soon as it was out. I was never going to use that expression again, I decided.

'I like being bold,' he told me. 'Thomas says it's more fun.'

'Thomas is right.' I laughed. 'But don't tell his mum I said so.'

Because I'd had such a lovely Christmas and was delighted to be starting the New Year working for myself and possibly even living in my own home with Charlie and a menagerie, Richard and Daisy's wedding wasn't the first thing I thought of when I opened my eyes next morning. Still, I knew it was going to be a long day, so I threw back the duvet and dived into the shower, then went out to get my hair blow-dried. I'd bought a dress in a very posh boutique that had opened recently near the café. I wasn't at all sure about it now.

At twelve the doorbell went and a young guy handed me a huge bouquet of white flowers.

Tamsin and I wanted to wish you and Charlie all the best for the New Year, the card said. It was signed *Love, James* and I felt sad for them again.

Brian Daly arrived at two and that made me a little nervous. I'd invited him in a moment of madness, mostly to save myself from having no one to talk to, but also because I stupidly hoped Richard might be a teensy bit jealous. Sally's email put paid to that wacko theory.

From: laydownsally@heatmail.com
To: lilyofthevalley@goodoldireland.com
Do you fancy this guy or not and if so, why the hell are you going to his wedding? Come to think of it, you haven't mentioned him in the same way at all recently? Is his appeal beginning to wane or are you going to be sick all over your new frock when you see him? And you're going with Brian? Whose horrible, slimy brother is

430

Charlie's father? (What are you going to
do about that, by the way?)
Are you hoping the groom might still be
harbouring a secret desire for you? Well,
I'd check first to see if someone is
cattle prodding him up the aisle because
otherwise I've got news for you. He's
getting married 'cause he wants to. Face
it, babe, men like him do exactly what
they want, no matter how much they pretend
otherwise.
Really, I think I'll have to go see the
credit union for a loan — you need me more
than you realize.
S xx
PS Is lawyer guy any way fanciable?
PPS Who the hell is this Daniel bloke you
keep mentioning all of a sudden??

I had to admit it, Brian Daly looked great in a monkey
suit, although his mood seemed a bit subdued. He kept
glancing at me as if he wanted to say something but hadn't
the courage. Frankly, whatever it was I prayed he'd keep it
to himself. I had enough to deal with today. Or maybe he
just hadn't quite got over our last meeting. I think we both
knew we needed to talk about the real problem in my life
– his brother – and what trouble that could cause me in the
future.

'How did it go in Cork, how's Charlie?' He wanted to

know everything. I relaxed as much as I could and told him all the news but all I could think about was him being Charlie's uncle.

As we arrived at the church I resolved to enjoy myself while at the same time saying a Hail Mary to St Anthony for the day to be over quickly.

Brian abandoned me almost as soon as we arrived, which annoyed me slightly. It turned out he was a great friend of Daisy's brother and knew all the family well, so he was off kissing cousins and back-slapping rugby types, which left me with far too much time to think.

'Lily, you look terrific.' Richard had spotted me the moment we walked up the aisle. 'How was your Christmas?'

'OK, yours?'

'Mum totally spoiled me.' There was an awkward pause. 'Hard to believe, eh? Me, of all people, getting married.' He looked like a goofy twelve-year-old. 'Can't think how I ended up here, really.'

'Well, it does tend to happen when you ask someone to be your wife.' I tried to keep the sarcasm out of my voice. Sally's email was still niggling.

'Are you OK?'

I was a bit peeved that he thought I wouldn't be. 'Yes, I'm fine, looking forward to the whole day really.'

'Richard, I need you.' Tom, the best man, raised his eyes to heaven and smiled at me before dragging the groom away.

'Apologies.' Brian slipped in beside me just as the music started. 'Small world, what?'

'Very.' I was glad he was here all the same. Sitting on my own had made me start to think and some of my thoughts were disconcerting. Why was I still so confused about things, I wondered? I just had to concentrate on how far I'd come since the initial dark days when I thought I'd never even survive, let alone flourish, as Milly kept reminding me.

Daisy looked amazing. There were literally gasps as she walked up the aisle, and judging by the jewellery and shoes worn by the congregation this crowd were not easily impressed.

As the ceremony started, I let my thoughts drift back to Alison and Richard and James and William Hammond and Dave. Now that I knew who Charlie's father was I needed to let them go, although I sensed I'd stay in touch with Richard, if not Daisy.

Before I knew it the priest was asking the age-old question about anyone knowing of any impediment. 'I'd hate this bit if I was getting married.' Brian winked at me. 'Just in case.'

'Surely as a lawyer you'd have all that nasty business taken care of,' I whispered back, laughing.

I was getting a bit bored. The priest had a monotonous voice and had taken to explaining every detail as he went along, so I began to daydream about Richard not going through with it. Or another guy – a male model – running in and yelling Daisy's name and her charging off down the aisle with him while the congregation gasped in horror – or applauded, depending on whose side they were on. I'd seen it happen on *Fair City*: it made for great TV.

I think I heard the voice long after everyone else realized something was up. All I can remember is that I looked around and saw a young woman in a simple dress and jacket standing at the back of the church, clutching the hand of a young boy who was a miniature version of Richard.

44

MARIE

'COME ON, MUM, PLEASE,' KIRSTIN MADDEN BEGGED. 'It'll be just a quiet night, honest.'

'Really, love, I'm not up to it.' Marie knew her daughters would be disappointed – which was the only reason she'd agreed to spend the day in town at the sales – but she'd never been much of a New Year's Eve type even when Dave had been the life and soul of the party, and she drew the line at going to the pub this year of all years.

'We're not leaving you at home on your own, Mum, no way,' Lola said for the third time.

'Please, I'll be fine, honestly, I told you that already. Besides, my feet are killing me after all that walking earlier.'

'Look, tell you what,' her younger daughter was at her most persuasive, 'stay here for a few hours, have a bath, relax, and one of us will come back for you about ten. How's that?'

'No, really I—'

'No excuses, Mum. Just so that we can ring in the New

Year with you, please? As soon as it's over we'll walk you home and then we can go back there if we feel like it.'

'We will feel like it,' Kirstin said, laughing. 'No question about it.'

'OK, OK.' Marie knew when she was beaten. 'Now go, both of you, and leave me in peace for a few hours.'

'Yes,' they chorused and went off punching fists in the air.

When Marie arrived the place was heaving. Every table was laden with almost empty glasses and there was nearly as much booze again on the floor. A brutal Beatles tribute band was belting out the hits and everyone under sixty was giving it socks.

Marie had never been much of a drinker and even though she downed a glass of lager in double-quick time to try and get in the mood, she realized she'd never catch up with most of this lot, so she stopped trying and resolved to sit it out. The heat was intense, and the place seemed to be overflowing with scantily clad women and sweaty men.

To their credit, most of Dave's friends dropped over and insisted on buying her a drink. For some, it was the first time they'd seen her since the funeral. She was touched by all the stories about her husband and had to stop herself from crying more than once.

This was a terrible idea, she realized after about an hour, feeling a bit panicky all of a sudden. She missed Dave, especially missed knowing he was there to take care

436

of her, bring her home whenever she wanted, fetch her crisps without her asking and loads of silly little things, like remembering she liked a splash of lime in her lager.

'Excuse me, I need to go to the loo,' she said to the two men who used to know Dave at school. They seemed relieved not to have to make small talk any more.

When she got back a woman she didn't know had squeezed herself into a corner of the banquette next to where Marie had been sitting. Her heart sank and she was more determined than ever to get home fast and into her nice comfy dressing gown.

Just as she feared, the other woman was on for a chat.

'I'm Nuala.' She nodded pleasantly at Marie.

'How're you doing?' Marie smiled and searched for one of her daughters.

'Me husband's abandoned me.'

'It happens.' Marie couldn't remember which drink was hers, although she knew she had several to choose from.

'He plays darts here so he knows all the regulars. I know a fair few, mainly the younger ones. My two sons bring me out for a drink some nights. They like it here 'cause the crowd aren't as old as our local and there's usually a good band on.'

Marie mumbled something and hoped one of the girls found her soon.

They chatted on for a few minutes. 'Are they Dave Madden's girls?' Nuala asked, pointing in the direction of her daughters, who were falling about laughing with two guys on the dance floor. Marie was relieved to see them. She tried to catch their eye.

'Oh yes, I think I'll—'

'Terrible shame, wasn't it?'

'Yes . . .' Marie hoped she wasn't going to make a fool of herself before she could escape. Her emotions were already running high since the band had played 'Here, There And Everywhere' a few minutes earlier. It was the first song she had danced to with Dave.

'My son used to fancy one of them.' Nuala smiled. 'Can't remember which one now. Lovely family, from what Joseph told me.'

'Yes.' Marie's voice was barely a whisper. Someone shouted, 'Thirty seconds to midnight!' but Nuala didn't seem to care.

'Although he was a bit of a ladies' man, apparently.'

Marie was half standing and just about to make her excuses.

'What?' She sat back down, all ready for a row. The cheek of the woman, the absolute nerve. Marie opened her mouth to let her have it. 'Now you—'

'Sure aren't they all, wha'?' She grinned. 'My fella is always eyein' up the young ones. Have to keep them on a tight lead, eh?' She waved to a crowd who were signalling to her to join them. 'Anyway, Happy New Year, love.' She disappeared.

Although her heart was thumping with indignation, Marie knew it had been said innocently. There was no intention to upset her, she was sure of it. Under normal

438

circumstances, Marie would have laughed and agreed with her. That woman was only saying what everyone knew, after all. Dave had always had an eye for a good-looking woman. And Marie knew that even now – with all that had happened – it wouldn't have bothered her unduly if she hadn't found those numbers and text messages in Dave's phone the other day, when she'd finally plucked up the courage to start clearing away his stuff.

As she half-heartedly joined in the countdown with her daughters glued to her side, Marie made only one New Year's resolution – to find out a bit more about her husband's friends.

45

WILLIAM AND BETH

'FIVE, FOUR, THREE, TWO, ONE, HAPPY NEW YEAR!' CORKS popped and streamers and balloons seemed to fall from the sky as the orchestra segued into 'Auld Lang Syne'.

'Happy New Year, darling.' William turned to Beth and kissed her on the cheek. 'You have to hand it to him, Dermot Bryant sure knows how to throw a party. I've never seen so much Dom P in one room in my life. Want another?'

'No, thanks, I'm taking it easy.' Beth looked around, enjoying the moment. A group of friends arrived to air-kiss and clink glasses and it was only when she found herself being lifted up and swung around by Ronnie Wilson, one of William's more outgoing colleagues, that Beth felt a bit faint.

'William, I need some air. Could you help me, please?' She was afraid she was going to pass out.

'Of course, are you OK?' He came to her aid immediately and ushered her outside to a huge balcony where people were smoking and dancing and waiters hovered with trays of bubbles.

'Sit down over here.' William was concerned. Beth hadn't been herself at all for the past few weeks. 'Can I get you a glass of water, darling?' He was at his most attentive.

'Yes, please.'

'Back in a jif.' William decided to have a little talk with her the following day. Something was bothering her, he was sure of it. She'd taken to calling in at the clinic at odd times and kept ringing him on his mobile asking him to come home early. As a result he hadn't had a minute to himself, his gym routine had gone to pot and he hadn't even managed to find time to drop down to see Lily with the expensive lingerie he'd picked up for her in Harvey Nicks – paid for in cash, of course.

'There you go. How are you feeling now? Plenty of doctors here anyway,' he joked as he sat down beside her and flagged a passing waiter for another drink for himself.

William liked this kind of party. Dermot Bryant knew everyone who was anyone in Dublin and it was *the* party of the Christmas season, complete with rock stars and best-selling authors, a handful of carefully chosen politicians and even the odd supermodel. William had been looking forward to it for ages: it would definitely be the main item for gossiping about in theatre later this week and besides, they'd already been snapped by more than one Sunday newspaper. William knew he looked the part, which always helped. He felt good and was still tanned this year, thanks to a mild autumn and a few wekends on the golf course.

'I'm OK now.' His wife interrupted his thoughts. 'Just needed some air, that's all.' She looked a bit less grey, he decided, pleased.

'Good.' William hoped she wasn't going to want to leave early. In fact, if she suggested it he'd offer to put her in a taxi. There was a fleet lined up outside Dermot's mansion, all paid for already, he'd overheard someone with no class mentioning earlier.

'More champagne, sir?' a waiter asked discreetly.

'Why not?' William was relieved of his glass and a fresh one was handed to him in seconds, just as a young RTE presenter strolled by. She reminded William of Lily and he resolved to text her later to say Happy New Year, the bubbly making him forget his normal paranoia with text messages.

'Maybe we could go soon, now that we've seen out the old year?' Beth smiled at him. It was so unlike her: other years she'd be flitting about, delighted to be in the thick of it. His wife loved parties and people – much more than he did, in fact – and she usually chatted away to everyone she met, regardless of who they were. One year he'd found her in the corner with a very old lady, happily exchanging recipes instead of mingling and being seen.

'Really?'

'I'm a bit tired, actually.'

'Would you mind if I stayed?' William looked around and spotted a few people he wanted to see. He didn't like the look on his wife's face as soon as he suggested it, so he quickly added, 'Or I could take you home in a taxi and then come back myself for an hour or so.'

Normally one of them staying and one going wouldn't have been a problem – they'd done it often when they'd had to relieve a babysitter – although it was mostly Beth who went home early.

'Do you really want to?'

'Well, yes, I'd like to.' He leaned over in a gesture of solidarity. 'What's the matter, darling? You're normally the life and soul of a party like this.'

'I'm pregnant, William.'

For a second he thought she was joking. He waited, but no elbow in the ribs came. 'Pregnant?' was all he managed.

'Yep. Are you pleased?'

'Well, I . . . of course, but darling, we agreed our family was complete. I mean, our life is pretty much perfect as it is . . .'

'Well, these things happen, I suppose.' She clearly wasn't upset about it. 'Anyway, I thought it might be a nice New Year present for you if all goes according to plan, which please God it will.'

William didn't like surprises. 'It's a shock, I have to be honest.' He looked at his wife. 'Are you sure?'

'Of course.' She laughed. 'It's not so unusual. I mean I'm barely forty, some women my age are only starting their families.'

'Are you worried about your age?' William asked quickly.

'No, not really, although of course I'll need to look after myself. But I'm healthy, that's a good start . . .' Her smile was overbright. 'It'll mean a few changes, that's for certain.'

'Such as?' He didn't like the sound of this.

'Well, your new car, for instance. You probably should think about cancelling it. A two-seater, top-of-the-range whatyamaycallit will hardly be suitable now.'

'But . . . but . . .' William couldn't believe his ears. He adored his car, it was a symbol of who he was. He'd been looking forward to the new model for months. It was being brought into the country ahead of schedule especially for him, and after the diesel fiasco they were giving him sat nav at no extra charge. 'But you've always had the family car, darling. We can change the Volvo for an even bigger version, if you want . . .'

'It's not that, it's just I want us to be able to do more together − and not in a car that's always crammed with bottles for recycling or ice-cream wrappers or school-books. Besides, you're going to have to take the other two out a bit more, now that there'll be a new baby in the house. And you hate driving my car anyway. Last week you told me it smelt of sour milk.' She'd obviously given it some thought. 'A two-seater is for a single man.' She sounded as if it was already agreed. 'Also, while we're on the subject of changes, I was thinking we could convert the big old garage that we never use into a home gym. That way you wouldn't have to be out so much in the evenings.'

William felt his carefully designed life falling down around his ears.

'And anyway,' Beth continued, clearly on a roll, 'I

intend getting back into shape as quickly as I can after-wards, so I can use it too. It'll be so much easier for both of us.' She patted her stomach. 'I'm prepared to work hard, I've become a bit flabby lately. Who knows, I might even start before the baby is born.'

William was lost for words.

46

JAMES AND TAMSIN

'JAMES, WHAT TIME IS IT?'

'Twelve thirty.' He put down the book he was reading and turned to his wife, who was struggling to sit up in bed. 'Are you OK? Can I get you anything?'

'No, I'm fine, I must have dozed off. I didn't want you to be on your own for the New Year.' She flopped back down on the pillow. 'I'm sorry, I just feel so worn out at the moment.'

'I wasn't alone, you were here beside me.' James kissed her on the head. 'Happy New Year, love.'

She gave him a sad smile. 'It hasn't been much of a Christmas, has it?'

'No.' There was no point in arguing that one, he decided.

'I can't seem to pick myself up after all that's happened,' she told him. 'I hadn't realized how much I was pinning my hopes on Alison's little boy.'

'I know that.' He'd been pretty geared up for it himself. 'Would you consider talking to someone?'

'James, I'm a psychologist, for God's sake. I spend my life helping other people handle exactly this type of stressful situation in their lives.' She looked worried. 'It's just that, for once, I don't seem able to follow my own advice.'

'Are the antidepressants helping at all?'

She shook her head. 'Not really.'

'Maybe you should go back to the doctor then?'

'James, will we be OK, do you think?' She ignored his suggestion.

'What do you mean?'

'You know, as a couple. Will we survive this awful time?'

'Don't worry, we'll be fine.' He'd never heard her talk like this. 'We're a strong unit, nothing can change that. Now, why don't you just get some rest?'

'You know, sometimes, on top of everything else, I hate you for being with Alison. I feel that maybe it put a curse on us . . .'

'You never said that to me before,' James said quietly.

'I've felt so angry with you a lot of the time lately. And I wonder if God is punishing you – and by association me – by not giving us a child.'

'That's ridiculous,' he told her.

'Well, that's how I feel.'

'Look.' He jumped out of bed. 'I've said I'm sorry. I've begged your forgiveness. I told you about it in the first place because I couldn't bear to have it sitting there between us for the rest of our lives.' He sighed. 'But the one thing I can't do is change what happened. And I need for us to try and get on with our lives, otherwise I'll go crazy.'

'I am trying to get on with my life, James, really I am. Every day I . . .' She started to cry and it was as if she was in physical pain.

'I'm sorry.' He made to hold her, his earlier frustration diminished.

'No, it's me. I'm torturing myself and I want to punish you sometimes too. Just give me time, please?'

He shushed her with his finger. 'You don't have to explain anything to me. Take as long as you need.'

'It's just so hard. I feel so . . . lonely.' She'd told him this many times over the past days. 'I feel empty inside.'

'I know.' He cradled her to him. 'I know you do.'

'I wanted to give you a baby so badly.' She was crying softly now.

'You're all I need, you know that,' he told her again. 'Anyway, love, let's try and put this year behind us and start afresh. Maybe tomorrow we could go out for a long walk. Will you do that with me?'

'I'll try.' She swallowed and his heart went out to her. They lay there in silence for ages.

'I love you, darling,' he whispered then, before he turned out his bedside lamp, but she was already asleep.

47

LILY

From: laydownsally@heatmail.com
To: lilyofthevalley@goodoldireland.com

What the fuck's going on? Are you seriously telling me the wedding came to a halt because a floozie turned up out of the blue with Richard's illegitimate child in tow? And then a fight broke out? In that tiny little church in the arsehole of nowhere in rural Ireland where the last exciting thing to happen was electrification? Actually, fuck the expense, I'll call you. This is too much for a woman with the worst hangover in all of Oz to get to grips with while typing. Anyway, the noise of this lousy keyboard is giving me an even worse headache.

S xx

I could hardly believe it myself. All hell had broken loose, I told Sally when she rang minutes later.

'Start at the beginning and don't dare leave anything out,' she ordered.

'Sure your delicate constitution can take it?' I asked.

'Yep, I'm munching painkillers as we speak,' she said, trying to sound cheerful.

'Well, actually it was awful. I felt really sorry for everyone. Daisy legged it, her mother slapped Richard very hard and then I didn't see Brian for hours because he was suddenly in great demand for lawyer-type negotiations.'

'How was Richard, was he mortified?'

'He certainly wasn't happy. He escaped as soon as possible. Tom – that radio presenter I told you about who was best man, remember? – well, he went a funny shade of purple. Oh, and then Richard's mother tried to make polite conversation with the woman, in an effort to get better acquainted with her newly acquired grandson, I presume.'

'Was she gorgeous, the woman I mean?'

'No, ordinary, I thought. Seemed nice though. Great body but . . .'

'So she was a BOBFOC?'

'A what?'

'Body off *Baywatch*, face off *Crimewatch*?' she said and I laughed. It was so typical of Sal always to cut to the chase.

'Jesus fucking Christ, I'll never complain about

weddings being boring again.' Sally's laugh crackled down the line. 'Did you talk to Richard?'

'Only briefly,' I told her. 'He *was* really upset at all the trouble he'd caused. It seems this woman has been telephoning him for weeks now and he's been putting her off. All she'd say on the phone was that she needed to see him.'

'Typical man, eh? Don't deal with it if you can put it on the back burner.'

'Apparently he eventually told her he was getting married and that he'd meet her after the whole thing was over . . .'

Sally snorted. 'Red rag to bull comes to mind.'

'I felt really sorry for Daisy too. What a nightmare.'

'You're over him so.'

'D'ya know something, Sal, with all that's happened I've been over him for a long time. I guess it took him almost getting married to make me realize it.'

'And now he's single again.'

'Yeah, funny that.'

'So what did he say, about the child I mean?'

'Oh, he admitted he'd shagged the mother but said he wasn't sure if the child was his, although the entire congregation thought he was the spit of Richard, from what I overheard. He said that it had been a fling after he'd finished school and took a gap year in New York. She's from Belfast apparently, although she'd no accent, as far as I could tell. Anyway, she was a waitress in some Manhattan hotel where he worked part-time . . .'

'Well, she obviously served him some lovely desserts.'

Sally wished she'd seen it all happen. 'So where did you end up?'

'In Kinnity Castle. No one knew what to do and all the younger crowd, friends, etc., were dying for a drink. So we went there anyway – not immediate families, obviously. You should have seen the manager's face when Tom told him the wedding was off. I had to wait on Brian, who didn't come back for hours. When he did he was pretty pissed off with Richard, as most people were, so we headed home. Tom and some of his mates were downing shots like water. I so wouldn't want to be any of them this morning.'

Next day the café opened again and I was raring to go. I had the lights and ovens on, coffee brewing and was making a list when Orla arrived. She'd been back home for Christmas and we hugged each other warmly.

'Tell me everything. How did Charlie get on?'

'Fantastic. I had a lovely time with him.'

'And the wedding?'

'Now, you'll need a coffee for this . . .' I was off again. Even Violet knew not to disturb us so she and Naomi concentrated on getting the tables spotless and everything ready front-of-house for 8 a.m.

Our weekly delivery of flowers arrived bang on time and I'd ordered the first hyacinths of the season, so the café smelt gorgeous and reminded everyone that spring was on the way. Naomi went off to collect the newspapers and it wasn't long before all our regulars came in – like old friends now – moaning about the cold and their credit card bills and useless presents and too much drink in about equal measure, it seemed. I revelled in it and had just found a spare minute to text Daniel Williams when he walked in the door.

'Happy New Year, I was just about to send you a message,' I told him, feeling good at the sight of him. His hair was longer than I remembered and he looked as healthy as always, despite the festivities.

'I thought you might be on my case early all right,' he teased. 'I guess that,' he lowered his voice, 'declaration of love as you got on the train was because of my house as opposed to my irresistible charms, eh?' He winked at me.

'What was that about a declaration of love?' Mrs Pearson, a devout Catholic and regular at ten o'clock mass, asked as she popped in for coffee with her cronies. Her new hearing aid was working, it appeared.

'I'd say anything to get my hands on his house,' I said, laughing.

'You wouldn't be the first, dear.' She tutted and smiled at us fondly.

'That's how rumours start.' Daniel pretended to look serious.

'Tell me all,' I said as I handed him his coffee. 'And what are the chances of taking me to see the house today? I can't sleep thinking about it.'

'Put that in a takeaway cup, so.' He handed me back the coffee. 'But I only have an hour.'

'Me too. Have to be back for lunchtime.' I whipped off

my apron. 'Thanks. I've been so excited, I drove out the road to see if I could spot it as soon as I got back in from Cork, even though it was pitch black.'

'Can't be seen from the road,' he told me as we headed for his car.

'Yes, thank you, I discovered that.'

'Now close your eyes,' he instructed as we rounded a bend a little while later, 'and don't open them until I tell you.'

I did as I was told and he stopped the car, pushed in a gate and drove a short distance further on.

'Now, as I said, the best thing about this place is the view.' He was helping me out of his jeep. 'So you can look at that first.'

It took me a second to get my bearings. 'Oh my God,' I said quietly. 'Oh my God,' I screamed then. All I could see was miles of blue sea held in place by a ribbon of pale cream sand.

'Like it?'

'Are you crazy?' I swung around to make sure there was a house. 'I love it!' I threw myself at him. 'Thank you, thank you, thank you.' It felt right somehow, being here with him.

'Get off me.' He laughingly took my hand, then both of us pulled away at the same time. 'You haven't even heard the price yet.'

'I don't care, I'll work my arse off, sell the apartment, whatever it takes,' I told him, embarrassed at how much I liked him touching me. 'Will you let me see inside?'

'It's open.' He strolled after me as I broke into a run.

He was right: it was nothing special, but it was clean and dry with three bedrooms, a plain white kitchen, a decent-sized bathroom with a separate loo and a huge, open-plan sitting/dining room. But it was the position of it, overlooking a small, secluded cove, that made my heart stop.

'Most times you can walk all the way back to the main beach, so exercise won't be a problem.'

'I can't believe this is happening to me.' I felt like bawling. 'It's perfect. How old is it?'

'Thirty years or so. It's fine, wiring and plumbing are all OK for another few years and the roof is sound. It's just a bit boring, I suppose, not pretty or anything.'

'I don't care. I love it. You don't know what this means to me, if I can afford it,' I told him, eyes shining. 'I was getting desperate.'

'Charlie, I presume?'

'Yep, he was so sad when I left him this time. Didn't want me to go. And the only thing that stopped me from howling at the moon was the thought of us being together sooner rather than later, thanks to you. Now,' I looked around, 'all this place needs is a fresh coat of paint and—'

'I've already organized someone to do that, as part of the sale. I was just waiting for you to come back to choose the colours, if you liked it. By the way, there is one condition attached and it's not negotiable.'

He must have seen my face drop because he said

quickly, 'The house comes complete with Max. He lives here.'

'Max?' I said stupidly. I'd been prepared all along for a catch, but not in the form of a sitting tenant.

'Yes, the man who lived here had a mutt named Max. He goes with the place.' He took one look at my face and stuck out his tongue. 'Gotcha.'

I threw a punch at him then and he pulled me towards him as he grabbed my arms in an effort to protect himself, and this time I was sorry to pull away. 'As long as Max is not a two-legged beast I'll have him,' I said, moving reluctantly to look out the window. 'Anyway, I've already promised Charlie a dog, so Max is perfect – I think.'

'Crikey, you're unputdownable today, I'll say that for you.' He laughed, scratching his head.

'Daniel Williams, you have just provided me with the best thing anyone has ever given me. Ever ever ever.' I bit my lip, but this time the tears that threatened were joyful.

'I haven't *given* you anything,' he joked.

'Thank you so much.' I meant it.

'Pleasure. Now I must get back to work so can we talk money, solicitors, etc., on the way into town? Oh, and keep it to yourself for the moment. There've been a few locals asking about the place. Best if you don't go shouting about it just yet.'

'Fine,' I told him and wished my heart would stop hammering. 'But can I just tell my aunt?'

'Of course.'

'That is, as soon as we've agreed a price.' I was nervous.

'Make me an offer,' he said, then noticed my face. 'Stop worrying, we'll sort something out!' he said quickly.

The high I felt for the rest of the day was akin to giving birth, I reckoned, and in a way I just had. I'd conceived a whole new life for me and my child. All I had to tackle now was the thorny issue of his father.

At four o'clock that afternoon a woman came into the café. She looked around nervously before making her way to the counter.

'Hello, how are you?' I asked as I polished the counter top.

'Fine,' she said in a wary Dublin accent.

'Good,' I beamed. 'Lovely day.' I made small talk but she didn't seem that way inclined. Each to his own, I decided. 'What can I get you?' I asked pleasantly. 'Or should I leave you to choose for a moment?'

'Coffee, please,' she said quietly.

I was becoming quite American in my approach to people ordering coffee. I wanted them to spell it out. 'What would you like?' I said – patiently, I hoped – pointing to the twenty or so varieties on the board.

'Oh, just plain black.' She shrugged.

'OK, why don't you take a seat and I'll bring it to you. Anything else? The crumpets were only made an hour ago?'

'No, thank you.' She didn't smile.

'No problem.' I busied myself and noticed she took a seat in the quietest corner, away from the window.

'Afternoon, Lily,' Tom Mangan, a local handyman, greeted me as I brought her coffee over. I noticed her head jerk up at the mention of my name. 'Any crumpets left?'

'For you, anything.' I winked at him. He was one of my favourites.

'There you are.' I laid out a proper napkin in front of her, and left a little porcelain dish with two miniature cupcakes in the centre of the table. 'Just a taster,' I explained. 'We do it for all our new customers and I don't think I've seen you in before.' I fixed everything just so. 'Enjoy.' It sounded a bit too trendy, so I smiled at her in a friendly way as I turned to go.

'You're Lily,' she said quietly. If I hadn't seen her re-action to Tom's greeting earlier I probably wouldn't have heard her, but I think I'd sensed something was coming and so was on the alert.

'Yes.' I waited.

'I wonder if I might have a word with you?' I noticed her hands were trembling. 'I'm Marie Madden, Dave's wife.'

458

48

RICHARD

RICHARD WAS FEELING AND LYING LOW. HIS DAYS consisted of watching endless reruns on TV with the curtains closed and ordering in pizza or Chinese. Under any other circumstances he might have enjoyed it.

The flat was straining under the weight of beer and other assorted bottles and a pile of cartons and boxes that was beginning to stink, but he hardly noticed. Luckily, Daisy – or her parents, more likely – had removed all her stuff so he didn't have to face the prospect of her knocking on his door without warning or, worse, letting herself in and finding him scratching his balls with a three-day stubble and red eyes.

Tom Dalton had left several messages and he'd had a text from Lily, but luckily the gang in work were leaving him alone. He knew he'd have to get his act together at some stage but right now all he had the energy to do was crack open another beer. Every time he thought about his wedding-day fiasco he was mortified, so he tried his best not to. Drinking helped.

Next day when he woke around eleven he just about made it to the bathroom before throwing up. He'd really given it a lash the night before. The telly had been brutal so he'd started on his stash of dope, not very clever after all the alcohol. Just as he was making coffee his phone rang. He saw Tom's number come up and pressed reject. Two minutes later there was a knock on the door.

'Richard, it's me, mate. Let me in.'

He ignored it and turned on the telly. His phone rang again and then the knocking started in earnest.

Five minutes later he flung open the door. 'Would you ever fuck off and leave me alone.'

'I've left you alone.' Tom strode past him. 'And by the looks of things it hasn't done you much good. Now, jump in the shower. We're going out for lunch.'

Richard surprised himself by doing what he was told. He had known Tom long enough to realize he wouldn't give up without a fight.

They had a big plate of pasta in a great little place in Temple Bar and Tom wanted to know what his plans were.

'I suppose I'll have to go into the café, for a start.' Richard would've rather gone for a bikini wax. 'They've been leaving me alone but I've had two texts from Hazel already today about ordering stuff urgently.'

'That seems like a plan, anyway. Why don't you do that this afternoon and then take it easy tonight? Or do you fancy a few pints after I finish the show?'

'I do, yeah, but my liver doesn't.'

'That bad, eh?'

'Cleared out everything I had, gin, brandy, the lot. Even some of those cheap liqueurs you made me buy years ago in Torremolinos when we were into getting trollied.'

'Charming.' Tom made a face. 'Has it been that rough?'

'Yeah,' Richard said. 'I really fucked up, didn't I?' He didn't expect the 'You sure did' he got in reply.

'Daisy's out to get you, I thought I'd better warn you. She's been on the blower loads. So has Trudy.'

'I can't blame her. Jesus, it must have been awful.' Richard knew she'd never forgive him.

'So, get up off your arse and start trying to apologize.'

'I just keep thinking about what a mess I've made of things and how I have to sort things out with Shauna now too . . .'

'She said she wrote to you years ago?' Tom looked puzzled.

'She did, yeah. She wanted to meet. To be honest, I just kept putting her off. I mean, it was just a fling.' Richard couldn't believe this was happening to him. 'Anyway,' he said tiredly, 'I'll deal with it but right this minute I've a head fit to burst open, so I'm a write-off.'

'What I don't understand is, how did she know you were getting married?'

'I told her, can you believe that?' Richard said. 'I actually thought it might get her off my back once and for all. I think I even mentioned the date. Anyway, sure Daisy's a model, she's been in the papers, on TV3, you name it. Christ, Shauna must have been completely pissed with me to actually turn up at the church, though.'

'I think you can safely assume she was,' Tom agreed. 'It took guts as well.'

'Yeah, she was sparky, as far as I remember. Anyway, let's change the subject for now, eh?'

Tom ignored him. 'I suppose she'll be looking for money, Child Support or whatever?'

'Fuck off. I said let's change the subject.'

Tom knew when he was beaten. They talked about football for a while. 'Look, mate, I've gotta get into the studio,' he said eventually. 'We're pre-recording a piece in an hour and I've done no bleedin' work for it.'

'You'll survive.' Richard laughed at him. 'You've probably interviewed whoever it is four or five times before anyway.'

'No, that's the problem. It's Phil Collins and I know sweet fuck all about his music.' They left and Richard headed for the café. He pulled up outside, then thought about it and drove off again. They could do without him for one more day, he decided.

After an hour's kip he felt marginally better so he jumped in the shower again and shaved. Before he slipped back into his old ways he grabbed a few black sacks from the local shop and emptied his garbage. Then he gathered up all his shirts and took them to the laundry and left some other bits into the dry cleaners on his way. He knew he had to face his mother at some stage but that could wait. He needed a bit of fresh air, so after making a few calls to the wholesalers he hit the road and headed for Wicklow.

49

LILY

OH GOD NO, SHE'S FOUND OUT, WAS MY FIRST REACTION when Marie Madden told me who she was. I hoped my face hadn't given me away. 'Would you just excuse me a moment, while I put an order into the kitchen and grab a coffee?' I asked, even though there wasn't a sinner in the place. 'Takeaway,' I mumbled as I made my escape. I needed a moment in private to panic.

She watched me scurry away, I could feel it. I headed for the kitchen, where I fluted around until I could no longer avoid her.

'Sorry about that.' I wasn't sure why I felt guilty as I sat down beside her a few minutes later with a triple espresso for courage. 'Can I top up your coffee?' I asked, hoping for another reprieve.

'No, thanks.' She moved her cup away. 'I wanted to talk to you about my husband,' she said. I could tell she was nervous because of the way her eyes kept darting about. 'I know you . . . knew him.'

I had to keep reminding myself that I had nothing to

worry about. 'Yes, although not very well at all,' I told her. 'Actually, he was supposed to give me a quote for some work on the shop but I never heard from him, so . . .' Stop rabbiting on, I told myself.

'He's dead.' The way she said it made me think she'd assumed I already knew.

'*What?*'

'You didn't know?' She seemed relieved.

'No.' I was genuinely shocked. 'Of course not. As I said, he was—'

'He was with you on the night he died.' It was a statement, not a question.

'What? No, I haven't seen him for weeks, months even.' I still couldn't believe it. He'd always seemed so . . . ebullient, I suppose. Dead didn't suit Dave.

'I want to ask you something and I really need an honest answer because it's driving me mad. And I can't seem to . . .' She sighed. 'I was going to say move on, but I'm not anywhere near that yet. I suppose what I'm trying to say is that I can't even start to grieve properly until I know.' She twisted her napkin as she spoke. 'Were you having an affair with him?'

'No.' I never imagined I'd be so glad to be able to say it.

With that one word she crumpled. 'It's just that I'm beginning to think . . . You see, Dave was always streets ahead of me in the looks department and after the kids were born I sort of . . . lost interest in him.'

I sensed she felt she was saying too much and was still unsure as to whether to completely trust me or not.

'You met him on the night of his death,' she said, confirming my thoughts.

'Did I? When?'

She mentioned the date and I had to think quickly. 'The last time I saw him was . . .' I did a quick calculation. 'Yes, it would have been on or around the date you said. I can't recall exactly without my diary,' I apologized. 'I do remember that I texted him and asked him to meet me for a drink. I needed a bit of help with this place before I opened. It was a small job – probably way too small for him – but I wanted his advice. I only saw him for an hour or so. I was in town so we met up. He promised to think about it and ring me the next day . . . and I haven't heard from him since.' I was still shocked at what she'd told me. 'So what happened?'

'What time did he leave you?' I sensed she believed my story.

'About nine or thereabouts.' I tried to think. 'I was driving back here, so I just had one glass of wine, and as far as I can remember I was home before ten.'

'Well, he went to our local and had a couple more there. He left about eleven. He was giving some young one a lift home and he had a heart attack in the car.' She paused and I could see the pain. 'And I've been driving myself mad, wondering if there was something going on between them because she wasn't someone he really knew, as far as we can tell.'

'Have you spoken to her?'

'Yes, but only at the time, to ask her all about how it had

happened. To be honest, I didn't think anything of it. She said she'd met him the previous night and they'd been chatting at the bar. She asked him for a lift because all her friends were drunk . . . She was very young and it would have been typical of Dave to want to look after her. I'd say she reminded him of the twins – his daughters,' she told me.

'Yes, he mentioned them to me . . . once,' I added quickly, not wanting her to think we were bosom buddies.

'Did he?' Her eyes lit up. 'He adored them, that's why I think he'd have been very protective of that girl – Kylie – in the pub that night.

'How did you meet him?' she asked me now.

'My sister . . .' I knew I had to choose my words carefully because at that moment I realized she was just like me, searching for answers she'd probably never get. That's what death does to you, it robs you of any possibility of answers. Besides, she was nice, in a salt-of-the-earth Dublin way – the sort of decent person who'd be kind to you in times of trouble, I imagined.

I fetched myself another coffee and told her about Alison's death, which at least got me off the hook there, because she was full of sympathy for me.

'You know, meeting you has been a big relief,' she said after we'd worn ourselves out talking. 'I feel I can put it all out of my mind now and get on with grieving. It was just too much at first. All the stuff about the girl in his car, then seeing a text from you. So many questions, d'ya know?' She seemed to be talking more to herself than me, so I didn't answer, but I knew all right.

'Dave liked style and a bit of finesse. If he had been . . . making a play for someone it wouldn't have been her, I felt. She was – well, rough – and common with it. She wasn't very nice to my girls when they went back to talk to her after the funeral and to tell you the truth she wasn't very . . . I dunno, warm towards me when we met, although maybe that was just my imagination. I was hardly thinking straight at the time.'

'I can imagine,' I said gently.

'I suppose I've had a bit of an inferiority complex for years where Dave was concerned,' she said softly and I thought how sad it sounded. 'I always felt he was too good for me. And we sort of grew apart, I suppose – even though he treated me like royalty. Oh, I knew he had an eye for the women, but I always assumed he just looked. Then some stupid bitch made a remark about him in the pub on New Year's Eve . . .'

'What did she say?'

'Oh, just that she'd heard he'd always been a bit of a ladies' man. She didn't realize I was his wife.' Marie's smile was forced. 'It was innocent enough – I knew by her face it was just idle gossip, something to say, you know how it is. But after what happened the night he died, I started putting two and two together and getting five. Then I found a couple of messages from you and it just sort of got to me really.'

'How did you find me?'

'It wasn't hard. When I was going through stuff I found a brochure for a beauty salon with your sister's name on it.

467

It also had your name scribbled on it. I made a few enquiries, checked his work diary . . .' She smiled at me. 'When I saw you first I was frightened. You're exactly his type. Dave liked class. He always said you could smell money.'

'Well, he wouldn't have smelt it from me,' I assured her.

'Do you only work here then?' she asked, surprised.

'No, I do actually own it. What I meant was I've never had a penny really. All this only happened because of Alison's death.'

'I see.'

'She had a child, a little boy called Charlie. He's three. There was a trust fund . . . I only found out . . . later.' I'd no idea why I was telling her all this.

'I'm so sorry. What's happened to him?'

'I'm looking after him – or at least I will be shortly. He's with my aunt, just until I get our house sorted. I can't wait to have him with me, he's all I have . . .' I felt embarrassed yet happy saying it. 'I suppose in a sense all this is for him.' It was odd, but it was the first time I'd thought of it that way.

'You're lucky then,' she said with confidence. 'You have a reason to go on. He'll make you so proud one day, and he'll keep you young, and teach you so much. My girls still do that.'

'You sound very wise.' It was true. 'I'd say Dave was a lucky man.'

'Did he ever mention me?'

'Yes, actually, he did.' It wasn't a lie, but the rest was.

'He mentioned something about me catering – a surprise party for you, as far as I remember. It was one of the first things he contacted me about. That and my sister's death. He was quoting her for a job, or something . . .'

'Really?' Her eyes lit up. 'It probably would have been for my birthday. I'm fifty next month. He was on at me to throw a big do. Dave loved surprises.'

'That might have been it,' I told her. 'I know I wrote it down at the time . . .' I let my voice trail off.

'Thank you.' She grabbed my hand. 'I'm so glad I plucked up the courage to come and see you. You've no idea what a weight's been taken off my mind. I was torturing myself with it.'

'It's hard when someone you love dies suddenly . . . It leaves you with so much extra stuff to deal with, on top of the grief.'

Marie left once we started to get busy. As I watched her go I knew that she was a lot happier than when she'd arrived and I was glad.

50

LILY

JANUARY IN WICKLOW WAS A GREY AND DREARY MONTH with hardly a local, never mind a tourist, in sight. The countryside was naked and the sea looked angry any time I drove out the coast road. The car parks were deserted and the picnic tables dotted about the edges needed to have kids climbing all over them. I longed for the first splashes of yellow to appear in the gardens and window boxes and tried to cheer up our customers by introducing an 'energy-boosting' menu to keep us all going. Aunt Milly insisted I buy an industrial juicer and try out a few healthy specials – the recipes for which she personally researched – and I have to say our younger customers really took to them.

Everyone around me was complaining that the days were crawling by and a lot of our regulars came in looking damp and grumpy. Too many hard-to-keep resolutions or strenuous exercise classes, Orla reckoned, as everyone ordered skinny lattes and vegetable soup and brown salad sandwiches – no butter, no mayo. The new menu was a hit for about three days but by the end of the first week they were all back on the white chocolate chip muffins.

The house purchase was going through without any difficulty, which my aunt reckoned meant it was destined for me. She and Charlie were coming to see it the following weekend and I couldn't wait.

Daniel invited me to have dinner with his mother at their house. It seemed she wanted to check out her new neighbour. I was terrified she might not like me and veto the sale, so I dressed carefully – like a nun, according to Orla, who laughed outrageously when she saw me – and took her a huge bunch of late winter grape hyacinths and early daffs and snowdrops.

'You look very sedate,' Daniel said when he came to pick me up. 'Like you're going to meet a priest or something. What's up?'

'Nothing,' I said casually. 'Just felt like being understated for a change.'

'Well, you managed it.' He laughed as we snaked along my favourite road with the purple hills on one side and the vast expanse of frothy waves providing a backdrop on the other. It still gave me a thrill each time I realized that this would be my route home from work each day.

'I hope you're not trying to impress my mum?' Daniel asked.

'Whatever gave you that idea?' I shot him one of my looks.

'Oh, I dunno – the flowers, the homemade cupcakes, the all-black outfit and the flat shoes – nothing much, I guess.' He poked me in the ribs, then burst out laughing so I was forced to clock him one.

As soon as he introduced me to his mother I realized why he'd been trying to keep a straight face earlier. She was much younger than I'd expected – a well-known local artist, as it turned out – and a hippie. I nearly died with mortification when she strolled out to meet us wearing a long, flowery kaftan-type dress and sandals, even though it was winter.

'She's much more likely to be put off if she thinks you're a Bible-thumper,' Daniel whispered as we followed her indoors.

Luckily for me, she was also a very nice woman and warm, home-baked bits and pieces seemed to convince her that I wasn't going to be the neighbour from hell. Listening to her stories I knew it was much more likely that I'd be feeding her up and mothering her rather than the other way round. It was also a great relief to know that she wouldn't be knocking on my door all the time looking for company.

'The way you talked, I thought she was a little old lady with a bun and roundy specs and an apron.' I could have killed Daniel as he dropped me back.

'I never implied anything of the sort,' he said indignantly. 'She spent three months in Zanzibar on her holidays last year, so she's not about to crawl into a rocking chair any day soon.'

'But you said she relied on you when your dad died . . .'

'To run the business, yes – but that's because she has no

interest. If I'm honest I was afraid she'd sell it from under me.' He laughed again at my face. 'And donate all her money – my inheritance – to a benevolent fund for ageing tree-huggers or something.'

By the time we pulled up at the shop we were giggling like teenagers.

'Would you like to come up for coffee?' I asked him, not wanting the evening to end. I'd knocked back a couple of glasses of wine pretty smartly at dinner to hide my embarrassment, whereas I knew he'd hardly drunk anything. 'One for the road maybe?' I suggested then, anxious to keep the atmosphere going.

'Better not, I've a group in first thing in the morning. Got to be at the airport at six thirty.'

'Where on earth do you get your energy?' He looked as fresh as the proverbial daisy.

'It's the company.' He tipped the side of my nose with his finger. 'You're a funny girl, Lily Ormond, do you know that?' Without warning he leaned over and kissed me – very lightly to start with – then leaned away slightly so that he could see my face in the half-light. Afterwards, I don't know which of us decided we wanted more first, but thirty seconds later it was definitely more satisfying than any kiss I'd ever tasted.

'Don't you have a girlfriend who might object to that?' I asked him, still unsure about his friend Zanna.

'No, but don't you have at least two boyfriends on the go at once?' He raised his eyebrow at me, then didn't wait for my reply. 'Goodnight.' He grinned and leaned over to open the door for me.

'I don't have even one boyfriend.' It seemed important to set him straight.

'Glad to hear it,' he said softly and pulled my hair.

Next day Richard called in and I was pleased. I'd phoned him a couple of times and we'd been texting, but I still hadn't seen him since the day he nearly got married and I was concerned about him.

'Hi.' He still looked sheepish even now – over a week later.

'Hi, yourself.' I greeted him warmly. 'Coffee, or something stronger?'

'Coffee – black and strong – would be great, thanks.'

He looked the worse for wear. I watched him as I made up a pot of espresso and frothed some milk for myself.

'So, how've you been?'

'OK, I guess.' He shuffled about. 'Was it a complete disaster?' He was looking at his feet.

'Unmitigated,' I told him.

'Go on then, get the lecture over with.' He sounded like a schoolboy as we sat down at a table in the window.

'I'll leave that to everyone else in your life,' I told him. 'I'm not in a position to lecture anyone.'

'Well, I've started to clear up the mess,' he said. 'I have a son, can you credit that?'

'Me too,' I said softly. 'Can *you* believe that?'

He smiled.

'Had you really no idea?' I asked him.

'Truthfully, somewhere at the back of my mind I knew there had to be a reason Shauna was always trying to see me. I'm not that vain.' He grinned. 'But I dunno, I just never let myself go there. As long as she didn't say it out loud then I guess I could avoid it.'

'Well, she definitely picked her moment,' I said, not sure he deserved that.

'I probably deserved it.' He was reading my thoughts, it seemed.

'No, I don't think so,' I told him truthfully. 'What are you going to do now?'

'We've spoken. It was all a bit fraught on the day, I needn't tell you, but things calmed down eventually. Anyway, I'm going to meet them both next week. He knows about me.' He smiled. 'His name's Cillian.'

'Good for you.' I meant it. 'I don't think you'll be sorry.'

'No, but I am sorry about Daisy. She doesn't want anything to do with me. I loved her, you know, in my own way. I'm just a typical stupid male, I guess, always wondering if there isn't more around the next corner,' he said and it didn't hurt at all to hear.

We chatted for a good while and the light faded and eventually the girls called goodnight. Daniel Williams walked by with a young woman in tow and made a face at me as he passed. I laughed in spite of myself and stuck out my tongue at him in response, then spent the rest of the evening wondering who the hell the girl was.

'Got any scraps to eat?' Richard asked eventually.

I gave in and prepared a plate of cold meats and cheeses and added some olives and sun-blushed tomatoes and a bit of pesto. 'That's all you're getting.' I put down a basket of fresh bread and some butter and stole the black pepper from a nearby table. 'Wine or water?'

'Maybe one glass of wine?'

'That didn't take long.' I grinned. 'I thought one of your texts said you were off drink for the rest of January?'

'Well, I was off it for a couple of days after my binge, but hey, you gotta live, eh?'

'That's true.' I handed him a glass and a quarter bottle of wine and we tucked in.

'So, d'ya fancy meeting up some time then?'

'A date, do you mean?' I was joking.

'I suppose so. Yeah, why not?' He shifted about a bit and looked uncomfortable.

'So what is this, a "let's start again"-type conversation?'

'Sort of. I'm definitely single now.' He gave me one of his 'please love me' looks.

'Richard.' I was getting a bit tired of all the game-playing with him. 'What is it you're trying to say?'

'I just thought . . . you know, maybe we could get together some time, have a bit of fun . . .' He was struggling to make it more palatable, I could tell. 'I'm not ready for anything else at the moment,' he said quickly.

'Sorry, Richard, it's out of the question,' I told him in a flat voice. I felt oddly disappointed. He hadn't grown up at all, it appeared. 'The truth is, I won't have much time for "a bit of fun" in the near future. As you know, I'm a mother now and my child is coming to live with me.' I stood up. 'Actually, I need to phone him, so I'd better close up here.'

'Can I call you some time?' He seemed about to say more, then drained his glass.

'No, I don't think so but thanks, you've helped me clear up a few things in my head.' I walked him to the door. 'Good luck with your own son, by the way. I hope you get a second chance with him.'

'Lily, is this because of . . . you know, my arrangement with Alison?'

'What do you mean?'

'Because if it is, I just want you to know that I wasn't suggesting anything like that.' He looked genuinely upset. 'I wasn't implying that you were . . . well, you know.'

'What?' I asked.

'Nothing,' he said and I let it go. But I knew exactly what he meant. I just wasn't ready to hear it said out loud. It was still too big for me.

51

LILY

HIS WORDS HAUNTED ME FOR THE NEXT FEW DAYS, BUT I couldn't, or wouldn't, let myself think too much about what he'd meant. I was beginning to feel I'd never be able to face it, so I convinced myself that I'd no real proof. It could still turn out to be something else entirely, I reasoned. It wouldn't be the first time I'd got it all wrong.

I finally had the long–overdue chat with Brian Daly. We had some formal business to do, but first I took him to lunch at a little French bistro near his office. I felt it was the least I could do: he'd been a good friend to me over the past few months.

'We need to talk about Kevin,' I said after a while.

'Lily, I want you to know that the Kevin thing was as much of a shock to me as it was to you.' Brian looked as strained as I felt. 'Let's just say it took me a long while to discover what it took you less than a month to figure out about Kevin. Oh, we get on well enough and all that, but Kevin is out for only one person in life and that's himself.'

478

I couldn't deny he was spot-on. 'What I don't understand is why he's come forward after all this time? I mean, he and Alison were never an item – in the traditional sense – or I'd have known about it.'

'I'd no idea either. He said that after Alison died he realized that he was all Charlie had left. I know what you're thinking,' he added quickly as he saw my face.

'I'm Charlie's legal guardian,' I said quietly. 'And nobody comes into his life unless I say so.'

'I understand that.'

'Brian, I know he's your brother and all that but I don't trust Kevin. And I don't think he'd be any good for Charlie right now. I'm not even convinced he sees himself as a hands-on father, so what does he want?'

'Nothing that I know of.'

'So why didn't he talk to me about this? Christ, is that why he . . . made a play for me?' I wondered aloud. 'I thought at first he was interested in Orla, and so did she.'

'I don't know. He came to me and I asked him not to talk to you about it. I wanted to tell you myself. I'm just sorry the way it came out . . .'

'Brian, I want to see the letter she left. I want proof before I think about this any more. It's been on my mind since we had our conversation and it's wrecking my head, to be honest. Besides, I have a horrible feeling he's not going to go away where I'm concerned.'

He said nothing for a moment and I was prepared for an argument.

'Fine,' he said eventually.

'Do you believe Kevin?' I felt I had to ask. 'And I'm sorry if that's an unfair question.'

He shook his head. 'No, it's not. And yes, I do believe him. Why else would he be doing this?'

I sighed. 'OK, let's go back to your office and get this over with.'

'Lily, it's not a very long letter and I don't think it's very . . . personal or anything,' he warned. 'I think she just wanted me to have it in case anything ever happened to her . . . but like all of us she never really thought it would.'

My heart sank. This letter was my last chance to get some answers to the one question I could no longer avoid. 'How do you know that?'

'She wrote it in my office one day. She asked me to witness her signature but I didn't read the contents or anything so I don't know what's in it.'

'I see.' We ordered coffee which neither of us really wanted, I guessed.

'You'll be glad to know we've finally arranged a date for Charlie to move in with me,' I told him as we walked back to his office a short while later. I saw his face light up. He knew about the house purchase; all the paperwork had gone to him as my solicitor.

'Can I come and see him?' he asked.

'You'd better,' I warned him. 'You'll be my chief babysitter if I ever get a boyfriend. I've nothing planned, mind you,' I added quickly.

Ten minutes later he handed me a brown envelope. My heart started beating faster the second I saw my name written in her bold handwriting. She'd drawn a little flower in the loop of the Y in Lily, just as she'd always done. When we were children she said it was because the name Lily made her think of the scent of summer flowers and when we were very small she used to make me smell my name whenever it was written down, insisting that if you tried hard enough you could get the perfume. Also on the front of the envelope was the date and a note that said *Statement of Alison Ormond – only to be opened by her sister Lily Ormond in the event of her death, and then only if an issue arises in relation to the father of Charles Ormond. Otherwise to be retained by Brian Daly, Solicitor, and left unopened.*

'I'll leave you for a couple of minutes,' Brian said quietly.

I looked at the envelope for ages and ran my hand over her writing, hoping to feel her close. Then I said a quick prayer and tore it open. It was much shorter than I would have liked and not at all personal.

In the event of my death, I wish to place on record the identity of the father of my son Charles Joseph Ormond. In doing so I would also make it known here that I have instructed my solicitor Brian Daly that sole custody of my son Charlie is granted to my sister Lily who is to be given full responsibility for his upbringing. In late 2002 I had a relationship with a man and it continued for a number of years. This relationship was purely physical. The man in question was married and at the time of writing he and his wife are trying for their first child. I wish it to be known that I consider the man in question to be a decent and trustworthy person, however because of the nature of the relationship I do not envisage him playing any part in my son's life. His name is James Weldon.

I don't know how long I sat there before Brian returned. He went quietly to his desk and waited for me to speak. For a split second after I read the letter I'd wondered if I could trust him but I dismissed the notion when I saw the worried look on his face.

'Did Kevin know of the existence of this letter?' I asked him eventually.

'No, of course not,' he said quietly.

'I'm going to kill him.' I bit my lip and handed Brian the page.

If I'd had any lingering doubts – and I hadn't – they would have disappeared as soon as I saw his expression when he read Alison's letter.

Neither of us spoke for a while, then eventually he said, 'I'm very sorry. This is all my fault.' He put his head in his hands. 'I believed him, Lily.'

'Why?' I asked him. 'Why would he put me through this?'

'I haven't the faintest idea, but if it's not too much to ask, maybe you'd let me speak to him first. I might have more of a chance of getting an answer to that question.'

'No,' I said, quietly.

'Please.' Brian looked really upset. 'I promise you I'll get some answers. I know what buttons to push where my brother is concerned.'

'How do we know how many more lies he's told?' I asked bitterly. 'Do you know for a fact that he ever had anything to do with my sister?'

'I know they'd gone out a couple of times.' He was choosing his words carefully. 'I introduced them,' he said with a wry smile. 'It didn't last long. Afterwards he said it was nothing. I didn't even know Alison was pregnant until after she'd had Charlie. I asked her directly if there was anything I should know – in a personal capacity – and she said no. I was relieved, to tell you the truth. Kevin would have been the last person I'd have wanted to be the father. Apart from that, my relationship with Alison was purely professional and it wouldn't have been appropriate – in fact, if she had said that Kevin was the father I'd probably have insisted that another solicitor handle her affairs, for obvious reasons.'

'That still doesn't tell us why he lied.'

'No,' Brian said. 'But if you give me forty-eight hours, I'll be able to tell you, I promise.'

52

JAMES AND TAMSIN

JAMES WAS WORRIED: IT WAS A VERY FROSTY NIGHT AND
Tamsin was late. He'd been delighted when she'd phoned
him in the office earlier to tell him she was meeting Maria
for a drink. He knew how much she relied on her best
friend, and this year Maria and Dan had gone to Australia
for Christmas, to see his sister Helen, which meant they'd
been away for a month. James had felt a teeny bit
optimistic as he drove home to feed the dogs, knowing that
Tamsin would tell her friend all about their attempts to
adopt Charlie. He hoped it would bring her some relief.
Colin Johnson, his boss, had phoned as soon as he arrived
home.

'James, I meant to see you before you left. I was just
wondering how things were going?' his old friend asked.

'Sorry, boss, I ran out a bit early.' James laughed. 'Had
to feed the monsters. Tamsin's out tonight, I'm happy to
report.'

'That's a good sign. How's she been?' Colin didn't want
to let on, but his wife had insisted he keep more of an eye

on them, having called to see Tamsin the previous day.

'The same, really. Very quiet.' James got worried even thinking about how low she'd been. 'It hasn't been easy. By the way, say thanks to Anne for dropping by yesterday. Tamsin's spending far too much time on her own at the moment.'

'And how are you holding up?' Colin always worried about James because James took care of everyone else.

'I'm OK. Tired but, you know, I'm fine really. Why, has my work been suffering?'

'Good grief, no, nothing like that. In fact, I think you should take a holiday, get some heat in your bones.'

'You know what, Colin, you could be right. Maybe that's just what she needs. I'll talk to her about it later. Thanks.' James was touched.

'Oh and by the way, we'd like you two to come to dinner on Saturday week, catch up and all that. How about it?'

'Great, I'll let you know tomorrow. Thanks, Colin, you're a good friend.'

Now, at almost ten o'clock, she still hadn't arrived home. He'd tried her mobile twice but it had rung out, not surprising if they were in a pub or restaurant. She never heard it. James knew she wouldn't have more than one glass of wine, so that wasn't a problem. He wished he'd thought to tell her he'd collect her, so that she could relax.

He was just about to call Maria when the doorbell rang. She's forgotten her keys again, James thought. He smiled to himself and shooed the dogs out of the way, wondering why they were barking. Normally they could smell her a mile off and merely wagged their tails furiously until she'd petted them. As soon as he saw the policeman, he feared the worst. Garda John Murray asked to come inside and told James as gently as he could that there'd been an accident and he needed to get to the Mater Hospital as quickly as possible.

Later James couldn't remember anything about the journey. Thankfully the Garda drove, but if the fresh-faced young man had any details he wasn't letting on.

The relief when he saw her was unlike anything James had ever experienced. She was bruised and her arm was broken and they were still doing tests, but at least she was alive.

'Oh James, I'm so sorry.' She burst into tears as soon as she saw him.

'Shush, darling, don't. It's OK, I'm here.' He kissed her and tried to wipe away her tears, but she was hysterical and eventually they had to sedate her and ask him to wait outside while they finished their tests, which they'd assured him were all routine.

Later Garda Murray explained that it appeared a car driven by a young man had taken a corner at speed and ploughed into Tamsin, who'd been travelling in the opposite direction. He'd admitted responsibility and a breath test showed he was well above the legal limit for alcohol intake.

'Thank God your wife was driving a jeep, which held

up remarkably well,' the officer said. 'Otherwise it might have been much worse, from what I've been told by my colleagues.'

'It's the dogs,' James told him unnecessarily, still in shock. 'We need the jeep for them.'

They brought him strong tea and eventually let him back in to see her, after confirming that there appeared to be no further damage.

James had the difficult task of telling both their parents, but at least he was able to reassure them immediately that she was going to be fine. Her mother came straight away and his mum and dad went to be with the dogs and look after their house. The Irish were the only people he knew who believed that houses needed to be minded.

After her mother was persuaded to leave, James sat by her bed all night and watched her while she slept.

It was bright outside and he was dozing in the chair when she woke up.

'James.' Her voice was barely audible but he jumped anyway, alert for the slightest sound.

'It's OK, love, I'm here and you're grand.'

'What happened?'

He told her as little as possible in order to avoid upsetting her.

'Is the other driver OK?' she wanted to know.

'He's alive. They didn't say much, just that he was badly smashed up but he's not in any danger.'

'It wasn't my fault,' Tamsin said quickly. 'I mean—'

'No, it wasn't your fault. He's admitted everything.

Apparently he'd been out drinking with some of his mates.' James didn't want to think about what could have happened.

'I'm so sorry.' She was getting upset again and he hugged her as best he could and tried to soothe her. Eventually she fell asleep and her parents came in to let James go home and shower, and he was back by her side before she even noticed he'd gone.

Much later that day she was able to sit up, although she was very sore and needed assistance. She asked for some tea, and after several cups and a half-slice of toast they were able to talk a little bit more.

'James, all I can think of is . . .'

'Never a good sign, you thinking.' He held her hand and kissed it.

'No, let me say it please. I know I've been selfish.' She closed her eyes and sighed. 'I think I've been very lucky and I want to try and, you know, start living my life again.'

'That's all I want, darling.' James had tears in his eyes. 'And I'm sorry for everything I put you through.'

'We'll be OK, me and you. We're a family, aren't we?'

'Yes, love, we're a family.'

53

LILY

I SLEPT BADLY YET FELT LIGHTER WHEN I WOKE UP. AS I lay there going through it all again in my mind, I knew I had to accept that I'd probably never really have answers about why my sister had done what she'd done. No matter how much I'd give to have one final conversation with her, it wasn't going to happen. The only things I still had to decide on were what to do about James and what – if anything – to say to Kevin Daly. Thankfully I had the sense to realize that I was too nervous where James was concerned and too angry with Kevin to act rationally in either case, so I resolved to do nothing for the moment.

I must have fallen back asleep because when I awoke the second time I could smell warm bread. Jumping up, I nearly had a heart attack when I discovered it was after nine. A quick call to Orla put my mind at rest and after a lightning shower I headed down to face the day, feeling a bit tired and emotional but otherwise OK.

The girls insisted on feeding me before I did anything

and Violet brought me the paper and a fresh pot of coffee as I sat in the window and people-watched and fell in love with Wicklow all over again. A class of very young school-children zig-zagged like snakes towards the charity shop, each one carrying a toy. The line was topped and tailed by a teacher, both of whom waved even though I barely knew them. Jack Donoghue, a local electrician, blew me a kiss and Maud, one of our regular pensioners, swatted an elderly man with a bunch of flowers and raised her eyes to heaven when she saw me. Her husband, I assumed, laughing, enjoying being part of it all, even if I was a blow-in.

'Morning.' Daniel Williams appeared out of nowhere.

'What are you doing creeping up on people?' It came out a bit sharper than I'd intended. I was still feeling vulnerable after that kiss.

'Charming.' He pulled out a chair and sat down without being asked. 'Who stole your rattle then?'

I laughed in spite of myself and we chatted as Naomi brought me scrambled eggs and bacon and a pile of hot toast.

'I only came to tell you that my solicitor called and apparently we're ready to close the sale, provided you have the rest of the finance in place.' He nicked a piece of toast.

'Yes, I do. Oh my God, that's great.' My animosity was instantly forgotten.

'So I'm back in the good books then?'

'For the moment,' I laughingly admitted.

'Terrific, because I wondered if you'd like to have

490

dinner with me tonight? We can toast our first successful business venture together, perhaps?'

My mouth was full of egg so I shot him a 'what exactly do you want from me' look. My recent experiences had warped my judgement.

'I take it that's a no then?'

'Maybe.'

'So when did I go from being the nicest guy in the world and the one who saved your life and made you the happiest girl ever, ever, ever – at least I think that's how you put it?'

'I'm off men at the moment.' I wanted to tell him about Kevin Daly – and Richard.

'Well then, consider me your guardian angel.' He got up. 'I'll pick you up at seven. Oh, and I've booked that new place in Gorey that you've been trying to get into for ages. Seems like it's owned by one of my ex-girlfriends.' He smiled sweetly.

'As opposed to the current one you had in tow the other night?' I could have kicked myself for asking.

'My cousin Andrea, but thank you for your interest.' I knew he was teasing but I wasn't in teasing mode at the moment. 'See you at seven, and try to smile, for God's sake, otherwise you'll frighten what little passing trade there is.' He grabbed a piece of bacon.

'Fine,' I said through gritted teeth. I was not going to miss eating in the hottest place in the south-east for anyone. Anyway, I really wanted to go and besides, I owed him bigtime.

'My treat,' I said quietly without looking up.

'Sorry?' he enquired with a smug look.

'I'll pay,' I told him in what I hoped was a bored voice.

'Well, it's better than a slap with a wet fish, I suppose,' he said and I giggled. 'Actually, I'd settle for the old Lily back.'

He was gone before I had a chance to apologize.

Brian Daly dropped by just as the lunchtime rush was starting. It was turning into one of those days.

'Would you have ten minutes to talk?' he asked quietly.

'Not really,' I told him, glancing at my watch.

'Lily, we're well covered if you need to take some time out.' Orla had overheard him as she stocked up the chiller cabinet.

'Are you sure?'

'Positive.' She smiled at me.

'Thanks a mil,' I told her. 'Could we get out of here?' I asked Brian. 'I think I need some air.'

'Fine.'

'How about I make us a sandwich and we sit on one of those wooden benches just out the road?' I suggested.

'Is it not a bit chilly for a picnic?'

'I'll make us two hot chocolates. Deal?'

'Deal.'

It was what could only be described as bracing as we sat on a bench in the car park in full view of passing cars.

'I wonder why they picked this particular spot for a picnic area. It's a wind tunnel. And wouldn't the kids be playing with the traffic?' I was thinking of Charlie.

'It is rather busy.' He smiled and as if to emphasize the point a jeep roared by.

'Who's that?' Brian asked as a horn was tooted and a very large hand waved madly in our direction through an open window.

'Daniel Williams,' I told him, waving back and trying not to look too interested.

'Nice guy,' Brian said. 'Seems like a decent sort.'

'He is.' I spread out our food and cupped the hot chocolate for warmth. This was a mad idea, I decided. It was grey and breezy, not helped by the choppy sea all around us.

'I spoke to Kevin last night,' Brian said quietly after a pause.

'Oh?'

'There's no easy way to say this.' He looked wrecked, I noticed for the first time.

'Say what?' My heart was working overtime again.

'He found out that there was a lot of money coming Charlie's way.' Brian kept his eyes on my face.

'How?' I wasn't surprised but I was shocked nonetheless.

'I'm sorry, Lily, but it appears to have been my fault. It seems he saw your file open on my desk. I should never have left him alone in there.' He banged his fist on the bench and gritted his teeth. 'My landline was acting up and an important call came through. I was gone for less than a minute but it was totally unprofessional of me and something I'd never normally do.'

493

'I see.' I felt relieved that my instincts not to trust Kevin were so spot-on. Shame it had taken me so long in the first place.

'I'm always so careful but, Lily, this is very serious for me. I should have known better. And with Kevin, of all people. I'm very sorry,' he said again. 'It is completely unacceptable that because of me he was in a position to . . . abuse you and—'

'He didn't abuse me, Brian. Don't give him any more power than he deserves.'

'I will report him to the police, of course, and I'll have to tell our senior partner. You'll be assigned another member of staff immediately.' He looked devastated and my heart went out to him.

'What will the guards do? It's his word against yours,' I said gently. 'And as for another solicitor, I don't want one.'

'But, Lily, you don't understand the implication of what I let happen. It's—'

'Nothing happened. He didn't get away with it and that's all that matters. As long as you give me your word that he will never come anywhere near me – or Charlie – again, I'm happy.'

'He's leaving for London this evening. I got him to sign a document relinquishing any claim on you or Charlie. Not that he ever had any – thank God we had that letter. I just did it as a double precaution. Also, I taped our conversation and if my father gets to hear about this his inheritance is out the window and he knows it.' But, Lily, I don't deserve to get off so lightly. I think you should take independent advice on the matter.'

'Thankfully, very few of us get what we deserve,' I told him. 'I'm just glad it's over.'

54

LILY

THE NOTION OF GETTING AND NOT GETTING WHAT WE deserve stayed with me as I helped the girls cope with the last of the lunchers.

'Sally asked me to pass on a message,' Orla told me cheerfully as we grabbed a quick coffee as soon as we could. 'She said she got your email last night and if you don't call her in the next twenty-four hours and explain it all in precise detail she will personally arrange for both your kneecaps to be broken in a paramilitary-style shooting that cannot be traced back to her. Make any sense?'

'Yes.' I laughed. 'Perfect sense.'

'So when are you going to let me in on it all? I feel neglected.' She made a face and then smiled at me. 'Are you OK?'

'Yes, I am and listen, Orla, I wouldn't want you to feel neglected for the world. You've been the bestest friend – as Charlie would say – these past few months.' I felt ashamed that I'd been so wrapped up in myself. 'And the only reason I haven't told you everything that's been going on is that I needed to lose myself in work and not feel I had to talk, or that you were watching me. Does that make sense?'

'Yeah, and I know you've had a lot on, but a trouble shared and all that rubbish . . .'

'I know that and I can't think of anyone except you and Sal that I'd want to share it all with – so how about, in the next day or two, I bring you out for a slap-up meal, ply you with alcohol and tell you everything, on condition that you wire your jaw so that it doesn't hit the floor and permanently deform your face, OK?'

'And then can I ask Sal any questions I have so that you don't have to talk for twelve hours non-stop?' She grinned.

'Perfect,' I told her. 'You can fill in the bits for each other.'

'I can't wait,' she said, still grinning as she went off to the kitchen after we'd exchanged hugs.

'And Orla, thanks. I mean it. You saved my life.' I winked at her over Naomi's head.

Just when I was thinking of texting James, he phoned.

'Lily, I was wondering if I could come and get a selection of your best bits and pieces?' he asked after we'd exchanged greetings.

'What exactly did you have in mind?' I was intrigued.

'Em, cupcakes as well as those lovely ones you do with the fruit and flaky pastry . . .'

'Eccles cakes?'

'Yes and some of that brack thing, oh, and that drizzled lemon cake maybe.'

'You having a party?' I asked and he filled me in on Tamsin's accident, while quickly assuring me that she was fine.

'It's just the hospital food,' he explained. 'I'm trying to encourage her to eat. She's lost a lot of weight recently,' he told me and it sounded like he blamed himself.

'James, could I come and visit her?' I had to stop putting these things off. 'And see you both?'

He hesitated.

'I could bring the goodies?' I suggested. 'Save you coming all this way?'

'Lily, I don't want her upset . . . or anything. She's still very fragile. Maybe another time.'

'Please, James? It's important.' I was afraid of what would happen if I avoided the meeting for too long. 'I'll only stay a few minutes.'

'I suppose so, then. Actually, she asked me to apologize to you. She feels she may have been . . . a bit too pushy . . . about, you know – the whole thing.'

'Tell her thanks for that.' I didn't know what else to say so I decided to wait till I was face to face with them both. 'If I said I'd see you about four?' I checked the clock. 'Will you be there too?'

'Yes, but Lily, just a quick one, OK? And no mention of what's . . . gone before.'

'I understand.' We said our goodbyes and I hung up and begged Orla for one last favour.

* * *

On the way I rang Daniel. 'Would it be OK if we made it eight instead of seven?' I asked him. 'I have to go to Dublin for an hour.' I knew I'd be stuck in the traffic getting back to Wicklow and I wanted to glam myself up for our dinner.

'After the look on your face when I merely beeped my horn in friendly greeting at you earlier, I'm hardly going to argue with you today,' he said pleasantly and I was smiling as I hit the off button.

'Hi,' I put my head round the door of the private ward less than an hour later. 'I come bearing edible gifts, the best kind, don't you think?'

'Lily, hi.' Tamsin tried to hoist herself up and I was shocked by her appearance. Apart from the bruises, her face was all sucked in and she had the kind of dark circles normally sported only by heroin addicts.

James helped her by putting an extra pillow behind her head, then came to give me a hug. 'You're good to come.' He took the pretty wicker basket that Orla had made up. 'My goodness, this smells divine.'

'Thanks a million.' Tamsin smiled weakly. 'The food here is, well, not for the faint-hearted.'

We chatted for a while and I could see she was tiring.

'Lily, I understand James apologized to you on my behalf, but I wanted to say it myself too,' she said eventually. 'I know now that I was out of order, putting you under so much pressure . . .'

499

I raised my hand to stop her but she said quickly, 'I went a bit mad, I think, but I'm OK again. We've accepted that we're not going to have any children and we're not putting ourselves through the wringer any more, are we?' She smiled at her husband. 'Not even the whole adoption thing,' she said quietly. She leaned back then, as if the air had gone out of her.

'We've both agreed enough is enough.' James reached for her hand and squeezed it. 'We need time to heal, mentally as well as physically.'

'I need to tell you something,' I took a deep breath, 'and I hope that it will help you to heal.'

'What is it?' I could see James was apprehensive.

'It's a very long story and not for today, but Alison left a letter.' I could see Tamsin's face cloud over. 'Ironically, I only had access to it because someone came forward claiming to be Charlie's father.' I wasn't sure which one of them to look at. 'It was all very messy . . . and not easy to deal with. Anyway, it turns out he wasn't, thank God.' They both looked puzzled. 'It was difficult for me, and I wish she'd said more in the letter, but there you go. We don't always get what we want, eh?' I tried to smile. 'Anyway, one good thing came out of a bad situation, at least.' I saw them watching me closely and noticed Tamsin's hand was gripping her husband's. 'In the letter Alison confirms that you're Charlie's father, James.'

I think time stopped for all three of us then. Certainly it did for me because I knew there was no going back from this moment.

'Lily, this isn't . . . You're not . . . making this up?' James asked.

'No.'

'Oh my God, oh my God' was all Tamsin said, tears streaming down her face.

'Lily, I need to know what this means,' James said quietly.

'Thank you for telling us,' his wife added. 'Even just knowing . . . you've no idea.' I saw then that they were both crying.

'Tamsin, I need to ask you something first. Are you certain that you can cope with the reality of this? What I mean is, the fact that Charlie was born as a result of a relationship between your husband and . . .' I started to cry too, then, and the rest of the words remained unspoken. 'Between your husband and my sister?' I asked eventually.

She didn't rush in, which I was happy about. 'That's something I gave a great deal of thought to before we . . . before I approached you initially,' she said slowly. 'And all I can tell you is that in my heart I know that James and your sister . . . Alison . . . had a special bond in spite of the circumstances.' I sensed she was choosing her words carefully to avoid upsetting me unnecessarily. 'That made me very sad – and very unhappy initially, if I'm honest.' She paused for a moment. 'But I can truthfully say that if you'd agreed to my . . . mad suggestion, that first day we met . . . I knew that I would love that little boy as if he were mine and James's.' She looked at him and smiled and I envied them what they had. 'It's the next best thing, you see. And a very good second best, if your sister was anything like you,' she said quietly.

All three of us had to swallow hard then.

'In that case, what it means,' I bit my lip, 'is that I would like Charlie to get to know his father – slowly – and eventually to spend some time with you. But, and it's a big but' – I knew I had to be absolutely upfront with them – 'I have sole custody of him. I am his legal guardian. The letter makes that clear too. So, he lives with me. And all of this happens on my terms. I hope that doesn't sound hard, but I need us to be straight with each other. Can you understand that?'

'Yes,' James whispered.

'We'll do anything,' Tamsin said quietly.

'He's all I have left, you see,' I told them with a little smile. 'And I need him so badly.'

'Thank you,' they said in unison and I knew they were decent people and was glad for them.

By the time Daniel collected me I was an emotional wreck. I'd had to redo my make-up twice because I was crying so much.

'You're very quiet,' he said as we looked at the menu. 'Is everything OK?'

'Yeah.' I really wanted to share it all with somebody, but I was scared.

'This is supposed to be a celebration, remember?' He was teasing. 'So, are you excited about the house?'

'Yes, wildly excited,' I told him and I meant it.

'Then I don't have to send back the champagne I arranged earlier?' he said as a waiter appeared with an ice bucket. 'Otherwise I'm afraid I've just spent the entire profit we made on the sale of the house on a taxi ride for no reason,' he told me.

'That driver thought all his birthdays had come together all right, when we told him we were going to Gorey.' I laughed at the memory. 'So, what are you having?'

'No idea. You're the foodie. Advise me. Is it any good even?' he asked as he browsed the menu.

'Yes, it sounds amazing. I want at least two starters and three main courses.'

'Well then, you order.' He sat back and looked relaxed as his glass was filled.

'Seriously?' I was thrilled.

'Yep, I'll be your guinea pig.' He made an oinking noise which the waiter tried gallantly to ignore.

'So, tell me about Charlie's visit the other day. I was sorry I missed him.' He'd been in London when Charlie and my aunt had arrived unexpectedly to give the house the once-over.

'It was a complete surprise, I only got the call on the day,' I explained. 'You see, I made the near-fatal mistake of mentioning the house to him on the phone the other week and Aunt Milly said he'd been driving her mental ever since. She got a chance of a lift when one of her neighbours had to visit a relative in Loughlinstown Hospital. How lucky was that?' I asked, and went on to explain how

I'd collected them from the hospital, which is barely half an hour from Wicklow town.

'God, he was so excited.' I laughed, remembering Charlie's face, and suddenly all my earlier tension disappeared. 'Your mother was great with him, by the way. He was fascinated by the colours in her kaftan. He followed her about for ages.'

'She said he was gorgeous,' Daniel said. 'Which for my mother is quite something. She's not big into kids.'

'Really? Well, she did very well then.' I filled him in on how the day had gone.

'Pity they had to go back the same day,' he said. 'That was quite a journey for your aunt. It must have taken a bit out of her.' I was touched that he sounded concerned.

'I think it did, although she denied it,' I told him. 'Her own excitement kept her going. One was as bad as the other, I swear. She looked about five years of age.'

Daniel laughed at the picture I painted.

'Anyway, Charlie immediately picked his room and he wants a Thomas the Tank Engine duvet like his friend in Cork has, apparently. Oh, and a black and white spotty bean bag for the dog as well.'

'So no negatives then?'

'Only when he saw the sea, initially.' I told him sadly. 'He still associates it with the night Alison died, obviously. He was a bit upset at first, just like he was the last time, although Milly insisted he wasn't nearly as bad. I spent ages assuring him it was a different sea altogether.' Before I could stop myself, I was remembering the night she died all over again, and I said a silent prayer that it would get easier soon. 'Anyway, at least I was ready for it this time and I had a number of distractions planned.' I took a deep breath and made a big effort not to get too morbid. 'But Max was the saviour, in the end. I'm going to have a hard job keeping them apart, especially at night, once the bean bag arrives. My aunt says he has a tin of baked beans in a brown paper bag in his bedroom in Cork, with his toy puppy sitting on it, practising "stay" and other commands.'

Daniel smiled.

'He wanted to bring the dog back with him to Cork as well, you see, and now every night when I ring him he asks to speak to Max, so we have this ridiculous conversation where he kisses the phone his end and I bark like mad my end.'

'Hey, women get paid good money for that sort of conversation,' he told me and this time it was my turn to smile.

'Your mum is really good to look after Max until I get organized, by the way. Will you tell her I appreciate it?' I asked and he nodded.

'And you're happy Charlie's coming to live with you?' he said in a gentle voice.

'Happier than I ever thought possible,' I told him truthfully.

'Good.' He seemed satisfied. 'Now feed me, woman, because I'm so hungry I'd eat the leg off the lamb of God right now.'

* * *

505

Two and a half hours later another equally happy taxi driver got the fare of his life and we were still laughing when we pulled up outside the café.

'Imagine, very soon you'll be able to drop me home and walk to your own place.' I got a tingle down my spine when I thought of it, and not just because of my new house.

'So will there be other nights like this then?' He raised his eyebrows at me as I opened the door to the flat.

'If you're lucky,' I told him and we both laughed and then he leaned over and kissed me and just like that one other time it started off innocently enough and suddenly we were inside, in the hallway, and if there'd been anywhere to sit or lie down we'd have been stretched out and glued together, I reckon.

Again, it was me who pulled away first.

'If you do that once more,' I said only half jokingly, 'I will take it your intentions are serious – and I'll assume we're a couple and I'll tell everyone, so be warned.'

'What'll you do, put a notice in the window of the café?'

'No, I'll take out an ad in the *Wicklow People*.' I was making it up as I went along, fuelled by half a bottle of bubbly. 'And what's more, I'll send a copy to my friend Sally in Oz, and she'll put it on the internet and then all your old girlfriends will find out and you'll be ruined.'

'And why would you do that to me?' He pushed my hair back from my face.

'Because . . . well, just because . . .'

'Because what?'

'Because I've had it with men who aren't honest,' I told

him softly, the emotions of the day rolling back in to knock me for six. 'And because my sister, my lovely sister whom I adored, spent the last few years of her life having sex with men who were lying to their wives or girlfriends and today I agreed to let one of them spend time with Charlie – my Charlie – because I just found out he's his father.' I was stone-cold sober now but still I had a need to say it out loud to him. 'You see, Daniel,' I swallowed noisily, 'I don't really think my sister had a number of affairs . . .' My voice faltered for a second. 'I think she got paid for it . . . for sex. And that made her a—'

'Don't.' He pulled me over to the stairs and sat me down, then knelt down in front of me. 'Don't torture yourself.' He put his arms around me and held me like a baby while I cried my eyes out.

'And what's more, I've known for ages, but I refused to accept it,' I told him and neither of us said anything for a bit.

'It must be the truth,' I said quietly. 'It has to be, there's no other explanation . . . and God knows I've tried to think of one.' I said it just to finally say it out loud, because talking to somebody meant there was no going back. I also knew I had to give Daniel the opportunity to back off now, while I was still able to let him go easily. I was sure he'd run a mile once he knew the truth about our family.

'It must be,' I said again, just to make sure he'd heard. He looked at me then and I could tell he was struggling with his own thoughts.

'I know it is, Lily,' he said eventually. 'Alison told me.'

55

LILY

'WHAT DID YOU JUST SAY?'

'I said I knew about it already.'

I still thought I'd misheard. 'What did you know?'

'Look, can I come up? I can let the taxi go and get another one.'

'No, just tell me what you knew.'

'I knew that Alison was . . . got paid for sex.' He looked directly at me.

'And she told you this herself?'

'Yes.'

'Send the taxi away,' I said after what seemed like ages.

'Come on, let's have a cup of coffee.' He took my hand and led me towards the flat a minute later.

'Actually, no.' Suddenly I knew I didn't want to talk to him there. 'Let's go for a walk.'

'Lily, it's freezing and you're wearing high heels and a see-through top. I don't think so.'

'Well, I'm not talking to you up there, in the flat. It's where . . . it all happened.'

'Fine, I understand now.' He sounded relieved I wasn't cracking up. 'Come on so.' He took off his jacket and put it around my shoulders. 'I'll treat you to coffee and a brandy in the only greasy spoon in Wicklow.' He put his arm around me and we set off down the main street and headed for the port.

'And now for a complete contrast,' he said as he held open the door. 'Let me introduce you to Wicklow's best-kept secret.' He was trying to distract me, and it worked.

The smell of bacon and chips and sausages cooking in real dripping or lard or something filled my nose as soon as we got inside. The place was a ready-made, de-clutter your life TV show but it was perfect. The walls were stained and the shelves were bursting – one even held a large frame containing those old currency notes from all around Europe and there were treacly black beams holding it all together.

'Wow!' I hadn't even known of its existence. 'It's fantastic . . .' I looked around the spotless, Formica-filled room. You could see the kitchen and there were bottles and plates and crates everywhere, but it was organized chaos. '. . . although I'd say your chances of getting a brandy in here are very slim.' I made an attempt at humour to hide the sick feeling in the pit of my stomach.

'I know the owner.' He winked. 'I can't believe you like it. Why on earth did I go to all that trouble to get a table in Gorey tonight when I could have just brought you straight here?'

It was still early enough that the place was empty

although Daniel told me that once the pubs closed it would be jammed with punters looking for soakage. 'So, what'll you have?' he wanted to know.

'Actually, a big pot of tea would be great,' I said.

I watched him chatting to a fat Italian man with a handlebar moustache and a minute later he came back with an old-fashioned, squashed aluminium teapot and a mug for me, and coffee and a small brandy for himself.

'So tell me, please. What do you know?'

'Lily, I don't know a huge amount.' He seemed to be warning me. 'I was only with her for a few days, remember. But what I did learn was that Alison had a number of . . . men in her life – whom she slept with on a regular basis,' he told me simply. 'That's it, in a nutshell.' He watched me as I stirred the thick, black tea.

'And got paid for it?' I needed it hammered home.

'Yes.'

'So she was . . . a prostitute?' I said. There it was, out in the open at last, the one word I'd tried to avoid using, even to myself. And it was me who'd finally said it. I was shocked that I was shocked.

'Yes,' he said very quietly.

'And you're absolutely sure?' What a ridiculous question.

'It's what she told me.'

'Straight out, that's what she called herself?'

'Yes.'

'God.' I felt icy cold in the stifling heat.

'But you knew, didn't you?'

'Yes,' I answered truthfully. 'But funnily enough, now it's like I just found out this minute.'

'How come?'

'Because I kept expecting someone to guffaw and tell me it was all in my head. Can you believe that?'

He nodded.

'A rational explanation, something I'd missed, you know?' I laughed. 'You see, Daniel, she just wasn't that type of girl.'

We sat in silence for a while then and he acted as if my snivelling was completely natural.

'So, what do you know?' he asked after a while.

I told him briefly what I'd learned and how for a long time I assumed she'd just had a number of affairs or something. I told him about William and then Dave dying and how it all just didn't seem to fit until eventually Richard more or less said it straight out. I explained how even then I was convinced I was putting two and two together and getting forty. He listened carefully and I knew from the way he kept nodding that none of it was new to him.

'For a long time I wouldn't let myself think about it.' I could feel the tears threatening because finally it had been confirmed beyond doubt. 'I guess I just needed to hear the word out loud,' I told him. 'But still, even now that I know for sure, I don't want it to be true.' I had to bite my lip to stop it quivering.

'Oh Lily, come 'ere to me.' He came over to my side of the table then and put his arms around me and let me cry noisily and didn't appear to be fazed or mortified at all.

'I'm OK,' I told him eventually and he went back to his own side but held on to my hand across the table.

'Can I ask you something else?' Daniel nodded. 'Why on earth didn't you tell me earlier?'

'It wasn't my story to tell, Lily.' He looked at me for ages. 'It was her secret. I had to let you figure it out for yourself.' He paused. 'Tonight, when we talked, I knew you had.'

'Yeah, I had,' I said and tried not to sound bitter. 'But keeping it all bottled up nearly ruined my life,' I told him. 'Christ, for one brief moment along the way I was even planning revenge . . .' My voice trailed off.

He sighed. 'I'm sorry it's been so hard on you.'

'You've no idea.'

'No, I haven't,' he said softly.

'I could have ruined more lives . . . if I'd gone ahead with my plan.' I didn't look at him.

'But you didn't.'

'No.'

'And you still love your sister just as much, in spite of it all.' It wasn't a question.

'Yes.'

'And you love her little boy as if he were your own.'

'Yes.'

'Then I'd say that's a good result.'

'Daniel, did she say why she did it?'

'For the money,' he said simply. 'She was determined to build a life for the two of you and she wanted a really good standard of living for you, especially. She told me you both had to go without when your mother died, and that you minded much more than she did.' He was being careful, trying to make sure I wouldn't get upset; I could tell from the way he kept his eyes on my face and paused for a second here and there, stirring his coffee, giving me a breather. 'She talked a lot about your father, about how he controlled you both. She sometimes wondered if she did what she did partly because she liked the idea of controlling men for a change. But mainly she did it because it offered her a chance to build a better life for herself – and for you. At one point she said she spent so many years smiling and doing exactly what she was told by your father that it was no problem to smile and pretend that she had something special going on with each of the men. And then Charlie came along and instead of protecting you like she had done for so long, she was protecting her child, as well, in that she was building a secure future for him with the money she was earning.'

I swallowed hard and he noticed and kept talking. 'It came about because a friend of hers – someone she worked with, as far as I remember – was making huge money from it. The whole internet thing was just taking off. The woman ran a sort of high-class escort service. She introduced Alison to a doctor or someone and it started from there. It was a million miles away from men in macs and women standing on street corners. And she was very careful, by the way,' he said as if trying to reassure me. 'Someone always knew who she was with and where.'

'And then she got pregnant. Did she mention the father?'

'Yes, I gather she became very attached to him. But he was married, as most of the men were. And he loved his wife – the usual – but they were having problems . . .'

I was just about to tell him more, but then I decided that that was a story for another time.

'Did she consider having an abortion, do you know?' I poured some more tea and cradled the warmth. It was something I'd wondered about a lot. In some ways it would have been the easy option for her.

'No, I don't think so. She said having Charlie was the best thing that had come out of it all.'

'I see.' I was trying not to get too upset.

'And she talked about you often. About how much she loved you and had tried to protect you because you were so outspoken to your father that you normally came off much worse than she did.'

I nodded, remembering.

'Lily, did he hit you?' he asked softly, taking my hand.

'No, but he punished us – me, really. I was always in my room, or not allowed out because I gave cheek. But I think Ali had to put up with a lot too, or else I've blocked it out,' I said. 'Sometimes I can't remember things, and sometimes I have different memories. It's weird.'

'He sounds like a complete bastard,' Daniel said and his lips were tight.

'Well, he didn't abuse us or anything but yes, it was tough. He turned my sister into the sort of woman who

514

said "How high?" when men asked her to jump. And me into the sort of woman who doesn't trust anyone, who nearly gave away a child because I was afraid I wouldn't be able to love him properly . . .'

'I'm sorry,' he told me, not for the first time. 'But Lily, you'd never have given Charlie away.'

'Do you think not?'

'I know it.' He smiled.

'Did she know about the money at that stage?' I wanted it all tied up now. I just couldn't face any more stuff coming out later.

'No, I don't think so. I don't know anything about any money,' he said simply.

'My father left a lot . . . It's complicated.' I sighed. 'I'll tell you about it, if that's OK? But not just now.'

'You don't have to.'

'No, I want to.'

'She had decided to give it all up – the men. I do know that. She felt she'd made a difference to your lives and wanted . . . I dunno, something else for the three of you. I was simply the person she spoke to because the time was right, I suspect. And she said that talking about it had helped her come to a decision. That was why she wanted us to meet again, in a year.' He looked sad. 'It was all going to be different, she was determined.'

'That simple?' I wasn't sure.

'Yes, actually it was that simple.'

We talked for a while longer, until I nearly fell over with tiredness, and then he walked me to my door.

'Thank you,' I said. 'It's like the final piece in the jigsaw.'

'I don't know it all,' he said anxiously. 'I wouldn't want you to think that.'

'You know enough for me to be able to move on with my own life at last.'

'You knew it all along, Lily. And you were doing just that anyway,' he told me. 'Look at what you've achieved in a short time.' He tilted up my face. 'I think you're amazing.' He kissed me then, more gently than ever.

'Goodnight,' he said softly.

'Yeah.'

'I'll drop in tomorrow, just to make sure you're OK. Call me if you need me.'

'Thanks.' I meant it.

He tapped me on the nose and made to walk away. 'No worries.'

'Can I ask you one last question?'

'What's that?'

'Did you sleep with her?'

He looked disappointed that I'd asked. 'Does it matter?'

'I dunno.'

'Well, it shouldn't. That's between me and her.'

'Maybe I need to know.'

'And maybe I'll tell you some time. But judge me as you find me, Lily. And decide if you think you can trust me based on that. Goodnight,' he said quietly and started to go, then changed his mind. 'Oh and by the way, we are a couple, so put a notice in your window,' and this time he walked away without looking back.

56

LILY AND CHARLIE

THE HOUSE LOOKED LIKE A GIANT CHRISTMAS TREE. There were lights everywhere, thanks mainly to Aunt Milly and Daniel's mum – or Sara, as she'd insisted I call her. Between them they'd indulged all their childhood fantasies, I reckoned. The garden was practically a fire hazard with tealights and candles all over the place – in jam jars hanging in the trees, on sticks plunged into the ground to guide a path to the door and all along the window ledges.

Charlie's eyes were the only things that came close for sparkle appeal. He was in his element as he toddled around with Squirt held high above his head. This was because we'd earlier caught Max sniffing at him in a rather alarming, lip-smacking way that Aunt Milly reckoned would have meant curtains for the tortoise if she hadn't wandered into the room at precisely that moment.

'Bold boy,' Charlie kept repeating to a bemused-looking Max.

'Is it any wonder the poor animal is confused?' Sara

laughed. 'Every time he says it he plants a big wet kiss on the dog's mouth.'

'Down.' Charlie had found a new word. The only problem was that he sat on Max every time he said it, in order to ram home his command.

Daniel had been going around all day with a drill in his hands and said he'd never felt so needed by so many women. Orla, Violet and Naomi had done all the food, supervised, of course, by my aunt, who insisted everyone say 'Yes, chef' or 'No, chef' in response to her requests. The whole shebang was a circus, really.

The first of the guests arrived about eight and Daniel escaped to change.

'You OK?' he asked, planting a big kiss on my head.

Every time he came close I had to pinch myself that it really was me he was after.

'Yeah, excited. It's my first-ever housewarming, did I say?'

'Only about a million times.' He laughed.

'Don't be long,' I warned him. 'I may need you when James and Tamsin get here. I'm very nervous about it.'

'Back in a jif,' he promised, as Charlie and I went to meet and greet our visitors.

Everyone had brought a present for me for the house and something for Charlie, so that eventually, instead of saying hello to new arrivals, he simply said, 'Can I have my present now, thank you?' and held out his hands.

'Look who I've found,' Daniel said on his return. 'I

introduced myself.' He smiled at me and gave me a look that said, 'It's all going to be OK. Chill.'

I glanced over his shoulder to find a very fidgety James in tow, with Tamsin holding back a bit, still looking frail.

'Hi there,' I said a tad overenthusiastically, in order to hide my nerves. 'Charlie, come and say hello.' I held out my hand and he shot past me, mainly because he'd just spotted a very large, brightly wrapped box in James's arms.

'For me?' he said, skipping the pleasantries altogether at this stage.

'Are you Max?' James asked, getting down on his hunkers. Immediately I saw the resemblance. They had exactly the same jawline.

'No, I'm Charlie.' He put his hands in his pockets and seemed to throw back his shoulders in a gesture that clearly said Max had two chances of getting his paws on that parcel – slim and none.

'But this is for Max,' James said, without taking his eyes off him.

'Max bold.' Charlie made a last-ditch effort to secure the booty. 'Max very bold boy.'

'Oh well, in that case, I think you'd better have it.'

'I'm very good,' Charlie said and lunged at the parcel. I'd tipped James off that if he wanted to make an immediate impact a train of any description should do it, and we all watched as my little boy's eyes almost popped out of their sockets when he tore off the wrapping and discovered a million bits of track and carriages and engines and even a painted stationmaster along with a rake of passengers.

'What do you say to James and Tamsin?' I asked him.

'Tanx a million,' he said and threw his arms around the man he'd only just met but who was going to play a big part in his future, I suspected.

I looked up and Tamsin was fighting back tears. 'Thank you,' she mouthed.

'I found this woman trying to gatecrash,' Daniel announced at that precise moment, in an effort to lighten things. 'Do you know her at all?' His smile was much more relaxed this time, I noticed.

A face I hadn't seen in years peeked out from behind his back.

'Sally,' I screamed and finally I did burst into tears.

Unfortunately, so did Charlie, who got a fright because he thought I was upset. I lifted him up and held him tightly, right next to my heart, where he belonged.

'How on earth did you find us, out here in the sticks?' I just couldn't believe she was there, standing right in front of me.

'Long story.' She danced me and Charlie around the room. 'Let's just say I've missed far too many important nights in your life this last while, so if you've any plans to get married could you please do so in the next month?'

Everyone who heard her cheered at that and the slagging started in earnest then.

'Lily, I can't thank you enough.' James caught me on

my own in the hall. 'You've no idea what this means to us.'

'Isn't he a dote?'

'He's simply the most amazing little boy,' he said shyly. 'He's a credit to you – and to Alison.'

'He has your jaw,' I told him.

'Really? That's exactly what my wife said.' He sounded very proud.

After that, it was the nicest night of my whole life as I held my baby and entertained all my friends – old and new – in my first-ever house.

'I'm so hot,' I told Daniel much later. I hadn't seen him for ages and every time I'd spotted him in the crowd my heart had lurched. Once or twice I managed to catch his eye and when he'd smiled at me I wanted to burst with happiness.

'Tell you what, let's sneak outside and catch some air,' he said now, grabbing a bottle of wine and two glasses.

'Great idea.' I followed him and we hid in a quiet corner of the garden on my new swing chair – a present from Aunt Milly.

'Isn't this perfect?' I sank into the cushions and tucked my feet up under me.

'I'd say it's damn near perfect.' He poured and handed me a glass.

'To you,' he said simply. 'I wish you and Charlie many years of good health in this house.'

'Thank you, it's all I pray for really.'

'You deserve it.' He smiled and took my glass away and kissed me.

'Imagine, a while ago it felt like I had nobody except him and my aunt and now look . . . We've made so many new friends – or aunties and uncles as Charlie keeps calling them, in the hope of even more goodies. And he's got a father, although he doesn't know it yet.'

'And what about you, are you content?'

'Oh yes,' I told him.

'And you're OK with everything you found out?'

'I'm fine. It's taken me a while, but yes I am.'

'She was a good person,' he said. 'I knew it the minute I laid eyes on her.'

'She was,' I agreed. 'And I loved her so much. Still do, no matter what.'

'That's the way it should be. And are you happy with me?' he asked softly.

'I can't imagine not being happy with you.' It seemed easy to say it now, but in a way that was how it had been with him, right from the start.

'So you've decided you trust me then?' He grinned.

'I trust you completely.'

'Good.'

'And how about you? Are you OK with everything?' I asked him, still feeling just a teeny bit anxious. 'We're not exactly the Waltons, that's for sure.'

'How d'ya mean?'

'You know, all the things about . . . me and Alison . . . and Charlie. Hardly your average family, eh?' I grinned.

'And for all that Alison told you about her life, you didn't really know me at all, did you? And when we met, I wasn't what you thought I'd be, was I?'

'Oh, I think I knew you long before I ever met you,' he said simply. 'And no, you're not what I imagined, you're even better.' He put his arm around me. 'You have all the lovely bits of Alison and much more besides. And you're a great mother. I adore watching you with Charlie when you think I'm not looking.'

'Thank you.'

He took a sip of his wine. 'I didn't sleep with her,' he said quietly. 'Just in case it still matters.'

'It doesn't. I thought it might, but not any more.' I kissed him and it felt like the first time and I knew I'd never get enough of this man, no matter how long he stayed.

'Mammy,' Charlie called.

'Over here, love,' I shouted and he toddled over, fire engine in tow. I lifted him up on my lap and within minutes he was asleep.

'He needs me so much.' I pushed back his hair and Daniel went and fetched a rug and put it over him. 'And I'm glad he has a father too, just in case . . .' It was my one worry.

'And who knows, some day soon he might even have a stepfather,' Daniel whispered, and that was when I knew I was happy, really happy, for the first time in my life.

THE END

ACKNOWLEDGEMENTS

It was the dedication in my last book – *The WWW Club* – that jinxed me, I'm convinced of it. Something about a new husband and a long and healthy life. We were both crocks within months. But at least his stint in surgery was planned, whereas I – having never been in hospital a day in my life – ended up in St Vincent's twice while writing this book! Both stays were unexpected, and the first was made a lot easier because of the kindness and support of Enda McDermott, Ann O'Doherty and Claire Glennane.

Not long after I'd finally escaped their clutches, I went walking in Wicklow (to celebrate!) and met Ian and Sean. Nothing wrong with that, they were lovely. I just wasn't very fond of their brand new ambulance. They were paramedics, you see, and together with several hunky firemen they had the unenviable job of stretchering all seventy-something kilos of me – including my broken leg – off the edge of the cliffs. Major thanks due there.

Needless to say my amazing family rallied round and kept me going, as usual. And my friends Dearbhla (best mate and general dogsbody), Caroline (organic veggie and Indian food provider), Ursula and Dee have stuck with me through thick and thin – and plaster. So too have Dave Fanning and Frank Hession, although the jury's still out on Diarmuid Gavin, because he went off on a TV job around the world without me when I broke my leg. The texts from Tahiti did nothing to improve my mood.

Patricia Scanlan kept me positive and reminded me that these things happen for a reason – not what I wanted to hear. Claudia Carroll brought me to the hairdressers anytime I threatened to become violent, and Mary Canning never once avoided my calls when I begged her to bring me for coffee so that I could moan for Ireland. Oh, and Anna Nolan called round with pink champagne (to match the Barbie pink cast on my leg) and then *I really* couldn't walk – even with crutches.

My editor, Francesca Liversidge, would have been forgiven for drinking a lot herself as she waited for me to *finally* deliver this book! You were brilliantly supportive as always. Thanks to everyone in Transworld – from Larry Finlay down, you've been terrific. As have Gil and Simon Hess as well as Declan Heeney and Helen Gleed O'Connor, who gave me buckets of TLC when I needed it.

Marianne Gunn O'Connor was a friend as well as an agent, despite losing her lovely mum, Mary, during all this. And Pat Lynch is still the best listener I know. Thanks also to Vicki Satlow who does tremendous work for me in Europe.

I first got the idea for this book when I was involved in

a report on prostitution for *Prime Time* on RTE Television and I'm grateful to the women who spoke to me then and shared their varied and complex stories. Thanks also to Kieran Henry, who told me all he knew about air-sea rescue.

And Gerry McGuinness, your love makes me very happy – most of the time. I'm still not sure about the day you reminded me that my career as a writer didn't depend on having the use of both legs – and suggested I ditch the chocolate and start keeping my fingers in shape by using the keyboard on the computer! Ouch!

Finally, to everyone who reads my books, a million thanks for your support and feedback, especially Anna and Marie Hughes, who always send me such lovely messages.